FORBIDDEN PASSION

Suddenly he had dropped the wet cloth and his hands were on her throat, framing her face. Her breath coming in short rasps, Brietta watched his lips moving toward hers. The whole world seemed to start spinning when he kissed her, his lips setting fires inside her that felt deliciously wonderful, yet dangerous.

Her heart pounding, afraid of the desire this Indian was making her feel, Brietta shoved at his chest.

Her face aflame, Brietta placed her fingertips to her lips, still tasting his kiss there, still dazzled by it. She was afraid to breathe, much less speak. For a moment her world and the Indian's had become one.

But how could it have happened? Such a love between them was forbidden! She knew it, and so must he.

CASSIE EDWARDS

SAVAGE
Persuasion

LEISURE BOOKS ⦁ NEW YORK CITY

A LEISURE BOOK®

Published by
Dorchester Publishing Co., Inc.
276 Fifth Avenue
New York, NY 10001

The name "Leisure Books" and the stylized "L" with design are trademarks of Dorchester Publishing Co., Inc.

Printed in the United States of America.

I dedicate *SAVAGE PERSUASION* to many special friends and fans. With love this dedication goes to:

THELMA ANDERSON
JANELLE GORTNEY
MORNING STAR
COLEEN "FIREWOMAN" SHEETS
DEBORAH ABRAMS
LINDA "WATERFALL" MARONEY
CHAQUITA DE RUY
EDNA PARKER
PAT STRAUMANN
DOROTHY TURNER
JEAN HENDERSON
GLORIA COOLEY
RUTH KIGER

AUTHOR'S NOTE

The Cherokee, *Ani-yun-wiya*, meaning the "Real, or Principal People," were an emigrant tribe of Indian. The first Cherokee settled in the Arkansas Ozarks in the early 1800's, seeking wild game. The arrival of the Cherokee in the traditional hunting grounds of the Osage tribe resulted in rivalry and enmity between the two groups.

The Cherokee, as a result of many hostile acts on the part of the Osage, assembled and armed themselves to avenge the wrongs done them.

SAVAGE PERSUASION is the story of two proud young Indian leaders—Cherokee and Osage—who managed to find friendship despite the fact that it was forbidden between their two tribes. It was a friendship that would be sorely tested in many ways.

POEM

Close your eyes, and hook your dreams up to a star!
Let them take you, wherever you want to go, either
near or far.

With our dreams, we could go back in time,
through an open door,
And for a little while, live as our ancestors did,
hundreds of years before.

They woke, and gave prayer. When they saw the
hues of dawn of Grandmother Sun,
Their days were of hunting, hard work, fun and
more prayer when day was done.

And how peaceful it must have been, to travel the
beautiful waters of blue,
Yet no one realized the hard work, love, and prayers
that it took to carve a tree into a canoe.

Our ancestors were proud, and regal, a gift for a
gift, a trade for a trade.
If my dream could get me where I want to be, I'd
unhitch my star, and would have stayed.

Let your dreams take you ever so high!
High enough, to look into Heaven's eyes!

BY:

Linda "Waterfall" Maroney
who is very proud of her
heritage, which is Cherokee,
Blackfoot and Mic Mac.

PROLOGUE

There is a destiny that makes us brothers:
No one goes his way alone.

—Markham

1807—THE ARKANSAS OZARKS

The sun was slowly setting, casting long purple shadows across the land. A young Indian brave was making his way along a river in a wooded glen. As night drew a mantle of darkness over the rushing water, the ferns and vines of the riverbank, and the verdant hillsides, the whole world seemed to be lost in a sudden deep sleep.

Clad only in a brief breechclout, Pale Moon had gone into the forest to seek the vision required of him before he could be called a man. He had been taught by his chieftain father that power would come to him at the time of his vision, and to prepare for it he must isolate himself, fasting and thirsting, and praying in an abject, humble manner.

Along with that newly found power would come a new name—a name that he would carry with him as he rode among his people, a great Cherokee warrior, until the day he drew his last breath!

Pale Moon had been gone from his village for a full day and night, wandering, hoping to find that special place where he would be blessed by *Wah-kon-tah*, the great spirit. Pale Moon was now thirteen and had much to prove to his people, the proud Cherokee. He was the next-chief-in-line, always to be admired and respected. He had to prove that he was worthy of such devotion.

Under the trees, the darkness was solid, yet Pale Moon continued feeling his way through the forest, a destination now in mind. From the high bluff that he sought, he could gaze upon the vast sky and feel as one with the stars. He could turn his thoughts to *Wah-kon-tah*. *Wah-kon-tah* would see Pale Moon's worth and bless him with a vision, and also a name befitting his new status as a man.

His knees weak and his pulse racing, Pale Moon moved onward. The trees that loomed above him were an even deeper black than the night. He hadn't eaten for two days, for his father had said that when one fasts he is blessed more quickly and grandly.

As always, Pale Moon had listened to the teachings of his father and knew that his reward for doing so would be twofold.

In the past it had always been so.

His father was a wise leader, trusted and admired by all who knew him.

"Except for the Osage," Pale Moon whispered to himself. "They have become the *ha-ma-ma*, the enemy of my people!"

Knowing that this was not the time or place to think of enemies, Pale Moon concentrated on the climb to the bluff. Sweat pearled his brow as he fought his weakness, his bare feet slipping and sliding on the dew-laden grass of the steep embankment as he moved steadily upward. Above him now were the smiling faces of the stars, though the moon was hidden behind a shadow of cloud.

Pale Moon sighed with relief as the ground leveled off. Sinking down on a patch of earth, he surveyed the view around him. He was high above the treetops now, where heaven and earth seemed to become one entity. Stretching out on his back, he fixed his eyes on the dark sky, allowing the twinkling stars to hypnotize him.

The long hours passed, yet Pale Moon still did not sleep. He did not want to miss any sign in the heavens which might herald his vision. He fought the urge to sleep. He fought the gnawing hunger at the pit of his stomach.

And then a faint glow of pink began seeping along the horizon where the sun was ready to shine its face upon Mother Earth for another day. The forest was coming alive with song and sound —the birds in sweet melody and the bobcats and grey timber wolves howling from their distant haunts.

The elk, in scattered herds, would soon gracefully traverse the open landscape. Deer would dash hither and yon. Buffalo would awaken and roam the prairie.

Pale Moon rose to his knees and folded his arms across his bare chest, casting his eyes toward the heavens in search of some good omen from the Great Spirit.

He called aloud and said, *"Wah-kon-tah*, Great Spirit in all places, it is through you that I am living. You are the supreme ruler! Nothing is impossible to you! If you see fit, bless me today with a vision!"

His heart pounded wildly and his breathing quickened when he saw an eagle swoop downward into the shadows of Mother Earth, then rise again into the sky, soon disappearing into a strange brown cloud.

Pale Moon, like the great eagle, seemed to be rising to an even higher plane, for when the darkness of night turned to light, a wondrous sort of uplifting sensation filled his eager heart, and he knew that he had been blessed and that a great destiny lay ahead for him!

"And I shall now call myself Brave Eagle!" he cried to the heavens, still in awe of the eagle that had flown so courageously into the brown scud of clouds. "Beautiful brave eagle, you and I are now, and always shall be, as one!"

"I, too, saw the eagle. . . ."

A voice behind Brave Eagle, speaking in the Osage language, caused him to bolt to his feet. As he turned, his hand flew to his waist, where he usually carried a sheathed knife for protection. But he found nothing. He had been instructed by his father that one must go defenseless into the wilderness to face *Wah-kon-tah*. Only so would he prove that he was brave and worthy of a vision!

Face to face with a young Osage brave of the same height and age, whose copper skin and dark eyes mirrored his own, Brave Eagle found he could not look upon the other boy with hate and loathing. Brave Eagle's heart was filled with too much love and peace at this moment.

"I too saw the eagle," the young Osage repeated softly, this time in Brave Eagle's Cherokee tongue. "I share your vision, Brave Eagle. You choose the name Brave Eagle. I will choose the name Brown Cloud for where the eagle so bravely flew. It is destined now for us to be friends forever—*tso-ga-li-i i-go-hi-di*. No matter that we are of different peoples and beliefs."

"How do you know me?" Brave Eagle questioned, his gaze intense. "How do you know that I am of the Cherokee nation?"

"I know you as you know me," Brown Cloud said, daring to take a step closer to Brave Eagle, normally his archenemy. "Can you tell me that you do not know me? That I am not the son of Chief Climbing Bear, Osage by heritage? My father and your father are enemies. They speak of sons, do they not?"

"My father, Chief Silver Shirt, speaks of your father with much anger in his heart," Brave Eagle replied. "Your people refuse to talk peace with the Cherokee. How can you say that we are to be

15

friends? How can you say that we are to be brothers?"

"It is because we shared the same vision today," Brown Cloud said, daring to reach out a hand and rest it on Brave Eagle's shoulder. "Is that not so, Brave Eagle? Do you not see the meaning in that? Your destiny is my destiny. My destiny is yours. The Great Spirit has made it so."

Brave Eagle's eyes wavered. He glanced down at the hand on his shoulder. It was the hand of an enemy! Yet, did not Brown Cloud's words speak truth? Today was designed by the Great Spirit! Surely the two young leaders had been brought together for a purpose! How could Brave Eagle not do as the Great Spirit indicated? If he did not follow the dictates of his heart, he would forever walk in shadows, his heart burdened!

"Yes," Brave Eagle finally said, looking Brown Cloud directly in the eye. "Our destinies are now intertwined. I accept that it is so."

A spider suddenly appeared on the ground between Brave Eagle and Brown Cloud. As though by magic, it began to weave a lacy web from one boy's bare foot to the other's.

"It is another sign," Brown Cloud said, watching the spider spin its intricate pattern, feeling the stickiness of the web against the flesh of his foot. "We shall mark ourselves with the design of the spider to prove our loyalty to one another."

Brave Eagle nodded. He knelt and let the spider crawl onto the palm of his hand, then gently released it on the ground away from him.

He and Brown Cloud anxiously left the butte and searched in the forest, first for the wing bone of a dead bird, then for a sacred red bud tree.

Once these were found, they began the ritual that was meant to seal their friendship.

"We shall mark ourselves with the design of the spider where no one else will see it," Brave Eagle said, settling on the ground facing Brown Cloud as Brown Cloud sat down opposite him. "We must keep the secret of our brotherhood from our separate peoples, because such a union is forbidden." He held his knees apart. "The inner thigh will bear our small, private tattoo."

Brown Cloud nodded. Then with the wing-bone, he pricked out the geometrical figure of a spider on the inner thigh of Brave Eagle's right leg, then rubbed some charcoal from the red bud tree into the opening of the skin. This beautiful design would last a lifetime. It was the symbol of all the mysterious powers that both Brave Eagle and Brown Cloud would discover now that they had been transformed from boys to men today, their shared vision a thing of wonderful meaning for them both!

"It is done," Brown Cloud said, then watched as Brave Eagle pricked out the identical figure on his own inner thigh.

"It is done," Brave Eagle said, casting aside the wing-bone and charcoal. He clasped his hands to Brown Cloud's shoulders. "We are now brothers, in this *un-a-liy*, place of friends. As long as this is so, never shall I call you my enemy. But cross me once, betray me once, Brown Cloud, and all of my vows to you will be cast to the wind! Forgotten!"

"Today we have joined our hands and hearts in friendship," Brown Cloud said, placing a doubled fist to his heart. "Never shall I break the vows spoken to you today."

"Nor shall I, mine to you," Brave Eagle said. He moved to his feet, Brown Cloud following his lead.

They eyed each other warily for a moment, then, as brothers, embraced.

CHAPTER ONE

It matters not how deep entrenched the wrong,
How hard the battle goes, the day how long;
Faint not—fight on!
Tomorrow comes the song.

—*Babcock*

1819—THE ARKANSAS OZARKS

"Brietta, supper is getting cold. Where do you think they are? Do you think the Indians caught them this time?"

Brietta Russell untied her apron and hung it on a peg in the wall of the crude, dark cabin. "You know how I feel about that," she said solemnly. "Anyone who makes money dealing in human flesh, no matter if it is Indian flesh, will get exactly what they deserve in the end."

"Everyone is aware of black slaves, but who would have thought anyone would deal in Indian slavery?" Rachel said, shuddering at the thought of the many Indians that her uncles had captured and sold for a meager sum of money. The slavers then took the Indians to the West Indies or the lower Mississippi valley for slaves. "And that our own kin could stoop so low . . . it sickens me."

"I do not wish to refer to our uncles as kin any longer," Brietta said icily. "To me they are two heartless men I am anxious to be free of."

"I feel as if I have aged ten years since we arrived in these Arkansas Ozarks," Rachel said, gesturing with one hand at the squalor around her. "Just look at this place. It's no better than a pigsty." She looked down at herself and at her faded cotton dress, the hem dragging on the floor since she had used up the last spool of thread six months ago. "Brietta, you and I look no better than St. Louis street urchins. All of our dresses are so faded and ugly you can't tell them apart on wash day. You are probably wearing my dress right now. And I am probably wearing yours."

"God willing, all of this will change soon," Brietta said hopefully. She gazed at her twin sister, mirror image of herself, except that Rachel's eyes were blue and Brietta's were green.

Most of their acquaintances in St. Louis had said that Brietta and her sister were uncommonly beautiful girls. Their faces were framed by dark, natural ringlets that hung down their backs to their waists. Their noses were straight and well-formed, their cheekbones delicate. It had always embarrassed Brietta when someone had commented on her lips—saying they were shaped as though a sculptor had molded them.

Now Brietta could only wonder what people would think of her and Rachel. They weren't allowed to meet anyone face to face any longer. Since their two failed attempts to escape, they were now forbidden to go outside the cabin together. Their uncles feared that if they did, they might try running off again. They took turns doing outdoor chores, taking what time they dared to breathe in the wondrous scents of the wild flowers that wafted through the air from the forest and distant meadows.

They were prisoners—prisoners of their own uncles.

Rachel flipped the skirt of her dress around her legs as she went to the table and dipped a finger into the milk gravy. She hungrily sucked the gravy from her finger as she smiled almost wickedly at Brietta. "Perhaps the Indians *have* captured our uncles today," she said.

"They deserve no less than that," Brietta said, lifting her chin. She looked around the drab, one-room log cabin, hating everything about it. Where was the dream of a better life that had prompted her family to leave St. Louis? So many dreams had died when her parents were found dead in their wagon one morning where they had stopped along the White River before entering the

Arkansas Ozarks. Her parents had been knifed to death—and—scalped. It was a mystery why no one else had died that night.

Brietta had drawn her own conclusions, though they could not be confirmed. She had always suspected her two uncles. They had laid claim to all of the Russells' possessions far too quickly after the burial—even Charles and Martha Russell's twin daughters.

It seemed to Brietta that from the moment her parents had agreed to let Ray and Patrick Russell travel with them from St. Louis, her days of true happiness and peace had been numbered. Had her parents been more astute, had they seen the greed in Patrick's and Ray's eyes that Brietta had seen, perhaps everything would have been different. If they had only listened when she tried to warn them.

But to them, she had been only a girl of fifteen with foolish notions.

Brietta went quickly to Rachel. She grabbed her sister's hands and peered intensely into her eyes. "Did you place Papa's rifle beneath your pillow today, like I told you?" she asked, her voice drawn with worry.

"Yes," Rachel said, her voice just as concerned. "Did you place Mama's pearl-handled pistol beneath yours?"

Brietta nodded. "You know that I did," she said, releasing her sister's hands. She went to the ladder that reached into the loft where she and Rachel slept each night, and stared up into the darkness overhead. "If ever our uncles are going to try to seduce us, tonight will be the night. We're headed back for St. Louis tomorrow. They know that once we get there, among decent kinfolk, they'll never have a chance again.''

Rachel turned to face the large stone fireplace and peered wistfully into the flames. "I didn't think our uncles would ever agree to return to St. Louis," she murmured. "I thought that we would be here with them 'til we died. The two times we tried to run off they gave us such terrible beatings. I—I thought I'd die then—and even hoped to.''

Brietta drew Rachel into her gentle embrace. Somehow she'd always felt as if she were her sister's protector, perhaps because she had been born one hour before Rachel. "I don't want to hear any more talk like that," she scolded. "We'll soon be free of our uncles. I promise you that."

"They won't allow it," Rachel said, relishing her sister's comforting arms. "I just know they'll find a way not to allow it! If I'm raped, sister, I truly will want to die!''

"We're lucky Uncle Ray and Uncle Patrick haven't tried to force us to bed with them before now," Brietta said, the thought giving her a heavy, sick feeling in the pit of her stomach. "I don't know why they haven't, except that perhaps there is still some trace of loyalty to Papa left inside their dark hearts. But I've seen a strange sort of light in their eyes of late—as though they're seeing right through us. That's why I decided we'd best keep firearms handy at night."

Rachel stepped away from her sister. "We'll shoot them if they try, won't we, Brietta?" she asked anxiously. "God won't condemn us for doing it?"

"Yes, we'll shoot them," Brietta said matter-of-factly. "And I'm sure God would even give his blessing. Though they are not twins like us, Ray's and Patrick's minds think identically. They are two of the most evil men who walk the earth."

She went to the cabin door and opened it and was met by a lovely sunset. Though anxious to return to St. Louis where she could be safe from the clutches of her uncles, she would miss this Ozark country. It was a land of raw beauty—a lovely, lyrical land of craggy peaks and fertile valleys, and of gently flowing rivers fed by chattering streams. In the spring the air was scented by the blossoming azalea, laurels, rhododendrons, and magnolias. In the fall the mountains flamed with the scarlet of maples and the gold of oak, birch, and cottonwood. In the winter it was a vast wonderland of white.

Rachel moved to Brietta's side and inhaled the clean pine smell drifting along on the evening wind.

Then her glance fell on the dark forest that lay not far from the cabin. She had always feared that there were Indians there, possibly hiding and watching her. Many times she had almost felt eyes on her, branding her.

But never had she seen anyone, white or redskinned, except for her uncles.

"But what of Indians?" Rachel blurted. "Surely they are more evil than Patrick and Ray. They were merciless when—when they killed Mama and Papa."

Brietta turned to Rachel. "Never will I believe

that Indians killed them," she argued. "I truly believe it was—"

Rachel shook her head frantically. "No!" she cried. "I can't believe that our uncles could do that. No matter how awful they are, they couldn't do that to their own kin!"

"I'm sure they are capable of it and I wish that I could prove it," Brietta said, heaving a sigh. She looked at a precariously leaning shack at the far end of the yard. "I've often wanted to go in the shack and search for—for the scalps. But they keep the door locked. And even if I could get inside, I would be afraid of what I might find. What if I did find Mama's and Papa's scalps hanging in there? What then?"

"You don't want to go in there anyhow," Rachel said, paling. "That's where Uncle Ray and Patrick have kept their Indian prisoners before selling them to the slavers. The place is evil, just like our uncles."

"The only reason our uncles are agreeing to return to St. Louis is because they are afraid that too many Indians suspect they are in on the Indian stealing," Brietta said, closing the door. She moved listlessly to the table and sat down. Rachel drew out a chair and sat opposite her. "The only thing that's saved them in the past is the still out back. As long as they had their home-brewed whiskey to bribe the Indians, they didn't fear them. But now that the still has broken down, they have nothing to bargain with."

"I'm not so glad the still broke down," Rachel said, taking a sip of coffee as she hungrily eyed the food on the table. She and Brietta didn't dare eat before Ray and Patrick.

"Why would you say that, Rachel?" Brietta asked, stiffening when she heard the sound of arriving horses outside. She always dreaded the return of her uncles. She never knew what sort of mood they would be in.

Tonight she suspected a mood that might lead to disaster. At the breakfast table Patrick and Ray had made too many snide references to what they planned to get from their nieces that night. Brietta had known that they had not been referring to anything as wholesome as food.

"Because, Brietta, while they're so drunk they can't see straight, they're no threat to us," Rachel said, eyeing the door warily when she heard her uncles laughing and joking just outside the door, only footsteps away. "Whiskey seems to have been a good substitute for women in these parts where women are scarce. But now?"

The door burst open. Brietta and Rachel could not help cowering beneath the burning gazes of their uncles. The men were powerfully built, their clothes reeking of perspiration, and their faces hidden behind thick red whiskers that matched their long, stringy hair. Although Ray was the oldest of the two by a couple of years, Patrick was no less mean. Their minds seemed always to be conjuring up ways to wreak havoc.

"Now ain't that sweet?" Ray said, sauntering into the cabin. "Our nieces sittin' polite-like, waitin' on us?" He licked his lips as he eyed the table laden with food. "I've been waitin' all day for this. Just look at that chow, Patrick."

Patrick closed the door. He was strangely quiet, his gaze burning on Rachel as he leaned his rifle against the wall. "Chow ain't what I've had on my mind since dawn," he grumbled. "But it'll satisfy my cravings for the moment." He jerked a chair out from the table and settled his massive weight onto it. Ray followed his lead and sat down opposite him.

"Have some mashed potatoes, Uncle Patrick?" Rachel asked weakly as she handed the dish of potatoes to him. When their eyes met and held, terror gripped her insides. He was looking at her as he never had before. It was as though he was touching her intimately. She could hardly bear to sit there, acting as though she didn't realize what he wanted from her.

Her jaw tightened and her heart raced. She was glad to know that she had options he would never expect. The rifle!

If it became necessary, she most certainly would use it!

She flinched when his hand grazed against hers as he took the dish from her.

Brietta was quietly observing what was transpiring across the table from her; then she looked slowly at Ray and saw that he was now as interested in her. She had been right to dread this night!

The dishes of food were passed around the table. Though half starved from the long wait, Brietta and Rachel could do no more than pick at their meat and vegetables as Patrick and Ray amused themselves with vulgar conversation. The twin sisters were forced to listen, their hatred for their uncles building by the minute.

"We had fun today, didn't we, Ray?" Patrick said, chewing on a mouthful of fried chicken and potatoes. "We gave them Injuns quite a chase, didn't we?"

"Yeah, no need in capturin' the varmints today, since we won't be here to trade 'em off tomorrow," Ray said as he poked his mouth full of turnip greens. "We popped them off one by one, didn't we, Patrick? Did you see them hit the dust as they fell from their horses? The damn Osage are a dumb lot."

Brietta shuddered as she envisioned what her uncles were describing. She did not think of Indians as savages the way most people did.

Her uncles were fools, she thought. The Osage were surely going to seek vengeance for the deaths of their loved ones. She only hoped she and her sister would be leaving the Ozarks soon enough to escape their retribution.

"Yeah, God in his mercy refrained from endowing the red man with human feelings or smarts," Ray scoffed. "So why concern ourselves with how they are done away with? One less Injun don't matter none to us. We don't have no more use of them since we're leavin' these parts for St. Louis tomorrow."

Ray narrowed his eyes as he looked at Brietta. He wiped his mouth clean of food and grease with the back of his hand and smiled slowly. "Cat got 'cher tongue tonight, Brietta?" he asked, chuckling. "Ain't you got nothin' to say about your two uncles takin' you back to St. Louis tomorrow like you asked us to do? I thought you'd be pleased as punch. Or is it because you've got unfinished business here in the Ozarks, like me?"

Brietta paled, understanding the implications of his words. She glared back at him with a set jaw. She refused to respond. She was trying to find the courage to be able to fight him off physically, later.

"She ain't got nothin' to say to the likes of you, Ray," Patrick said, laughing boisterously and spewing unchewed food from his mouth all over the table. "But she's regrettin' like hell that we've proved not to be a carbon copy of her daddy." He leaned his head over the table, closer to Rachel. "Ain't that the way you feel, Rachel? Don't you wish we were more like your daddy? He was a refined, educated man. We're just dumb bumpkins, ain't we?"

His gaze raked over her, stopping at her heaving breasts which strained beneath the too-tight confines of the bodice of her cotton dress. "But we're not dumb enough not to know when there's a good amount of woman flesh sittin' across the table from us," he said thickly. "My, but you've grown up, overnight, it seems. You ain't a girl no more, Rachel. You've developed into a woman. You're almost as pretty as your mama was." He shrugged. "Not as well endowed, mind you, but enough for my liking."

Rachel's face flamed with color. She slammed her fork on the table and scrambled out of her chair. "I can't take any more of this," she cried. She flung the skirt of her dress around her legs as she rushed toward the loft ladder. "I'm going to my bed. I can hardly wait for morning to come so I can leave this horrid place!"

She stopped and gave her sister a pensive stare.

"Are you coming, Brietta?" she asked, her heart thumping.

The thought of what she might be forced to do during the next hour or so frightened her so much she felt weak all over. But she still had the strength to pull the trigger, if she must!

"Hell no, she ain't goin' to bed yet," Ray spat, glaring at Brietta. "She's goin' to sit right here and eat until I tell her to leave."

Patrick motioned toward Rachel. "But you go on to bed," he said, his eyes gleaming. He looked at Ray menacingly. "And don't keep Brietta here for no reason." He flung a hand in the air. "Hell, if she ain't hungry, let her leave. Don't you know these two pretty things need their beauty sleep before headin' out on the long trip to St. Louis tomorrow?"

Ray understood Patrick's eagerness to get the twins to bed. He smiled slowly at Brietta. "I don't know what I was thinkin'," he said, pushing his half-emptied plate away from him. "Go on, Brietta. Go to bed. Me and Patrick'll clean up the table mess."

Knowing this was out of character for her two uncles, who were frequently guilty of making messes and not cleaning them up, Brietta quivered with fear. She slowly slid her chair back, not taking her eyes off her uncles as she edged backwards toward her waiting sister.

Then she turned, and she and Rachel climbed the ladder quickly, falling into each other's embrace when they reached the loft.

"I'm so frightened, Brietta," Rachel cried, clinging desperately to her. "I'm afraid to go to bed.

30

Perhaps we'd best take the guns downstairs now and shoot our uncles while they're sittin' at the table unaware."

Brietta stroked Rachel's back. "No," she whispered. "We will shoot only in self-defense. Perhaps they won't come to our beds tonight as we've feared. You know that they are often filled with nonsensical talk. Let us pray that they will drink up the rest of the whiskey in their jugs tonight and leave us be."

"I shan't get one wink of sleep worrying about it," Rachel said, easing out of Brietta's embrace. She stretched out on her bed, leaning her chin on a cupped hand as she peered through the dark at her sister. "I'm not going to change into my nightgown tonight. I'm going to sleep fully clothed, ready to flee, should the need arise."

"Yes, that's best," Brietta said, nodding. "And so shall I."

Brietta climbed into her separate bed and drew a blanket up to her chin. She reached beneath her pillow and the nearness of the pistol made her feel more courageous.

Rachel felt beneath her pillow too; the shape of the rifle made her breathe more easily. Sighing, she allowed herself to relax just a bit.

Brietta fought sleep as long as she could, then drifted off. Raucous laughter below in the main room of the cabin startled her back awake.

And then the dreaded moment came. She grew tense when she heard the creak of the ladder, knowing that someone was climbing it. She looked over at Rachel to warn her, but found that her sister had fallen sound asleep.

Her horrified gaze was drawn from her sister to Ray's silhouette, which had just appeared at the head of the ladder. She edged back farther on her bed and clung to the covers, trembling. When Ray turned to her, his hands were already unbuttoning his breeches. She slid her hand beneath the pillow and closed her fingers around the gun.

Her heart pounded as she watched him stop long enough to pull across a blanket that hung on a wire between the two beds.

Brietta sucked in a wild breath when Ray let his breeches drop around his ankles, and then stepped out of them and kicked them away. Embarrassed at what he was now fondling with one of his hands, she looked away, gulping back a feeling of revulsion. She trembled when the mattress sank beneath Ray's weight as he climbed onto the bed with her. She cried out in alarm when the covers were suddenly jerked away from her.

"What the hell?" Ray demanded loudly, his eyes staring at her fully clothed body. "Why are you still dressed? Damn it, girl, don't you know that you're supposed to shed your clothes when you go to bed for the night?"

Brietta froze as his heavy hands groped over her, familiarizing themselves with her body through her dress.

But when he roughly shoved the skirt up her legs and started pulling at her undergarments, she hesitated no longer. She pulled the pistol from beneath the pillow and aimed it straight into his face.

"Now you get off me right quick, Uncle Ray, or I swear I'll shoot you," she said, her voice weak.

"You know that Mama and Papa never meant for you to treat me and Rachel like you've been treating us. You know that Papa would turn over in his grave if he knew you were touching me in an indecent way. Now get off my bed and away from me or I'll do exactly what Papa would do if he were alive. He would not hesitate to shoot you, Ray. Nor will I."

"You're full of surprises tonight, ain't you?" Ray said, slowly moving his hand from the waistband of Brietta's undergarment. "Now, easy like, girl. Don't do anything you'll be sorry for later."

Brietta kept the pistol on Ray, determination etched on her face. "Sorry?" she said, emitting a low, sarcastic laugh. "Uncle Ray, I could shoot you without blinking an eye and most definitely without ever shedding a tear. You're beneath contempt. I don't know why Papa didn't see it. But you watched yourself while you were around Papa and Mama, didn't you? You were always on your best behavior. It was only when you were away from them that you let down your guard and showed your true self to me and Rachel. Now get off my bed or I'll show you a side of me you've never seen before."

"All right, damn it, I'm goin'," Ray said, slipping slowly from the bed. "Just don't let your finger slip on that—"

A loud gun blast on the opposite side of the blanket stole Ray's words from him. "Patrick?" he said.

The sound of gunfire had made Brietta grow limp all over. Though she knew that the plan was to shoot their uncles should they try to enter their

33

beds, she could not help but worry that their plan had gone awry.

What if Patrick had jerked the rifle away from Rachel and shot her?

Brietta had not even heard Patrick come to the loft. During that nightmare exchange with Ray, she had been aware of nothing but her tormentor.

Forgetting the danger of letting down her guard with Ray, Brietta scrambled from the bed. Still clutching the pearl-handled pistol in her hand, she shoved past him and pulled the blanket aside. Relief flooded through her when she found Patrick on the bed, writhing with pain, grabbing at his bloody left shoulder.

A sick feeling assailed Brietta when she looked at Rachel. Her sister's dress was hiked up past her thighs; her hands were still holding the rifle in a tight grip. "Rachel, are—are you all right?" she managed shakily.

"I shot him before he—he—" Rachel said, but stopped short and screamed when she saw Ray sneak up on Brietta, grabbing the pistol from her hand, then slapping her across her face.

"You little bitches!" he said from between clenched teeth. "What'd my brother raise? Two little savages?"

Rubbing her sore and throbbing cheek, Brietta inched away from Ray. "I should have shot you when I had the chance," she said, anger flaring in her eyes. She glanced at Patrick who was naked from the waist down, then glared at Ray again. "I wish Rachel's aim was more accurate. Then we'd have been rid of you both forever!"

"And, smart-ass, how do you expect you'd make

it back to St. Louis?" Ray mocked. "Two women alone would get no farther than a savage Injun camp." He laughed throatily. "When they got done with you, you'd be fast regrettin' havin' shot your uncles."

"I would prefer Indians over you two any day," Brietta said tightly.

A sudden commotion downstairs drew Ray's attention. "What now?" he said, groaning. Keeping his aim steady on Brietta he managed to get back into his breeches. "You stay put, do you hear?" he commanded. He glanced at Patrick and frowned. "Damn it, Patrick, how'd you let a woman get the draw on you? Like me, you were too anxious for what was beneath her skirt. I think we've both learned lessons tonight."

"Ray, quit your jawin' and get downstairs and see who the intruders are, then get the hell back up here and take care of things," Patrick said, wincing when renewed pain stabbed through his wounded shoulder.

"Yeah," Ray grumbled, starting down the ladder.

As soon as Ray was out of sight, Brietta went to another ladder—one that led to a trap door in the roof. "Rachel, we've got to get out of here," she said, her feet already on the bottom rung. "Come on. We must leave before Ray gets back."

Rachel came out of what had seemed a trance. She scrambled over Patrick, jerking away from him when he grabbed for her.

"You bitches!" he said, his voice weak with pain. "You won't get far! Ray'll come after you!"

Brietta reached a hand to Rachel. "Pay no

attention to him," she said. "We have to try to escape now—or it may be never. Ray is so angry at us, there is no telling what he'll do." She glanced over at Patrick as he lay on the bed, groaning. "Patrick isn't able. So it's two against one, Rachel. Let's go."

Brietta climbed the ladder with Rachel right behind her. When she reached the roof she flung the trap door open, then grabbed a rope that had been secured to the roof, placed there for quick escapes from possible Indian attacks. She threw the loose end of the rope over the side of the cabin, leaving it dangling in the wind.

"I'll go first," Brietta whispered, clutching the rope. She gave Rachel a weak smile, then let herself down the side of the cabin to the ground.

Brietta steadied the rope as Rachel began her descent, and when they were safely on the ground, they tiptoed behind the cabin and looked around to the front.

"It's Indians!" Brietta whispered, fear engulfing her. "That's who we heard downstairs! Indians!"

"Let's hurry away from this place," Rachel whispered back.

"If they hear us, there's no telling what they'll do," Brietta said, still eyeing the Indians sitting straight-backed on their horses. Apparently they were waiting for their companions who were inside, wreaking havoc. "What do you think they are doing to Uncle Ray?"

"Brietta, let's not stand here discussing it," Rachel exclaimed. "Let's go! Now!"

Brietta nodded. For a moment they clasped their hands together as they ran silently into the dark forest. But finding it awkward to run while holding hands, they slipped away from each other and ran onward, their chests heaving, their breath coming in raspy, choked sounds. A sudden desperation seized Brietta when she remembered the marshes nearby, where one could get lost and never be heard from again.

"Rachel, keep close!" Brietta said in a harsh whisper, afraid the Indians might hear her if she spoke any louder. "The marshes, Rachel! We must stay away from the marshes!"

Rachel stiffened when she heard Brietta trying to warn her of something, but her sister seemed so far away! And it was so dark! Rachel could no longer see Brietta.

Rachel stopped and clawed at the darkness around her, trying to see her sister. "Brietta, where are you?" she said, her voice thin with fear. "Brietta, I'm—I'm frightened!"

Brietta's heart pounded as she stopped and searched for Rachel. "Rachel!" she cried, an awareness of her solitude sending spirals of dread through her. Frantically, she began to run in one direction, then another, and another. "Rachel, oh, Rachel, hear me!"

Terror-stricken, Rachel began running again, reminded of the many nights she had lain awake in the cabin listening to the night noises, hearing the coyotes bark and the hoot owls uttering their calls among the trees.

But the sound she now heard made all other night noises pale in comparison. The hair bristled at the nape of her neck when loud screams of pain echoed through the forest from the cabin.

"Uncle Ray?" Rachel whispered.

The cries of pain reached Brietta, causing her to stop dead in her tracks. "Uncle Ray?" she whispered, feeling ill when she let herself imagine the torture the Indians could be inflicting on her uncle. Perhaps both Uncle Ray and Uncle Patrick!

Fearing for Rachel's welfare, she looked around for her sister again. She had never felt as empty, for she was certain now that Rachel had somehow gotten lost in the darkness.

The total aloneness was overwhelming.

CHAPTER
TWO

The little leaves hold you as soft as a child,
The little path loves you, the path that runs wild.

—*Eastman*

The stars were fading as a faint glow of pink lit the
horizon. The figure of an Indian warrior on horseback on a high butte overlooking the vastness of
the forest was silhouetted against the lightening
sky. Brave Eagle let his brown gelding's reins rest
loosely within his hand as he became lost in
thought.

Twelve winters had passed since his shared
boyhood vision with Brown Cloud, and their bond
was no less now. In this *un-a-liy*, place of friends,
their hearts and thoughts had wandered often

together. When they had dared to, they had ventured farther, walking together with *Wah-kon-tah* along the peaceful valleys and divides.

Yes, they were friends still, yet no peace had been found between their fathers.

It was an elusive thing, he thought, this word "peace."

"I see you have come again, my friend."

The voice of Brown Cloud broke through the stillness of the early morning and made Brave Eagle turn and smile, knowing that only his Osage friend had the ability to sneak up on him without his being aware of another's presence.

Brave Eagle looked down into Brown Cloud's dark eyes, knowing that once again he had come to their special meeting place on foot, his horse tethered somewhere in the forest behind them.

Brave Eagle's smile faded when he recognized the look in his friend's eyes. It told him that Brown Cloud was once again filled with the demons of alcohol.

A quick anger seized Brave Eagle. The white traders did not always bring beneficial items to sell to the Indian. They sometimes carried a strange liquor called *pe-tsa-ni*, firewater. Brown Cloud was obsessed with a desire for a feeling of great importance, and the white man's firewater produced just such a false feeling of superiority in him.

It was a weakness in his friend that Brave Eagle could not accept, or ever understand. Brave Eagle loved his own body too well ever to put a bad spirit into it. He could not understand why Brown Cloud could not see the dangers in the firewater.

"*Twi-lu-gi,*" Brave Eagle said, dismounting.

even the mention of women since the death of his wife, Snow Dove?"

Brave Eagle eased his hands from Brown Cloud's shoulders. He turned his eyes to the sky which was now turning a pale blue where the sun was a magnificent globe of orange peeking over the horizon. "It is not my wish to think of her at all except to wish that no harm befall her," he said, his voice drawn. "Spare her, Brown Cloud. Should you find her and the white man she is kin to, spare her." He turned slowly to Brown Cloud, his face a mask of icy coldness. "Or you will have me to answer to."

Stunned by Brave Eagle's insistence, Brown Cloud was at a momentary loss for words. *"Hawa,"* he finally said, nodding. "All right. No harm will come to her. But, Brave Eagle, should I find her, she is rightfully mine. It is I who killed her kin and burned her house. It is I who claim her now, as I should have then. It was only because of my haste to come to you that I did not go after my spoils of war." He thrust out his chest. "But now I go. She will be mine, Brave Eagle, to do with as I please—except that I will keep my promise not to harm her."

The thought of the white woman in the possession of Brown Cloud's Osage warrior friends, and Brown Cloud whose logic and reason were so clouded by firewater, made a strange sort of revulsion surge through Brave Eagle. Although Brown Cloud promised that he would not harm the white woman, Brown Cloud could not speak for the rest of his tribe, who would look upon her as something to toy with and torment. All white people were the Osages' enemy. The white people, even more than the Cherokee, had encroached on the Osages' hunting grounds.

Brave Eagle remained silent for the moment. Brave Eagle himself would search for the white woman. Although it was hard to understand why he should care so much, he was driven to seek her out, to make sure that she was not harmed. She had had the face of innocence. She had spoken to his heart as no woman had since the death of his beloved Snow Dove! Though she had not said a word, his heart had pounded out the message that this woman was different. That she was special in many ways.

But the white man accompanying her—what of him? From all observations, he had not been kind to her. While Brave Eagle watched from his lookout point in the forest, he had heard the white man speak to the woman harshly. Brave Eagle had even seen her glare at the white man, as though she hated him.

"Brown Cloud, she is not yours," Brave Eagle said before he even realized the words were on his lips. "You have no true claim to her."

Brown Cloud's dark eyes narrowed. "And you do?" he asked, daring his friend with an angry stare.

"It is not for either of us to lay claim to her," Brave Eagle said bluntly. "She belongs to neither."

"She will be mine once I find her," Brown Cloud argued. "I shall kill her male companion and claim her!"

"And so you will scalp her companion while she watches? You believe after that she will go with you willingly?" Brave Eagle mocked. "I think not, foolish friend."

"We shall see who is foolish!" Brown Cloud said, tightening his hands into fists at his sides.

A keen sadness assailed Brave Eagle. He placed a gentle hand on Brown Cloud's shoulder. "Up to now only fathers and firewater marred our friendship. Must stubbornness over a woman neither of us have met destroy it now?" he asked.

"Perhaps," Brown Cloud said, his features stern and unchanging. "Is she worth it, Brave Eagle?"

"Perhaps," Brave Eagle said, again envisioning her loveliness. He dropped his hand from Brown Cloud's shoulder. "I must go. This has not been a peaceful meeting between brothers. We must turn our thoughts to *Wah-kon-tah* to guide us into respect and love again." He swung himself up onto his saddle. "Ride in peace, Brown Cloud. Let love, not hate, be your companion."

Brave Eagle wheeled his gelding around and rode away, feeling for the first time in twelve winters a division of heart and spirit between himself and Brown Cloud.

Yet he had seen it coming.

It had become harder and harder to reason with his friend, whose love for firewater seemed to outweigh his love for his friend. Until now, Brave Eagle had not let Brown Cloud's strange behavior get in the way of their friendship. But his patience had run thin, especially now that someone else was involved!

Brave Eagle would not let anything happen to the white woman.

The cold nose of a squirrel sniffing at her hand awakened Brietta with a start. She bolted to her feet, then laughed when she saw that she had frightened the poor squirrel so much that it had tumbled over headfirst before fleeing.

Brietta's laughter was short-lived when she looked around her and recalled her circumstances. While she had slept, she had escaped the horrors of yesterday. But now that she was awake she was fully aware of how alone she was and that somewhere out there in the depths of the forest her sister was just as alone, just as lost!

"Rachel . . ." Brietta said to herself, placing a hand to her mouth to stifle a sob. "Where are you?"

She looked warily around her. The morning sun was just creeping through the trees overhead; the sounds of the birds and forest animals echoed around her as they had done early in the morning when she was awakening in her bed in the cabin.

"I wonder if Rachel might return to the cabin, hoping that I might also, since it is the only place we both are familiar with," Brietta whispered to herself. She peered in the direction whence she had traveled through the dark, ghostly hours of night. "Dare I return to see? What will I find? Did the Indians kill both Ray and Patrick? What if Indians are waiting for our return?"

Downhearted and afraid, Brietta saw no choice but to go back to the cabin. She must do everything within her power to find Rachel. Together they might have a chance against the evils of the world.

Alone, they were at the mercy of everyone and everything.

Her dress ripped, her hair tangled, Brietta moved through the forest again. Although her stomach ached unmercifully from hunger, she did not want to waste any more time on herself. Having taken the time to sleep had been selfish. She should have continued looking for Rachel through the entire night!

"I shall find her," she whispered harshly. "I . . . shall . . ."

She trudged onward, her back aching, her arms and legs burning where sharp briars had pierced the cotton of her dress, snagging on her tender flesh.

And after what seemed an eternity she became aware of a different smell in the air.

She stopped and sniffed hard, then grew pale with worry. What she was smelling was the distinct odor of smouldering ashes. She looked desperately around her, wondering if there had been a recent fire in the forest, perhaps caused by lightning.

But there was no other sign of a fire.

She had gained her bearings now and knew where she was. And what she was seeing puzzled her. It was a void where she now realized the cabin should be standing!

Lifting the hem of her dress into her arms she broke into a mad run, then stopped abruptly when she came to the clearing and saw the true horror of what had happened after she and her sister had fled the previous night. The cabin had been burned to the ground. Nothing was left but ashes.

She turned her gaze slowly along the ground, close beside the cabin. Her eyes locked on the macabre sight of her Uncle Ray. He was dead, his scalp missing.

She turned around, hung her head, and retched.

CHAPTER
THREE

No sister flower would be forgiven
If it disdained its brother.

—*Shelley*

The breeze was light, yet it stirred the ashes of the burned cabin into the air, as though ghostly apparitions were dancing in the wind around Brietta. She wiped her mouth clean with the sleeve of her dress and turned slowly back to the ruins, willing her eyes not to return to her uncle's body.

And what of her other uncle? Had Patrick died in the loft, too weak from his gunshot wound to flee?

Not knowing Rachel's fate, Brietta had to wonder if she was now the only survivor of those who had so hopefully left St. Louis to find a new life in the Arkansas Ozarks.

She looked back at her Uncle Ray and shuddered at the thought of burying him. Without his scalp, and with his eyes transfixed in such a grotesque death stare, he looked like some strange sort of being that was not of this earth.

"I must bury him," she whispered to herself, tears flooding her eyes anew. "And then I must continue searching for Rachel. I have to believe that she is not dead. That hope alone can help keep me sane!"

The shack that she had always wondered about had also been burned to the ground. She went to it and stared at the remains of what had once been stored there, realizing that she would now never know the true fate of her parents.

But in the ashes she saw the remains of a shovel. Finding it almost too hot to hold, she picked it up gingerly and went beneath the shade of a tree to begin digging. Tears mingled with sweat as she dug deeper and deeper, then stopped when she thought the hole was big enough to place her uncle in it.

Sobbing, she returned to her uncle's body. The sick feeling grabbed her at the pit of her stomach again as she stooped and placed her hands at his armpits and began dragging him toward the hole. He had been a massive man, one who had loved to eat, and she could only manage to get him across the dried earth an inch at a time. She stopped frequently to catch her breath and wipe the torrent of tears from her face.

But finally she had him in the hole and covered by a mound of dirt, glad that his grotesque corpse was no longer in sight.

Pushing dampened strands of her hair back from her face, Brietta stared down at the grave. She knew what was required to make the Christian burial complete. She must say words of kindness over the grave. And she would find that hard. She had never liked her uncle. How could she say anything that would fit the occasion without lying?

Firming her jaw, Brietta sank to her knees beside the grave, knowing that she must get this over with so that she could flee this place of death.

If the Indians returned . . . !

"Uncle Ray," she began softly. "Though you never showed me any love or respect, I hope that in that world you have now entered, you are treated kindly. May God have mercy on your soul. Amen."

She rose to her feet and looked away from the grave. Now she must decide which way she should travel to find civilization before Indians found her. She had heard of a Fort Smith that was several days' ride from here. She had heard of a new mission being erected somewhere close by.

She stared at the barn, which had also been burned. Either the Indians had stolen the horses, or the animals had perished in the fire as Patrick surely had.

Sighing heavily and straightening her back, Brietta began walking. No matter which way she went, her fate was now in God's hands. Surely in His wisdom, He had also spared Rachel.

Pushing her way through the forest, she fought twisting vines that hung from the trees, and thorn bushes that grew in masses on the ground beneath the trees. The more she walked and the more time she had to think, the more she hated men. She hated her uncles, who had raided the Indians and taken slaves. She hated them for lusting after her and Rachel. She hated those warriors who had killed and scalped without mercy.

After walking without resting for some time, Brietta realized how hungry she was, yet she was afraid to stop for any reason.

Rachel.

She must search for Rachel!

Her sister had to be alive!

Unable to walk much further, Brietta managed to make her way toward the shine of water she glimpsed through an opening in the trees ahead. Panting, she began a slow run, then ran faster when she saw thick, juicy grapes hanging from a vine, just ripe for the picking, beside the river.

Brietta fell to her knees beside the grape-vines and began plucking and eating the sweet and juicy morsels until her stomach felt comfortably full. Revitalized, she went to the river and knelt down beside it. Splashing her face and hair, she relished the feel of the water that was washing away the dirt and sweat. She held her head back and combed her wet fingers through her hair, untangling it.

Again she leaned over the water.

But before she could fill her hands with the cool, clear liquid, she screamed and almost fainted with fear when she found another reflection in the water beside hers.

It was the face of an Indian warrior!

Brave Eagle was taken off guard by the woman's sudden reaction to seeing him, then understood. Had she not fled her home because of atrocities committed by Indians? If she had seen Brown Cloud scalping her kin, perhaps she would never get over her fear of Indians—any Indians, even though it was the Osage who had done the killing and scalping.

Brietta scrambled to her feet and slowly backed away from Brave Eagle along the embankment of the river, her heart hammering inside her chest. All she could think about was how horribly her uncle had been murdered.

Would she be next?

"Do not fear me," Brave Eagle tried to reassure her in the English language, which he had learned from white traders. "No harm will come to you. I come as *i-gi-na-le-i*, friend. I am of the *Ani-yun-wiya*, Cherokee, nation. We are at peace with your people. Let me help you."

Though the white woman's eyes were filled with fear, Brave Eagle could not help admiring her beauty. She had flawless features and liquid curves —and eyes that could mesmerize.

Since the death of his beloved Snow Dove, he had not allowed himself to see anything special in any woman. Even his five-year-old son, Rising Fawn, had been kept from his view, upon his request; Brave Eagle's mother cared for him. He had not been able to look upon his son without seeing the gentle face of his beloved dead wife in every feature!

But he could not deny his cravings for a woman any longer.

And not just any woman.

He wanted this woman standing before him. Surely, his desire for her was forbidden by the Great Spirit!

"If you are a friend, then let me pass by you and go on my way," Brietta said, finding herself puzzling over her reaction to him. Never had she been so close to an Indian. Never would she have thought that an Indian could be so handsome. Tall and robust, this man was a perfect human figure, his features regular, his forehead and brow suggesting heroism and bravery.

His eyes were fathomless, the pupils midnight black, and his nose was aquiline. He seemed dignified and proud, and most certainly unwavering beneath her glare!

Her gaze lowered, and she blushed when she saw the scantiness of his attire. If the wind blew even slightly and lifted the flaps of his breechclout, he would surely be the same as naked!

"It is not wise for Brave Eagle to let you go, to wander alone in the forest," he said, his speech slow and reserved, even somewhat musical, yet frank. "I will take you to my home. There you can eat well. There you can rest."

Brietta's eyes glittered mutinously as she looked up at him again. "Do you truly believe that I can be swayed by gentle words into accompanying you to a village of—of savages?" she interrupted, regretting having said the word "savage" the instant it left her lips. Brave Eagle's expression changed from compassionate to harsh. If she were to come out of this ordeal alive, she must try to be more diplomatic!

Brave Eagle called upon his reserve of iron will and self-control, so that he would not react to this white woman's verbal attack. He had been called "savage" numerous times before, but coming from this woman, the insult cut more deeply than ever before. He had come to protect her and she was not grateful.

Yet again he reminded himself of the horrors she had witnessed. He had to make sure they were not repeated. He must save her from the Osage at all cost! Even if he had to hand her over to the white pony soldiers at Fort Smith, it must be done.

Perhaps that would be best. She was a danger to him. The dark droop of her lashes over her eyes . . . her lips of fire . . . her slim and sinuous body. . . .

"Do not fight my decision," he said quickly, grabbing her wrist. "It is best that you go with me today. Tomorrow we shall see. . . ."

"Tomorrow you will probably place my scalp along with the others that wave on your scalp poles!" Brietta put in, trying to free her wrist from his tight grip. She looked up into his dark, determined eyes. "Please let me go. I must search for my—"

"So, my friend, you have found her," Brown Cloud said as he rode up and dismounted. He walked slowly around Brave Eagle and Brietta, his eyes appraising her. "I thank you for doing me this service."

He stopped and glared at Brave Eagle. "Brave Eagle, release her to me. She is mine."

Terrified, Brietta looked desperately from Brave Eagle to Brown Cloud. Fighting off one Indian was bad enough. Now there were two and she had no hope of escaping.

"My Osage friend, she goes with me," Brave Eagle said flatly, tightening his grip on Brietta's wrist. "I cannot honor your claim to her."

Brietta looked up at Brave Eagle, then slowly over at Brown Cloud, wondering what claim the Cherokee warrior was talking about. The other Indian was Osage. Why would he declare that she was his? He had no more claim on her than the Cherokee warrior who called himself Brave Eagle!

Her mind was swimming with questions. Who was this Osage Indian? Could he have known her uncles? Could they have made a bargain with this Indian before the tragedies of last night? Was this Osage warrior responsible for everything that had happened at the cabin?

Brietta's thoughts were brought back to the ordeal at hand when Brave Eagle released his grip on her wrist. Holding himself erect, he faced the Osage warrior.

With this release, Brietta saw a possible chance of escape. Slowly she began to back away from the quarreling Indians.

"We have been best friends for twelve winters, Brown Cloud, but this time I cannot comply with your wishes. I have found the woman," Brave Eagle said. "She is now mine. If you wish to challenge my right to her, so be it!"

Brown Cloud's vision was blurred from the firewater he had been consuming while searching the forest for the white woman, and he swayed before Brave Eagle's defiant stare. He was stunned by his friend's insistence on possessing the white woman. Indeed, she was lovely, but was she worth losing a best friend?

Still, he had never backed away from a challenge.

Brown Cloud drew a knife from the sheath at his waist. "We fight with knives!" he said, brandishing his weapon before Brave Eagle.

Brave Eagle frowned. He had smelled the firewater on his friend's breath and he could hear the slur of his speech.

"No," he said, taking his knife from its sheath and tossing it on the ground beside him. "You are in no condition to fight with knives. The *pe-tsa-ni*, the demon of alcohol, is muddying your sense of logic. It will also affect your skills with your weapon. We will arm wrestle only, my friend."

Refusing to listen to sense, Brown Cloud lunged for Brave Eagle, his knife unsteady in his grip. Brave Eagle stepped quickly aside, and the blade missed him.

He continued to elude Brown Cloud's thrusts, and his adversary tripped and almost fell several times. Brave Eagle knew that if his friend were sober, he never would have started the fight. And understanding this, he continued stepping aside, keeping his anger at bay.

Brietta scarcely breathed as she continued to move slowly backward. She was waiting until they became fully absorbed in their fight before turning to make a mad dash into the forest.

Brave Eagle knew of only one way to stop the fight. He grabbed Brown Cloud's wrist, halting the knife so that the blade gleamed beneath the sun's rays. Sweat pearled Brave Eagle's brow as he pushed against Brown Cloud's wrist, trying to make him drop the weapon. He was amazed at his friend's strength. He had thought him weakened by the demon alcohol.

But Brown Cloud held his arm steady, his muscles bulging.

"You do well, friend," Brave Eagle said in a grunt, continuing to try to disarm Brown Cloud. "But . . . I . . . will be the victor! She . . . will . . . be mine!"

"No," Brown Cloud grunted, the muscles of his arms aching fiercely. "She . . . will . . . be mine!"

Brietta smiled as she listened to them claiming her, knowing that now was the time to turn and run. They were too busy glaring into one another's eyes even to notice.

Lifting the hem of her dress above her ankles, Brietta turned and ran—and ran, and ran. She welcomed the darker depths of the forest, hoping that somehow she could find a peaceful refuge where neither Indian could find her.

Finally, Brave Eagle jarred the knife from Brown Cloud's grasp, then quickly wrestled him to the ground and pinned him there, straddling him. He held Brown Cloud's wrists to the ground for a moment longer, looking into the eyes of a man defeated, feeling strangely less than victorious himself.

Brave Eagle rose to his feet, then stiffened when he discovered that Brietta was no longer there. His gaze searched frantically for signs of her; then he doubled his fists at his sides, and rage filled his eyes.

He turned and glared down at Brown Cloud.

"She is gone! She belongs to neither of us now!" he stormed. He grabbed up his knife and placed it quickly in its sheath, then began running toward his tethered gelding. "But she will! I will find her again!"

As Brave Eagle rode away, Brown Cloud buried his face in his arm, struggling to get his breath.

Then he grabbed his knife, rose shakily to his feet and mounted his stallion and also rode away. "She will be mine!" he shouted into the wind. "I will make it so!"

Pain was wracking Brietta's side from the exertion of running. But she would not give in to it. She must not stop, or else she would become a captive again.

Her heart skipped a beat when she heard the thundering of hoofbeats coming up behind her . . .

CHAPTER
FOUR

You kissed me! My heart, my breath, and my will
In delirious joy for a moment stood still!

—*Hunt*

Panic seized Brietta when she heard the horse
drawing closer. She took a quick look over her
shoulder. She could tell that the approaching
horseman was an Indian, but at this distance, she
still could not tell which one.

Breathing hard and determined not to give up
easily, she focused her attention straight ahead
and began running even harder through the deep
shadows of the forest. Suddenly, with a jerk of her
body, she fell clumsily across a log that lay in her

path. She cried out with pain when her head hit the ground with an impact that momentarily stunned her.

Through a haze, Brietta heard the horse come to a halt somewhere close beside her. She could hear the animal's heavy wheezing. She could smell the scent of its sweaty lather.

Blinking her eyes nervously, she raised herself on one elbow. When she touched her head, her hand came away wet with blood. She winced in fright when she felt strong arms engulfing her.

When she looked up into dark, scalding eyes, a part of her was glad that it was Brave Eagle and not the Osage Indian. She had been aware of the other Indian's drunken state, for she had come to recognize that look after her uncles had consumed a good amount of whiskey. She had smelled liquor often enough on their breaths, and had seen the same vacant look in their bloodshot eyes. She knew better than to trust anyone who was a drunk.

But what of this Cherokee warrior? Although it was apparent that his mind was not twisted by alcohol, what was his reason for showing so much kindness and concern for her? Was it all to mislead her?

She could not let down her guard.

Not with Indians.

Not with anyone!

"You are hurt," Brave Eagle said, seeing the wound on her scalp. He felt her pain as though she were one with him. How could he explain this attraction? It seemed to go deeper than anything he'd known before.

If he was smart, he would turn and run away and never look back!

But he could not. She needed him as never before. Wounded, she was at the mercy of everything on two and four legs in the Ozark wilderness!

"I'll be fine," Brietta said, grimacing when she saw the blood on her fingers. She forced herself not to show alarm over her injury. She could show no weakness before this Indian.

"You have lost much blood," Brave Eagle said, parting her hair so that he could get a closer look at the wound. "Brave Eagle will treat it with herbs. Brave Eagle will make it well."

"I can care for it myself," Brietta said, moving his hand away. "Please go on your way. You need not concern yourself over me."

"We must get away from here or I will be forced to fight with Brown Cloud for your honor again," Brave Eagle said, taking it upon himself to lift Brietta up into his arms. "I will take you to water. There I will bathe your wound."

With all of the strength she could muster, she shoved at Brave Eagle's chest as he carried her toward his horse. "Let me down," she demanded, growing dizzy as she used her waning strength to fight him.

When he lifted her onto his buffalo-skin saddle, which was stuffed with dried grasses, she gave up. She soon found herself even glad to feel him mount behind her; his body was like steel against hers as he drew her backside against the front of him, anchoring her safely to his body. A tremor went through her as his arm snaked around her waist and held her in place while he sent his horse into a hard gallop.

But the pain in her head soon overtook all her other senses. She hung her face in her hands and closed her eyes, moaning.

"We will soon find water," Brave Eagle said, eyeing her bobbing head, afraid that she had perhaps lost consciousness due to the loss of blood. "White woman will be all right. You shall see the magic of my medicines soon."

"Brietta," she found herself saying before she had thought consciously of revealing her name to him. She raised her eyes and looked over her shoulder at him. "I have a name. It is Brietta. Brietta Russell."

Brave Eagle's eyes lit up. "Brave Eagle," he said, his chest proudly swelling. "I am called Brave Eagle."

Brietta smiled weakly at him before again sinking her face in her hands.

Touched by Brietta's sweetness and glad that she was no longer fighting him, Brave Eagle felt his heart soar into the heavens like the eagle that he had seen on the morning of his boyhood vision. That day he had started down the long path in search of his destiny. Was the Great Spirit looking down upon him even now, saying that this woman was part of his destiny?

Soon he would see.

But he must remember to be cautious with his heart. He had lost one woman. Would it be wise, he wondered, to chance losing another? The heart healed so slowly!

Brave Eagle hauled back his reins and stopped

his gelding beside the shine of a stream that twisted beneath a low overhang of clustered maple trees.

Brietta blinked her eyes nervously as she raised her head, worried when she discovered that her vision was still blurred from the blow to her head. If she were given the opportunity to escape, she needed to be able to see more than two feet ahead of her. As it was, she could hardly make out the outline of her hand as she held it out before her.

"We are here," Brave Eagle said, sliding out of his saddle. He placed his strong hands at Brietta's waist and gently lifted her from the horse. Allowing her to lean against him, he led her to the embankment and to a soft bed of moss.

When he reached for the hem of her dress, Brietta tensed and slapped his hand away.

"Your wound must be bathed," Brave Eagle said, his dark eyes filled with compassion as he looked down at her. "Give me a portion of your dress. I will use it to cleanse your wound. Nothing else."

Blushing, feeling foolish for having misinterpreted this Indian's motives, Brietta ripped a portion of her dress away and meekly handed it to him. She watched him guardedly as he went to the stream and dipped the cloth into the water, then went away for a moment into the deeper depths of the forest. She had to surmise that he was now searching for the herbs that he had mentioned earlier.

Sighing deeply, she lay down on the ground and closed her eyes, knowing that she was defenseless against this Indian, yet strangely not fearing him any longer. Surely no one so gentle could cause her harm.

Yet she could still see her murdered parents, scalped so unmercifully. Even more recent, the discovery of her scalped uncle reminded her just how savagely vicious an Indian could be!

Could they be gentle one minute—cruel and unjust the next?

"This will hurt but for a moment," Brave Eagle said as he returned and settled himself on his haunches beside her.

Brietta looked quickly up at him. Her eyes held Brave Eagle's as he leaned over her, his brow knit in a worried expression.

Then, realizing that her vision had cleared somewhat, she let her gaze take in his finely chiseled, bronzed face. Her heart pounded when she became aware of his bare, wide, and muscled shoulders, and his hard, flat stomach which tapered to narrow hips.

Brietta averted her eyes quickly from that part of his anatomy that was clad in only a brief breech-clout. When she looked up at him, she found that he was still looking at her, but this time with strange lights moving in the depths of his eyes, and with a smile that softened his strong jaw and well-defined cheekbones.

Suddenly he had dropped the wet cloth and his hands were on her throat, framing her face. Her breath coming in short rasps, Brietta watched his lips moving toward hers. The whole world seemed to start spinning when he kissed her, his lips setting fires inside her that felt deliciously wonderful, yet dangerous. . . .

Her heart pounding, afraid of how this Indian was making her feel, Brietta began shoving at his chest.

But it was all in vain. He grabbed her wrists and held them to his chest, his lips now at the hollow of her throat, setting flames anew within her.

And then he eased his grip from her wrists and moved away from her, his back to her for a moment, his mood turned somber.

Her face aflame, her heart still beating in an erratic fashion, Brietta placed her fingertips to her lips, still tasting his kiss there, still dazzled by it. She was afraid to breathe, much less speak. For a moment her world and the Indian's had become one. He had been a man, she a woman, with no difference in skin color affecting how they felt about each other.

Even now, as she stared with wonder at his muscled copper back, she knew that he had awakened a desire in her that surely could never die.

But how could it have happened? Such a love between them was forbidden! She knew it, and so must he.

Did he not, even at this moment, feel awkward because of their shared kiss?

Did he not, even now, turn his back to her, perhaps ashamed of what his feelings had led him to do with a woman forbidden to him?

And what dangers did she face? Would a moment of sweet passion turn to a vicious rape?

Alarmed at how his feelings had gotten out of control, Brave Eagle stared angrily into the rustling stream as it rushed across the pebbled ground. Minnows darting to and fro seemed to imitate his erratic heartbeat. Not since Snow Dove had he let his emotions go astray in the wonder of a woman's kiss.

But the kiss of the white woman who called herself Brietta was different.

Like the softness of a rose, or the touch of a butterfly's wings, both of which were sent to Mother Earth with the blessings of the Great Spirit, her kiss was a wonder.

A renewed stab of pain in her head made Brietta sway and moan. She closed her eyes and clutched her head, her fingers coming away from the wound freshly bloodied.

Brave Eagle flinched as though he had been shot when he heard Brietta's cry of pain. With a wildness in his eyes, he turned and looked at her, then alarm set in when he saw a fresh stream of blood spiraling from her head wound. Casting aside his desirous feelings for this white woman, he went to her and urged her down on the ground.

"Keep your eyes closed, and soon your wound will feel much better," he said, quickly mixing a compound of herbs and several drops of water in the palm of his hand. He held this mixture with one hand, then began softly dabbing the blood away from the wound with the cloth in his other.

When Brietta gasped and her hands circled into tight fists at her sides, Brave Eagle frowned, again feeling her pain as though it were his. "Soon it will be over," he tried to reassure her, applying the herbal mixture. "And then I will take you to my village where you can eat and rest."

Brietta's eyes flashed open at the mention of his village. She had heard of white women who were held captive, forced to do Indian labor—and even worse.

She would never submit to such treatment!

Although she had to admit that what he was applying to her scalp was beginning to make it feel better, she scooted away from him on the ground, refusing to let him continue. "I will go nowhere with you," she said, stubbornly tilting her chin. "Do you hear? Nowhere! I will be no one's prisoner! No one's!"

Brave Eagle moved to her side again. Looking forcefully into her eyes, he drew an imaginary line in mid-air to signify that what he said was final, and he wasn't having any further argument about it.

"You will go with me," he said matter-of-factly. "But hear me well, Brietta, it will never be as a captive. When you are well, you will be free to go. It is as simple as that." He began smoothing the herbal mixture onto her wound again. "Brietta? Do you now see that I intend you no harm? That I am a *tso-ga-li-li*?"

Brietta closed her eyes and allowed Brave Eagle to continue his ministrations. "*Tso-ga-li-li*?" she murmured. "How do I know if that word means friend or enemy? I do not know the Cherokee language."

"Then Brave Eagle will teach you," he said, again matter-of-factly. He paused, lifted his hand from her scalp, and looked down at her with his night-black eyes. *"Tso-ga-li-li*? It means I offer you friendship, Brietta. Friendship."

His thumb lightly caressed her flushed cheeks, and his words were so gentle and caring that Brietta could not speak for the moment. She feared that anything she said might reveal to him exactly how he was making her feel. Her every heartbeat was revealing to her just how much she wanted him to kiss her again.

And was it just friendship that he was offering her? She could see passion burning in his eyes, which surely mirrored the same in hers.

She looked away from him, afraid of many things at this moment—above all her feelings for the handsome Cherokee warrior!

Stung by defeat at the hands of his best friend, Brown Cloud thrust his heels harder into his horse, forcing his mount into a gallop beneath the dark canopy of trees. He had wasted too much time before deciding to go after the white woman, still determined not to let Brave Eagle have her.

In this part of the forest, where the sun was elusive, and in his drunken haze, he had lost sight of the white woman's footprints, and now even Brave Eagle's horse's tracks. It was with a wildness that he now ventured onward, hoping that somehow he might be lucky enough to come across them together, for he had to believe that Brave Eagle had caught up with the woman and had captured her.

"U-yo-i-," Brown Cloud grumbled to himself. "She will be mine! I have much to prove to Brave

Eagle! He shames me too often for my love of *pe-tsa-ni*! Why does he not know that firewater makes one strong, not weak? I must prove him wrong. I . . . must. . . ."

Brown Cloud's words blew away into the wind. Then he caught sight of something beside a stream up ahead that made him blink his eyes over and over again to see if it was a mirage, or real.

When his vision became more exact, his lips lifted into a smug smile, for he now realized that he had outdone Brave Eagle after all! He had found the white woman before his friend! Brown Cloud's worth would be proven—he was able to beat Brave Eagle in this challenge!

Drawing his horse to a plunging halt, Brown Cloud's eyes never left the woman who was eating blackberries ravenously from vines which twisted along the embankment of the stream. He could not help but marvel at her skill at eluding Brave Eagle. It made winning her from Brave Eagle even more of a victory.

And wouldn't she draw many valuables from the white slavers?

His heart pounded at the prospect!

Smiling victoriously, Brown Cloud dismounted and secured his stallion's reins to a low tree limb. Moving stealthily beneath the low-hanging branches of the trees, he circled around behind the woman. Not a sound did his moccasined feet make. Nor did he allow himself to expel great breaths of air, for he did not want to alarm her and chance having to draw a knife to force her to do as he wished. A strip of leather was hanging from his waistband. Soon he would have her wrists tied. He would have her on his horse. When he entered his village with his prize, would he not be the envy of those who surveyed her?

Only a footstep away from the white woman, Brown Cloud paused for a moment to steady himself, then lunged toward her and clasped one hand around her mouth, while with his other hand he twisted her wrist behind her.

"You thought you could get away from Brown Cloud?" he snarled, jerking her around so that she could look at him. He smiled smugly down at her, glad to see intense fear in her eyes. "You eluded Brave Eagle, but not Brown Cloud. I now have proven who is the most cunning of friends!"

Rachel Russell was cold with fear as she stared up at the Indian who spoke in English skillfully enough for her to make out what he was saying.

And none of it was making sense!

Who was Brave Eagle? What did this Indian mean by saying that she had eluded a person called Brave Eagle?

And not only did this Indian reek of whiskey, he looked down at her with such an evil, victorious glint in his eyes that tears began to stream across her cheeks. Rachel wondered if Brietta had found the same fate in this forest that seemed to have no beginning and no end.

Now it seemed that they never would see one another again.

"Come," Brown Cloud said, jerking Rachel roughly around and giving her a shove toward his

horse. "You are now mine. If you try to escape
again, I will have no choice but to kill you."

Rachel looked over her shoulder. "Again?" she
murmured. "What—do you mean? I don't know
you from Adam. Who—"

Her words were stolen and her breath seemed
suddenly lodged in her throat when Brown Cloud
jerked a menacingly long knife from the sheath at
his waist. When he placed it at her throat, her head
began spinning, and soon a blackness engulfed her
as she fainted and crumpled to the ground in a
heap at his feet.

Brown Cloud's eyes wavered as he slowly lowered his knife. "Her courage fails her so quickly?"
he marveled. He frowned, now wondering if she
would be as valuable.

Then he shrugged, knowing that the white slaver
would not know of her lack of courage anyhow, for
Brown Cloud was going to place her on a stake in
the midst of his village for all to mock.

Smiling devilishly down at her, Brown Cloud
slipped his knife into its sheath. Bending to one
knee, he lifted Rachel into his arms and carried
her toward his horse. He would proudly place this
white woman out in full view, for even Brave Eagle
to see—to prove Brown Cloud's cunning prowess!

Stumbling in his drunken stupor, Brown Cloud
grabbed for his horse, then lay Rachel across his
saddle. "White woman, soon my people will take
much pleasure from touching your hair and snow-
white skin," he said, clumsily pulling himself up
onto his horse.

The flap of Brown Cloud's breechcloth whipped

across Rachel's ashen face as he lifted his reins and rode away in a hard gallop.

In another part of the forest, an Indian was crouched behind flowering lilac bushes, watching Brave Eagle ministering to Brietta. "Running Wolf has seen how Brave Eagle fought Brown Cloud to win white woman," he whispered to himself, frowning thoughtfully.

Running Wolf was small in stature, his hair drawn back in one long braid down his back; his skin was the identical tone of bronze as Brave Eagle's. Running Wolf chuckled to himself. A plan was forming in his brain—one that would turn friends into bitter enemies! He would steal the white woman away from Brave Eagle to cause problems between the two blood brothers. Brave Eagle would think that Brown Cloud had stolen her away. Friends would become enemies over this woman! Running Wolf would make it so! He had not appreciated being forced to atone for Brave Eagle's sins—sins that Brave Eagle still commited by secretly meeting with the Osage brave, Brown Cloud.

Unable to hear the words being spoken between Brave Eagle and Brietta, Running Wolf settled himself more comfortably on his haunches and became lost in thought. He would never forget the day that he had been singled out from Brave Eagle's other nephews and cousins to bear the guilt for his powerful relative. A great warrior was not allowed to atone, personally, for crimes he committed. Brave Eagle had committed this crime one and one-half years ago—the crime of having been discovered consorting with an Osage!

By family agreement, Running Wolf, the smallest in stature, had become Brave Eagle's scapegoat. The ruling of the family had been that Running Wolf would spend two years hiding from vengeance at the *City of Peace*, where fugitives from vengeance found sanctuary.

"I am dishonored because of Brave Eagle," Running Wolf whispered to himself. "Somehow I must find some way of avenging the wrong he has done me! This woman. Surely she is the way!"

Running Wolf grew tense. His hand moved to his sheathed knife when Brave Eagle lifted Brietta gently up into his arms and began carrying her toward his gelding. His eyebrow quirked, wondering about how gently Brave Eagle treated this white woman.

But did it not prove just how much she meant to him?

Smiling smugly, Running Wolf nodded. "Yes, she will cause many hard feelings between blood brothers," he whispered. "Perhaps even a war between the Osage and Cherokee. Would my people not come for me, to ask me to fight with them? Yes, this plan is perfect! Perfect!"

He stalked toward his Appaloosa pony as he heard Brave Eagle's gelding ride away. In one movement he had swung himself into his saddle. With the skill of a panther, Running Wolf followed just close enough behind Brave Eagle not to lose sight of him—or the woman!

CHAPTER FIVE

While that heart is still unwon, oh! bid not mine
   to rove,
But let it nurse its humble faith and
   uncomplaining love.

—*Moultrie*

Tall stands of hardwood ranged along the lower slopes, changing to hemlock, pine, and balsam as the land rose higher. Brietta clung to Brave Eagle's arm that held her firmly before him on his saddle as he urged his horse onward. She wondered how much longer it would be before they reached his village.

And once there, what fate awaited her? Would

this tribe of Cherokee resent Brave Eagle's kindness to her?

Her only hope was that he was a man of power in his village, a voice of authority, one who set down his own rules.

She questioned him with her eyes when he drew rein beside a gently flowing river, then dismounted. Yet she did not complain when he placed his hands at her waist and lifted her from the horse. She was weary from the long journey in the saddle and was glad to place her feet on solid ground.

"Why have we stopped?" she asked. Her head was beginning to pound again. She had felt a slight trickle of blood on her forehead which she now brushed away with the back of her hand.

"We will spend the night here," Brave Eagle said, seeing that Brietta's wound was bleeding slightly again. "You need the rest. We ride on to my village at the rise of the sun."

Sighing, tired and aching, Brietta still chose not to argue with him. After all, did this not give her another opportunity to escape? While he slept, she would sneak away.

But this time she would not be on foot. She would steal his horse! He would not be able to find her all that easily a second time!

"Whatever you say," she said, avoiding looking into his eyes. He had such a way of disturbing her. She had never seen anyone as handsome.

And the way he spoke! So musically! So musically and so kind . . .

Leaning the right side of her face in her hand to soothe the more pronounced ache at her temples,

Brietta sat down on the ground while Brave Eagle built a fire.

A short while later, she grimaced and emitted a soft gasp when he urged her up from the ground and toward a tree. Then he tied her to it.

"What do you think you're doing?" Brietta asked in a half shriek. "You said that—that I wasn't a captive, yet you are tying me to a tree?"

"I cannot leave for the hunt and chance that you will try to flee and get lost in the forest without my protection," Brave Eagle said, securing the rope at her wrists only enough to make sure she did not work herself free. "You are not safe without me. You must be made to understand that."

"I did not ask you to become my protector," Brietta said venomously. "Let me go! Release me at once!"

Brave Eagle tied the final knot. He leaned away from her, his gaze devouring her. Reaching a hand to her cheek, he touched it gently, then flinched when she jerked herself free of his touch.

He smiled slowly as he rose to his full height over her. "Your words and actions do not match what you feel in your heart," he said, daring her with a bold stare. "When we kissed, it was not the kiss of a woman who hates. You kissed with feelings—feelings of a woman who cares. So, white woman, Brave Eagle refuses to listen to anything but the message you sent to my heart with your kiss."

Brietta was taken aback by what he was saying. Her face flamed with a blush, knowing that it was true. Even now she was being awakened anew by passionate feelings as he stood over her in a display

81

of sinewed shoulders, eyes that were dark and knowing, and a breechclout that was not hiding all that well what was defined beneath it. She could not deny to herself, or aloud to him, that if he surrounded her with his hard, strong arms, and pressed her against him, surely all of the fight would melt from within her.

Afraid that he might be able to read her thoughts, she looked quickly away.

"I won't be gone long," Brave Eagle said, going to his horse to grab a rifle from its leather sheath. "The rope will be removed upon my return."

"And for what purpose, may I ask?" Brietta said sarcastically, turning her eyes to glare rebelliously up at him. "Just so that you can tie me up again when it is convenient for you to do so?"

When he ignored her sarcasm and walked from her sight, she became aware of just how alone she was, and of the darkness that was creeping up on her as the sun faded from the treetops, replaced by a few twinkling stars and only a thin slice of a moon.

A blast from a gun from the darkness of the forest made her recoil and look more intensely in the direction of the sound. Her heartbeat quickened when Brave Eagle did not return immediately after the gunshot blast. Her thoughts went wild. What if it hadn't been him firing? What if somebody else was close by? Surely no one else could be as kind to her, or as thoughtful as Brave Eagle.

Brietta shook her head, realizing just where her thoughts had taken her. For a moment she was actually thinking that she could trust Brave Eagle. Must she remind herself that no men were to be trusted? Even her own kin had treated her badly! Even her own kin had planned to rape her and Rachel!

"Rachel," Brietta whispered to herself. "Where, oh, where are you? If only we could be together. . . ."

Relief flowed through her when Brave Eagle came into sight, the campfire casting dancing shadows on his muscled, bronzed body. She now understood what had taken him so long. He had stopped somewhere farther down the river and had cleaned the rabbit that he was carrying by its hind legs. She scarcely breathed as he positioned it over the fire on a spit, then came to her and knelt down on his haunches before her.

"How decent of you to finally untie me," Brietta said sharply as he worked with the knots in the rope that was holding her in place around the tree.

"Only long enough for you to eat," Brave Eagle said, his voice edged with warning. Their eyes met and held as Brave Eagle paused before untying the remaining knots.

"While we sleep your wrists will be tied to mine," he added, his voice void of emotion. "It is for your welfare."

Anger flared in Brietta's eyes. "Just as you have appointed yourself as my—my guardian is for my welfare," she fumed. "I was doing just fine until you and—and whatever his name was came along. I could get along just fine now!"

"If you want to test that theory, I will let you go," Brave Eagle said, dropping the rope away from her. He gestured with a hand toward the farthest stretch of the dark and beckoning forest.

"Go. Search for your own food. Search for a safe place to sleep. Without a weapon see just how many coyotes you can keep from your beautiful white skin. Their teeth would soon mar its beauty." He paused and frowned. "Even worse than that, beautiful white woman."

Paling at the thought of what he described, knowing that what he said was true, Brietta swallowed hard. "Must you make it sound so—so dreadful?" she said, a shudder encompassing her. She rubbed her wrists where faint lines had been pressed into her flesh from the rope. "People have learned to fend for themselves from the beginning of time. So shall I."

In her mind's eye she was envisioning Rachel cowering away from a pack of coyotes, and the thought sickened her. If only Rachel could have found someone who wanted to protect her as Brave Eagle had taken upon himself to be Brietta's protector. Deep down inside, where her private feelings were hidden, she was glad for Brave Eagle. Glad!

She now doubted she would try to escape even if given the chance. It was at this moment that she knew that he was her only chance of survival.

At least until she was stronger and could steal a weapon and horse from him.

After she arrived at his village . . .

After she was stronger and had the ability to go and search for her sister . . .

"You are free to go," Brave Eagle persisted, rising to his full height. He folded his arms across his powerful chest and looked with a silent rage down at her.

When Brietta did not move, a slow smile tugged at his lips. "White woman, why do you not go?" he taunted. "The path is no longer cluttered with my objections. You can leave to wander as long as you wish. Brave Eagle will say no more about it."

Brietta was speechless and could not deny that his sudden change of heart made a strange sort of hurt sting her insides. Slowly she rose to her feet, smoothing the front of her dress down with her trembling hands. Her eyes wavered as she looked into the dark and damp forest, then at the pleasantness of the campfire and the rabbit dripping its juices into the flames, sizzling tantalizingly.

Then she looked up into Brave Eagle's dark and brooding eyes. "Do you want me to go?" she murmured. "If so, I will go."

"You do as you wish," Brave Eagle said, stubbornly setting his jaw, his arms still stiffly folded.

A sudden anger flashed in Brietta's eyes. She stood on tiptoe and spoke into his face. "You want me to beg to stay, don't you?" she dared to say. She dropped back away from him, flustered when he didn't say anything, just continued to stare down at her with eyes that troubled her deep into the core of herself.

She flipped the skirt of her dress around her and began stomping away from him and the smell of the cooking rabbit which was making her stomach gnaw unmercifully. "Then I have no recourse but to leave," she said, everything within her rebelling against her stubborn decision.

But he was giving her no other recourse!

He truly seemed to want to be rid of her!

And shouldn't she be glad? She was now free to

make her own choices again. She was now free to search for her sister without any interference.

Brave Eagle's jaw loosened and his arms dropped suddenly to his side, stunned that Brietta was foolish enough to leave his protection.

Not only that!

He had thought that she had feelings about him—that she would not want to leave him if she were given the chance! Although they had not spoken of it, he knew that something special had been exchanged between them and he wanted the chance to delve further into it.

Never had he looked on a white woman with favor before! Never had he hungered for anyone but women of his own heritage.

Taking quick strides, he went after Brietta. When he caught up with her he stepped into her path, stopping her. Their eyes locked and held.

Brietta swayed with a passion she could not deny as the fire's glow danced over Brave Eagle's muscled body and in his night-black eyes. Her heart pounded. Her pulse raced. She swallowed hard.

And she could not move, as though some unhidden force was holding her in place.

"White woman . . ."

"Brietta," she said, interrupting. "Please do not continue calling me white woman. My name is Brietta."

"Brietta?" he repeated softly.

"Brave Eagle?" Brietta murmured, her voice sounding foreign to her in its huskiness.

The unseen force that had seemed to hold Brietta in place now seemed to be making her move into Brave Eagle's arms as they snaked slowly around her waist. Her long and drifting hair curled farther down her back as she tipped her lips to meet his kiss and he surrounded her with his muscled arms, pressing her against his hard body. Her blood quickened as a great gush of wondrous feelings flooded through her. She coiled her arms around his neck and leaned into his embrace, too overwhelmed by desire to fear what she was allowing to happen. Pleasure was spreading through her into a delicious, tingling heat. His lips were drugging her, his powerful hands now at the curve of her buttocks, drawing her ever closer to the hardness beneath his breechcloth.

And then Brave Eagle released her and was standing at arm's length, looking down at her with an exquisite tenderness, even though she could see the pulse racing violently through the corded veins at his neck. She had always heard that Indians had tremendous control over their emotions. This Indian was proving it now, for she knew that the same hungers she felt raged through him too.

And she was glad that he had found it within himself not to take these feelings any farther—that this was not the time for two strangers to become lovers.

Shame engulfed Brietta for being so wanton. She looked quickly away from Brave Eagle and stifled a sob of regret behind her hand. In her lifetime she had only been kissed by one man—her father.

And now suddenly to have been kissed twice in such a short time by a stranger, and not only a stranger—an Indian!

Surely being alone had turned her into someone

she didn't know, or perhaps didn't want to know.

Unless what she was feeling was true love.

What then?

In the white man's culture it was forbidden for a white woman to love an Indian.

Trying not to be offended by Brietta's strange reaction to his kiss, Brave Eagle was torn with indecision. Should he try and comfort her, explain to her that her feelings for him were not wrong? Or should he ignore her and let her come to terms with herself all alone?

Unable to bear her soft sobs, not caring why she was crying but only wanting to make things right for her, Brave Eagle went to Brietta and gently gripped her shoulders. Slowly he turned her around to face him. With much care he placed a finger to her chin and lifted it, forcing her eyes to meet his. When he saw her fresh flood of tears, he could not help but draw her into his arms.

"Do not cry. Tears are *u-yo-i*, no good," he said, running his fingers through her hair. "No harm came to you because of the kiss. Let us settle down by the fire and eat. Then we will sleep. Tomorrow you will see that what happened tonight was nothing to regret."

Relishing his strong arms, yet knowing that she should fight off the need of him, Brietta wiped the tears from her eyes and eased away from him. Again she wiped her eyes. She sniffled. Then she smiled clumsily up at him. "I'm very hungry," she murmured.

"The food should be ready soon," Brave Eagle said, taking her hand and guiding her to the fire. He helped her to the ground, then parted her hair and looked at the wound. "I will bathe your wound and then it will be time to eat."

Brietta's love for this Indian was growing to an intensity that frightened her anew. When she looked up at him, and he down at her, she experienced a melting sensation that dizzied her.

Again she looked quickly away from him. She did not look in his direction again until after they had eaten and he was on one blanket asleep by the fire, and she was on a blanket far away from him. He hadn't bound her hands after all. His horse was near. His knife would be easy enough to steal from its sheath.

Yet she could not make herself take advantage of the situation. She looked heavenward, the sky a black velveteen sheen through the treetops. "God, have mercy on me," she prayed. "I love him. I love him. Please tell me what I am to do? Please?"

Rachel was trembling with fear, having been forced to sit and watch Brown Cloud consume a jug of whiskey that he had taken from his buckskin pouch at the side of his horse. He had not built a fire. He had not killed any game and fed her. His intent was only to drink whiskey and keep her prisoner.

Even now she lay at his side on the ground. Her wrist was tied to his wrist while he was in a drunken stupor of sleep, the forest dark and menacing all around them.

What, she wondered, were his plans for her when he awakened and sobered? Would he rape her before taking her to his village?

Or did he plan to hand her over to his many

warriors and let them have turns with her?

She had heard many vicious stories about the Osage and how they treated their captives. She had always hoped that these tales were false, blown out of proportion by trappers to make the white community fear and hate the Indians even more than they already did—mainly to scare the settlers into leaving, to search for land elsewhere.

Rachel curled up into a ball, the coldness of the ground reaching through her clothes, chilling her. She cried softly. "Brietta," she whispered. "I miss you so! Where are you? What is your fate? Shall we ever see one another again?"

She closed her eyes and let herself drift into a restless sleep.

Running Wolf sighed with exasperation as he waited patiently for Brietta to fall asleep. The aroma of the food had almost tempted him into giving himself away. Never had he been as hungry! He did not often stray so far from the City of Peace. If his absence was felt, then the time he was forced to spend there would be lengthened. It was imperative, even, that he get this white woman back to the City of Peace before the morning sky became flecked with the colors of the rising sun.

His eyes widened and his lips curved into a smile when he saw that Brietta was finally relaxed in a deep sleep and lay far enough away from Brave Eagle so that she could be abducted without awakening him. It would be quickly and easily done. Her absence would soon cause much hate between friends. Brave Eagle would blame no one but Brown Cloud. He had fought no one else but his blood brother for possession of her!

Running Wolf crept stealthily into the camp, his eyes darting from Brietta to Brave Eagle. Soon he was standing over Brietta, peering down at her loveliness, understanding the fascination of both the Cherokee and Osage warriors who were enamored of her. If he let himself, he could also see her worth. As it was, he must remember that he wanted her for only one purpose—To cause hate and jealousy between friends! To make enemies of friends!

In one lunge, Running Wolf was on his knees, his hand locked around Brietta's mouth. When her eyes flew open and looked desperately up at him over his clasped hand, he was not dissuaded by the fear in their depths. He wrestled with her for a moment, keeping one hand locked in place over her mouth, while with his other hand he jerked her up from the ground and held her against him.

Half dragging her, Running Wolf stole Brietta from the camp. When he reached his Appaloosa, which was far enough away from Brave Eagle's camp for Brave Eagle not to hear Brietta should she scream, Running Wolf released her long enough to grab a rope from his buckskin saddlebag.

"Who are you?" Brietta cried, backing away from him. "Please let me go. If you don't, Brave Eagle will come for you and kill you. He has already fought one Indian for me today. Do you not see that he won that challenge? He will again. You'll see!"

Running Wolf grabbed her by the wrists and locked them together. "I mean you no harm," he said in clear enough English, tying her wrists. "Soon I will even release you. But for now you must go with me." He smiled into her eyes. "White woman, you are most beautiful."

"You are mean and ugly," Brietta cried, her eyes blazing with anger.

"Many have called me puny, but never mean and ugly," Running Wolf said. Then he shrugged. "But it does not matter."

He led Brietta to his Appaloosa and lifted her onto his saddle. "We must leave now and ride hard," he said, looking back over his shoulder in the direction of Brave Eagle's camp. "When Brave Eagle awakens, he must not be given cause to follow me. Instead, his angry heart will lead him to Brown Cloud's village. There he will challenge Brown Cloud again, for he will think Brown Cloud abducted you, not I."

"You do this as a vengeful act?" Brietta asked, wincing when he mounted behind her and held her in place with his thin arm. She stiffened her upper lip. "Now Brave Eagle will hate you two-fold!"

Running Wolf shook his head. "My cousin?" he said, slapping the reins and sending the Appaloosa into a gallop. "His hate for Brown Cloud will blind him of hate for his cousin."

"You are Brave Eagle's cousin?" Brietta gasped, her hair flying in the wind. "You do this to your own cousin?"

"What he has done to me, his cousin, is far more than Running Wolf can ever do to him," Running Wolf said bitterly. He slapped the reins again. "No more talk! It is a waste of time and energy!"

Brietta sighed nervously, wondering where all of this would end. It seemed that her life kept getting more and more complicated, yet she had expected to be treated much differently at the hands of Indians.

Thus far, she felt more protected than endangered.

CHAPTER SIX

The firefly wakens; waken thou with me.

—*Tennyson*

The stirring of the birds in the trees overhead awakened Brave Eagle. Stretching his arms and yawning, he turned his gaze to where he had placed a soft pallet for Brietta the previous evening. He had had to fight off his yearning for her the entire night. Even in his dreams he had ached for her.

Brave Eagle was stunned for a moment when he saw that Brietta was gone, then bolted to his feet. A hurt anger washed through him, and he knelt to study the empty blankets, wondering how he could have trusted her so much that he had not tied her wrists to his as he had originally intended.

But she had seemed sincerely trustworthy!

Shaking his head and touching the blankets as though they were she, Brave Eagle could not help but worry about her fate. Had he not warned her? Why hadn't she listened? He had volunteered to protect her. Had she so little faith in his abilities to do so?

Or had she been playing a game with him all along?

Then Brave Eagle noticed something else. He rose slowly to his full height and studied drag marks on the moss that lined the banks of the river.

He turned his eyes back to the blankets and studied them again. It suddenly struck him that had Brietta left willingly, her blankets wouldn't have been in such disarray. They were twisted as though she had battled someone!

He looked back at the drag marks and began following them into the forest, seeing an occasional scattering of leaves, as though someone had wrestled there.

"*U-yo-i!*" he shouted, doubling his hands into tight fists at his sides. "She did not steal away in the night by herself! She was abducted!"

His eyes filled with rage, Brave Eagle glared into the distance where the shadows of the forest deepened. "Brown Cloud!" he shouted, his voice echoing back at him. "Why have you done this? How could you have done this to me? A man's word is a precious thing, to be remembered, and above all, honored! We fought for her! I won! I found her again when she ran away! She is rightfully mine. Must friends become enemies because you do not fight with honor?''

He lowered his eyes, again shaking his head. ''It must be so,'' he murmured. ''Or why else would you have taken her?''

Torn with anger and hurt, feeling betrayed by his long-time friend, Brave Eagle gathered up his blankets, stomped out the fire, and went to his horse. After securing his camping gear, he swung himself onto his steed and rode away, swearing to himself that he would not let Brown Cloud have Brietta for long. By sunset she would be in Brave Eagle's possession again. Then, if Brown Cloud came for her again, he would be met with weapons!

His long, sleek hair whipping in the wind, his shoulders squared and his jaw tight, Brave Eagle forced his mount into a gallop, his destination Brown Cloud's village.

''Soon, Brietta!'' he shouted, doubling a fist into the air. ''You will be safe again soon!''

Filled with a desperate fear, not knowing what the next moments held for her, Rachel rode into Brown Cloud's village with him. Her eyes innocently wide, Rachel looked slowly around her. Dawn was only now breaking along the horizon, enabling her to at least be without an audience as she was forced to go with Brown Cloud into the Osage Indian village by his arm locked possessively around her waist. There were no people visible outside. Even the dogs seemed too lazy to stir as the lone horseman and his captive ventured farther into the camp.

Having never before been among Indians, Rachel looked inquisitively at their dwellings that looked like inverted birds' nests with a small aperture in the top for the smoke to escape. These brushlike tents were arranged in a circle, with one larger dwelling that stood in the center. She had to surmise that this was the chief's tent, for it was richly covered with woven mats and skins of animals.

Brown Cloud drew rein in front of one of the tents and dismounted, leaving Rachel peering questioningly down at him, her heart pounding.

"What now?" she murmured, her voice quavering. "What are you going to do with me now that you have brought me to your village?"

"You shall see," Brown Cloud mumbled, grabbing her wrist and jerking her from the horse.

Rachel fell in a heap at his feet. Cowering, she looked around her as Indians began to leave their dwellings, moving silently toward her and Brown Cloud. She tried to edge away from them as they approached her, but she had no place to go. They were now on all sides of her, looking down at her with wonder in their eyes.

"*Twi-lu-gi*! Welcome! I have brought a captive for us all to enjoy!" Brown Cloud boasted, as he smiled from Indian to Indian. "Do you not see her fair skin? Do you not see her strange-colored eyes? Soon you can touch the softness of her hair and her skin."

Because he had not consumed any alcohol since late last evening, Brown Cloud's mind was clear. His step was sure. He grabbed Rachel up from the ground and walked her toward the center of the village, where a large stake had been thrust into the ground long ago, close to where an outdoor fire sputtered.

Panic seized Rachel. She glanced over her shoulder at Brown Cloud as he pushed her onward, twisting her arm behind her. "Please don't place me on the stake!" she cried, tears streaming down her cheeks. She looked back at the ashes of the outdoor firepit. "Please don't burn me! What have I done to deserve this? What?"

Her pleadings reached Brown Cloud's heart, making his eyes waver momentarily. The white woman was so beautiful! She was so innocent!

Yet he had to prove to Brave Eagle who was the most cunning! He had to prove to his people that he had much prowess! It had been many sleeps since anyone had been brave enough to capture a white woman to put on display in the Osage village. No one wanted to displease the white pony soldiers.

But it was time to prove something to them—that they did not own the Osage!

"Be quiet, white woman," Brown Cloud ordered gruffly. He let go of her and gave her a shove toward the stake. "Nothing you say will save you." He chuckled as he grabbed her by the hair, holding her face close to his. "Beautiful woman, not even Brave Eagle will save you. Never will he come into my village warring over a mere white woman!"

Her eyes wild, Rachel looked up at Brown Cloud with a pleading gaze. "Who is this Brave Eagle?" she asked.

Brown Cloud moved Rachel up to the stake and began tying her in place. "You are not only beautiful, but clever as well," he said, laughing beneath his breath. "You pretend not to know Brave Eagle. Yes, white woman, you are clever, but not clever enough. I will not be fooled by anything you say. You are my captive. I won you back from Brave Eagle by finding you. You are mine, fair and square. That is final!"

Tears streamed down Rachel's cheeks. Her words were falling on deaf ears. She flinched and screamed when Brown Cloud placed his hands at her bodice and ripped her dress down the front to her waist, revealing her breasts. She shuddered violently when his gaze fell on her breasts, then sighed heavily with relief when he walked away from her without touching her.

But her relief was short-lived. One by one the women of the village began passing by her, then the men. She turned her eyes away and closed them, wanting to die.

On a high bluff overlooking Brown Cloud's village, Brave Eagle sat stiffly on his saddle, peering intensely at the activity below him. A sick feeling spiraled through him when he saw the Osage women filing past the captive on the stake, touching and taunting her.

Believing the white captive was Brietta, it took all of the restraint he had been taught as a child not to ride immediately into the village and reclaim the white woman whose loveliness had stolen his heart.

But he still had claim of his senses. He knew better than to ride into the Osage village alone, especially to reclaim one of their captives. Only he and Brown Cloud knew the full story of the blood brothers' claims on the same woman!

"But soon they all will pay for his carelessness," Brave Eagle whispered to himself, having forgotten his brotherly feelings for Brown Cloud. Brown Cloud had gone back on his word! He must pay for that! It was time for war!

With deep regret and sadness, Brave Eagle rode away. It was with a heavy heart that he would fight Brown Cloud and his people—especially since he was certain that Brown Cloud's actions were caused by his consumption of firewater. The firewater had stolen his reason from him!

Casting all thoughts of Brown Cloud aside, Brave Eagle rode with a determination he had never felt before.

Each jolt of the horse seemed to be turning Brietta's stomach inside out. The entire night long, Running Wolf had stopped only once, and that was to take time to eat. After consuming a quick meal of berries, persimmons, and hazelnuts, they had ridden onward, Brietta's fears mounting. What sort of people would she find in the City of Peace?

A wave of dizziness suddenly swept through Brietta. She grabbed for Running Wolf's arm, which held her tightly against him, afraid that she might fall from the horse.

Again the dizziness seized her and her temples began to throb, causing her to think that it was her head wound at fault.

But when a bitterness rose up into her throat and she knew that she was about to retch, she realized that something else was bothering her.

She must have eaten a poisonous berry while she had been foraging through the bushes in search of food.

Choking back the urge to retch, feeling suddenly feverish, Brietta looked over her shoulder at Running Wolf, terror in her eyes. "Stop!" she cried. "I'm ill. Please. Stop. I'm sick to my stomach!"

Seeing Brietta's flushed cheeks and the desperation in her eyes, Running Wolf panicked. He could not afford her becoming sick and perhaps dying, and then having Brave Eagle find out that she had been with Running Wolf at the time. Brave Eagle would never allow Running Wolf to leave the City of Peace. He would be condemned to die there an old man!

"I'm going to be ill at my stomach," Brietta pleaded again, this time more shrilly, becoming more ill as the moments passed. She was willing herself not to throw up just yet.

But she could only hold it back so long.

Running Wolf wheeled his Appaloosa to a stop. He quickly dismounted, immediately helping Brietta to the ground.

She ran to a thick stand of bushes and moved behind them, hanging her head in her hands. Over and over again her throat spasmed until there was nothing left to spill from her insides.

Sobbing, she continued to hang her head in her hands as she moved to a tree and sat down beneath it, limp.

Concern for Brietta's welfare building, Running Wolf went to her and knelt down before her. "You are better?" he asked.

He touched her brow, then flinched and drew

his hand away when he felt how hot she was. He now knew for certain that she was ill, perhaps so much so that she might not recover. He looked desperately from side to side, then down at her again, knowing what he must do. He must flee. Chances were that the white woman would not survive such an illness. Brave Eagle must never find out that she had been abducted by Running Wolf.

"I . . . need . . . water," Brietta whispered, raising her eyes slowly to look up at Running Wolf. She grabbed at her parched throat. "Please give me some water."

Not wanting to take the time to give her a drink from his pouch, desperate to separate himself from ever knowing her, afraid of Brave Eagle should anything become of this white woman, Running Wolf moved to his full height over her. He stared down at her for a moment longer.

Then he turned and rushed back to his Appaloosa and in one leap was back in the saddle.

Panic seized Brietta. Her eyes widened in horror at the prospect of being left alone so ill in the vastness of the wilderness. Surely she would not survive! If she did not get water into her system soon, she would surely dry up to nothing. She was burning up with a temperature that was ravaging her body. She had thrown up so much she felt as though nothing was left inside her to nourish her through her weakness!

Lord, she was going to die!

"Please!" she cried, crawling toward Running Wolf's horse. She reached a hand out for Running Wolf. "Do not leave me like this. Please . . ."

Running Wolf's eyes wavered. He swallowed hard. His insides quivered strangely when his eyes met Brietta's and held, knowing that perhaps leaving her to die alone was the most cowardly act of his life.

But he had no choice. He must not take the chance of Brave Eagle ever realizing that it was he, not Brown Cloud, who had abducted the white woman. If she died, Brown Cloud would have to pay!

And that would, finally, mean Running Wolf's vengeance would be fulfilled.

With this in mind, Running Wolf looked away from Brietta and sank his heels into the flanks of his pony and rode away in a brisk gallop.

Brietta sobbed as she watched him leave, then collapsed back on the ground, breathing hard. Never had she been as hot. Never had she been as ill.

How could she survive?

"Brave Eagle," she whispered. "Please find me."

She closed her eyes and sank into unconsciousness.

CHAPTER
SEVEN

I want your strength to help;
Your laugh to cheer;
Heart, soul and senses need you, one all all.

—*Alford*

To stifle her sobs and pleas, Brown Cloud had tied a cloth across Rachel's mouth. Her lips were parched and dry, and she recoiled as the young children of the tribe came to taunt her and poke at her with sticks.

Then her eyes widened and her heart began to race with hope when her gaze was drawn elsewhere. She could not believe her eyes! A holy man was arriving at the village on a squat donkey, his long, black robe dragging the ground on either

105

side of the animal, his white collar tight beneath a narrow, pointed chin.

It was like a scene from the Bible. How often had she read the passages where Jesus entered the ancient cities on donkeys? Could this holy man have heard about her dilemma? Had he come to rescue her?

But surely not, she thought woefully. Who would have carried the news to him? This was surely the missionary she had heard was to head the new mission being erected in the area. He had come to try and heal the Indians of their savage ways.

When he saw her there, a captive, she wondered anxiously, what would he do? What would the Indians do to him? Surely he would be an obstacle to their plans—especially Brown Cloud's!

Scarcely breathing, Rachel waited for the missionary to get closer. Perhaps he could persuade the Indians to release her.

Brown Cloud had turned away from Rachel to go to his father to explain her presence in the village, but he stopped short and frowned when he heard the bray of a donkey. His insides stiffened when he caught sight of the missionary on his donkey moving into the village, the Osage people parting to make room for him while they ogled him and his unfamiliar attire.

Brown Cloud had heard about the new mission. He had gone and viewed it from afar. He had seen this man with the long, black robe instructing people in the way it should be built. Brown Cloud knew this man to be the holy man of the mission and he did not know just how to receive him into his village. A holy man was surely similar to a shaman, to be treated with reverence. Should it be the same for even a white man's shaman?

Missionary George Cutright sucked in a shocked breath when he saw the girl tied to the stake. He whispered a quick prayer beneath his breath. He had not thought that the Osage were taking white captives—especially defenseless women! It had been rumored only that they raided other Indian villages for slaves.

He had thought those rumors were false, for he so badly wanted to be able to convert these people into the Christian faith.

Now there was proof before his eyes of just how hard it was going to be!

Brown Cloud met Missionary Cutright's approach. He stood boldly in the path of the donkey, causing it to stop. He folded his arms across his chest. "You have come to my village," he said flatly, his eyes narrowing with suspicion. "Why do you?"

"I plan to visit everyone in these parts," Missionary Cutright said, glancing from Rachel back to Brown Cloud. "Those who live in cabins and those who live in earthen lodges. Today I chose to introduce myself to your people."

Missionary Cutright cleared his throat nervously when, out of the corner of his eye, he saw Rachel squirming to get free. It was hard to sit on the donkey, a free man, while she was so helpless on the stake, a captive.

But he had to be diplomatic if ever she was going to be set free.

"Do you speak for this village of Osage?" he asked quickly. "Are you Chief Climbing Bear?"

"I am Chief Climbing Bear," a voice said in a gruff manner behind Brown Cloud.

Brown Cloud turned on a heel and faced his father, who was moving among his people with a solemn and ponderous dignity, always full of commanding reserve, whose countenance was awesome to a son who had never been able to walk in his footsteps. His chieftain father, who was in his fiftieth summer, was a stoic man, his feelings hidden deeply inside where no one could see them. Tall of stature, his nose bold and his eyes fierce, Chief Climbing Bear wore a gold-dyed buckskin shirt and leggings with a matching feather headdress. Fond of ornaments, he displayed much jewelry. Silver bracelets shone at his wrists and beaded necklaces hung around his neck, and a bear claw armlet marked him as a man of distinction.

But today it was not his father's presence that was disturbing Brown Cloud. He was frustrated at this holy man's untimely arrival. Now it was going to be awkward to explain why he had brought the white woman to the village.

And it was already awkward enough between father and son. Brown Cloud's chieftain father did not understand his son's need for firewater. He called his son weak and foolish.

Today Brown Cloud had wanted to prove that his father was wrong. The white woman in his possession was proof of so many things!

"Brown Cloud, I awaken today not only to find a white woman in our village, but also a white man,"

Chief Climbing Bear said, gazing intensely at Brown Cloud. "The holy man comes of his own volition. But the woman is here because you brought her. You will explain?" He awaited an answer, his eyes never leaving Brown Cloud. He ignored the missionary, who had come uninvited.

"The white woman was taken after I slew her kin—a vile man who abducted many of our people and sold them into slavery," Brown Cloud said, squaring his shoulders proudly. "I bring her to you, father, as proof of your son's prowess." He smiled at his father. "Do you accept the gift with a fond heart?"

Chief Climbing Bear studied Brown Cloud in silence a moment longer, looked slowly over at Rachel, then walked past Brown Cloud without any further comment. He glowered at Missionary Cutright as the holy man slipped from his donkey. He watched with much suspicion as the missionary reached inside his saddlebag and plucked out his Bible, then faced the Osage chief as he clasped the book before him with both hands.

"Your reason for being here is *u-yo-i*!" Climbing Bear growled. He waved a hand in the air. "Go. We need no white holy man among the Osage. Your presence dishonors our shaman!"

"It is with much love that I have come to you today," Missionary Cutright said. "I wish to extend an invitation to you and your people to come to my house of worship anytime you feel in need of anything, be it holy or of this earth. I have been sent by God to the Ozark wilderness to be a comfort to those who are in need."

He shifted his Bible to one hand and clutched it

tightly. In a gesture of friendship, he stretched his free hand out to the chief. "My name is Missionary Cutright," he said softly. "I am honored to be in your presence, Chief Climbing Bear."

Chief Climbing Bear folded his arms across his chest and tightened his jaw, refusing to accept the holy man's friendship.

Missionary Cutright held his hand out for a moment longer, then eased it to his side. Not to be beaten by the stubborn Indian, he refused to budge, even though he knew that the Indian chief was waiting for him to go away in defeat. Boldly, he looked over at Rachel, then back at the chief.

"You have a white woman hostage," he said somberly, again clutching the Bible with both hands. "I pray that you will take pity on her and release her to my care. No woman deserves to be treated that way, no matter the reason you chose to put her there." He cleared his throat. "I beg you to release her. I shall take her away. You shall never be bothered by her again."

Brown Cloud's heart skipped a beat when his father went to the missionary's donkey and opened the saddlebag, searching through its contents. Surely his father wasn't going to trade the captive! Surely she didn't mean that little to him— someone Brown Cloud had perhaps lost his best friend over!

No! He could not give her up, yet he could not defy his father by arguing for the right to keep her!

Chief Climbing Bear walked away from the donkey and stood face to face with the missionary again. "You do not have enough payment for the captive," he said, glancing at his son as Brown Cloud emitted a nervous sigh of relief. He frowned at Brown Cloud, then gazed intensely at the missionary again. "If you bring payment enough you can have her. Bring horses. Bring white man trinkets. She will be yours."

Missionary Cutright swallowed hard with regret as he looked at Rachel. It ate away at his heart to see the fear in the young woman's eyes. It made him suddenly aware of what he was up against in the Ozark wilderness. The Indians had the upper hand. Could it ever change? What would it take to convince them that what they were doing with the white woman was wrong!

Of course the army could be contacted, but it would take two days to get to the fort and two days back. By then the lovely young woman could be dead. The only other alternative was to return to his mission and gather together as many belongings as he could, then return to the Osage village with his offerings, hoping they would be adequate to free her.

"I shall return soon," Missionary Cutright said, placing his Bible back inside his saddlebag. He slipped back onto his donkey and took up the reins. "I will make payment for the woman." He paused and pleaded with the chief. "Perhaps you could release her from the stake? Soon she will be mine. I would like for her to be able to travel back to the mission with me. If she continues to hang in the sun—"

"Go!" Chief Climbing Bear ordered. "Until she is yours, you will not dictate to me about her!"

Inhaling a nervous breath, Missionary Cutright nodded, then urged his donkey around and ambled away.

Chief Climbing Bear turned to Brown Cloud and placed his hands to his son's shoulders. "My son, you have brought misery to your people when you chose to bring this white woman to our village as captive," he said. "But now that she is here, we shall see that we are paid well for her, and soon. It is not healthy for her to be here." He gestured with a hand toward the stake. "Remove her. Take her to your dwelling. Keep her from sight. No one but those we wish to show her to will know that she is here."

Brown Cloud hesitated for a moment, feeling disgraced again in front of the villagers. Then he nodded, knowing that he had no choice but to do as he was commanded by his powerful father. *"Ha-wa,"* he said, trying not to reveal his shame. "Whatever you say, father."

In a slow stride, Brown Cloud went to Rachel. She recoiled at his touch, wary of the chief's decision for her to be placed in Brown Cloud's dwelling. Once she was so accessible to him, he might decide that she was his for the taking.

She trembled as he loosened her bonds and gave her a shove. Holding her torn bodice together in front, she stumbled along behind Brown Cloud, fear almost overwhelming her.

Brave Eagle was dressed in breechclout, moccasins, and a war shirt ornamented to represent his life story—the breast containing a prayer for protection, and on the back the symbol of victory woven in beaded tapestry.

With black ash smeared on his face—the color associated with warring—Brave Eagle had, with the blessing of his chieftain father, Silver Shirt, assembled his warriors together to sing and dance, with the object of arousing their courage and enthusiasm for war. While his father, the elders, and the women and children of the village sat in a wide circle around them, the warriors were divided into four groups who seated themselves facing the center in the four corners of the dance ground. They carried clubs, bows, lances, and shields. The drummers were seated in the rear.

A roll on the drum, followed by three sharp beats, was the signal for the war dance to begin. At the third beat the warriors rose and danced with a rapid hop-step toward the center. Lances were extended, clubs raised as if to strike, and it appeared as if each group was about to attack the one opposite it.

They then came together with a yell. The drum-time became slower and the step changed to a slow toe-heel. The warriors formed an irregular circle and began acting out war experiences, Brave Eagle in the lead.

At first, their movements were slow and stealthy. By their gestures they showed the way of advancing on an enemy, by hunting out and following up the track, discovering the enemy, and preparing for the attack. This took three rounds.

Then with a double drum-beat as a signal, the time and step changed again to a rapid hop. Arms and legs were now lifted at sharp angles, the body was bent and raised with sudden and varied movements, as in a charge, or as if dodging arrows or warding off blows of weapons.

, Each warrior acted out his story without regard to what the others were doing, so that at the same instant one might be seen in an attitude of attack, another of defense, drawing the bow, striking with the war club, some listening or waiting an opportunity, and others striking a foe. This took place while the warriors circled around four times.

Then the drum-time changed for the rapid flat-foot step. With this step, the warriors divided into groups of three. In each group, one warrior took an attitude of defense while the others attacked him. He swung his shield from face to face and thrust his lance, all in time with the music. The attackers pretended to snatch at his weapons and fight him off. Clubs were struck together and lances and bows were struck on the shield.

The lone fighter gradually drove the others back. Once more drummers increased their beat to rapid hop-step time. At first it was rather slow, but the time increased, reaching its climax as the dance ended.

There was at once a total silence in the Cherokee village. Chief Silver Shirt rose from among the others who had proudly viewed the activity of their warriors and went to Brave Eagle. One hand leaning heavily on a cane, he clasped his free hand onto his son's shoulder and gazed intensely into his dark eyes.

"Ride with courage against our enemy the

Osage," Silver Shirt said solemnly "It is good that you no longer regard Brown Cloud as your friend and that you have chosen to ride against him, even if it is because of a woman that you do this thing. It is with much relief in my heart that you finally see the worthlessness of Brown Cloud."

"I shall bring the woman to our village and you shall see that she does not deserve to be treated as a captive," Brave Eagle said, his jaw tight. "Though white, father, she has the courage and fire of a man!"

Without responding, Chief Silver Shirt scrutinized Brave Eagle for a moment longer, then stepped back from him, his chin boldly lifted. "We shall see," he said, then again hobbled up to Brave Eagle, this time giving him a fierce hug. "Ride with care, my son."

His father was not one to show much emotion, and Brave Eagle was taken aback by his attitude now. Even when Running Wolf was assigned to atone for Brave Eagle's choice of friends, he had not realized the depth of his father's feelings about his having been friends with Brown Cloud for so long, in secret. It had hurt his father deeply.

But Brave Eagle's feelings as he embraced his father were equally clear. How could he not regret having to kill his longtime friend—a friend who carried the identical tattoo of a spider on his inner thigh. To love for so long, how could one kill so easily?

"I will return safely," Brave Eagle said, easing from his father's arms. His eyes locked with his father's, knowing the pain inside his father's heart over his lameness that rendered him incapable of warring. Then he ran to his gelding and quickly mounted.

Raising a doubled fist, he shouted to his warriors. "It is time!" he said. "Let us ride! Soon the Osage village will be no more!"

Whooping and firing his rifle in warning, Brave Eagle led his warriors from the village, their horses galloping hard, dust flying in the wind behind them. Brave Eagle looked stern and determined, yet within his heart he was torn. If he came face to face with Brown Cloud with a weapon, could he truly kill his old friend? Could Brown Cloud truly kill him? Was this how it was meant to end? Had *Wah-kon-tah* planned this from that moment when two young braves had met face to face to exchange boyhood visions?

If so, what was the use of visions?

To kill his feelings of love and devotion to Brown Cloud, Brave Eagle forced his thoughts back to the moment when he had seen the white woman on the stake and to why she was there. Brown Cloud had gone back on his word! He had placed this barrier between the two friends! At that moment, another Osage and Cherokee had become enemies! And Brown Cloud had to pay. He had to pay dearly!

Never would Brave Eagle forget the sight of his chosen woman shackled to the stake! At that moment, never could he have hated anyone as much as he hated Brown Cloud!

"Death to the Osage!" he suddenly shouted, and

more war whoops rose from all those who hungered for the fight.

Morning sounds awakened Brietta. Lethargically, she looked around her, finding it hard to remember who or where she was. Her whole body seemed aflame, as though someone had set a torch to her.

But slowly it came back to her. She had been abducted by another Indian. He had spoken his name. Running Wolf. And he had disclosed more than his name to her. He had said that he was Brave Eagle's cousin! How could he be kin to Brave Eagle, who was so gentle and caring? Running Wolf was heartless. She would never forget how callously he had left her to die!

"Water," she whispered, clutching her aching throat. "I . . . must . . . have water."

Her body seemed to be made of stone as she inched heavily along the ground, looking for signs of water through the trees ahead. Thus far she had only seen trees and more trees! Was she never to drink again? Was she never to taste the wonders of the refreshing, cold water she had cupped so often in her hands while out in the forest searching for wild greens for supper? She felt as though she were dying. Just how much longer would it be before she took her last breath?

"Brave Eagle," she whispered harshly. "Where are you, Brave Eagle? Please . . . save me. . . ."

Unable to move any farther along the ground, exhausted to the point of blacking out again, Brietta curled up on her side and began crying, the tears hot against an even hotter cheek.

"Somebody," she gasped. "Please help me. . . ."

Her eyes closed slowly, the long droop of her lashes like dark wisps of satin against her flushed cheeks.

Again she drifted off into a restless sleep. The leaves above her swayed in the breeze, the shine of water reflecting on their silver undersides. The stream that meandered just ahead was hidden behind a thick stand of redbuds, their opened pink blossoms filled with the hum of bees.

CHAPTER EIGHT

You are the white birch
In the sun's glow.

—*Wagstaff*

The gag removed from her mouth, Rachel sat huddled in the dark corner of the Indian dwelling, her eyes never leaving Brown Cloud. Now attired in a buckskin dress which had been forced on her by Brown Cloud, she looked cautiously around her as the fire in the firepit glowed from the center of the room. The dwelling was small; it looked as though it had been built for only one person. Woven mats hung on the walls, along with a vast display of weapons. The bows were the most

Cassie Edwards

colorful of them all, with designs of the moon, stars, and lightning streaks depicted on them.

She looked past these at the blankets rolled neatly along one of the walls, then at the herbs and foodstuffs hanging to dry over the fire.

When Brown Cloud tipped a jug of whiskey to his lips, Rachel's pulse began to race. Although getting drunk had always seemed to cause her uncles to lose interest in her and Brietta, she did not know if it would have the same effect on this Indian. She had heard that whiskey caused many men to become violent.

"You fear me so?" Brown Cloud said, suddenly looking at her as he wiped his mouth dry with the back of his hand. "You did not fear Brave Eagle. Why you fear me? I have not harmed you—only bound you so that you could not flee from me. That is the only difference in the way Brave Eagle and I have treated you."

Rachel raised an eyebrow at the repeated mention of Brave Eagle! How was she to know who he was? Why did Brown Cloud seem obsessed by the man? She started to ask him about Brave Eagle again but did not get the chance. A commotion outside the dwelling drew Brown Cloud quickly to his feet. He went outside.

Rachel moved to the entrance flap and listened, growing cold inside when she realized that Brown Cloud was bargaining with someone—over her. She shoved aside the entrance flap so that she could see the man he was talking to. She was still more horrified when she recognized a man who had dealt with her brothers many times. It was René, a French slaver.

120

He was disgustingly obese with bulging eyes and yellowed teeth, waist-length black hair that was matted with filth, and a thick mustache that carried some of the remains of his last meal. She was familiar enough with the man to know that she soon would be his, but not to be used by him personally. She would be sold to the highest bidder.

It was a fate worse than death. If given the choice, she would even prefer to stay with the Indians!

"So, one who calls himself by the name René, you have come to make trade with Chief Climbing Bear and his son Brown Cloud?" the chief asked as he circled two pack mules heavy with gifts for his people.

Of late, he had welcomed white traders more often than in the past. They offered guns, hatchets, knives, awls, scrapers, fleshers, bolts of cloth, and many other items in exchange for slaves and furs. This gave the Osage a ready market for their captives—and a twofold purpose for war on their enemies. Chief Climbing Bear knew that their desire for the trader's merchandise made the warriors eager to go on slaving expeditions.

For the sake of getting ammunition for their new rifles, Chief Climbing Bear's warriors were willing to take captives among enemy tribes to sell to the whites.

The chief's only interest was the preservation of the Osage!

"*Bonjour*, René has brought you many articles of worth today," the trader said, untying the buckskin that was covering his wares. He threw it aside

121

and let the sun reflect on the barrels of rifles, sharp hatchets, and different sizes of pots and pans. A bolt of red cloth took the eye of an Osage woman whose curiosity drew her to it, to touch the cotton fabric.

René smiled smugly down at her, then looked up at Chief Climbing Bear again. "Do you have something of equal worth to trade?" he demanded.

Brown Cloud's eyes followed his father's gaze when he saw his father look past him toward Brown Cloud's dwelling. It was apparent what his father had in mind as part of the trade with the French slaver today.

The white woman!

Although she had been brought to the Osage as Brown Cloud's captive, the woman was now the possession of the chief of the village, whose word would be final when her fate was chosen.

Brown Cloud shifted his feet nervously on the ground. He wanted to persuade his father that the white woman should at least stay long enough for Brave Eagle to see her there, to prove Brown Cloud's cunning to his longtime friend. He did not voice this desire aloud. His father's eyes were stern as he looked at Brown Cloud, his arms folded tightly across his chest.

"Get the white woman," Chief Climbing Bear ordered. "René has valuable items to trade for her."

Brown Cloud tarried a moment, then knowing that he had no choice, he went inside his lodge and stared angrily down at Rachel. Without saying a word, he went to his jug, lifted it to his lips, and took several deep swallows of the whiskey.

Rachel edged away from him slowly. "I don't want to go with that man," she murmured, her pulse racing. "He—he will sell me later to someone else. The thought frightens me. René is an evil man. Please don't force me to go with him."

Brown Cloud set his jug aside, stunned that the white woman would choose to stay with the Osage. How could this woman with eyes of the sky fear any white man, when the men that she had lived with had been the most evil of all men Brown Cloud had ever known? Had she closed her eyes to their evil?

Knowing that he had no choice but to hand her over to René, Brown Cloud grabbed Rachel by one wrist and yanked her up. He leaned her against him and gazed down at her face, shaken to the core when tears began streaming from her eyes.

"Please," Rachel sobbed. "I'll do anything. Just don't give me to the evil Frenchman."

The entrance flap opened suddenly, spilling the morning light into the dwelling. Chief Climbing Bear stepped around Brown Cloud and took Rachel away from him. "Come, white woman," he said, giving Brown Cloud a glaring frown. "My son, you come also. You will accompany the Frenchman and the white woman as far as the Great River. Then return to me. We have much to discuss, you and I."

"*Ha-wa*," Brown Cloud said humbly. His jaw tightened as his father took Rachel from the dwelling, then he looked toward the jug of whiskey with desperate eyes. He bent to one knee and grabbed up the jug, drinking until it was empty.

Then he rose to his full height, wiping the

wetness from his lips with the back of his hand. He staggered as he lifted the entrance flap and stepped outside. His eyes blazed with silent fury when he realized that the bargaining was already over. Rachel was on one of the mules, with several Indians that the Osage had captured from other villages tied in a long line behind her.

Many warriors were already on horseback, and Brown Cloud's horse was quickly brought to him. Mounting, Brown Cloud did not look the white woman's way again. The sound of her sobs was a torment, making him feel that somehow his plans had gone awry. Brown Cloud knew that Brave Eagle would never forgive him now.

Rachel clung to the reins as she was forced to ride beside the Frenchman's mighty palomino. She tried to evade René's leering smile as he looked her way and shuddered with fear when she saw him taking occasional swigs from a whiskey bottle.

Filled with a desperate need to free Brietta from Brown Cloud, Brave Eagle urged his mount up the steep bluff that overlooked Brown Cloud's village, to survey once more the position of the stake.

Once at the peak, Brave Eagle shifted slightly in his saddle, cupped a hand over his eyes to shield them from the sun's rays, and peered down at the village. Quickly his eyes scanned the landscape. He clenched one fist when his gaze fell on the empty stake.

His eyes were filled with fire as he searched for Brown Cloud's lodge. "He has taken her there!" he whispered, his throat constricting at the thought of

Brown Cloud forcing himself on Brietta. The thought sickened him, especially when he recalled how close she had come to letting him love her, drawing away from him only because she was not ready to give herself completely to any man.

How dreadful it would be if she were forced by someone for whom she had no feelings at all. Brave Eagle would cut off his own arm to prevent such a thing.

"She loves me," Brave Eagle gritted from between his teeth. He clenched his rifle hard as he withdrew it from its buckskin sheath at the side of his horse.

"She loves only Brave Eagle!" he shouted, his voice echoing back to him in the lilting breeze.

He waved his rifle in the air as he looked over his shoulder at his warriors. "We ride to rescue the white woman from the Osage!" he commanded. "Kill if you must to rescue her, but spare the innocent women and children! Burn the Osage dwellings, also, if that is your desire!"

Moments later, the Cherokee warriors were thundering into the Osage village. Whooping and shooting their rifles, the horsemen rode through the village, leaning down alongside their horses as shots were fired at them.

Brave Eagle leveled his rifle and aimed at a guard who had him in his direct aim, and with much regret sent a ball through his chest.

Screaming, women and children fled from their dwellings as torches were set to them, sending them up in flames until hardly a wigwam was left untouched—except for Brown Cloud's and the great chieftain's lodge.

Brave Eagle drew rein at Brown Cloud's wigwam. In one lithe motion he was off his horse and inside the lodge. With a single glance he knew that he was too late. Brown Cloud and his captive were gone!

Seized by determination, Brave Eagle stormed from the wigwam and quickly mounted his steed. Fixing his eyes on the chief's lodge at the center of the village, he rode toward it at a brisk gallop.

Once there, he dismounted and started to go inside, but stopped short when he found Chief Climbing Bear lying just outside the door, blood streaming from a wound in his upper right chest.

Regret he could not deny swam through Brave Eagle. Although the Osage chief and Silver Shirt had been enemies for many moons, Brave Eagle deeply regretted the attack on his friend's father.

Ignoring the warriors who were setting torches to the chief's lodge, Brave Eagle dropped to one knee, lifted Chief Climbing Bear's head and held it up. "The white woman," he said urgently. "Where is she? Where is Brown Cloud?"

Chief Climbing Bear fought for breath. Sweat pearled his brow; the pain in his chest was intense. He clutched at his wound. "What is the white woman to you?" he asked, forcing himself not to gasp when the pain intensified. He looked past Brave Eagle at the flames now engulfing his dwelling, then gazed up into Brave Eagle's eyes with hatred. "You do your father's work? He is no longer capable of warring himself, of leading the warring party?"

Considering his father's pride, Brave Eagle

would not disclose the affliction which was slowly crippling Silver Shirt. Brave Eagle knew that his father would not want his enemy to know that he had been disabled by some unknown disease. He would not want the Osage chief to know that a man of his stature could become so weakened, so quickly.

"My father sent me with his blessings," Brave Eagle said, then his eyes narrowed. "And if you live, my father will come and show you just how capable he is of warring," he said, feeling that the lie was necessary to save the honor of his father. "It is because of the woman that I came today without my father. This is my fight—not my father's!"

Chief Climbing Bear sucked in a deep breath of air when the pain grabbed him again. He closed his eyes and breathed in heavily, then directed his gaze at Brave Eagle again. "I ask again . . . what is this woman to you?"

"That is not your affair," Brave Eagle said stubbornly. "It is a matter between Brave Eagle and your son. Now, where can I find them? Or do I have to place you on the stake where you displayed her to your people? Do I allow my warriors to disgrace you, the powerful chief of the Osage, while your people watch?"

"I shall never tell you," Chief Climbing Bear hissed, then glanced up at a Cherokee warrior as he knelt down beside Brave Eagle.

"I discovered from one of the Osage women that Brown Cloud left with the white woman not long ago," the warrior said. "It was said, though, that the white woman now belongs to René, the French trader. Brown Cloud only escorts them to the Great River."

Brave Eagle laid Chief Climbing Bear's head back down on the ground, then rose to his full height. He bolted onto his horse, and as his warriors gathered around him on their sweat-leathered steeds, he looked them each in the eye as he spoke.

"We must separate," he shouted. "Some of you come with me. We go one way. The rest go the other! We must find the white woman before she is taken from the Ozarks." He raised his rifle into the air. "Search well, my warriors. We will meet back at the village on the next sun's rising!"

Sorrow swept through him when he looked around at the destruction of the Osage village. All of the lodges had been burned, or were in the process of burning. The women and children were standing around in groups, clinging to one another. The warriors had been stripped of their weapons, as well as their pride.

Then Brave Eagle wheeled his horse around and rode away, knowing that he had not seen the end of the destruction. His former friend was bound to retaliate somehow.

Brave Eagle shouted into the wind. "You are now my *ha-ma-ma*, Brown Cloud," he said. "Do you hear? My enemy! A friend never again!"

The sound of approaching horses awakened Brietta. She was so feverish she found it hard even to raise her head, and she blinked her eyes nervously as the horses grew closer.

Fearing that the riders might be enemies,

Brietta began to drag herself an inch at a time across the cushion of dead leaves beneath the trees. When she came to the flowering bushes, she found the strength to crawl around them, then swallowed a gulp of air, surprised when she found herself staring down into the cool pool of a stream, minnows darting peacefully around over the pebbles at the bottom.

"Water!" she gasped. "Oh, Lord, thank you. You've led me to water!"

She crawled on her stomach, closer . . . closer . . . but she could not fight the weakness that was gripping her. "Just a little farther," she whispered, her breath hot on her lips as she spoke. "I must get my temperature down. I must . . ."

Struggling not to lose consciousness, Brietta crawled until she reached the water. Her fingers trembling, she sank them down into the cool depths, then could not help but succumb to another bout of feverish unconsciousness.

As she sank back to the ground, breathing heavily, her arm dangling over the side, minnows began nibbling softly on her fingertips.

CHAPTER NINE

Oh fair she is! Oh rare she is!
Oh dearer still to me,
More welcome than the green leaf
To a winter stricken tree!

—*Sigerson*

Seeing the shine of water through the blooming bushes ahead, his thirst powerful after warring with the Osage, Brave Eagle led his warriors toward it. After dismounting and securing his reins to a low-hanging branch, he stepped around the bushes, already feeling the cool taste of the water on his parched lips.

Stunned at what he saw lying beyond the bushes,

131

beside the river, Brave Eagle's footsteps faltered and his heart skipped a beat.

Could it be?

Was that Brietta? Or a mirage?

He did not understand this!

How could she have managed to escape from Brown Cloud and the evil trader?

Wanting to touch her, to see if she were truly real, Brave Eagle commanded his warriors to stay behind to keep a look-out for Brown Cloud and his band, then crept closer to Brietta. He knelt to one knee beside her. Gingerly he touched her arm, which was dangling down into the water. When he felt its warmth, he knew that she was not only real, but was being devastated by a soaring temperature!

"*O-ge-ye*," he whispered. "My woman." He lifted her arm from the water and turned her over slowly so that he could peer down into her lovely face.

When she was on her back and her flawless facial features were fully revealed to him, it was as though someone had thrust a knife into his heart. Her thick lashes rested like a veil against her flushed cheeks. Her sculpted lips were ruby-red, the fever having given them the deep color. And each breath she took seemed to be an effort, making Brave Eagle's own breath catch as though an extension of hers.

He ran his hands through the soft glimmer of her hair, keenly aware, while she was so close to him and not defying him with her eyes, that her waist was narrow and supple, her hips invitingly curved, and her breasts perfectly rounded. He could not help but draw her up from the ground and surround her with his hard, strong arms, pressing her against him.

Never had he felt such a need to protect! To love! To possess!

And never had he felt so intensely helpless.

Brietta was very ill. And with no shaman nearby to chant his magic over her, it was for Brave Eagle alone to find a way to lessen his woman's temperature. If not, he would lose her—and this time not to another man.

This time—to death!

Drawing away from Brietta, Brave Eagle gazed down at her again, but this time in wonder. She had escaped two very clever men! She was surely the most awesome creature that he had ever known! She had proven that she was cunning. Not only that, she was brave and she was courageous!

Brave Eagle become filled with hope. Anyone who had defied so much would also defy the dark clutches of death!

"She won't die," he whispered, setting his jaw. "She will fight off this fever that has her in its grip. I will fight it myself, until she once again looks at me with her grass-green eyes!"

He once again gazed at her lips. He would fight any odds to gain a lifetime of kisses from those lips that had once been so passion-moist and sweet. Though she did not seem to want to accept such a truth, she had responded to his kisses, his touches. In time, she would willingly turn to him for love and the soft comfort that came with being loved intensely, solely, by one man. . . .

* * *

133

In her dark haze of feverish sleep, Brietta was becoming vaguely aware of the strength of arms around her. She had even heard a voice, but it had seemed to come from a deep, narrow well.

And had she heard her name being spoken? Had she even defined this voice as . . . Brave Eagle's? Had he come to her in a dream to comfort her?

Or was he real and was it his arms around her, his voice speaking her name so gently?

Oh, if she could just open her eyes to see! If she could just respond to him in some way!

But it was impossible. The fever seemed to have robbed her of not only her strength, but her ability to see or speak. That she could even hear was nothing less than a miracle. This alone gave her the courage to go on clinging to life.

Brave Eagle gazed at Brietta a moment longer, then looked at the river. Had he not come here for a cool drink to quench his thirst? Could the water not have the same effect on a body that was ravaged with fever? His mother had bathed his brow more than once when he had been feverish as a child. If such a small bathing could help lessen someone's fever, surely immersing the whole body into the water would reduce the fever much more quickly.

Gently placing Brietta on the ground, Brave Eagle went to his waiting warriors. "The white woman is now safe with me," he said. "Brown Cloud seems to have abandoned her here. Ride ahead and tell the others to return to our village. I will return there soon myself, with Brietta. Ride with care, my friends."

He watched his warriors mount and leave, then went back to Brietta. He knelt beside her, his hands trembling when he began unbuttoning her dress. As he began slipping the garment down from her shoulders, his heart pounded. Then his breath caught in his throat when her ripe body spilled from the dress as he slipped it on down to her waist, and past it.

Having her slim and sinous body revealed to him was perhaps his greatest challenge today, even more difficult than warring with the Osage. His blood raced hot through his veins as his eyes raked over her exquisite body which now lay so helpless before him. It was such a temptation to run his hands over her breasts, her long and tapering calves and silken thighs. His lips hungered to kiss her—to taste her sweetness again.

But having learned the art of restraint well, he forced his mind free of these temptations to help Brietta fight off the dangers of the fever. Touching her now, while she was unaware, would never be the same as touching her while she was awake and freely offering herself to him.

"And she will," he whispered, removing her clothes and shoes completely.

When she was finally, silkenly nude, he lifted her into his arms and began carrying her into the water.

"And she will," he whispered again, watching her expression for any signs of her awakening as he moved more deeply into the water so that she was, all but her face, completely immersed.

Cradling her close, holding her in one of his powerful arms, Brave Eagle quickly washed the black ash from his face with his free hand, so that if Brietta awakened, she would not be frightened by his fierce look.

Then he began lapping the cool water soothingly on Brietta's fever-ravaged face. He then held her with both arms, rocking her back and forth in the water, so that its motion continually caressed her body.

For what seemed hours to Brave Eagle, he held Brietta close to him in the water. Then, when the red flush seemed to fade from her cheeks, replaced by its normal creamy color, he smiled victoriously and could not help but lean down and kiss her softly on her parted lips.

Feeling comfortably cooled, her senses finally becoming more alert, Brietta felt the soft sensation of lips against her own and was very aware of the same powerful arms there again, holding her, that she had felt earlier.

She had felt these same lips before.

Suddenly realizing whose they were, Brietta's eyes flew open and a wonderful euphoria filled her when she found herself looking at Brave Eagle's handsomely sculpted face.

He had come!

Somehow he had heard her whisper his name over and over again in her feverish haze, bidding him to come to her!

He had come!

And he had done something to make her feel better. Twining her arms around his neck, Brietta returned his kiss with ardor, stunning Brave Eagle so much that he almost dropped her.

Quickly his hands were on her throat, framing her face. He reverently breathed her name as he drew his mouth from her lips, knowing that she was perhaps still too drugged from her illness to know what she was doing.

She had kissed him wildly—wantonly!

Her body had strained against his so that her breasts had crushed into his flesh, causing his desire to become a sharp, hot pain deep within his loins.

"*O-ge-ye,*" Brave Eagle said throatily, this time holding her away from him so that only their eyes met and held. "You are better, but not well. I will take you to my village, where the shaman will perform over you. In two sunrises you shall have reason to smile. Then if you still wish to kiss me with such passion, so be it. Brave Eagle desires you, always."

Now more aware of the circumstances she had awakened to, Brietta looked down at herself and at her bare flesh, and saw that Brave Eagle was holding her in his arms in the water. Embarrassment washed through her.

And that she had kissed him in such a way while she was unclothed was enough to make her hang her head with shame, never to look him in the eyes again!

"Let me down," she said, her voice quaking. She shoved at his chest. "Please, Brave Eagle. And why are you holding me in the water? Why am I undressed?"

Her eyes widened and her lips parted. "Oh, no," she cried, placing a hand to her mouth. "It was you who undressed me? Did you, Brave Eagle?"

137

She looked frantically toward the shore. "Where are my clothes?" she sobbed. "Please take me to them!"

Annoyed and hurt that Brietta seemed not to have any recollection at all of how gently he had treated her, and seeming not to be at all grateful that he had been the one to hold her for hours in the water to reduce her fever, Brave Eagle carried her briskly from the water and set her feet to the ground. His arms folded across his chest, he watched her with narrowed, angry eyes as she stooped quickly to gather up her clothes.

Then panic seized him and he fell to his knees beside her when her knees buckled and she collapsed to the ground, her clothes tumbling all around her.

Brietta clutched her head in her hands as a keen dizziness swept through her. She was too weak to fend for herself. The fever! Although no longer debilitating her by the moment, she was aware that her body was still hot to the touch and that she was still very ill.

"*O-ge-ye*, you try to be too brave too soon," Brave Eagle said, clasping his hands to her bare shoulders. He held her steady for a moment, then slowly began dressing her. "This weakness will pass. But not until we get proper nourishment in your body. And not until my village shaman speaks over you. Do you understand, Brietta, what is required of you? That you must not fight anything that I choose for you at this time? That only I know what is best for you?"

Brietta searched his face, aware of so much about him that had caused her to fall in love with him. Even while she had been so filled with fever, she had been able to envision his rugged, bronzed face, his bold nose and strong chin.

And never could she have ever forgotten his night-black eyes. As always before, they now stirred delicious feelings within her, even though she wanted to fight this thing that was growing between them.

It did seem that destiny had brought them together. Time and time again she had been thrown in his path!

"Thank you for caring," she said, smiling weakly up at him. She looked down at his deft fingers as they continued to dress her, laughing to herself as he was now at odds with her shoes, not seeming to know how they fit on her feet. One who wore only moccasins would be confused by leather sandals with their tiny snap buttons on the sides.

Trembling with weakness, Brietta murmured, "The shoes . . . Please leave them off. They are the least of my worries, Brave Eagle."

"*O-ge-ye*, your worries are my worries now," Brave Eagle said, wrestling with the shoes until he had them on her. Then he lifted her and carried her toward his horse. "Soon I hand your worries back to you. But for now, they are mine. Let it be so, Brietta."

Always in awe of how musically and poetically he talked, Brietta smiled and rested her cheek against his powerful chest. "I gladly give my worries to you," she murmured, then laughed softly as her eyes met his. "But Brave Eagle, when I am stronger, I will claim them again. Do you understand?"

Brave Eagle's eyes danced. He nodded. "Understood," he said, then gently placed her on the saddle. Mounting behind her, holding her against him as he lifted the reins, he caught a glimpse of a sudden forlorn look in her eyes. He had to believe it was because she missed her family. It was up to him to fill the empty spaces left in her heart because of her losses. She had filled his. He no longer thought of Snow Dove with a searing hurt. Brietta had taken her place in Brave Eagle's heart.

Brietta turned her eyes to Brave Eagle. "More than once you have called me by an Indian name," she murmured. "*O-ge-ye*. What is its meaning?"

"I call you my woman," Brave Eagle said, smiling down at her.

Too weary and weak to object to his so openly claiming her, or to think further of her sister's welfare, Brietta let her full weight rest against Brave Eagle and drifted off into a peaceful sleep, content, at least for the moment, to believe that as long as she was in Brave Eagle's arms, there was some hope for the future.

Missionary Cutright's haste to return to Chief Climbing Bear's village called for a horse instead of a mule to take him there. With another horse roped behind his, its back piled high with all sorts of belongings gathered from the parishioners at his mission, Missionary Cutright rode hard across the land.

His heart skipped a beat and his throat went dry when he looked into the distance and saw smoke billowing into the sky. From this vantage point he knew that the smoke could only be coming from the Osage village!

"Lord have mercy," he whispered, paling. "Am I too late to save the woman—perhaps even the Osage?" Who could have done this? he wondered. There were no soldiers in the vicinity. If there were, they would have come to the mission and made themselves known to him.

Afraid to face the destruction and death, yet knowing what was required of him at this moment, Missionary Cutright sank his heels into the flanks of his horse and hurried onward. When he entered the village, his suspicions were confirmed. He was stunned to see the devastation of the camp. All of their dwellings had been burned to the ground. The women and children were huddled everywhere, crying.

Yet, thank the Lord, only a few of the warriors had been killed. It seemed that whoever the perpetrators were, they had not been entirely heartless in their attack.

Dismounting, he was met by two warriors who took him to the ailing chief who lay on the ground close to his burned-out lodge.

Missionary Cutright knelt on his knees beside Chief Climbing Bear and said a soft prayer, then took the chief's hand and held it. "Who did this to your people?" he asked solemnly. He looked toward the stake that still stood in the center of the village. He gazed back down at the chief. "Where is the white woman?"

"The Cherokee came," Chief Climbing Bear said, coughing as pain shot through his chest.

"They destroy." He smiled slowly. "But they not get the white woman. She already gone."

"The Cherokee did this?" Missionary Cutright gasped, having always heard that the Cherokee in these parts were gentle and non-warring.

"Brave Eagle . . ." the old chief said.

"Brave Eagle," Missionary Cutright repeated thoughtfully. "I have heard his name." He forked an eyebrow. "But he is not the chief of his village. Chief Silver Shirt is. Why did Brave Eagle come and not Chief Silver Shirt?"

"Chief Silver Shirt his father," Chief Climbing Bear snarled. "Chief Silver Shirt give his blessing! He wishes me dead! Now I die!"

Missionary Cutright placed his hand to Chief Climbing Bear's heart as he gazed at the wound that was not life-threatening. "No," he said, smiling. "I don't think so." He laughed good-naturedly, glad to have found a sound heartbeat. "Not yet, anyhow."

He gestured toward the warriors who were standing around, staring down at their fallen chief. "Get him on a horse," he said in his gentle fashion. "I am going to take him to my mission." He looked around, as though to include everyone in the village. "You all will come. I will give you a place to live until you can rebuild your village. There you will get food and shelter." He smiled. "And perhaps a lesson or two about my God." He peered kindly down at the chief. "You will come with me? You and your people?"

Chief Climbing Bear thought hard for a moment, trying to envision what it would be like to live in a white man's dwelling. It did not please him at all, yet was it not the only way? His people came first and they were being offered shelter by this missionary until they could rebuild their own civilization again. And it would give them a place of safety while he sent his warriors far and wide, to friendly Osage villages where they would ask for assistance. His warriors needed weapons. They needed horses. Whatever they got from the friendly neighboring tribes, would be paid back twofold. Somehow . . .

"We will go with you," Chief Climbing Bear said, his voice solemn. "But only for a short time." He grabbed Missionary Cutright by the sleeve. "But you leave your God within your heart. My people already have their Great Spirit to whom they pray!"

"I understand," Missionary Cutright said, nodding. "The important thing is to get you safely away from here so that you can heal properly. Your people depend on you. As do I depend on my God."

As the old chief was being helped to his horse, Missionary Cutright dared to ask about the white captive again. "You said that the white woman was taken away before the Cherokee attacked," he said smoothly. "Who took her away? Where were they taking her?"

"That is Osage business," the old chief said flatly. "Never interfere in Osage business!"

A trace of fear entered Missionary Cutright's heart, yet he knew that someone greater than himself and the Osage chief was watching over him. A great calm overwhelmed him as he went to his horse and mounted. He waited patiently for all the women and children and warriors to get ready for the march to his mission. He had always taught that through evil came good. Today much evil had been done to the Osage, yet was it not leading them to his house of God?

But what of the woman he had come to rescue from the Osage? He would never be able to erase from his mind the vision of her as she had hung from the stake.

CHAPTER
TEN

I love thee freely, as men strive for right;
I love thee purely, as they turn from praise.

—*Browning*

Sage was burning in the firepit, cleansing the air of Brave Eagle's wigwam. Brietta lay comfortably on cattail mats, her stomach warmed with the broth that Brave Eagle had spoon-fed her. She could not help but feel blessed to have been taken in by this generously kind Cherokee.

Yet she feared this bond that was joining them as though they were one entity. She had learned too much mistrust from her uncles ever to totally give in to her feelings about this Indian.

145

And she was eager to go on her way—to search for her sister.

But for now, she was biding her time until she was strong enough to leave Brave Eagle by being attentive to the shaman who had worked vigorously at his craft from the moment she was brought to Brave Eagle's dwelling. Had the shaman's magic worked, she wondered? She no longer had a fever. And she could tell by flexing her arms and legs that her strength was returning—perhaps even enough to walk.

Seeing Brietta's eyes so bright and alert, and her flesh no longer looking as though it had been scorched by the heated rays of the sun, but instead the color of snow in winter, made Brave Eagle's heart soar with gladness. Even her head wound had healed over quickly.

Should she have died . . .

He would not allow himself to think further on that possibility. Brietta was not going to die. And she was there for him to gaze upon, to marvel over as though he were looking at her for the first time. She was now attired in a buckskin dress, its softness defining her every dip and curve, making him recall how beautiful she had been while naked in his arms.

His eyes dark and knowing, he smiled at Brietta as she looked his way, as though she had somehow known that his thoughts were about her.

When she returned his smile, everything within him warmed, and he loved her so much it dizzied him!

Brave Eagle swept an arm around Brietta's waist and drew her up from the cattail mats to snuggle next to him. He was glad when she did not resist this.

As though having never been strangers, they sat together as the shaman, mindless of two hearts that were pounding with wondrous, yet controlled desire, performed his rituals.

Almost swooning from the passion Brave Eagle's presence was evoking inside her, Brietta forced herself not to let it overwhelm her by focusing her full attention on the shaman. He was an aged man, his gaunt face grooved with many wrinkles and his wiry gray hair reaching the floor. He wore a long, loose buckskin robe, embellished with colorful beads and porcupine quills.

For many hours he had performed mysterious tasks for Brietta's benefit. When she arrived at the village, her face had still been hot with fever. She had been so weak, she could not stand. After being arranged comfortably on cattail mats in Brave Eagle's wigwam and fed broth, the shaman had been announced to her and had immediately begun what Brave Eagle had described as amazing feats.

Being a Christian, knowing only to pray to God, Brietta had for a time been frightened of the shaman's performance. But soon she became intrigued and could see why the Indians placed such emphasis on his healings. She now understood that this healing practice was meant to work mainly on the mind of the sick person, and by that means to produce a recovery.

To that end he had startled, amazed, terrified, and stimulated Brietta. The shaman had exerted his mental influence, in addition to his material

147

remedies, chiefly through the words of the songs that he had sung while administering his medicine.

As now the shaman was singing as he was shaking his rattle over Brietta.

"You will recover;
You will be well again.
It is I who say it;
My power is great.
Through my healings I will make you well again."

After singing for a while longer and shaking his medicine rattle, the shaman left the wigwam as abruptly as he had entered.

There was a strained silence between Brietta and Brave Eagle. Then Brave Eagle stood and offered Brietta his hands, encouraging her to stand.

"Go with me outside to view the stars," Brave Eagle said, smiling down at her. *"O-ge-ye*, you have seen that the powers of our Cherokee shaman are great. You are no longer ravaged by fever. You are now strong." He pulled gently on her hands. "Rise. Test my shaman's abilities. Walk with me outside."

His eyes like magnets drawing her to him, Brietta rose to her feet. At first she was unsteady, then with the support of Brave Eagle's arm around her waist, she became more sure of her steps and soon went with him outside, amazed at how well she was feeling.

His arm still locked around her waist, they walked slowly through the village, where the dark sky was filled with reflections from the outdoor

fires that were burning near the clusters of wigwams. Her gaze settled on one dwelling in particular. It seemed a natural extension of the soil,
dome-shaped and rising like an earth-colored
mound from the center of the village.

Brave Eagle followed her gaze. "That is my
father's council house," he said. "Many decisions
for our people are spoken around the fire there."

"Did you speak of me around that fire?" Brietta
asked softly. "Did your father approve of your
bringing me to the Cherokee village?"

"My father trusts my judgment in all things,"
Brave Eagle said. He chuckled low. "Even when it
involves a woman with white skin and green eyes."

"But why do you care so much about what
happens to me?" Brietta asked, having seen so
many beautiful women in the Indian village.
"Surely you have your pick of women. What about
me causes you to look past them?"

Brave Eagle doubled a hand into a tight fist and
clutched it to his chest. "The difference lies here,"
he said. "Within my heart. You make my heart
react as only once before in my life . . ."

His voice trailed off, realizing that he had said
more than he had planned to. Never did he wish to
speak of Snow Dove to Brietta!

And now Brietta must realize that there had
been another woman before her.

That was not good, yet sometime in the future,
when Brietta gave her heart totally to Brave Eagle,
she would have to know about even more than a
wife now dead.

There was also a son. Could she accept another
woman's son?

Even if it was Brave Eagle's?

Brietta looked quickly up at Brave Eagle, stung by what he had revealed to her, yet feeling foolish for such a reaction. He was a powerful, handsome man, who was surely in his early thirties. There had to have been many women before her, yet he spoke of this one woman as having been special.

Who was she? And where was she now?

Brietta looked quickly away from Brave Eagle. These were questions that she was not free to ask. These were questions that he would surely not answer, even should she ask.

"I shall take you to a special place to view the dark heavens," Brave Eagle said.

Brietta's breath was stolen away when he suddenly lifted her up into his arms and began carrying her up a steep embankment.

"Often I sit and study the stars," he explained. "There are reasons for each of them to be in the sky. I sometimes ponder over these reasons." He glanced down at her. "Do you ever?"

Her arm around his neck, his powerful chest heaving in his exertion to carry her up the steep embankment, Brietta looked up at the sky, soon defining the loveliness of the milky way. "Yes," she murmured. "I have often wondered about the stars and their origin. But their mysteries stay locked in the heavens."

"There are more than the stars in the heavens that one from time to time is forced to think about," Brave Eagle said, reaching the bluff that overlooked his village. Gently he placed Brietta to her feet and encouraged her to sit down on a soft bed of grass beside him. Suddenly quiet, he frowned as his eyes scanned the heavens.

Noticing the marked difference in Brave Eagle's behavior, Brietta touched his arm gently. "What?" she murmured. "What are you talking about? What could be in the sky that you would be forced to think about, so obviously seeing displeasure in it?"

Her hand on his arm stirred feelings within Brave Eagle that he was having to battle. He tried to ignore its warmth, its gentleness, and spoke with venom about something that all Cherokee dreaded. "Raven mockers are in the heavens," he said. "They come too often to my village of Cherokee."

"Raven mockers?" Brietta said, her eyes wide. "Brave Eagle, I have never heard of such a thing. What are they?"

"They are creatures who swoop through the air in fiery shapes, with arms outstretched like wings, to rob the dying man and woman of life!" he said with much bitterness, his eyes blazing down into hers.

"Oh, I see," Brietta said softly, looking intensely at Brave Eagle, in awe of how innocent he was to believe this myth that had surely been taught to him by his father and his father before him.

But was it any different than the beliefs told to her by her mother and father, which surely the Cherokee would find strange and forbidding?

They were of two separate peoples and customs, yet she could not deny how their hearts had become fused with something beautiful.

She loved him.

She would never love anyone but him.

A slow smile began to tug at Brave Eagle's lips. "Tonight we defied the raven mockers," he said, reaching a hand to gently cup Brietta's cheek. "You lived. My beautiful woman, you lived."

Beginning to be caught up in rapture that she knew she should fight, Brietta eased his hand from her cheek. "Please . . ." she murmured. "Perhaps we should return to your village."

Not to be dissuaded, having been patient long enough with Brietta, Brave Eagle placed both hands to her face and began easing her lips closer to his.

"You do not enjoy this time alone with Brave Eagle?" he asked, his dark eyes melting her reserve away. "Is not this a place made for lovers? My woman, you have regained your strength. You are well. Let us think of other things. Have we not long enough denied our feelings for one another? Your eyes tell me so much that your words have not. Now tell me with your kiss."

Her heart pounding, her knees weak from bliss, Brietta let his lips claim her as he drew her into his powerful embrace and began lowering her to her back on the ground. A moment of panic was all that she experienced when she felt his hand snaking up the skirt of the buckskin dress and slowly lifting the dress up past her waist, and then over her head.

But that moment of panic was gone and she was soon caught up in ecstasy as Brave Eagle's mouth moved from her lips to the hollow of her throat and her nipples, nipping them with his teeth as his hands kneaded them.

"Brave Eagle," Brietta whispered, running her

hands over the taut smoothness of his chest, then to his muscled shoulders. "Am I truly here with you? Am I truly allowing this?"

"Your heart leads you into allowing it," Brave Eagle said, moving over her, his kisses feathering Brietta's face, sending her into a whirlpool of desire. "*O-ge-ye*, I will be gentle. Everything I do with you, forever, will be done with tenderness."

"Oh, my darling, don't you know that I am aware of your sweetness?" Brietta said, hardly able to recognize this woman who had only a short while ago been a girl, unaware of womanly desires and dreams. "Do you not know how your embraces, your kisses affect me? Please kiss me again, Brave Eagle. Kiss me now. Hold me. Make love to me. What has happened these past several days has proved to me that tomorrow may never even come. Let us share what we can, tonight. I . . . so . . . love you."

"Your words are like the music of spring in my heart," Brave Eagle said, looking adoringly down at her. "These words I have hungered for, for so long! *O-ge-ye*, they will be locked within my heart forever!"

Brietta was unable to stifle a sob of happiness against his lips as he kissed her hard and long, his hands smoothing over her trembling, bare body.

Brave Eagle molded one of her breasts within his hand. The mere touch of its softness made his breath almost fail him, causing his mouth to part from her lips with a light gasp.

"Brave Eagle," Brietta whispered against his parted lips, her whole body trembling with need. "Please do not think less of me for what I am

153

offering to share with you tonight. Please . . ."

"Never . . ." he whispered back. *"O-ge-ye,* never." His mouth covered hers with a fierce kiss.

With a moan of ecstasy she returned the kiss, clinging to him. When he drew away from her to remove his breechclout, the realization of what she had agreed to seized her in a sudden fear. She had been taught not to share these sorts of embraces until the words of a preacher had been spoken over her and the man of her choice.

But she had learned, of late, that time—that life—was so fleeting! If she waited for everything to be proper, it could be too late!

And she so badly wanted Brave Eagle.

He brought to her something that no one else ever could. With his special loving of her, it brought her the tranquility and peace that at this time in her life, when everything had been taken from her, she so desperately needed!

For now, for this moment in time, she had Brave Eagle, and he had her!

As Brave Eagle's manly strength at the juncture of his thighs was revealed to Brietta, she swallowed hard, looked away, and clutched her arms about her chest, shivering.

Brave Eagle cast his breechclout aside and knelt down beside Brietta. He placed his arm tenderly around her waist and drew her against him. "You tremble so," he said, his lips buried in the depths of her hair just above her ear. "You are cold? Or are you still too weak to continue this that we have begun?"

"No," Brietta whispered. "It is not the cool of

night that my body is reacting to. Nor am I aware of any weaknesses.''

Brave Eagle drew away from her, his eyes sweeping over her with a silent, urgent message. Her long, drifting hair lay across her shoulders, a few strands covering the peaks of her budded breasts. "You will confess to me why you tremble so?" he urged gently, drawing her against him again so that her breasts touched his chest.

He rained kisses along her brow, his hands taking in the round softness of her buttocks, then around to where his fingers grazed the soft bush of hair at the juncture of her thighs. He was aware of the quick intake of her breath at the boldness of his actions, and then of her sigh and the response to his touch as she relaxed and let him have his way with her again.

"My love, you are the reason," Brietta murmured, lifting her lips to accept the offering of his as he bent over her to softly kiss her. With care, he lowered her to the ground, his tongue brushing her lips lightly, causing her to moan softly.

"Brietta, you have been in my dreams every night since that first time I saw you," Brave Eagle admitted, his heart thundering as he shaped his hands about her breasts. The touch of her nipples stiffening against his palms made euphoria claim him as never before when he sought pleasure from women. Not even while making love to Snow Dove had he felt such drugged emotions!

He let one hand wander down the full length of Brietta's body until once again he found the juncture of her thighs and that secret part of her that surely had never before been touched by a man.

"*O-ge-ye*, I shall always love you," Brave Eagle reassured her, caressing the damp valley that was awaiting his entry. When she parted her thighs, he knew that it was an open invitation to do as he wished.

"As I shall always love you," Brietta said, stunned by the strange huskiness of her voice, yet aware of the rush of rapture that was claiming her insides. She trembled again as Brave Eagle touched her lips in a gentle and lingering kiss, while his stroking fingers fully awakened her senses.

A blaze of desire fired her insides. Her body turned to liquid as Brave Eagle moved directly atop her and she felt the hardness of his manhood touching her thigh close to where she so strangely, sensually, throbbed.

She knew that there was no turning back now. What she had let begin, she must finish. She loved Brave Eagle. He loved her. Kisses were no longer enough.

Brave Eagle's stomach churned wildly as he pressed his hardness closer against Brietta. With one knee, he opened her legs wider. And while kissing her, caressing her breasts, he began his slow entrance inside her. When he found the part of her that had never been breached by a man, he knew that he was the first with her. And realizing the pain that would accompany his full entrance, he kissed her more ardently to silence her outcry of pain as he made the lunge that claimed her completely!

Soft sobs arose from within Brietta when she

felt the stab of pain as he entered her. She clung to the corded muscles of his shoulders as he began his easy thrusts, the pain now smoothing away into something sweet, something magical. She moved her hips with him, her head spinning with delight. When he lowered his lips and suckled one of her nipples, she threw her head back into a deep, lingering sigh of pleasure.

Brave Eagle's tongue skillfully teased her taut breasts as he moved rhythmically within her. Her answering excitement pleased him. Theirs would be a future of such lovemaking—of such intimate sharing! He would soon marry her in a ceremony that would please her!

His hands moved from her thigh to her hip to her breast, wanting to memorize every inch of her body. His mouth slipped from her breast to kiss the column of her throat. And then he felt the familiar spreading heat encompassing him and could no longer hold back that which would deliver him to the heavens and back in a flash of ecstasy.

Gripping Brietta's buttocks, Brave Eagle lifted her closer. His body momentarily stiffened and then he released his warmth into her depths, shuddering with the rapture of release.

And when her body spoke in kind, he smiled down at her, knowing that she had just been introduced to how it felt to be a complete woman.

Embarrassed at how her body had reacted to Brave Eagle's loving, Brietta looked away. But she was forced to look up at him again when he placed a finger at her chin and encouraged their eyes to meet and hold.

"O-ge-ye, you turned your eyes away," Brave Eagle said softly. "Brave Eagle did not please you?"

Seeing the hurt in his eyes, knowing that his manhood was in question, Brietta placed a hand gently to his cheek. "Yes, you pleased me," she murmured, tears burning at the corners of her eyes, now knowing the true danger of having allowed the lovemaking of this handsome Cherokee. It was as though he had become the most important thing in her life—and she could not allow it!

There was her sister! What of her welfare?

Ah, but wouldn't it be easy to let herself think only of herself and stay hidden away from life while in the protective embraces of Brave Eagle?

Yes, it would be easy. Too easy. And she could not allow it. Soon she would leave him. As soon as she felt that her strength had completely returned.

"If Brave Eagle pleased you, why did you turn away, and why are there tears in your eyes?" he persisted.

Brietta sniffled, then smiled weakly up at him. "My darling, you must understand how a woman feels when she—she first gives herself to a man," she murmured. "It is not done lightly."

Brave Eagle drew her into his embrace. He hugged her to him, relishing the feel of her breasts against his chest. "I was the first with you,' he said flatly. "And I am the last!"

Brietta squeezed her eyes closed, tears streaming down her face. "Yes," she whispered. "You are the last." And so he would be. Even after she left him, she could never allow another man to touch her. No man's loving could ever compare with Brave Eagle's.

Brave Eagle eased her from his arms. He reached for the buckskin dress and with much devotion and care slipped it over her head, smoothing it down across the curves of her body.

She watched with sadness as he slipped into his breechclout, already missing him, wondering if she could really turn her back on him and leave his village.

Suddenly her eyes were averted. She gasped as she looked heavenward and saw several falling stars.

Brave Eagle stiffened his arms at his sides as he watched the heavenly display. "*U-yo-i!*" he said, his voice drawn. "It is raining stars! Star showers warn of impending disaster!"

Brietta looked quickly at Brave Eagle, seeing fear in his eyes, and hearing it in his voice, for the first time since she met him.

It soon overwhelmed her too, for if he had reason to be afraid, how could she not be?

CHAPTER
ELEVEN

My face in thine eye, thine in mine appears,
And true plain hearts do in the face rest.

—*Donne*

Brown Cloud had left Rachel with René even before they left the Ozarks behind. With his Osage companions riding at a fast clip on both sides and behind him, Brown Cloud rode with determination toward his village. Hidden beneath many mats at the back of his wigwam were two unopened jugs of firewater. Tonight he would sit before the fire in his dwelling and let the spirits of *pe-tsa-ni* claim him.

For a while he would be able to forget his differences with Brave Eagle. For a while Brown

Cloud would forget that his chieftain father had forced him to give up the white woman to the French slaver!

A strong odor of smoke wafting through the air stung Brown Cloud's nose and throat. His eyes narrowed as he peered through the trees ahead, knowing that just beyond lay the Osage village. Had the fires been kindled for the evening already?

He looked heavenward, through the thick canopy of trees. The setting sun was gilding the leaves. Soon it would be dark.

He frowned as he flicked his reins and nudged the sides of his horse with his knees. There would be no hero's welcome for him today. He had been dishonored when his father claimed the white woman as his own, to do with as he pleased.

Only for a short while had Brown Cloud drawn admiring looks from the villagers.

As he rode on toward his village, something began gnawing at his consciousness. Many things were peculiarly different than when he normally came this close to his home.

He glanced up into the trees again, keenly aware of the silence. Where were the birds that usually began nesting at sunset? Where were the squirrels that usually scampered around nervously, searching for at least one more acorn before the moon replaced the sun in the sky?

The silence was deafening.

And where there was silence . . . there was trouble!

The aroma of scorched ash became stronger as Brown Cloud rode onward. When he came to a clearing and was finally able to see the village, the devastation sent spirals of nausea through him. He stopped his horse and dismounted just in time to bow his head and retch.

The shrieks and cries of the other Osage warriors echoed through Brown Cloud, as though they were echoes of cries from the past when other Osage villages had been reduced to ruin and rubble by their enemies.

Would it ever end?

And why had it happened this time?

Which enemy was responsible?

Breathing hard, his stomach and throat still burning, Brown Cloud wiped his mouth clean with the back of his hand, then reached deeply within himself for the courage to look at the remains of his village again.

Not only had all of the dwellings in the village been burned—even his father's great lodge—but there were no signs of survivors. The village was even quieter than the trees in the forest.

"Is there not anyone alive?" Brown Cloud cried, raising his hands and weeping eyes to the heavens as he beseeched the comfort of *Wah-kon-tah.* "Great Spirit, I have already lost a mother to death. What now of my father? What of the mothers and children of our village? What of our Osage warriors?"

The sound of a lone horseman arriving behind him made Brown Cloud turn with a start, his hand automatically going for his knife.

But he soon replaced it, for the brave arriving was not his enemy.

Cherokee, yes. But not an enemy.

Brown Cloud recognized Running Wolf, the

Cherokee fugitive who was atoning for Brave Eagle's sin of befriending Brown Cloud. It did puzzle him, though, that Running Wolf was not at the *City of Peace*, where he had been banished until the time of atonement was over.

Brown Cloud stood his ground, awaiting Running Wolf's arrival. He motioned with his hand for his companions to retreat when they came and flanked his side, their rifles ready for firing. Left alone, he looked Running Wolf straight in the eye as the Cherokee's horse reined in before him.

"What brings you here at our time of sorrow?" Brown Cloud asked, not inviting the Cherokee to dismount. "What has taken you from the *City of Peace*?"

Running Wolf sat stoically stiff on his saddle. He looked past Brown Cloud, at the smoking ash of the village, then down into Brown Cloud's eyes. "I witnessed everything," he said, ignoring Brown Cloud's question. It would no longer concern Brown Cloud when the Osage heard that Brave Eagle had been responsible for the devastation of the Osage village.

And being the one to disclose this truth to Brown Cloud was another way for Running Wolf to avenge his weeks and months of being shamed for the sins of Brave Eagle! Running Wolf smiled to himself. He would tell Brown Cloud everything that he had witnessed.

Brown Cloud stepped closer. He peered intensely up at Running Wolf, his heart racing at the thought of finding out who the culprit was—and having the opportunity to go after him, to make him pay! His father was dead, somewhere in the ruins. Someone had to pay!

"You were witness?" Brown Cloud said, a sudden fire lighting his eyes. "Tell me who it was!" He doubled a fist at his side. "Tell me now, Running Wolf!"

"It was Brave Eagle and a band of his warriors," Running Wolf said.

There was a strained pause. Deeply within Brown Cloud's dark eyes, Running Wolf saw that the Osage found it hard to accept this truth.

"Brown Cloud, your father and many of your people are now captives of Brave Eagle and his warriors," he added quickly, surprised at the ease with which the lie passed his lips. "It was I who saw them taken away by ropes and led behind the Cherokee horses as though no better than dogs!"

Brown Cloud felt a sudden tearing at his heart, as though it was being pulled in two directions— sadness over the fate of his father and his devoted people warred with the hate that had guided Brave Eagle into doing such a spiteful thing.

And Brown Cloud knew that his friend had not done it solely for a woman. He had done it to a friend who had gone back on his word! He would never forget Brave Eagle's warnings after they found their vision. He had said that should Brown Cloud ever deceive him, the friendship would cease! He had warned Brown Cloud that one act of betrayal would cast all vows of friendship to the wind!

"But to go this far?" Brown Cloud whispered to himself, turning his back to Running Wolf. He did not even hear Running Wolf ride away. He was too distraught to think clearly about anything.

"We must go after them!"

The voice of one of his Osage companions broke into Brown Cloud's troubled mind. When the warrior stepped into the line of Brown Cloud's vision, only then did he respond, realizing that since his father was now a captive, it was up to him, the next-chief-in-line, to prove his prowess by stealing his father and his people back again from the Cherokee!

Doubling a fist in the air, Brown Cloud spun around and faced the warriors who stared back at him for guidance. "Death to all Cherokee!" he shouted, accepting a lance that was thrust into his hand and waving it in the air over his head. "Brave Eagle and his warriors must pay! Our people must be set free! Do you hear me, my warriors? Death! Death to the Cherokee!"

The warriors raised their weapons over their heads and echoed Brown Cloud's words until the hills and forests rang with their voices. Brown Cloud's jaw tightened and his shoulders squared proudly.

But his pride was short-lived. His jaw loosened at the thought of suddenly being at the reins that normally were held by his father. If he failed, if his father died, would he not be scorned forever by those of the Osage who lived to tell it?

Such news would be passed down from generation of generation of Osage. He would be a laughing stock!

Turning, his eyes scanned the smoking debris of the village, settling on the smouldering ashes of what remained of his own dwelling. His heart began to pound as his gaze moved over the mounds of ash. Perhaps his two remaining jugs of whiskey had stood up against the ravages of the flames.

Fear struck at his heart. Without the aid of firewater, he would lack the courage to make war with the Cherokee. He would fail, even before firing one shot against them.

Walking, then running, toward his wigwam's remains, Brown Cloud became aware of the sudden silence behind him and felt the eyes of his warriors on him, as though branding him. He understood too well how most of his companions felt about the *pe-tsa-ni*. They saw it as a scourge on a man's soul—as something wicked and frowned upon by the Great Spirit.

And they knew him well enough to know what he was seeking as he fell to his knees in the hot ashes and began brushing them aside.

Desperate, ignoring the heat against his knees and the palms of his hands, and of the eyes still on him, Brown Cloud dug through and scattered the ashes, then laughed throatily when his hand finally made contact with a stone jug. Circling his fingers around it, he pulled the jug free. Laughing, he stood and held it in the air for all to see.

"Pe-tsa-ni!" he shouted. He ignored the scornful eyes of those who did not approve of the firewater and smiled at those who shared his love of the whiskey. He nodded toward them. "Let us share in drinks, my friends! Soon we shall feel the power that it grants us! Then we shall attack the Cherokee!"

He moved to the outskirts of the village and sat down beneath a tree, resting his back against its trunk. The cork in the jug was smoking, having been half burned. Brown Cloud spat on it to cool it off, then grabbed it with his eager fingers and gave it a yank. When the cork popped free and the fumes of the whiskey wafted up from the jug, he licked his lips, tipped the jug to his mouth, and drank greedily until his stomach felt the fire and he felt the familiar stronger pumping of his heart.

A hand on his shoulder reminded him that he was not the only one eager to extract that feeling of great importance from the *pe-tsa-ni*. He lowered the jug from his mouth and smiled at his three companions who waited their turn. Handing the jug over to one of them, he looked past them at the others, who never participated in the drinking of firewater. They had disbanded, each one going sullenly through the village, sifting through the remains of their dwellings.

His gaze moved to where his father's great lodge used to stand so supremely, and his gut twisted when again all that he saw was the glow of smouldering ashes.

His gaze shifted back to the warriors who were mulling around, waiting for him to find the courage he needed from the firewater. So much depended on him.

And if his father should die?

Everything depended on him! He would be in charge. He would be the leader of his band of Osage!

Fear gripping him, Brown Cloud accepted the jug back into his hands, closed his eyes, and gulped down many deep swallows until he no longer cared about anything or anyone.

When that jug was empty, he searched through the remains of his wigwam until he found the other one. Staggering, laughing crookedly, he carried this jug to his waiting friends. While the sober Osage settled down on the ground and watched, awaiting orders from Brown Cloud, his body continued to crave more and more of the whiskey and he fed this hunger until drinking was all that mattered.

And no one dared to go against the Chief's son—the one who would one day be chief himself. Even now they were not sure if he already was, for none knew the true fate of Chief Climbing Bear.

The air was warm and drenched with a flood of mellow, evening light. Through wide valleys Running Wolf rode, crossing little streams and flowery meadows where bees hummed at their work. The trees all around him seemed to grow in an orderly fashion and were the most exquisite shade of soft green imaginable. Just ahead a fox trotted through the trees, then crossed Running Wolf's path from left to right, an omen of good luck.

Running Wolf nudged his horse's side with his knees, urging his handsome steed into a harder gallop into open terrain. Unknown flowers as bright as a rainbow covered the fields. The air was filled with sweet smells from plants that were being crushed beneath his horse's hooves.

Proud of his deceit and his act of vengeance against Brave Eagle, Running Wolf rode into the outskirts of the *City of Peace*. He held his head high, and much pride swelled his heart. He nodded as he was greeted from all sides by those who inhabited this place where fugitives from vengeance found sanctuary.

His gaze took in the familiar setting, a village with a multitude of peaked huts under the shade of an island of trees that resembled green umbrellas. Extending from the village was more broad meadow country sloping up toward a series of densely green hills. Behind these hills were serrated ridges, and behind the ridges rose a low and sprawling range of mountains.

Running Wolf rode on through the village and urged his horse into a canter. He had fooled Brave Eagle even before today. Though everyone thought he never left the *City of Peace*, he had made residence in a much more private place. It was not so much a prison as one of the huts crowded together among those who were living out their assigned punishments would have been. Where he had taken his belongings was a place of mystery and beauty.

Smiling, glad to have arrived at his home, he rode up to a cavern hollowed into the side of a hill and dismounted. Securing his horse, he walked into the cavern that was lit by a fire whose soft glow illuminated the many chambers that were divided by walls of hard, white, shining crystal that dazzled like frozen snow.

"And so is your deed done?"

A voice coming out of the shadows made Running Wolf turn and smile. "Yes, it is done," he said, his dark eyes gleaming victoriously at the man who stepped into view. "Today my vengeance against Brave Eagle is one step closer to being achieved."

Running Wolf looked down at the man's bandaged arm and frowned. "And are you able to ride tonight? You said that you wished to search for your nieces."

He would not tell Patrick Russell that he had been delivering one of his nieces to him when she had fallen ill. It was best not to let him know that he had ever seen her, or perhaps Patrick would hold him responsible for her death!

Running Wolf knew the wickedness in Patrick Russell's heart and had tolerated his companionship for only one purpose. He had thought perhaps to use Patrick in helping him achieve his vengeful acts against Brave Eagle, since Patrick hated Brave Eagle as much as he did. Brave Eagle had kept Patrick from stealing his Cherokee people to sell to slavers. Now that Patrick was of no further use to him, Running Wolf would see that he was guided to the white man's fort, and out of Running Wolf's life.

Combing his fingers through his long, stringy red hair, Patrick smiled through a thick stubble of whiskers at Running Wolf. "I ain't one to be kept down for long," he said, spitting over his shoulder. "I'm ready to take out on a horse as soon as you give the word, Running Wolf."

Running Wolf sank down on his haunches by the fire, staring into it. "When the moon rises full in the sky, then we shall become as one with the night," he said. "Too many risks have already been taken in the daylight. My luck could run out."

Patrick smiled slyly, eyeing Running Wolf's knife

sheathed at his waist. He had pondered all day whether to kill the small Cherokee or ride with him until his worth was used up. He had decided that Running Wolf was worth much more to him alive than dead.

At least for now. He had been lucky to have escaped the wrath of the Osage shortly after the damnable Injuns had set fire to his cabin.

It had been a close call that he didn't want repeated.

Yes, he thought further, he would stick with Running Wolf a while longer. Having an Injun companion was better than having no companion at all.

He joined Running Wolf beside the fire. "Wait until you see those nieces of mine," he said, placing a log on the fire. "Now those two are somethin' else."

Running Wolf looked guardedly at Patrick, hearing more in this white man's voice than mere affection for his kin. It made a protective feeling for the remaining white woman spiral through him. This crude white man would never be allowed to abuse the woman.

Turning his eyes back to the fire, Running Wolf thoughtfully patted his sheathed knife.

CHAPTER
TWELVE

She is a woman; one in whom
The spring-time of her childish years
Hath never lost its fresh perfume.

—*Lowell*

A campfire was casting its dancing light onto the canopy of trees overhead where Rachel sat half-heartedly eating beans from a tin plate. Hating even more than fearing the obese Frenchman, she glared at René. It was hard for her to comprehend anyone as greedy—as cruel. This Frenchman who traded in human flesh was as evil as her Uncle Patrick and Uncle Ray! She had to find a way to escape! Even the dark shadows of the forest would be more welcome than remaining at the mercy of René!

Her eyes never leaving the Frenchman, Rachel hungrily scooped another spoonful of beans into her mouth. He had eaten voraciously and was now leaning back on one elbow, his legs stretched out before him, tipping a jug of whiskey to his lips. He drank as greedily as he ate.

Rachel recoiled when René eased himself back to a sitting position and set his jug of whiskey aside to leer at her. She had feared that his male hunger would be the next thing that would need to be fed. She scooped several more bites into her mouth, knowing that she needed every bit of her energy to resist this man who turned her stomach to look at him!

"*Ma cherie*, and so you find our food to your liking?" René asked, sitting down beside her and reaching to toy with the ends of her hair. "My beauty, I have fed you. Now perhaps you would like for me to help you with a bath?"

Rachel dropped her plate to the ground and slapped his hand away. "Keep your hands off me, you pig," she hissed, looking at him through narrowed eyes. "Though I know how badly I need a bath, I'd die before I'd undress before you. Get away from me. If you plan to sell me to the highest bidder, it shall be done with my hair matted and filth covering my body! I do not want to be responsible for helping you get more money for me!"

René laughed throatily and rose back to his full height, standing over her with his fists on his hips. "*Bien*. Have it your way, *Ma cherie*," he said. "And so I sell you to whoever wants to stand your stench. I can assure you the man will not smell any better than you."

The thought of being sold to someone no better than the Frenchman, perhaps even more vile in his dress and occupation, made Rachel's eyes waver.

Yet she was determined not to do anything to please the Frenchman. If she did not bother to bathe and make herself sweet for him, perhaps he would leave her alone.

But she doubted that. He reeked of dried perspiration and all sorts of ungodly odors. It surely wouldn't matter to him if the woman he bedded smelled as unclean!

Suddenly René leaned over and grabbed Rachel by the wrist. "I have wasted too much time on talk with you," he said between gritted teeth. "It's time you join the others in the tent for the night." He laughed throatily. "How will you like sleeping with a pack of wild Injuns? That's what you're going to get. By morning you'll be begging ol' René to have mercy on your sweet little soul."

Her eyes wide, her heart thumping, Rachel stumbled along beside René as he moved toward the small tent that already housed the Indian captives. Everyone would be squeezed into it like turtles in their shells! What might transpire during the night frightened her, yet anything was surely better than being with the Frenchman.

Rachel jolted to a stop as René turned her around, her back to him. She winced and cried out with pain as he clamped both of her wrists together and began tying them behind her.

"*Ma cherie*, you will have no way to fight back should the Indians want to have fun with you,"

René said, chuckling. "But should you decide that you wish to be spared, scream. René will come and rescue you. *Avec plaisir*!"

"You are a vile man," Rachel said, sobbing. "I shall never ask your assistance! Never!"

"We shall see," René said, giving her a shove that caused her to stumble into the tent, onto her knees.

Rachel steadied herself on her knees, breathless, as she looked slowly around her and at the Indian slaves who sat hunched together, staring angrily at her. They did not care that she was no more free than they.

Then René's large hands were giving her another shove, making her fall awkwardly forward. When she landed, she lay there for a moment, stunned, then looked slowly up into the soft brown eyes of an Indian maiden.

"I'm sorry," Rachel whispered, picking herself up and sitting with her knees locked against her chest beside the Indian woman.

"White woman treated badly," the Indian maiden whispered, moving closer to Rachel. "So is Osage woman. The Frenchman—he is bad!"

Rachel looked quickly at the maiden, surprised at her ability to speak in the English language. "You are of the Osage tribe?" she whispered, leaning her face closer to the maiden whose face revealed that she was young, perhaps the same age as Rachel.

"Yes, but my Osage shame me," the maiden said, lowering her eyes. "One who was greedy stole me from my village and sold me into slavery to the Frenchman. I wish to die." She looked slowly up at

Rachel. "I will help free you if you will, in turn, steal a knife and sink it deep into my flesh!"

Rachel paled, taken aback by the maiden's request. "I could not do that!" she whispered, repelled at the thought of what she asked, yet moved deeply by the pleading in the maiden's dark eyes. "Never could I kill you!"

"It will free Frodina's soul!" the Osage maiden begged. "Cannot you see? Frodina has been shamed. Never can I look into the eyes of my people again!"

"But what happened was not your fault," Rachel softly argued. "You were forced! You have been wronged, not shamed!"

"You will not kill me?" Frodina asked sullenly.

Rachel shook her head back and forth. "No," she murmured. "Never could I do that!"

"Turn your back to me," Frodina said softly. "Let our hands meet. I shall loosen your bonds. You can flee when the white men sleep."

"Only if you will agree to escape with me," Rachel whispered, looking from side to side at the Indians who had distanced their thoughts from Rachel and the Indian woman, their heads humbly bowed, most seeming to be drifting off into sleep. "We can be friends, you and I. I so fear the forest alone!"

Frodina was quiet for a moment, obviously contemplating the offer. Then she nodded. "We will escape together," she whispered. "Turn. Let our hands loosen each other's bonds."

Her heart pounding with the hope that escape was perhaps only moments away, Rachel turned herself so that her back was against Frodina's. She scarcely breathed when Frodina's fingers began working with the knots. She wanted to let out a shout of joyous victory when she felt her wrists become freed.

She turned and finished untying Frodina's wrists, then they faced one another, smiling.

"We did it!" Rachel whispered to Frodina, her eyes dancing. Without much thought, she grabbed Frodina into her arms and hugged her, then, embarrassed, fell away from her.

They sat stiffly side by side, staring at the entrance flap of the tent as they listened to the men disbanding by the outdoor fire to go to their bedrolls. The longer she waited, the more Rachel's heart pounded. Her knees were weak and the pit of her stomach felt strangely hollow. She knew that if she got caught escaping, René would punish her severely. Then he would force her to do anything else that he pleased to continue the punishment.

Everything was finally quiet. Rachel and Frodina exchanged questioning glances, then nodded and crawled from the tent together. Fear of being caught dizzied Rachel, yet nothing would keep her from trying.

Cautiously, she looked around her. From all that she could tell everyone was asleep—even the sentry posted at the side of the tent to keep watch on the prisoners. His knife was drawn and rested on his lap, his hand having fallen away from it. His bobbing head and snores attested to how soundly he slept.

Rachel and Frodina's eyes met and momentarily held, then Rachel nodded. She moved her lips, and without speaking aloud, mouthed the words, "Let's go!"

Thinking that Frodina was behind her, Rachel lifted the skirt of the buckskin dress and began running toward the darker shadows of the forest.

But when she realized that Frodina was not following her, she stopped and began retracing her steps.

When she stumbled over something in the dark, she caught her balance and stopped to look down. There was just enough moonlight spiraling through the trees to reveal a slim body, lying lifeless on the ground.

A keen dizziness swept through Rachel as she fell to her knees beside Frodina. "Why?" Rachel sobbed, her eyes locked on the knife lodged in Frodina's chest, one of her hands still clutched around the handle, crimson with blood.

"Why did you do it?" Rachel cried, cradling her face in her hands. The knife! she thought, trying to piece together how this could have happened—the knife on the sentry's lap had been too accessible for the maiden who wished so intensely for death.

And since Rachel had refused to kill Frodina, she had done the terrible deed herself.

Rachel stared down at Frodina. The lovely Osage maiden needed a Christian burial, but Rachel was not equipped to give her one.

And she had to flee! She was alive—she had to think of her own welfare!

Kneeling, she moved her trembling hands to Frodina's eyes and gently closed the lids. "We could have been good friends," she whispered,

179

then rose to her feet again and began running blindly through the forest, tears streaming from her eyes.

Survival.

No matter what, she must survive.

And what of Brietta? Had she been forced to endure as much as her twin sister?

The tears finally dried in her eyes, Rachel continued running until she found herself traveling over a meadow splashed with moonlight.

Her footsteps faltered when, up ahead, she could define in the darkness two men on horseback riding toward her. Fear grabbed her at the pit of her stomach, and she looked desperately from side to side, searching for cover.

But she had left the trees too far behind. All that surrounded her was vast stretches of ankle-deep grass and wildflowers.

Having no choice, Rachel stood her ground and awaited the horsemen. With a thudding heart, she watched as they came closer and closer, then reined in before her.

Her mouth parted in a gasp when she recognized one of the men.

"Patrick?" she said, shock registering in her eyes. Her gaze settled on his injured arm. "Uncle Patrick? I thought you were . . ."

"Dead?" Patrick said, laughing as he dismounted and went to Rachel. He lifted her hair from her shoulders, then walked slowly around her, studying her. "Naw, I ain't dead. Seems life ain't been all that grand to you since you fled in the night from our cabin. It's a good thing I managed to escape the fire and came along tonight and found you, ain't it?" He frowned and held his face into Rachel's. "Where's your sister?" he hissed. "Where is your goddamned sister?"

"I don't know," Rachel said, backing away from her uncle. She glanced over his shoulder at the slight Indian who was just slipping from his horse. She tightened inside as he came to her, looking at her strangely. It seemed that she got herself out of one fix just to get mixed up in another! She had fled one evil man only to fall into the clutches of another man who was just as evil and perhaps even more dangerous.

And what of this Indian? What could she expect from him? Something about her seemed to dismay him.

But what? Surely he had seen a white woman before.

She cringed when he touched her arm, then drew his hand back quickly, as though she were a hot coal.

Running Wolf was puzzled at having found the white woman. He thought he had left the white woman at the creek, dying! How could she be so well now? She was like a spirit—someone who had come back from the dead. Someone with magic powers! Her loveliness made him want to protect her from abuse at the hands of this white man.

He would protect her at all cost.

She would be his!

"Why are you with this—this Indian?" Rachel said, yet not feeling endangered by the Indian's presence. There was a gentleness in his eyes as he looked at her, and he made no advances toward her except to touch her that one time.

Yet, if any man chose to ride with her Uncle Patrick, what could there be good about him?

Evil begat evil.

"My Cherokee friend here patched me up and gave me a place to stay until I regained my strength," Patrick said, slinging an arm around Running Wolf's shoulder, which the Indian quickly shrugged off. "Then he agreed to help me find my nieces. Ain't that kind of him? A friend for life, wouldn't you say so, Injun?"

Running Wolf's eyes narrowed at the crude use of the insulting 'Injun'. He did not respond to Patrick, but instead turned to Rachel again. "You will come with us to the *City of Peace*," he said softly. "There you will be comfortable. There you will be fed and given a place to sleep without interference from anyone."

Patrick's jaw tightened as he glared at Running Wolf, then laughed absently as he nodded. "Yeah, you'll be seen to, all right," he said, taking Rachel by the elbow. "Come on. You'll ride with me."

Running Wolf looked at Patrick with coldness in his eyes. "She rides with me," he said, a warning in the way he spoke. "And at the *City of Peace* she will sleep alone while I watch over her to see that no one annoys her."

Rachel was stunned by the Indian's interference in her uncle's plans. She began looking at the Cherokee in a different light. She saw hope in Running Wolf's kindness. Perhaps he could help her find Brietta!

Not fearing the Indian any longer, for it was obvious that there was no true friendship between her uncle and the Cherokee, Rachel allowed him to help her onto his Appaloosa. She smiled smugly at Patrick as he glowered up at her, then grew cold inside as he silently mouthed several obscenities beneath his breath to her. She felt a strange sort of comforting in the touch of the slight Cherokee's arm as he mounted behind her. She felt somehow that as long as she was with him, she would be safe.

Especially from her Uncle Patrick!

Her hair blew in the wind as the horse began galloping across the meadow. She even felt strangely free while in this Cherokee's arms. She looked at him over her shoulder and was touched to her soul when he smiled at her.

The wind whispered gently through the trees as morning replaced night. René stirred in his bedroll and licked his lips, thirst arousing him into a full awakening.

Groaning, he lifted his bulky body up from the ground. Closing his eyes, he yawned and stretched, then opened his eyes again and looked toward the tent where the prisoners were housed. It had been a peaceful enough night.

And what of Rachel? How had she fared with Injuns as her bed partners?

Chuckling beneath his breath, he smoothed his hands through his thick, black hair and sauntered to the tent. He grabbed the entrance flap and opened it, then paled when he discovered that Rachel was not among the prisoners.

She had escaped . . . !

"*Merde*! The Osage warrior tricked me!" René shouted, dropping the entrance flap angrily.

"While everyone slept, he came for the white woman!"

Controlling his anger so that he would not make a spectacle of himself, René began planning his revenge. He would show Brown Cloud that he was not to be messed with! And all of Brown Cloud's people would pay for his one mistake! He would burn the whole village, sparing only those who begged!

The others he would take as prisoners!

CHAPTER THIRTEEN

If the heart be true and the love be strong,
For the mist, if it come, and the sweeping rain,
Will be changed by the love into sunshine again.

—*MacDonald*

Brietta was awakened by much excitement and noise in the Cherokee village. Even before she saw Brave Eagle, who had awakened even earlier and had left his wigwam, a beautiful Indian maiden had come to Brietta, fussing over her. First, Brietta breakfasted on corn cakes and pork, then was given different attire from that which Brave Eagle had already given her to replace her soiled cotton dress.

She gasped in awe when she looked at the long

skirt woven of feathers with a fringe of down. The vest was short and adorned with colorful beads and porcupine quills. The moccasins offered to her were also as decoratively beautiful.

"Why are you doing this?" Brietta asked, although she had received no answer the many other times she had questioned the tiny young woman with perfect facial features and copper coloring enhanced by different shades of makeup on her face. "Why are you treating me so—so specially today?"

Again she was ignored and Brietta had to assume that the Indian woman did not speak the English language as did Brave Eagle.

Brietta sighed and slipped into the lovely garments, relishing the softness of the fabrics against her flesh. Then, at the urging of the woman's delicate hands, she sat down beside the firepit and let the maiden continue to have her way with her.

Brietta curled her nose up in distaste as something that smelled like fish was smoothed across her face, and the full length of her arms.

"The fish oil and eagle fat keeps skin smooth and attractive," the maiden said in perfect English, so suddenly that it caused Brietta's breath to catch in her throat.

But her surprise was not altogether because the Indian had suddenly spoken in perfect English—the voice was not a woman's, but most identifiably a man's!

She gazed in wonder at the Indian, searching for manly features but finding none. Perfume of burned sweetgrasses clung to the Indian's long and flowing black hair. He wore a dress of doeskin whitened with clay and trimmed with the milk teeth of elks and the tips of turkey feathers and porcupine quills. This Indian was a vision of loveliness.

"You do know the English language," Brietta said, looking wide-eyed up at the Indian, watching every feminine gesture and movement, in awe of her discovery. "Why didn't you before now? I have asked you many questions."

The Indian shrugged. "Questions that needed no answers," he said, handing Brietta a mirror. "I do. You see. That is answer enough, do you not think so?"

"There is such a thing as politeness," Brietta said, frustrated by the Indian's nonchalant attitude when Brietta saw no reason for nonchalance at all. Her life was in a turmoil! Her heart was torn! She loved Brave Eagle, yet knew that she must turn her back on such a love. It was not only forbidden, but useless. Her life must center on finding her sister. Nothing else.

"Sun Flower polite enough," Sun Flower said, his fingers now busy mixing bright red mineral dust with animal fat for the rouge to be applied to Brietta's face. "But you want me to explain things to you, I explain. Brave Eagle wants you not only to be lovely, but happy. It is my duty to honor his wish. He is the next-chief-in-line. One day his commands will reign supreme in this village of Cherokee."

Brietta quirked an eyebrow, her curiosity about this Indian overpowering her frustrations. This man who was dressed as a woman even had a woman's name! Brietta badly wanted to ask Sun

Flower what had happened to make him choose the life of a woman over that of a powerful warrior.

But she knew she must keep her questions centered only on herself, and not delve into a stranger's personal affairs.

"Why is it so important that you fuss over me so much today, or is this the way it will be each day I am here now that my health is so improved?" Brietta asked. Her lips parted in another gasp as she stared into the mirror, watching Sun Flower apply the rouge to her forehead, temple, and cheeks.

Once the rouge was applied, she found that it did improve her appearance. Through her sickness she had grown much too pale.

"I shall make you lovely every day if Brave Eagle commands it," Sun Flower said, setting the rouge aside and picking up another small container, stirring the ingredients with his fingers. "But today is most special. You will meet Brave Eagle's father. You will also witness the wedding of Brave Eagle's cousin and his chosen woman. There will be much celebration. You will see. You will enjoy."

This news brought a mixture of feelings to Brietta—fear at having to come face to face with the powerful Cherokee chief, excitement at witnessing an Indian wedding ceremony—and anticipation, knowing that she was only biding time until she could flee, to search for her sister.

Sun Flower began applying an ointment of sorts around her eyes. "Sun Flower, what is that you are doing?" Brietta asked softly, intrigued. Everything the Indian did, he did with much care and skill, and in such a way as to enhance Brietta's appear-

188

ance. When she looked into the mirror again, she saw a woman that she herself could even call beautiful.

"Sun Flower is shading facial depressions around your eyes with black pigment paste made from redbud charcoal, yellow limonite, and animal fat," he said, applying the finishing touches, then stepping away to look at the final product. He clasped his hands together and smiled. "Brave Eagle will be very pleased."

"Brave Eagle is pleased," he said, as he entered the wigwam.

He knelt down beside Brietta and gently brushed her cheek with a kiss. "You are beautiful," he whispered, so that Sun Flower could not hear. "My father will approve. How could he not?"

He rose and stood with his arms folded across his chest. "Finish, Sun Flower," he said, nodding to him. "Time is passing quickly. My father awaits our arrival."

Brietta's breath was stolen as she looked up at him. Oh, but did he not cut a striking figure? Today he was dressed in a full regalia, in his newest buckskins, generously decorated with necklaces of wampum and beads. His glossy black hair was trailing down his back, braided and decorated with dyed bristles of deer hair and shells. His posture was such that there was no doubt that here was a person of stature, a future chief!

Brietta sat straight-backed as Sun Flower began grooming her hair. Long hair seemed to be greatly prized by the Cherokee women, who wore it hanging long down to the hips.

His fingers nimble and quick, Sun Flower gathered Brietta's hair into a small mass and let it hang down her back, ornamented with colorful strings of beads and other attractive attachments.

The final touches were added when Sun Flower anointed her with perfume made from a mixture of horse mint and columbine seed. "This perfume will aid you in doing away with evil," he said as he stepped back away from Brietta and smiled triumphantly, admiring his handiwork.

Brietta once again surveyed herself in the mirror and realized that she was deserving of the admirable glances from both Indians. She could hardly believe it was her own reflection looking back at her. Sun Flower had transformed her into something enchantingly beautiful!

"*O-ge-ye,*" Brave Eagle said, offering Brietta a hand. "Come."

Brietta laid the mirror aside. She smiled warmly up at Brave Eagle as she clasped her hand in his and rose slowly from the cattail mats. Only a moment of dizziness made her realize that she still was not quite ready to head out into the mysterious maze of the forest alone. Perhaps one more day and she would be strong enough.

Today was a day of excitement and intrigue to help get her mind off her sister.

"It is time to go to my father," Brave Eagle said, walking Brietta from the wigwam. He stopped for a moment and looked skyward. "The sun is brilliant overhead. The sky is clear. Both are good omens."

Proudly, Brietta began walking beside Brave Eagle. Her insides quivered at the wonder of coming face to face with the powerful Indian chief she had heard so much about. And she was afraid of the importance that Brave Eagle was placing in her meeting his father. Surely she was being taken to him for approval.

A part of her wanted to be looked upon with disfavor by Chief Silver Shirt, for would that not make it easier for Brave Eagle when he discovered that she was gone? If his father did not approve of her, surely Brave Eagle would think her disappearance a good omen and would soon forget her.

But on the other hand, if Brave Eagle's father saw the same worth in her that Brave Eagle had seen, would it not make it even harder for her to leave? She so badly wanted to be free to love this handsome Cherokee warrior until her last dying breath. If given even the least encouragement, would she truly ever be able to leave him? Last night she had found paradise in his arms, and hungered, even now, to ride on gossamer wings again with him to that land that knew no grief or unhappiness—only joyful bliss.

She continued walking with Brave Eagle through the village. Along the edge of the forest she could see many teepees pitched in groups of semi-circles, each group belonging to distinct bands of Indians. Last evening, Brave Eagle had told her that invitations had been sent to neighboring tribes by way of bundles of tobacco, and acceptance had been sent back from the various bands in similar fashion.

He had told her that meat of the wild game had been put away with much care during the autumn in anticipation of such feasts. Wild rice and the choicest of dried venison had been kept all winter, as well as freshly dug turnips, ripe berries, and an abundance of fresh meat.

The invitations had brought many visitors to the Cherokee village. It was alive with joyful, celebrating Indians. Trying not to let the throng of people frighten her, Brietta held her chin high as she walked beside Brave Eagle, looking neither to her right nor her left. Nevertheless, she could feel eyes following her. She could feel bodies pressing forward, taking a closer look at her. Hardly a sound could be heard in the village now, except for the distant neighing of the fenced-in ponies and an occasional barking dog.

She kept her gaze locked on distant sights—on the peach trees that were prevalent in the fields and the abundant crop of corn and beans. She could see that the Cherokee had a number of fowls, hogs, and some cattle. The women's patches of maize and potatoes were already sufficiently advanced to harvest.

Walking steadily onward, coaxed by the firm grip of Brave Eagle's hand on her elbow, Brietta caught a glimpse of Sun Flower standing with a group of women, blending in as though one of them. "Brave Eagle," she whispered, nudging closer to him. "I am so puzzled about something."

"What puzzles my beautiful woman?" he whispered back, leaning closer to her, yet still looking straight ahead.

"Sun Flower," Brietta murmured.

"Sun Flower?" Brave Eagle said, grinning wolfishly.

"Yes," Brietta said, still peering at Sun Flower.

"I found Sun Flower to be somewhat different."

"Different?" Brave Eagle teased. "How different?"

"Brave Eagle, I am sure you know what I am referring to," Brietta said, giving him an annoyed glance.

"Sun Flower is a squawman," Brave Eagle said nonchalantly.

"A squawman?" Brietta said, looking quickly at Brave Eagle, her eyes wide. "I have never heard such a term as that."

"That is because you are not Cherokee," he said, then smiled down at her. "Not yet anyhow."

"What is a squawman?" Brietta persisted, even though she had already guessed.

"Squawmen are young men who have shown weakness or cowardliness in their first warring engagement," Brave Eagle tightly replied. "They are compelled to live as squawmen, dressed like squaws and doing the work of squaws, never getting a chance to redeem themselves."

"Why, that's terribly sad," Brietta said, once more glancing at Sun Flower, still in awe of the Indian's intense loveliness. "That must mean that Sun Flower will never father a child."

"Never," Brave Eagle said flatly. "Squawmen are forbidden to marry lest they beget cowardly sons who might endanger the survival of our tribe."

"What a horrible punishment," Brietta gasped.

Brave Eagle's gaze found Sun Flower in the crowd. "Do you see him among the women, Brietta?" he asked quietly.

"Yes, I do," she murmured.

"Does he look unhappy? Misplaced?"

"No. Not at all."

"Then so be it," Brave Eagle said. "Sun Flower is content."

Brietta smiled weakly at Brave Eagle. Then her gaze settled on the larger dwelling that she had seen the previous evening—the council house. By daylight she could see that it was built up on a rise of land. It was a long, narrow structure, handsomely fashioned of bark, sixty feet or more in length. Its ends were beautifully rounded and the roof gracefully arched.

The snow-white birchbark sides were decorated with striking totemic designs in brilliant, but harmonious colors. Its buckskin entrance flap opened to the *council circle*, a large, cleared space where the Indians were now gathering—surely a place where the Cherokee held their tribal dances and pow-wows.

To focus her concentration on something besides her pounding heart, Brietta studied the drawings on the front of the council house. They seemed to be representations of streaks of lightning, the moon, and the rising sun, and also rough sketches of dogs and various other animals. It was a grand display compared to the plain exteriors of all the other dwellings in the village.

A slow dread began to creep through Brietta as she walked up the incline which led to the door of the council house. She inhaled a nervous breath as Brave Eagle stepped ahead of her and lifted the entrance flap. He gestured for Brietta to enter, smiling reassuringly down at her.

Smiling weakly back at him, Brietta stepped past him into the dwelling, and found herself looking down at a powerful man sitting straight-backed on a raised platform that was spread with bear skins, before a slow-burning fire in the center of the lodge.

There was no doubt in Brietta's mind that she had come face to face with the Cherokee Indian chief, Silver Shirt. This man was most identifiably a person of stature, of intelligence. He was solidly built, with a muscular body, and wore a fine, lightweight red cloak draped over one shoulder like the toga of a Roman senator.

His headdress was a crest of eagle feathers which hung long and colorfully down the straight line of his back. He wore a necklace of bear claws and large silver earrings. His forehead was high and broad, and his large, piercing dark eyes expressed firmness and decisiveness.

He displayed his age well, with only a few creases cutting lines across his copper face. He had a very prominent nose and jaw muscles, giving him an air of severity.

Then her gaze fell on the cane that rested on his lap, seemingly out of place with this man of outward strength.

A stirring in the shadows drew Brietta's eyes into a squint as she looked past the chief to see who else was in the council house. The light given out by the fire was too dim to distinguish who was standing at the far wall, except that Brietta felt that she was being scrutinized by more than one set of eyes from the veiled darkness.

As Brave Eagle stepped to Brietta's side, he motioned with a silent nod of the head for her to sit down on a cushion of milkweed down before the fire, opposite his father. He eased down beside Brietta and folded his legs. Clasping his hands onto his knees he gave his father a nod and a smile, then waited for his father to speak. His father had only half-heartedly accepted this audience with Brietta and Brave Eagle today.

But after Brave Eagle had explained his full intentions for Brietta to his father, of his plan to marry her, and that nothing anyone said would dissuade him from this decision, his father had had no choice but to acquiesce. It was best for a father to have an audience with a son's future bride before the wedding.

The chief did not rise. He bowed graciously from the waist and raised his hand in greeting. "And so this is the woman you speak so warmly of, my son?" he then said, leaning forward, his dark eyes squinting as he looked more closely at Brietta. "She is called—what did you say, my son, that her name was?"

"Her name is Brietta," Brave Eagle said, keeping his eyes straight ahead, yet so wanting to look at Brietta and comfort her with his eyes, since he could not humble himself in front of his chieftain father by comforting her with words.

"A lovely name," Chief Silver Shirt said, straightening his back and loosening his jaw when Brietta smiled at him, the smile alone making him understand the attraction of his son to this woman, even though her skin was not the same as the Cherokee's.

"Thank you," Brietta said, her heart pounding as she endured the chief's scrutiny.

"And your life has been touched by sadness of

late, Brietta?" Chief Silver Shirt asked, lifting a long-stemmed pipe to his lips and lighting it. "You are now without a home? You are now without parents?"

Tears stung the corners of Brietta's eyes with the mention of her parents. Deep within her heart, she hoped that she still had a sister. If God was in his Heaven, she still had a sister.

"Yes, both my father and mother are dead," she said, her voice slight.

She could not find the words to explain about her sister and how they had gotten separated in the forest. Even she could not understand what had happened. When she allowed herself to ponder it, she felt absolutely foolish to have let it happen!

Chief Silver Shirt took a long drag from the pipe, then rested the stem on his lap. "We welcome you as part of our village," he said. "The hearts of the Cherokee are good towards the whites."

Brietta smiled humbly at the chief, feeling a part of the betrayal her very own kin had committed when they stole and sold Indians into slavery.

But as far as she knew, most had been Osage. Her uncles had been afraid to go into Brave Eagle's territory. He was out for blood should anyone interfere in the Cherokee way of life.

She had heard her uncles say more than once that Brave Eagle's law was an eye for an eye.

Chief Silver Shirt averted his gaze, now looking at Brave Eagle. Smile wrinkles flashed around the dark slits that were his eyes. "You have chosen wisely, my son," he said. "You have my blessing. Now go. Join the celebration. Dance with abandon. Begin teaching Brietta the ways of our people

197

today. If she is to become as one with us, she must understand what is required of her."

Brietta looked quickly at Brave Eagle, wondering what the chief meant when he said that she was going to become as one with the Cherokee. Just how much did Brave Eagle expect from her today? Hadn't she already given too much of herself to him? She had given up her virginity while being held within his arms. She could not give of herself any longer. She had other responsibilities than to these Cherokee. Her first priority was to her blood kin—to her sister!

Brave Eagle rose to his feet and offered Brietta a hand. "Come," he said, smiling down at her. "My people will eat and dance the whole day through, into the night. *O-ge-ye*, you will enjoy the ways of the Cherokee. Come. Let me show you the way."

Knowing that she had no other choice, and drawn into the mystique of his eyes, Brietta clasped her hand in Brave Eagle's and slowly rose to her feet. When she was standing before him, he swept an arm around her waist and began walking her to the entrance flap.

But a movement behind her drew her eyes quickly around. Her lips parted in surprise when she found a small child standing beside Chief Silver Shirt, a boy of around the age of five, his dark eyes locking with hers. She felt as though she were looking at Brave Eagle when he was that age. The features were almost identical! This young brave would one day be such a handsome warrior!

But who was he?

Turning her eyes up to Brave Eagle, Brietta stopped in mid-step. "Who is the boy?" she asked, shaken by the child's sudden appearance and by his total silence as he stood in the dark shadows of the council house while she was scrutinized by the chief. He was an obedient child.

Brave Eagle's eyes wavered as he gazed down at Brietta, then turned his attention to the boy. He and the child stared at one another for a moment, then Brave Eagle reached a hand out for the child. "Rising Fawn, come to me," he said. "It is time for father and son to acknowledge one another again. It has been too long between hugs."

Brietta's eyes widened and her heart skipped a beat. She watched with astonishment as the child broke into a run and jumped into Brave Eagle's waiting arms. A son! Brave Eagle had a son!

A part of her felt betrayed, but another part of her melted inside as she watched Brave Eagle being so attentive and sweet to the child.

CHAPTER FOURTEEN

I wonder, by my troth, what thou and I
Did, till we loved? Were we not wean'd till then?

—*Donne*

Leaving the council house beside Brave Eagle, Brietta edged closer to his side. "You never told me that you had a son," she whispered. The throngs of Cherokee stepped aside as Brave Eagle and Brietta made their way toward the large outdoor fire, around which the wonderful-smelling foods had been prepared. "Your wife. Where is your wife? I feel so foolish, Brave Eagle. I—I gave of myself willingly to you last night— you betrayed us both, your wife and me, by taking me to your bed with you last night!"

Brave Eagle swept an arm around her waist and walked her past the fire and tempting foods, to land that had been cleared in the center of the village. *"O-ge-ye*, for so long I betrayed no one but myself," he whispered back, leaning down so that his words only went as far as her ear. "I refused to let anyone else into my heart since my wife's death. Till you, my woman. Till you. It is the worst of betrayals to a man to turn his back on the murmurings of his heart and forbid himself to love again."

Brietta stopped and turned to face Brave Eagle, her lips parting in a light gasp. "Your wife is dead?" she said, no longer caring that everything she did and said was being observed by the entire village. "Brave Eagle, I'm so sorry. Now I understand so much."

She looked past Brave Eagle at the entrance of the council house, seeing the small child standing beside Chief Silver Shirt, who leaned into his cane. The child was peering intensely at Brietta with his dark eyes filled with wonder. "And Brave Eagle," she murmured. "How sad for your—your son."

"The years soften the sadnesses," Brave Eagle said, imploring her with his fathomlessly dark eyes. "My son and I have sweet remembrances of a woman fair and pure. Now we have you, *o-ge-ye*, to take her place in both our hearts."

Brietta's eyes wavered and she blushed. Only moments ago she had spoken of a betrayal to Brave Eagle, accusing him of it when she was, in truth, the one who secretly planned a betrayal that would most surely never be forgiven. As soon as she was strong enough, she was going to flee the Cherokee village and the man whose love had touched her in so many ways she had never thought possible.

"Why didn't you tell me earlier about your wife and son?" Brietta said, her voice breaking. But had she known earlier, would that have kept her from falling in love with him? Would knowing that she had become so important to him in so many ways have made her flee, knowing that she could never be everything to him that he desired?

"*U-yo-li*. It was best unspoken," Brave Eagle said, his voice void of emotion.

"But what of your son?" she continued. "How could you not speak openly of him to me? He is such a handsome, sweet young man. How could you not boast of him to me?"

"*O-ge-ye*, I not only denied him to you," Brave Eagle said, his jaw firming. "But also to myself. While I carried hurt around inside my heart for my wife, it pained me too much to look into my son's eyes. In them, I saw her. Because of this I have kept myself from my son since my wife's death. Because of this, I do not speak of him to anyone. Now do you understand?"

Stunned by this confession, that Brave Eagle had not been a part of his son's life since his wife's death, Brietta could not think of anything appropriate to say to him. She did not dare ask how long his wife had been dead. In truth, she did not even want to know. If it had been a few months, she would fear having been chosen by him as only a means to forget his wife!

Brietta was glad when Brave Eagle took the initiative to change the direction of their thoughts when he took her by one elbow and guided her toward the cleared land just ahead. His people had gone on ahead of them. Some were sitting on blankets in a circle, while within this circle dancers were preparing themselves for an exhibition, the tomtoms already beating out a steady drone behind those who would only be watching.

Brietta scanned the crowd with her eyes, then narrowed in on two people in particular. The young man and woman were sitting separate from the others, on a platform that was covered with piled animal skins and drapings of flowers. She did not have to ask Brave Eagle who the couple were. They were the ones to be married today.

And didn't the young lady look ravishingly beautiful? She was attired in a dress similar to Brietta's. The difference was that she wore a wreath of flowers on her head, with the leaves of the flowers left on to shade her eyes from the rays of the sun. The fringes of her dress were skipping in the wind; her long, braided black hair blew back from her shoulders.

Brietta swallowed a quick breath of air as she became aware of her own garment again, knowing that it was as lovely—and as special. The ornaments on her dress chimed rhythmically in the wind as she was guided through the circle of people toward the platform where the young couple sat.

When they reached the platform, every nerve in Brietta's body tensed as Brave Eagle helped her up onto it, motioning with a nod of his head for her to sit down beside the lovely Cherokee woman.

Brietta leaned up and whispered into Brave Eagle's ear. "Why am I to sit here?" she whispered, wary. "Isn't this solely for the two who will be married? Won't we be intruding on their private affair by sharing the platform with them?"

"This is my cousin who is getting married," Brave Eagle said, sitting down beside Brietta. He folded his arms across his chest. "He is honored by my presence. And since you are my woman, it is only right that you sit beside me."

The way he said that she was his woman stirred Brietta to remembrances of the previous night, and how wonderful it had been to be taken to paradise and back within his arms, knowing that to have shared this so willingly with him made him surely believe that he had full claim on her.

Yes, she understood how he might think that she was 'his woman', not having any suspicion that she was planning to leave him, as soon as her legs were strong enough to carry her far away from him!

Yet in a sense, she was his. She could never love another man as fiercely as Brave Eagle.

When a young Cherokee girl stepped up to Brietta and offered her a lovely wreath of flowers, she glanced at the bride-to-be's wreath, seeing the similarity, then questioned Brave Eagle with wary eyes.

"Wear it," he said, taking it from the girl and gently placing it on Brietta's head. "*O-ge-ye*, it will enhance your loveliness."

Brietta inhaled the sweet fragrance of the roses that lay close to her brow, wafting its luscious scent down across her face, and tried not to think about how it did not seem right that she would be sharing everything equally with the bride-to-be, when she, in truth, should only be an observer.

Somehow she felt as though homage was being paid to her as well, as though she was perhaps also getting married.

Her eyes widened with alarm, thinking that perhaps she had not been told the true reason why she was sharing this platform with the two Cherokee who were to be married today. What if, somehow, she was going to become Brave Eagle's bride at the same time, during the same ritual?

The thought made her start to rise to her feet, but Brave Eagle's hand on her wrist encouraged her to sit back down beside him.

She stared at him, trying to wriggle her wrist free from his tight grip. "Brave Eagle," she whispered harshly. "Let me go. I don't want to be here. This isn't right. Please let me go!"

"You will stay," Brave Eagle said, his voice emotionless. His eyes locked with hers. "*O-ge-ye*, you seem to have guessed your true reason for being here. Had I told you earlier, you would have fought my decision to make you my wife today. Now you have no choice but to let it happen. You would not make me look foolish in front of my people by leaving me. You love me too much."

Brietta's face flamed with anger. She leaned closer to Brave Eagle. "You will start a marriage like this?" she whispered, her voice breaking. "By being untruthful? First you do not tell me about a wife and son. And now you try to trick me into marrying you? Brave Eagle, I do love you. But I—I don't want to marry you. I have more things on my mind than marriage. I've things to do!"

"Brave Eagle will do them with you," he said flatly. He removed his hand from her wrist and twined his fingers through hers, holding her hand on his lap. "You will not be sorry, Brietta, that I have made the decision for both of us that we will be wed today. You will never want for a thing. Brave Eagle will make everything good happen for you."

The tomtoms began to beat more insistently. Dancers formed two circles, one inside the other, before Brietta and Brave Eagle and the serene lovers at their sides. Brietta inhaled a nervous breath, feeling trapped and frustrated. She did not want to make a scene and hurt Brave Eagle's reputation in front of his people. He was to be their next chief. He must be everything to his people.

All that she could see to do was pretend to go through the ritual with him, knowing that the ceremony was not a true Christian wedding, which would make it not a true marriage for her at all. Once she left the village, she would leave her vows to him behind her. After she was gone, she would not let herself wonder how he would look in his people's eyes. Perhaps he could lie and say that it was he who banished the white woman from his life.

The tomtoms beat with a furious accent on the first stroke. The dancers picked up the rhythm of the drums and began to chant, "*Hi-ya-ya-ya, Hi-ya-ya-ya,*" their feet beating out the rhythm, their bodies swaying and their arms tossing first right, then left as they shuffled about the ground.

The inner and smaller circle of dancers moved with the sun—from right to left. The outer went in the opposite direction. Both circles used the sidestep. Many singers from the village joined the celebration, forming a line to one side, those with tomtoms in the center. The circle of dancers moved completely around three times. Then, at a signal from the tomtom, the dancers, using the toe-heel step, closed in toward the center, where they formed a compact mass.

There they stopped, bent down, and gave a drawn-out wolf howl. They then turned and danced back to their original positions and at the signal of a tomtom they moved about as before.

After repeating these movements three times, the dancers joined the crowd of onlookers.

Brietta gasped lightly as Brave Eagle and the other Cherokee warrior left the platform and started dancing before their women in a suggestive sort of dance. Brave Eagle stripped himself to his waist, tossing his fringed shirt aside. The muscles of his back rippled while he swayed to the singing of his people and the beat of the tomtom. He stretched one muscled leg forward and spun around on a heel, his head bobbing up and down, as he chanted. He was six feet of sinew and muscle, but to Brietta he was light and shadow flickering as he moved, stirring something primitive within her.

When he stopped before her and offered her his hands, the magnetic pull of his dark eyes drew her to her feet, and just as the lovely woman beside her did, she stepped out onto the stamped-down earth and began dancing in rhythm with her chosen warrior, their eyes locked.

Unaware any longer that an audience was watching, Brietta clung to Brave Eagle's hands and swayed and moved seductively with him, her heartbeats keeping rhythm with the tomtoms, her breasts heaving with the rapture that was enveloping her.

Her breath was stolen when Brave Eagle drew her roughly into his arms, locking their bodies together as though they were one. They swayed and bent some more, Brietta keenly aware of his manhood pressed against her belly, their thin buckskin clothes the only barriers to their aroused passions.

And then the music ceased and Brietta was led back to the platform. She seemed to be in some sort of trance for the rest of the morning as the ceremonies of music, dance, and games were played out.

Even when she realized that the ceremony included that which was joining her to Brave Eagle, becoming his wife in the eyes of the Cherokee, she looked on, her eyes hazed over with a wondrous, intense love for Brave Eagle and that which he was offering her in return.

Suddenly, Brave Eagle rose above her and drew her to her feet before him, and just as quickly had her in his arms and was carrying her through the shouting, chanting Cherokee. Brave Eagle smiled broadly, for his people had accepted a white woman as his bride, the warrior who would one day reign over them all.

Although he had just taken another wife, it was known to all that he had not been without a woman to share his bed since his wife died. He was aware that all unmarried women of his village envied his bride, for so many had tried every way to win him over for their own.

"You are now my bride," Brave Eagle said, beaming down at Brietta as she clung around his neck. "Forever, Brietta, you are mine. Say that you are happy?"

Brietta felt drugged, her cheeks sore from having smiled so much during the ceremony. Somewhere deeply within, a part of her was rebelling at what had happened today.

But on the surface, where her feelings were so finely tuned to this handsome Cherokee's, she was exceedingly happy. And she would not let knowing what she must soon do erase these few hours of bliss with Brave Eagle. When she fled into the night and he discovered her gone, his hate for her would be boundless.

Oh, but how he would hate her! Yet, she would love and miss him with all of her heart.

"Yes, my handsome Cherokee warrior, I am happy," she murmured, pressing her cheek against his smooth chest. She smiled to herself when she felt the pounding of his heart against her cheek. It was so strong—so quick! And it was because of his eagerness to bed her again. She could not deny the same feeling. She would love him fiercely! Devotedly!

Even if tonight was her last time with him. She must find a way to flee tonight. Even if her legs were not strong enough, she must. It was cruel of her to delay the leaving any longer. Cruel to herself and to Brave Eagle. The longer she remained with him, the more she would love him, and he, her.

Brave Eagle carried Brietta into his wigwam where the air was purified with burning sweetgrasses. The fire in the fireplace was burning low, casting dancing shadows along the walls and curved ceiling. Fresh cattail mats had been spread on the floor, and a mug of refreshment sat awaiting them, along with a large platter of roasted meats and cooked vegetables.

Brave Eagle placed Brietta on a mat and sat down beside her. "Do you wish to eat and drink?" he asked, his hands framing her face. His lips lowered and brushed gently along the slope of her jaw.

Becoming limp with desire, Brietta shook her head. "No," she whispered. "I don't care for anything, but—"

Brave Eagle's eyes danced as he peered down at her. "But, what, *O-ge-ye?*" he teased, already disrobing her.

"It is you that I want," Brietta murmured, blushing at her boldness. "Oh, Brave Eagle, only you."

Now silkenly nude, Brietta watched as Brave Eagle disrobed himself and knelt beside her, his copper body glowing golden as she peered up at him through tears of happiness and regret—regret that she had only this one more night of bliss with the man she adored.

She opened her arms to him and spirals of ecstasy began spinning through Brietta as Brave Eagle spread out atop her, nudging her legs apart with his knees. She opened herself up to him as his manhood probed. She sucked in a wild breath of air as he thrust himself deeply inside her. She arched and cried out. His mouth covered her lips with a fiery kiss as their bodies strained together hungrily, his hands running down her body, stopping at the juncture of her thighs to caress her. As his body stroked within her, his fingers aroused in her a passion so keen she shuddered from the searing sensations.

Brave Eagle drew his mouth from her lips and nibbled at her neck. "*O-ge-ye*, do you wish for me to stop? Do I annoy you?" he teased, then flicked his tongue over one taut nipple, and then the other.

Brietta giggled as she clung to him. "Annoy?" she whispered, closing her eyes to the building ecstasy. "My darling, you have the ability to evoke many feelings in me, but at this moment it is not annoyance that I feel."

Brave Eagle slowed his thrusts. He drew his hardness partially from within her. He smiled down at her. "Then you want me to continue?" he teased. "If so, tell me, my wife. Ask me to make love to you. I want to hear you say it."

Brietta's body ached for completion. "Yes, darling," she murmured, perspiration beading her brow. "Make love to me. My husband, make love to me. I need you. Oh, how I need you."

She curled her legs around his hips and locked her ankles together behind him, and drew him back inside her. She gasped with pleasure as his body hardened and tightened, absorbing his bold thrusts again.

His body plunged into hers. Over and over again he pressed upward into her, filling her hard, filling her deep. Brietta said fierce words of love to him that she did not know she was capable of saying. As her fingers tightened about his buttocks, leading him harder into her, she told him repeatedly that she wanted him. Brokenly, between gasps, she whispered to him never to let her go—all the while, at the far recesses of her mind, knowing that her words were betraying that which she knew to be true—that she would be leaving him.

Somewhere deeply within her a small voice was crying the name Rachel . . . Rachel . . . Rachel. . . .

CHAPTER FIFTEEN

Thy smiles can make a summer
Where darkness else would be.

—*Jefferys*

After the fierce loving, Brietta lay happily in Brave Eagle's embrace, filled with euphoric, peaceful bliss. How wonderful, she thought contentedly to herself, it would be to stay like this with Brave Eagle forever and ever. She was not only loved, but felt protected. When she fled from this village, anything could happen to her while she searched for her sister. Perhaps if she asked Brave Eagle to join the search, he could help her find Rachel, and Rachel could return to this village and be as protected, as loved.

A warning shot through Brietta. Rachel was the exact replica of Brietta, except for their eye coloring. Would Brave Eagle become as enamored with her? Would he choose to have two wives instead of one?

"Brave Eagle," she said, rising quickly up on one elbow. "It isn't the practice of the Cherokee to have two wives, is it?"

Brave Eagle lay for a moment without speaking, then turned and faced her. "Polygamy is practiced among the Cherokee," he said, his eyes dancing. "It is not uncommon for a man to take a family of sisters in one ceremony. It is an act of benevolence that insures against a woman going childless and manless even in time of war."

Another warning grabbed at her heart. "You would never wish to have two wives, would you?" she asked warily. "Did you ever think of marrying sisters?"

"The ceremony is over and I married one woman," Brave Eagle said, brushing a fallen lock of hair back from her brow. "And no sister could ever be as beautiful as you."

Brietta turned her eyes from Brave Eagle, again shaken with warning. If he thought her beautiful, would he not think Rachel was as beautiful?

Yet the ceremony was over. In his eyes, he had married her, not Rachel.

Then guilt flooded through her for having put her jealousies before her sister's safety!

She turned to Brave Eagle again, to tell him that she had also hidden truths from him—truths about a sister—but his lips were already parting to speak to her.

"You are a courageous woman," he said. "You managed to escape from Brown Cloud and his warriors and the white slaver. That took much strength and courage, Brietta. I commend you for that. You are like no other woman I have ever known."

Brietta rose to a sitting position, gazing at him questioningly. What was this about Brown Cloud? About Brown Cloud's warriors? And a slaver? She had been abducted by his cousin! And she had not thought to tell Brave Eagle who had done the dirty deed. Until now she had not thought it was important, but it was apparent now that it was! It was apparent that Running Wolf's scheme had worked —making it look as though the guilt of her abduction lay on Brown Cloud's shoulders.

"Brave Eagle, Brown Cloud didn't abduct me," Brietta said quickly. "I was taken by your cousin. He called himself Running Wolf. He did it to make you believe that Brown Cloud abducted me. He did it to cause trouble between you and Brown Cloud."

Brave Eagle bolted to a sitting position beside her, paling. "What is this you say?" he gasped. "My cousin? How could it be? I saw you tied to a stake in Brown Cloud's village! I made war with the Osage because I saw you there. So how can you say that it was not you?"

"But it wasn't me, Brave Eagle," Brietta murmured, stunned. "How could you think that it was?"

"I do not understand," Brave Eagle puzzled. "What I saw, I saw! I know you well, *o-ge-ye*. I could never mistake you for another!"

217

"Only if . . ." Brietta said, her heart skipping a beat. She moved to her knees and faced Brave Eagle. "Only if it was someone who looked exactly like me! Brave Eagle, surely you saw my sister! She is my twin! We are identical except for . . ."

She clutched his hands. "You did not see the color of her eyes, did you?" she said in a rush of words.

"She was too far from me," Brave Eagle said, his voice drawn. "I saw her hair. I saw her face. That was all I needed to make war against the Osage! Against my best friend!"

Tears sprang to Brietta's eyes, fear clutching at her heart. "My sister was in a village that you attacked?" she dared to ask, in a mere whisper. "What happened to her, Brave Eagle? What happened to her?"

Brave Eagle rose to his feet, torn with regret over many things. He had made war with Brown Cloud's people over someone who had only looked like Brietta? It was not Brown Cloud who had stolen her away from him? Running Wolf had left the City of Peace purposely to wreak havoc on Brave Eagle's life?

He had succeeded, Brave Eagle thought bitterly. Running Wolf had avenged his forced atonement for Brave Eagle's sin of being friends with Brown Cloud!

He could not hate or condemn Running Wolf for this deed. Running Wolf had thus proved his prowess and that he deserved better than being sent away, as though unworthy of the name Cherokee!

Brave Eagle's silence, his refusal to answer her

question about her sister, made Brietta jump to her feet, her eyes wild. "Brave Eagle, what of my sister?" she cried. "What has happened to her?"

Understanding Brietta's fears and concerns, Brave Eagle grabbed her hands and held them affectionately tight as he bent to speak into her face. "Your sister was not among those at the Cherokee village," he said softly. "An Osage brave told me that she had been sold to a slaver. By now I am sure she is far gone from here." He stared down into tear-filled eyes. "I am sorry, Brietta."

"And still thinking it was me, you did not go after her?" Brietta said, her voice rising to a shrill shriek.

"I was on the slaver's trail when I found you beside the stream," Brave Eagle said, drawing her within his gentle embrace. "When I saw you, I thought you had escaped. My search was over. You were safely with me."

Brietta clung to Brave Eagle, sobbing. "Rachel," she cried. "My poor sister. Oh, Lord, my poor sister. She is now someone's slave?"

"Or soon will be," Brave Eagle said. He eased her from his embrace and held her at arm's length. "Why did you not tell me about her sooner? I could have helped search for her."

Brietta chewed on her lower lip nervously, afraid of confessing the full truth to Brave Eagle— that she had planned all along to leave him, to search alone for her sister. She had thought she could never have a future with him and had planned to return to her way of life, perhaps to Fort Smith, for assistance.

These past hours had persuaded her that she had

been wrong to ever think of leaving Brave Eagle out of her future plans. He *was* her future!

"The reason may be similar to the reason you did not tell me the full truth of your life before you met me," she said softly. "For so many reasons I now know are wrong, I felt it best to keep the secret of my sister locked inside my heart, Brave Eagle, just as you locked the secret of your wife and son within yours." Tears sprang from her eyes. "But I was wrong. I was so very, very wrong!"

"As I have been about so many things," Brave Eagle said, looking away from her, his thoughts now elsewhere. He had wronged Brown Cloud's people! He had attacked the village, thinking that Brown Cloud had wronged him—that Brown Cloud had gone back on his word and had sneaked into his camp and stolen Brietta from him! However Brown Cloud had found Brietta's sister, he had not stolen her directly from his friend. A friend had not betrayed a friend, as Brave Eagle had thought!

And yet, Brave Eagle had, in a sense, betrayed his loyalty to Brown Cloud! He had attacked his village wrongly!

Quickly drawing on his breechclout and placing a headband around his head to keep his hair in place, Brave Eagle readied himself to go out.

Brietta grew cold inside as she watched him, a strange hurt in his eyes. "Where are you going?" she said, panic rising within her. "Brave Eagle, don't leave me now. We must plan a way to save my sister! Now that I know her fate, I cannot do it alone. I need your help, Brave Eagle."

Brave Eagle grabbed his rifle. He went to Brietta

and gazed down into her tear-filled eyes. "She is
long gone," he said. "She has been taken to lands
far from the Cherokee. You must make a life
without her, Brietta. Your life is now with me and
my people. Put thoughts of your past behind you
and look to the future. Our future!"

"Never shall I forget my sister!" Brietta cried,
bewildered and hurt that he would want her to
dismiss her loved one from her mind so easily! She
lifted her chin proudly. "I won't, Brave Eagle. I
won't!"

"In time, you will," Brave Eagle said. He
brushed a kiss across her lips, then walked to the
entrance flap and lifted it. "I shall be gone for only
a short while. I must make things right between
old friends."

Brietta stared at the entrance flap for a moment
after he left the wigwam, a coldness seizing her at
his refusal to understand her feelings toward her
twin sister. And that he would put his feelings for
Brown Cloud before hers was almost too much for
her to bear!

"How could he?" she whispered to herself, still
staring at the closed entrance flap. "How could he
leave me so soon after disclosing to me the evil
that has happened to my sister? And he does not
plan to help me even when he returns!"

She turned her eyes away from the entrance flap,
a sob catching in her throat, knowing what he was
forcing her to do. Her plans had not changed after
all. She was still going to have to go and search for
her sister, alone.

But first she must go to Fort Smith and get the
assistance of the soldiers! Surely they would know

Cassie Edwards

a way to track down the evil slaver and find out with whom he had left Rachel!

"Yes, I must go to Fort Smith," she said, scurrying around and dressing in a simpler buckskin dress than the one she had worn during the wedding ceremony. Wearing it now would be a mockery of that which she had so intimately shared with Brave Eagle.

"He says that I must put my past behind me," she hissed, braiding her hair into one long braid down her back so that it would not get in her way while traveling on horseback to Fort Smith. "Well, I shall. *He* is a part of that past. Never shall I think about him again! I hate him! I hate him!"

Her heart was betraying her words, for it ached unmercifully. Never had she thought to be awakened by such wondrous feelings as those she had found in Brave Eagle's arms. Never would she experience such feelings again, with any other man. She would never love again. Never!

Fully dressed and clutching a rifle that she had found among Brave Eagle's many weapons, she listened at the entrance flap for the departure of Brave Eagle and his warriors. When she heard the thundering of horse's hoofbeats as they rode away from the village, and she also heard the others of the village still partaking in the celebration around the large outdoor fire, she knew that this was the best time to escape. No one would notice one small person slipping behind the domed wigwams. No one would miss the horse that she would steal.

Not until much later, after Brave Eagle returned and found her missing.

"He will come for me," Brietta whispered to

222

herself, choosing the horse that she would take flight on. It was not among those that were fenced. It was tethered to a tree, close by. It was already saddled.

She must make haste on her journey to Fort Smith so that she would be so far ahead of Brave Eagle that he would never catch up with her.

Moving stealthily across the stamped-down grass in her soft and silent moccasins, Brietta breathed a sigh of relief when she reached the horse and was able to mount it without being discovered. Leaning low over its mane, she urged it into a slow canter away from the village, then into a hard gallop once she reached a straight stretch of meadow.

Tears of regret streamed from her eyes.

Rachel huddled close to the fire in the cavern, hungrily devouring a platter of fish that Running Wolf had prepared for her as soon as she had arrived at the City of Peace with the slight Cherokee and Patrick. She kept giving Patrick wary glances, still finding it hard to believe that he was there, alive. She had imagined that the Indians had slain both of the evil brothers at the cabin for their dirty deeds.

She had prayed that they had.

"And so, my pretty niece, our lives become intertwined again," Patrick said, eyeing her greedily. He feasted his eyes on her firm, round breasts that were outlined beneath the soft fabric of the buckskin dress, and the ache in his loin grated on his nerves. "Aren't you glad to see your Uncle Patrick? Now we can go to St. Louis, as planned.

What we will share on the trail will liven you up a mite. When we reach St. Louis, you'll know what it means to be a woman."

He chuckled low, then grimaced when Running Wolf blocked his view of Rachel as the Indian purposely stood in front of her, glowering down at him. "What'cha doin', Cherokee? Get outta my way. I was havin' an enlightening conversation with my niece."

Running Wolf folded his arms across his chest. "She was not sharing in the conversation," he said sourly. "Nor does she wish to share anything else with you. White man, she is no longer your concern. You will be taken to Fort Smith and there you will travel onward without looking back. Do you understand?"

Patrick eyed the knife sheathed at Running Wolf's waist, then at the rifle leaning against the wall of the wigwam. He glowered at Running Wolf as he rose slowly to his feet. "That was not a part of the bargain," he hissed. "You agreed to help me find my nieces, not for me to then hand them over to you. They are of my blood kin, not yours! It is my duty to care for them. My brother would want it that way!"

"There is only one sister that I see here in my dwelling," Running Wolf said. "And she stays. You do not want her with you because she is your blood kin. You want her only because she is a woman—a woman you will force yourself upon. That will not be so, white man."

Rachel set her empty platter aside, and settled herself more comfortably on the cattmail mats, in awe of this Indian who had appointed himself her

Thrill to the most sensual, adventure-filled Historical Romances on the market today...

FROM  LEISURE BOOKS

As a home subscriber to the Leisure Historical Romance Book Club, you'll enjoy the best in today's BRAND-NEW Historical Romance fiction. For over twenty-five years, Leisure Books has brought you the award-winning, high-quality authors you know and love to read. Each Leisure Historical Romance will sweep you away to a world of high adventure...and intimate romance. Discover for yourself all the passion and excitement millions of readers thrill to each and every month.

SAVE AT LEAST *$5.00* EACH TIME YOU BUY!

Each month, the Leisure Historical Romance Book Club brings you four brand-new titles from Leisure Books, America's foremost publisher of Historical Romances. EACH PACKAGE WILL SAVE YOU AT LEAST $5.00 FROM THE BOOKSTORE PRICE! And you'll never miss a new title with our convenient home delivery service.

Here's how we do it. Each package will carry a 10-DAY EXAMINATION privilege. At the end of that time, if you decide to keep your books, simply pay the low invoice price of $16.96 ($17.75 US in Canada), no shipping or handling charges added*. HOME DELIVERY IS ALWAYS FREE*. With today's top Historical Romance novels selling for $5.99 and higher, our price SAVES YOU AT LEAST $5.00 with each shipment.

AND YOUR FIRST FOUR-BOOK SHIPMENT IS TOTALLY FREE!*

IT'S A BARGAIN YOU CAN'T BEAT! A Super $21.96 Value!

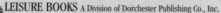 LEISURE BOOKS A Division of Dorchester Publishing Co., Inc.

GET YOUR 4 FREE* BOOKS NOW—
A $21.96 VALUE!

Mail the Free* Book
Certificate
Today!

4 FREE* BOOKS ❧ A $21.96 VALUE

Free *Books* *Certificate*

YES! I want to subscribe to the Leisure Historical Romance Book Club. Please send me my 4 FREE* BOOKS. Then each month I'll receive the four newest Leisure Historical Romance selections to Preview for 10 days. If I decide to keep them, I will pay the Special Member's Only discounted price of just $4.24 each, a total of $16.96 ($17.75 US in Canada). This is a SAVINGS OF AT LEAST $5.00 off the bookstore price. There are no shipping, handling, or other charges*. There is no minimum number of books I must buy and I may cancel the program at any time. In any case, the 4 FREE* BOOKS are mine to keep—A BIG $21.96 Value!

*In Canada, add $5.00 shipping and handling per order for first shipment. For all subsequent shipments to Canada, the cost of membership is $17.75 US, which includes $7.75 shipping and handling per month. [All payments must be made in US dollars]

Name _____

Address _____

City _____

State _____ *Country* _____ *Zip* _____

Telephone _____

Signature _____

If under 18, Parent or Guardian must sign. Terms, prices and conditions subject to change. Subscription subject to acceptance. Leisure Books reserves the right to reject any order or cancel any subscription.

(Tear Here and Mail Your FREE* Book Card Today!)

Get Four Books Totally
F R E E* —
A $21.96 Value!

(Tear Here and Mail Your FREE* Book Card Today!)

PLEASE RUSH
MY FOUR FREE*
BOOKS TO ME
RIGHT AWAY!

Leisure Historical Romance Book Club

P.O. Box 6613
Edison, NJ 08818-6613

protector. She could not believe that anyone, especially an Indian, would defy Patrick Russell! He put fear in most men's hearts, for he was evil through and through, and would kill someone as easily as he looked at them. Especially an Indian! Although this Indian was slight, he had the voice of authority, of thunder.

And yet there was such a softness about him, to care for her so quickly, so decidedly!

Patrick doubled his fists at his sides, then looked at the weapons again, feeling helpless. The damn Indian could move much more quickly than he.

"And so you plan to escort me to Fort Smith, do you?" Patrick growled. "I should've known that once you set eyes on my niece you'd want her for yourself. She'll be a good one in bed, all fresh and new, never touched by a man before. How often do you plan to do it to her every day, Injun? Ten times? Twenty? Then what will you do with her when she's all used up and haggard-looking? Give her to your other savages to rape?" Patrick laughed throatily. "Give it to her good, Injun. You damn savage, you ain't good for nothin' else."

Rachel jumped with alarm when Running Wolf pounced suddenly on Patrick, wrestling him to the ground. In a movement of the hand that was so quick it was like the strike of lightning, Running Wolf removed his knife from its sheath and had its blade at Patrick's throat. "White man, your words insult both me and the woman," he said, his teeth clenched. "Speak words of apology or your insults will be the last words you will ever say. My knife sometimes has a mind of its own. Even now I am having to hold it back from doing something it feels compelled to do." His lips lifted into a menacing smile. "So? What shall it be, ugly and stinking white man? Shall I let my knife do its will? Or do I release you and be merciful and lead you to Fort Smith?"

Patrick was scarcely breathing, afraid to. He wished he could slow his heartbeat, for the sharp point of the knife was too close to the throbbing vein in his throat. One slip and that would be the end for him! Even if he spoke, perhaps the movement it took to do so could cause the knife to pierce his flesh. And once it did and the Indian caught sight of the blood, he might want to spill even more! The Indian did seem angry enough to forget even considering taking him to Fort Smith. It would be much more convenient to kill him. He would have access to Rachel much more quickly! And surely that was all he wanted!

"I . . . apologize. . . ." he finally managed in an agonized whisper, which proved how hard it was for him to say the word. "Have mercy. Let me go. I won't bother Rachel again. I promise."

"A promise from a man like you is surely no better than that of a black widow spider should it have the ability to speak," Running Wolf said, lowering the knife from Patrick's throat. "But you had best honor the promise, for if you ever return to these parts, your death will be quick. I move in the dark like a panther. You would not even know that it was I who thrust the knife in your back should your ugly face ever draw near here again."

"Just get me to Fort Smith," Patrick said, sweat pouring from his brow as Running Wolf rose away from him. "That's all I want. You can have my niece. My life is worth more than her any day!"

"Running Wolf will take you from the City of Peace and point you in the direction of the white man's fort," Running Wolf said. "You are not worth the time wasted to take you all the way. You are a heartless man, and you are lucky that I did not kill you."

Panic flashed in Patrick's eyes. "You said that you would take me to Fort Smith," he stammered. "Now you won't? What if I get lost?"

"My mind has been changed by your thoughtless words," Running Wolf said, grabbing his rifle. "And what if you do get lost? Better yet for all concerned. You are of no use to anyone."

Patrick eyed the rifle, then looked slowly back up at Running Wolf. "You will give me a weapon for protection?" he dared to ask.

"You think I am foolish?" Running Wolf said, laughing absently.

"Then you won't?" Patrick gasped.

Running Wolf smiled at Patrick, then turned his eyes to Rachel, at the same time not letting Patrick out of his sight. "You will stay safely in my cavern," he said softly. "There is enough food. There is enough firewood to keep the fire burning. Soon I will return." His eyes softened. "You will be my princess, never wanting for anything. Life will be good. I will make it so for you."

Rachel was touched to the heart by his kindness, fear not entering into her thoughts at all about being left in Running Wolf's care. She was finding herself being drawn into more than liking him, into something that she had never felt for any other man. Her uncles had caused her to hate and mistrust men. But too much about Running Wolf scattered these emotions to the wind.

"You will stay?" Running Wolf asked, drawing Rachel's eyes back to him. "When I return, you will be here?"

Rachel rose to her feet and stepped closer to Running Wolf. "Yes, I will stay," she murmured. "When you return I will be here."

Running Wolf's face beamed as he smiled. "That is good," he said, nodding.

Rachel's heart hammered wildly as he continued to look down at her with his fathomless eyes. Although he was a slight man, and not very handsome of feature, his kindness, his warmth, were drawing her into caring for him. If she could have had her pick of men, this was the sort she would have chosen.

Running Wolf glared at Patrick. "Move ahead of me from the cavern," he said flatly. "And should you try to disarm me, your death will come quickly."

Patrick narrowed his eyes angrily, yet nodded in agreement. Then he looked down at Rachel, knowing that although he had given his word, one day he would return to claim her.

And Brietta, should she still be alive.

He walked ahead of Running Wolf from the cavern. Rachel followed them to the entrance and watched them ride away, feeling the first ray of hope within her heart for many a day. She knew that Running Wolf would return, bringing with him all of his kindnesses.

And couldn't he also help her find Brietta?

Sighing heavily, Rachel turned and went back to

the fire, easing down onto a cattail mat before it. "Brietta, soon I shall find you," she whispered to herself. "I know that I will. I know that you aren't dead. The good Lord above would not allow that to happen."

Tears misting her eyes, she thought back to that last night with her sister. How could they have been so careless that they had become separated from each other in the dark? Without her sister and the bonds that they had shared from birth, life was so bleak, so empty. . . .

"I love you, Brietta," she sobbed. "My sweet sister, oh, how I love you!"

CHAPTER
SIXTEEN

All night upon mine heart I felt her warm heart
  beat,
Night-long within mine arms in love and sleep
  she lay.

—*Dowson*

The mission stood up black against the dull red
glow of the setting sun seeping through thick,
swollen clouds. The glass of its windows shone in
the red reflected light with a murky luridness as
though within were the flames of hell.

Missionary Cutright stood in the doorway of the
mission, wringing his hands as he watched the
Osage warriors assemble in solemn conclave outside, listening to their beloved leader, Chief Climb-

ing Bear. The women and children obediently stayed within the confines of the mission, separate from those who were preparing themselves for war.

Chief Climbing Bear was proud that his neighboring tribes of Osage Indians had stood behind him and his people in this, their time of trouble, lending them all sorts of war paraphernalia and many horses. His wound healing well, Chief Climbing Bear was a striking figure as he stood before his warriors holding a long, steel-headed spear that was girdled with varicolored beads and ornamented with great tufts of eagle feathers and a picturesque plume at the tip. He began moving among his warriors with a solemn and ponderous dignity, silent and full of commanding reserve.

Then he turned and faced them all, peering intensely at them. The strenuous war career of this noted chief had ploughed deep furrows and written serious lines in his face; wounds and scars and battle left their mark on his fifty-five winters.

"The years of hate between the Osage and Cherokee are but one thread in the loom of time," he shouted, breaking the strained silence. "Today, my warriors, you must ride without your chief and lead an attack against Brave Eagle's village! Kill Brave Eagle for what he has done to the Osage! Even though he did not take Osage captives, he has brought much grief and shame to us!"

There were several shouts and weapons were raised in the air as Chief Climbing Bear looked among the dark, excited faces of his warriors. "This is only the beginning of our vengeance!" he shouted. He paused for a moment, then said,

"And, my proud warriors, die if you must to achieve our goal. You must always remember that death is but a change for the better and that it is more than anything unworthy and womanish to shun it!"

Several war whoops reverberated through the throng of warriors. Chief Climbing Bear thrust his spear into the air. "Before you fight, search for Brown Cloud," he continued, his voice now solemn. "See if he is still alive. If so, my son must be the one to lead the attack!"

He lowered his spear and looked into the distance, toward the fringes of the forest. "Then, my trusted warriors, we must rebuild our village," he said, his voice drawn. He looked toward the mission, then back at his warriors. "It is not right to keep our women and children surrounded by walls that were built by white men! They must once again have their own dwellings in which to carry on their lives!"

Missionary Cutright appeared suddenly at Chief Climbing Bear's side. He placed a gentle hand to the chief's arm. "Warring is not the way," he said, defying the chief as Climbing Bear glared down at him from his six-foot height. "It is not the way of God. Go to the Cherokee village and offer ways of peace. It is meant for all men to live as though one on this earth, with love and peace within their hearts."

Chief Climbing Bear politely lifted Missionary Cutright's hand from his arm. "You do not understand the true ways of man," he said scornfully. "Your words are but a puff of smoke as they come out of your mouth, snatched quickly away by the wind, leaving nothing behind that has meaning. Go. Leave us to our ways. We do not interefere in yours."

Missionary Cutright stared for a moment longer up at the chief, then realized that nothing he could say would change Chief Climbing Bear's mind and stepped away from him and returned to the mission. He went inside and looked at the women and children sitting quietly in the pews, their eyes wide and fearful. He shook his head sorrowfully and went to the altar and knelt before it. His hands clasped together in a prayful manner, he peered up at the statue of Christ that looked down upon him and began praying softly, while outside the war party continued.

"We begin our preparation for the fight!" Chief Climbing Bear shouted. "Dig the holes! Build the fires! Soon we will have ashes enough to place upon our bodies and faces!"

The fires built, the rituals began which prepared them for warring. All those who were going on this expedition collected together and formed a wide circle. An elderly Indian began to sing and timed the music by beating on a drum. The warriors began to move forward as well-disciplined troops would march to the fife and drum. Each warrior had a tomahawk, spear, rifle, or war club in his hand. They all moved together towards the east, the way they intended to go to war. At length they all stretched their tomahawks in the air and gave a hideous yell. Then they wheeled quickly about and danced back in the same manner.

Next came the war song. In performing this, only one warrior sang at a time, in a moving posture, with a tomahawk in his hand, while all the other warriors were engaged in calling aloud, "*He-uh, he-uh!*"

They constantly repeated this while the war song was going on. When the warrior who was singing had ended his song, he struck a war post with his tomahawk, and with a loud voice told what warlike exploits he had done and what he now intended to do. Some who had not before intended to go to war were so excited by his performance that they took up the tomahawk and sang the war song, which was answered with shouts of joy, as they were then initiated into the present marching company.

And then their prayers began. They were chanted in a high sing-song note and continued as long as there was breath in a progressively lower tone to the lowest key. This was repeated over and over again until the warriors were brought to a pitch of excitement.

Some chanted the death song for some deceased loved one. Others sought *Wah-Kon-Tah's* favor for their expedition. Some lay prostrate upon the ground, exhausted, crying and sobbing as if their hearts were broken.

The death song filled Chief Climbing Bear's soul with fear and bittersweetness, and when it ended he lay on the ground in an exultant fear-trance, afraid of what might be—death to his warriors!

And then he rose and led his warriors to the firepits, where the fires had burned down to ashes. They poured water into the holes and stirred the ashes with sticks. Then they dipped their hands into the mixture and smeared it on their faces and over their bodies, making them look fierce.

They then fell upon their faces while emitting more prayers to *Wah-Kon-Tah*, and after a few minutes, they rose to their feet and with much whooping and shouting mounted their horses which had been tethered close by during the ceremony.

"Return victorious!" Chief Climbing Bear shouted, walking among the jingling bridles of the horses, peering up at the determined, excited faces of his warriors. "Go now! Fight as though I were there leading you!"

Yelping and brandishing their weapons over their heads, the warriors rode away in a hard gallop, leaving Chief Climbing Bear standing in the sprays of dust stirred up by the hooves. Clutching his spear, his jaw tight, he watched until he could not see his warriors any longer, then stoically began walking toward the mission. In his mind's eye, he was a part of the battle, his son riding proudly at his side.

Then a raw bitterness entered his heart, shame filling him, unable to recall a recent time when Brown Cloud had had the ability to bring him honor. The firewater had claimed his son, heart and soul.

The forest was darkening all around her as she rode away from the man she loved, and Brietta began to fear the night that lay ahead of her. Although she had a weapon, if she took the time to sleep, she would not be aware of the creatures of night that might sneak up on her. A weapon would be of no use then.

"I must not stop," she whispered to herself, the dampness of evening chilling her. "I must ride onward and find Fort Smith. I cannot afford to waste time in sleeping. While I sleep, my sister could be taken farther and farther away from me." A sob caught in her throat. "Oh, God, please don't let me be too late! I must find Rachel now, or never!"

Birds scurried to shelter in the trees overhead, their chatter almost deafening. The baying of a wolf in the distance sent goosebumps along her flesh. She nudged her knees into her horse's sides and wove in and around the trees that constantly impeded her journey.

Determined to get to Fort Smith, she held her chin high and rode briskly onward.

Brown Cloud lay on his back on the ground staring up at the moon, yet not seeing anything but a haze of white through the drunken glaze of his eyes. The other warriors who had drunk with him lay close by, laughing and joking, while those who had remained sober still sat glumly aside, waiting for Brown Cloud to give them commands.

Brown Cloud did not even stir when a thunder of horses' hooves arrived at the ruins of his village. He did not even look away from the moon when he was surrounded by Osage warriors whose faces were painted for war. He did not even become alert when his name was spoken, not once, but many times.

Only when hands on his arms yanked him up from the ground did he become aware of someone besides himself and the moon. He looked in a bewildered fashion into the blackened face of his cousin, who was one of Brown Cloud's father's special warriors and rode at his father's side during battle more often than his own son.

"Blazing Arrow, why are you here?" Brown Cloud said, jerking himself free from his grasp. He swayed as he leaned closer to Blazing Arrow, squinting his eyes as he looked at his blackened face. "You are going to make war? With whom?"

Blazing Arrow folded his arms across his chest, his eyes two narrow slits as he glared at Brown Cloud. "You should not have to ask," he growled. "You should have been with your father during the preparations for warring. But I find you here, firewater clouding your brain! You are a fool, Brown Cloud. A fool!"

Brown Cloud stiffened. He clutched his hands angrily to Blazing Arrow's arms. "You speak to a future chief in such a way?" he said between clenched teeth. "You should die for such disobedience, Blazing Arrow. I could even order you banished from our tribe!"

"Then do it, fool," Blazing Arrow said, his eyes narrowing even more in his anger. "See then what your father would say to you. It is I he depends on—not you, his only son!"

"You are a mere cousin," Brown Cloud scoffed. "You are of less importance to my father than were you a dog sniffing at his feet."

Blazing Arrow wrenched himself free from Brown Cloud's grip. "I understand that it is the firewater that makes you speak so loosely, my cousin," he said. He looked away from Brown

238

Cloud at the devastation of their village, then back at Brown Cloud. "You have yet to ask about your father—of his welfare. I, too, blame that carelessness on firewater."

"My father," Brown Cloud said, weaving again as a dizziness came over him. "Is he well?"

"Wounded, but well," Blazing Arrow grumbled.

"Wounded?" Brown Cloud said, squinting as he tried to look more closely through his drunken haze at Blazing Arrow. "How badly? And where is he? Where are our people?"

"He was not wounded badly," Blazing Arrow said icily. "And our people? They are at the white man's mission until we rebuild our village."

"Rebuild?" Brown Cloud said, looking past Blazing Arrow at the remains of his and his father's dwellings.

"After we destroy Brave Eagle's village and see that he dies for his evil deed to our people," Blazing Arrow said.

Brown Cloud teetered, then steadied himself. "Kill?" he said, his voice drawn. "Kill Brave Eagle?"

"Your father has given the command," Blazing Arrow said. "It will be obeyed." He reached a hand to Brown Cloud's shoulder. "He also commanded me to search and find you so that you will lead us into battle. Though your body is ravished with firewater, it is no less your duty to follow your father's command. Come. It is time to go. Now."

Brown Cloud drew away from Blazing Arrow and turned his back to him. His heart pounded at the thought of going against Brave Eagle in such a way, the whole purpose to kill him. If it came right down to the moment of decision, could he kill his blood brother? Oh, why had it come to this?

Yet it was Brave Eagle's fault if his death came tonight at Brown Cloud's hands. Brave Eagle should have never spilled blood on Osage grounds!

Spinning around, steadying himself when once again he teetered from dizziness, Brown Cloud nodded. He half stumbled to his horse and, after several clumsy attempts, finally managed to mount his steed. He slapped the reins against his horse's mane and rode quickly away, soon hearing the thundering of the other horses behind him. He kept arguing to himself about this thing that he was about to do. He had no choice! He must defend his and his people's honor! And in the absence of his father, he must prove to be a great leader, one who could fight as fiercely as the chief whom everyone admired because of his great victories on the battlefields!

"I will prove that I am my father's son in every way!" he whispered to himself. "Even if I have to return to my father with Brave Eagle's scalp!"

Tears misted his eyes at the thought, then his heart skipped a beat and his knees grew weak when up ahead he saw the outline of several warriors shadowed against the landscape as they were riding toward the Osage warriors. When a cloud slipped away from the moon and it splashed its great white light on the leader of the approaching horsemen, he emitted a low gasp.

"Brave Eagle," he whispered. "I do not have to ride any farther. He has come to me!"

Brave Eagle had caught sight of the Osage warriors, whose faces were dressed in war paint. He did not have to guess who the warring was to be against. The Osage, with Brown Cloud in the lead, were out for vengeance. And Brave Eagle was the one whose scalp they would be seeking to take back as a trophy of war to the great Osage chief.

As Brave Eagle and his warriors rode slowly toward the Osage who were now awaiting them in a long line, their various weapons grasped tightly within their hands, there was no clink of steel or rattle of harness, only the soft rustling of the prairie grass under the unshod hoofs of their spirited steeds.

When they reached the Osage and were a few yards apart, they halted and sat on their horses facing each other, forming their own line of defense. Brave Eagle broke away from his warriors and rode out before the line, his eyes never leaving Brown Cloud, who also broke away from his warriors to meet Brave Eagle halfway between the two lines of Indians.

Horse to horse, face to face, they stopped. "We meet before battle, the last time ever to speak in peace with one another," Brown Cloud said, weaving, hardly able to keep himself in the saddle. "You must die, Brave Eagle. It is the only way. My father has ordered your death."

"That is understandable," Brave Eagle said, straightening his shoulders. "But listen well, my friend, before you lead your men against mine. It is with a heavy heart that I come to you to speak words of apology to you about my wrongful attack

241

on your people. I thought you had betrayed me. I discovered that it was not you at all, but someone else who had done the wrongful deed against me. It is with all sincerity that I come to you to ask you ,and your people's forgiveness. Even shall I lend a helping hand to rebuild your village. Even shall I bring you much food and many horses to repay you for this that I have done to your people. Listen well, my friend, for never have I apologized to anyone else, or offered so much. Especially to the Osage, our natural enemy!''

Knowing that apologies would never be enough for a father who hated all Cherokee, Brown Cloud knew that it was not for him to accept these kind offerings from Brave Eagle. Though it made an ache circle his heart to refuse his old friend, it had to be so! He was only the son of the chief, one who obeyed commands, not made decisions that would go against everything his father ever taught him about the marauding Cherokee.

"That cannot be," Brown Cloud said, his voice breaking. "My father gave a command. I must carry it through."

Brave Eagle's heart seemed to drop to his feet, unable to believe that Brown Cloud would not listen to reason. What Brave Eagle offered was more than should ever be expected to amend for a wrongful deed. Why couldn't Brown Cloud understand this?

Brave Eagle leaned closer to Brown Cloud and was seized with the reality of the condition of his old friend. Brown Cloud was drunk! Any decision he would make now would not be the same were he sober! The firewater caused his old friend to do many things, but this tonight might be the most disastrous of all!

"You are drunk, Brown Cloud," Brave Eagle said, stiffening in his saddle. "What you say you do not mean. Return to your people. Sleep off your stupor. Then let us meet and talk again."

Embarrassed and humiliated, Brown Cloud pursed his lips tightly together, his eyes two points of fire. "You think you are much better!" he shouted. "I will show you! I will show you!" He wheeled his horse around and joined his warriors.

Brave Eagle watched for a moment, stunned, then saw the danger in staying there any longer, alone, and quickly joined his warriors. Suddenly the horses on both sides plunged forward into a tearing gallop, each party uttering yells of defiance.

Brave Eagle felt the warm, silky hide of his steed between his knees, and felt the play of his gelding's muscles as he led it into a tearing gallop.

"*E-e-e-e!*" he screamed, defending himself, as he became a part of the big, spinning wheel of mounted warriors, horses' tossing heads, and dust.

Suddenly Brown Cloud made a lunge for Brave Eagle and wrestled with him while their horses snorted and shook their fiery manes. When Brown Cloud slipped from his mount and fell to the ground, his weapon thrown from his hand as he fell, Brave Eagle dismounted quickly and pinned Brown Cloud to the ground on his stomach, his knife poised in the air for the death plunge.

Everyone stopped and watched breathlessly as Brown Cloud groveled on the ground beneath Brave Eagle, breathing hard, his eyes wild, cowering as he looked sideways up at Brave Eagle.

Brave Eagle's eyes wavered. The hand in which he held his knife trembled as his eyes locked with Brown Cloud's. Within his old friend's eyes, he could see a marked fear, yet something more than that. His eyes were bloodshot and glassy, and he reeked of whiskey.

"I cannot strike you dead," Brave Eagle said, lowering his knife to his side. "I pity you too much." He jumped to his feet and stood over Brown Cloud, his old friend not yet moving from his prostrate position. There was a moment of strained silence while everyone looked on, then a choked sob of humiliation rose into the air from Brown Cloud, making a sort of sickness spiral through Brave Eagle. He stared down at his friend a moment longer, then mounted his steed and gave the command for his warriors to follow him from this place of humble endings between friends.

As Brave Eagle rode away, he drew a zigzag line in the air behind him with his hand to represent lightning, to keep his enemies from following.

The Osage did not try to stop Brave Eagle and his warriors from leaving. They stared down at their future chief, shamed for him. Brown Cloud rose slowly to his feet, brushing muddy tears from his cheeks as he walked to his horse. Shamed to the core, he mounted his steed and rode away in the opposite direction from where Brave Eagle had gone. Soon he heard the thunder of hoofbeats behind him. He could not look any of his warriors in the eye, for he had let them down.

Not only them, but himself.

And also his chieftain father.

244

His moment of humility had sobered him, making him realize exactly why his father could never put trust in him. He doubled a fist to his side, vowing never to touch firewater again!

He had much to prove to his father, and he would!

CHAPTER SEVENTEEN

Pale hands, pink-tipped, like lotus buds,
I would have rather felt you round my throat,
Crushing out life, than waving me farewell.

—Hope

The moon was covered by building clouds. Thunder rumbled in the distance, ominously low and prolonged as it rolled across the heavens. The picture of Brown Cloud lying prostrate on the ground was imbedded in his memory forever, and it was with a great sadness that Brave Eagle rode back into his village. At least he could be thankful that his warriors had been spared serious injuries or death. They had fought with much strength and valor a battle that they had not even prepared for with songs and prayers. It had been with a friendly heart that Brave Eagle had searched his old friend out, his tongue heavy with apologies—apologies that were ignored. How much better it would have been for Brown Cloud to accept Brave Eagle's apologies than to think himself capable of warring while his brain was soaked with firewater!

His warriors rode on without him, and Brave Eagle dismounted before his dwelling, eager to find solace in the arms of his wife. How good it was to have a woman to come home to. It had been so long since a wife awaited him like this—so very, very long!

His steps were eager as he went to the entrance flap and shoved it aside. Stepping inside his dark dwelling, he was puzzled at how the fire had been allowed to burn down to dying embers. Did his wife not know how to tend a fire?

Ah, but yes, he did have much to teach her about the Cherokee way of life. How to kindle a fire was only a small portion of what she would eventually learn from her tutoring husband!

Feeling his way around in the dark, along the cattail mats on the floor, he became puzzled anew, for where was his wife sleeping, if not snuggled in thick furs close to the fire pit? Did she not even know how to prepare skins for a bed in the Cherokee dwelling? That would seem to be the simplest of all things new to her!

Alarm set in when Brave Eagle suddenly realized what had happened.

"She is gone!" he said in a low gasp, the knowing tearing at his heart. He shook his head, unable to believe that she could have been so loving and devoted to him, and then deserted him the first time he left her alone.

"How can you do this?" he shouted, doubling his hands into tight fists at his sides. "*O-ge-ye*, do you not love me at all? Was I a fool to think that you could?"

Filled with a frustrated anger, Brave Eagle stomped from the wigwam and swung himself up onto his horse, ignoring the threat of the impending storm as lightning flared brightly in the sky. He was going to find his woman. He would not give her up this easily! If he had to make her a captive, so be it!

Yes, he would teach her many things—among them obedience to a husband!

Brietta rode more desperately, shivering as the lightning sparked the heavens above her with zigzags of light and the thunder rumbled around her like a giant bear growling. She must find shelter. Out in the open she was not only a target for any man who might happen along, but also for the lightning. She had seen cows fried on the spot in the pasture from lightning strikes. There were many ways to die and that seemed the least attractive of all!

The heavens erupted with another burst of lightning, lighting everything around Brietta enough for her to see ahead of her for some distance. She gripped the reins harder and her heart skipped a beat when for a brief moment she discovered that she was not alone on this meadow of violets and daisies. Ahead two horsemen were quickly approaching her.

"Oh, no," she whispered to herself. "In all this wide wilderness where there isn't a soul for mile after mile, how is it that I always manage to come across someone?" She gulped hard, fear gripping her insides. "And, Lord, why must it always be men?"

Her first instinct was to wheel her horse around and ride quickly in the opposite direction, but she knew that she couldn't get away from the men if she tried. They had most surely seen her at the same instant she had spied them. Not having any choice, she drew her reins tight and waited.

When the men drew rein before her, her voice caught in her throat when she uttered the name. "Patrick?"

Her gaze went to Running Wolf. "And you?" she said, wondering about this cousin of Brave Eagle's who seemed to be everywhere all of the time. "Again I am face to face with you?"

"Well, look who's here," Patrick said, his eyes raking over her. "And don't you look pretty in that Injun attire. Kind of looks right on you, you bein' tricky and all, like an Injun."

Thinking that Brietta was Rachel, Running Wolf was in awe of this woman who seemed to be everywhere at once. Hadn't he left her at his cavern? Hadn't she given her word that she would wait for his return? Why had she changed her mind and how had she managed to get this far so quickly?

And was it not strange that her flight was taking her in the wrong direction! The horse she had managed to steal from someone at the City of Peace should be carrying her away from the cavern, not toward it. Not knowing the terrain, perhaps she was riding in circles!

No matter what, he would not let her get away from him again. She would be his. He would make her love him!

"Patrick," Brietta murmured. "I thought you were—"

"Dead? Naw. Don't seem so. It's hard to kill a good man," Patrick said, chuckling. "And how about you? Seems you're makin' it on your own all right."

"As if you truly care," Brietta said icily.

"Why, sweet thing, I always cared," Patrick said, laughing beneath his breath.

"Not in the way that you should, or is decent," Brietta argued. "If father were alive and knew what your true intentions were all along, he would—"

Running Wolf edged his Appaloosa between Patrick's and Brietta's, blocking their view of each other. "Enough!" he said flatly. He looked at Patrick, then Brietta, then glowered at Patrick. "Ride on alone. You are pointed in the right direction. If you ride another day and night you will arrive at Fort Smith. Once there, white man, you forget you ever knew Running Wolf and the white woman. If ever you return to this area for any reason, you will be quickly dead! This woman will return with me to the City of Peace. She is mine. Remember that, white man. Mine!"

Patrick eyed Running Wolf questioningly, then a slow smile curled his lips. The Indian thought that Brietta was Rachel! Being twins, who could tell them apart except for kin who knew that the eye

251

coloring was what made the difference in their appearances?

Patrick chuckled low. "You ignorant savage," he spat. "You've got the wrong sister. This ain't the one you left in the cavern. It's her sister."

Running Wolf's eyes wavered as he looked quickly at Brietta, then his jaw tightened and his eyes became lit with fire as he glared back at Patrick. "You think I am blind?" he fumed. "This is my woman! Now ride on with you, white man, before I am forced to use my knife on you after all!"

"But Running Wolf," Patrick began, but was silenced quickly when Running Wolf removed his knife from the sheath at his waist, brandishing it in the air at him.

"Ride!" Running Wolf said in a hiss. "As I said before, my knife has a mind of its own. Right now it is hard to hold it back from your throat!"

Through Running Wolf and Patrick's confrontation something wonderful was revealed to Brietta. Her heart filled with joy, knowing that what Patrick had said to Running Wolf had to be true! Rachel was alive! Surely she was well! It seemed that Running Wolf had trusted her enough to leave her at the cave, or—or had he tied her there, forcing her to stay?

Brietta studied Running Wolf, recalling that he had left her to die, and the thought seized her with a sudden fear. What if he had been as heartless with Rachel? She would soon know, for she would continue pretending to be Rachel and accompany Running Wolf to this cavern where she would finally be reunited with her beloved sister!

Her heartbeat sped up, wanting to get there quickly, before it was too late.

"You foolish Injun, find out for yourself," Patrick growled, sinking his heels into the sides of his horse and riding away.

"Brietta, you're in the hands of a renegade Injun. Better it were me than him!" Patrick shouted over his shoulder, his laughter fading in the wind as he rode out of sight.

"Brietta?" Running Wolf said, quirking an eyebrow. "Still he tries to fool me? White woman, no one fools Running Wolf." His gaze softened. "I understand why you fled my dwelling. You did not know that it was with much kindness in my heart that I wanted you to stay. You are much safer there. Should the evil white man have taken you with him, he would have ravished your body. It is not my intent ever to violate you. I want to make you love me so that you choose to invite me to lie down with you."

Hope filled Brietta again. Surely her sister was unharmed. This Indian seemed to be truly sincere in his feelings toward her. That he had left Brietta to die was perhaps something that fear had led him to do.

Brietta smiled warmly at Running Wolf, eager to play the game with him until she was taken to Rachel. Then she would decide what her next move would be after Running Wolf saw the twin sisters and she could gauge his reaction.

"I was foolish for having left the cavern," she murmured, inching her horse closer to Running

Wolf's. "Please take me back." She flinched when a loud crash of thunder erupted close by. "I am afraid of the storm."

Running Wolf looked toward the heavens, seeing the moon being uncovered by the drifting clouds. "The storm is passing overhead," he said. "There is no danger in spending the night by a campfire and riding to the cavern before dawn." He looked at her, reaching a gentle hand to her cheek, which she allowed as a part of her pretense to be Rachel. "You must be tired. We will rest first, ride later."

He peered in the direction where Patrick had ridden. "But we must find a secret place should the white man decide to return and challenge my right to you," he said. "Come. We will ride a while, then make camp."

"Whatever you say," Brietta murmured, going with him willingly for more than one reason—not the least being that she was glad to be spared from Patrick.

Running Wolf's eyes wavered as he looked at her with a quiet longing. "Why did you not trust me?" he asked, sounding disappointed. "Why did you leave the cavern? I gave you no reason not to trust me."

Brietta thought quickly, wanting to sound convincing. "I became afraid," she murmured. "I wanted to search for you. Surely you can understand."

"And you found me," Running Wolf said, smiling. "Come. I shall give you only cause to be happy."

Brietta saw the sincerity in his words and actions and felt safe enough with him. Did he not treat her as royaly as Brave Eagle did? If he loved Rachel so much, oh, how wonderful for her sister! Perhaps both she and Rachel could make a life with their Cherokee warriors! Why should they ever leave this beautiful country where both were loved so dearly?

She nudged her horse with her knees and rode beside Running Wolf, hope filling her.

Humbled with shame, Brown Cloud sat on a bluff away from his warriors, who were eagerly rebuilding their village. He was praying to *Wah-Kon-Tah* for guidance. He had misjudged so many things, of late. Brave Eagle and Brown Cloud's father had preached to him of the evils of the firewater. Now at last he understood. It did not make him strong! It distorted his vision of life! Never would he touch it again!

"Brown Cloud?"

His cousin's voice behind him drew Brown Cloud to his feet. He turned and faced Blazing Arrow, forcing a smile of welcome.

"Brown Cloud, join the others," Blazing Arrow said sternly. "Though shamed tonight by Brave Eagle, let us replace the shame in your heart with an eagerness to make things right for our people." He glanced toward the warriors who were thrusting poles in the ground, bending and fastening them together, while others stretched out animal hides with which to cover them. "We will return to your father with good tidings to erase the bad. We will bring him to his village that is no longer only ash across the ground, but instead a place of rebirth where dwellings will be warming beneath the rays of tomorrow's sun. In this he will find happiness, not sadness over his son's shame on the battlefield."

"My father will never forgive me," Brown Cloud said, his voice breaking. "Seeing a rebuilt village will not take the place inside his heart of being able to shout into the wind that his son fought with valor—and won." He hung his head. "I deserve to be banished. I would not blame my father if he chose this punishment for my disservice to the Osage tonight."

"With the Great Spirit's blessings, all things are possible," Blazing Arrow said. "Now come. Let us walk among our brethren. Let us work side by side. What happened tonight is unfortunate, but already a thing of the past. We now look to the future."

"Yes, the future," Brown Cloud said, raising his eyes to meet Blazing Arrow's. "And it is to be a bright one, Blazing Arrow. Never shall I touch the firewater again! It is my shame!"

Blazing Arrow nodded, smiling to himself. His ploy of friendship was working and he knew Brown Cloud's weaknesses all too well—and that gave Blazing Arrow the advantage needed to one day take Brown Cloud's place at his father's side.

Together they walked from the bluff and entered the village. Brown Cloud did not receive looks of admiration, but neither did he receive looks of scorn.

Somehow the Osage warriors still saw him as their future leader.

Desperate to find Brietta, Brave Eagle rode hard through the night, then brought his gelding to a plunging halt when up ahead he saw two tethered horses, and farther still, the dancing flames of a campfire.

"Could it be?" he whispered to himself, hope filling his heart that he had finally found her. Yet, why were there two horses? Fear gripped him at the thought of Brietta having been abducted again.

He slapped his horse's reins and rode onward, stopping far enough from the campsite to tether his horse to a tree so that he would not startle awake whoever might be sleeping beside the fire.

His knife drawn, he wove stealthily in and around the trees until he was finally only a few footsteps away from the two sleeping figures on the ground. Slowly, he crept into the camp, his heart seeming to do a flipflop of delight when he discovered that the woman was Brietta!

He glanced at the man. He was shocked to discover that it was Running Wolf! How was it that Brietta was with him? Had he found her on the trail? If so, it was apparent that he was not forcing her to stay with him. He had not bound her arms or legs together.

He studied Brietta again. Had she left his Cherokee village of her own volition? Surely Running Wolf had not gone there to take her. He had a while longer to atone for Brave Eagle's crime. He surely would not go against the family agreement to enter the boundaries of a village that he had been banished from for a period of two years. The only answer could be that Brietta had fled the village and Running Wolf had come across her.

But what were his plans for her? What were his intentions? Anger-filled because of his lot in life,

257

could Running Wolf be planning to keep her from Brave Eagle?

Replacing his knife in its sheath, Brave Eagle went back to the grazing horses. He smiled cunningly as he roped Running Wolf's and Brietta's horses together behind his proud steed, so that once he fled with Brietta into the night, Running Wolf would be a long time in returning to the City of Peace.

Brave Eagle then returned to the campsite and knelt down beside Brietta. With the speed of lightning he clasped his hand over her mouth to keep her from crying out, while with his other hand he eased her up from the ground, from beneath her blankets.

Brietta awakened with a start and looked into Brave Eagle's eyes, and her heart sank. She had not forgotten how he had refused to help her search for Rachel. She was so close to seeing her sister again! She couldn't let Brave Eagle get in the way!

She began struggling against his solid hold. In only a few short hours Running Wolf would have led her to her sister! She could not depend on Brave Eagle to take her there, for surely he was so angry with her for having left his village, he would never cooperate with anything she asked of him again!

She pulled at his hands, but they held her like steel bands. Knowing that she had no other choice, Brietta grew limp within Brave Eagle's demanding hold and went with him to his horse. Before she could scream, he had a gag around her mouth and her wrists tied. Tears streamed from her eyes as he placed her in his saddle, mounting quickly behind her.

"Your bonds are only until I get you far from the ears of Running Wolf," Brave Eagle whispered, as he leaned close to her ear. "Then, *o-ge-ye*, we have much to talk about."

Brietta looked over her shoulder at him, seeing the fire in his eyes as he met her gaze with his own. Then she looked away from him as he sent his gelding into a thundering gallop across the land, the other horses following behind them.

CHAPTER EIGHTEEN

Could you but guess
How you alone make all my happiness.

—*Anonymous*

Angry, but glad that Brave Eagle had removed her gag and loosened her wrists, Brietta sat stiffly on the ground, watching him on his knees fanning the freshly built campfire with his hands. They hadn't traveled far, for they had not needed to put that many miles between themselves and Running Wolf's campsite since Brave Eagle had taken Running Wolf's horse.

"Brave Eagle, why did you have to interfere in my life again?" Brietta suddenly said, wincing when he rose to his feet and glared down at her.

"That is all that I am to you?" Brave Eagle demanded. "An interference?"

Brietta lowered her eyes, then dared him with a set stare. "You know my feelings for you," she murmured. "You know that I love you."

"Then you choose your words very unwisely, *o-ge-ye*," Brave Eagle said, turning his back to her again. "Your actions, also. A wife does not run from a husband. A wife awaits his return to the wigwam with open arms and a welcoming heart. You did neither, *o-ge-ye*. I returned home to an empty wigwam, so quiet in its emptiness that my heart cried out in its loneliness!"

"I only left because I wanted to search for my sister," Brietta said, rising. She touched Brave Eagle gently on the arm. "You placed your problems before mine. I had no choice but to leave, Brave Eagle, to try and find my way to Fort Smith. I was going to ask the soldiers' assistance in finding my sister. If you were not willing to help me, I had no choice but to go to the commander at the fort."

Brave Eagle turned scorching eyes to Brietta. "You are my wife. Your loyalty is to me!" he scolded. "And you shame me by going to white pony soldiers for assistance. This makes Brave Eagle look bad in his people's eyes!"

"I'm sorry," Brietta said, so wanting to ease into his arms and beg his forgiveness, yet knowing that she had been right to leave. Her sister had been an extension of herself long before Brave Eagle had entered her life. Brietta and Rachel had shared the same womb, the same heartbeat, and then the same troubled life. How could she be expected ever to forget her loyalty to her sister?

"You will return with me to my village," Brave Eagle said. "Your flight will be forgotten. You will take your place at my side, a dutiful wife, forever."

Brietta looked with disbelief up at him, finding it hard to understand how he could be so thoughtless of her feelings.

Then she wrenched herself free of him and doubled her hands into tight fists at her sides and lifted her chin haughtily. "I will not," she said, flinching when she saw the quick anger rise in his eyes again. "I am duty bound to find my sister. If you aren't willing to help me, then I have no choice but to go without you."

"I forbid it," Brave Eagle said flatly.

Brietta sucked in a wild, shocked breath of air. She squared her shoulders and tightened her jaw angrily. "You forbid it?" she said, her voice rising to a higher pitch. "It is not for you to forbid anything I do. Ever. In my eyes I am not your wife. We were not married by a minister, and for me to truly believe that I am married, I must be married in the eyes of the Lord!"

Brave Eagle's eyes wavered, stung by her words and denials of marriage to him! Yet he had to admire a woman who would take such a stand against him, a Cherokee who would one day be a powerful chief! He had never met a woman with such fire!

He had momentarily forgotten Running Wolf's involvement with her, and that Running Wolf had become a part of her escape—of her defiance of him!

"How is it that you were with Running Wolf?" he asked, forcing himself to ignore her reference to their marriage. As long as he knew deep within his heart that she was his wife, and that she truly wanted to be, he would not let her angry words inflame his heart into doing something that he would regret. Never did he want to have to force her, ever again, to do anything that she did not want to do. Even if it meant that he would have to travel from Cherokee country to look for her sister, who was so beloved to Brietta.

"Running Wolf?" Brietta said, stunned that he was actually ignoring her hurtful words and denial of being his wife.

"Do not pretend that you know not of whom I am speaking," Brave Eagle said. "Or do you also deny that you were with him when I found you?"

"No, I don't deny that I was with him," Brietta murmured. "But it was not by force. He thought that I was my sister. Through conversation, I discovered that she had been with him. He thought that I was her, having fled from where he had left her." She ran her fingers across her brow, frustrated. "Oh, it is too hard to explain! All that is important is that I know where my sister is! She is safe! And Running Wolf was taking me to her."

"Running Wolf knew where the slaver had taken your sister?" Brave Eagle said, quirking an eyebrow. "How could he know that? Running Wolf seems to get around much more freely than was intended. He was supposed to be confined at the City of Peace for a period of two years." He waved a hand of frustration in the air. "First he is here! Then he is there! He is not abiding by Cherokee law at all! He is too free to be atoning for my sin."

"The City of Peace!" Brietta said in a gasp. "I

remember now. That is where Running Wolf was taking me. My sister is there!"

Brave Eagle was taken aback by the discovery. "How is it that your sister is at the City of Peace?" he asked.

"Surely she was captured by Running Wolf—it seems an activity all Indians are prone to do," Brietta said, placing her hands on her hips. Then she regretted her words when she saw Brave Eagle's eyes soften with hurt. She looked away from him, then melted inside when gentle hands caressed her cheeks, turning her face so that their eyes could meet again.

"It is for Brave Eagle to erase the anger you feel for me in your heart," he said softly.

"And how do you intend to do this?" Brietta said, looking wide-eyed up at him, unable to control the harsh beating of her heart, nor the warmth growing at the pit of her stomach.

He did not respond in words. His response was in his lips, as he pressed them into hers with a sweet, quavering kiss. His powerful arms swept around her and drew her into his hard, muscled body.

As though willed by some unseen force, Brietta's arms twined around Brave Eagle's neck, and as he lowered her to the ground, she still did not fight the feelings that were being awakened within her again. Oh, how she loved him! And while she was in his arms, the world turned to something sweet, something wondrous! It was so easy to forget for a moment her worries and doubts.

Deep inside her heart, she knew that she was

free to take this moment to prove her love to Brave Eagle, for she knew that her sister was safe for now.

Brave Eagle leaned away from her, his hands deftly removing her dress. "You wear the dress of my people well, my wife," he said, his eyes dark with longing as he stopped to smooth his hands over her breasts, causing Brietta to sigh with pleasure.

His lips went to one breast and suckled on a nipple, setting fires throughout him as Brietta placed her hand to his head, drawing his mouth even closer. His hands moved along her silken flesh, stopping at the juncture of her thighs. Her body strained hungrily upward to meet his caresses, his fingers taunting her, stroking her fiery flesh. She closed her eyes, sensations searing her insides as Brave Eagle's mouth moved over her flesh, drugging her.

Brietta opened her eyes and looked adoringly up at Brave Eagle when he drew away from her to remove his breechclout. She admired his manliness, so obviously ready to travel with her to paradise and back.

She trembled with readiness as Brave Eagle moved over her. She arched her body to meet him as in an explosion of ecstasy he thrust himself inside her. Placing her hands at the nape of his neck, she urged his mouth to her lips. Her senses swam as he kissed her, the press of his lips so sweet, so soft. Tremors cascaded down her back, her whole body quivering as he cradled her close. Clinging to him, she moved her body rhythmically with his, his strokes sending waves of exquisite agony through her.

Overcome by passion's unbearable sweet pain, Brave Eagle's whole body seemed fluid with fire. He felt himself drawn into a chasm of agony and bliss. He pressed endlessly deeper within her, his breathing ragged as he drew his mouth from her lips, the sensations growing within him almost to the bursting point.

And then a sensual shock grabbed him and he knew that he could not hold back any longer. Holding her tightly in his arms, he gave in to a great shuddering in his loins, the explosion of ecstasy flooding him in great bursts of light.

Brietta felt Brave Eagle's joyous release. She soon joined him as a flood of bliss swept through her. She strained her hips up at him and cried out with ecstasy, as fulfillment was reached, and then too soon gone.

Brave Eagle's body subsided exhaustedly into hers as she still clung to him. He stroked her neck gently, his breath hot on her breasts as he felt comfort in their softness.

Combing her trembling fingers through Brave Eagle's hair where it fell away from his colorful headband, Brietta relished the calm sweetness of the moment, of their togetherness. It was at this moment that she knew she could not live without him, ever. And she did not want to feel ashamed that she had not spoken wedding vows with him before a minister. She could not deny to herself any longer that in her heart she was his wife.

In every respect.

"*O-ge-ye*, you fill me with much peace," Brave Eagle said, leaning away from her, so that their eyes could meet. "Is it the same for you while we are together in one another's arms?"

Brietta reached a hand to his cheek, her eyes moist with joyful tears. "It is the same," she said, smiling up at him. "I do love you, Brave Eagle. I do wish to still be your wife."

"You say you love me, yet you run from me," he said, frowning down at her. "Are you saying you will not do this again once I return you to my village?"

"Never will I do that again," Brietta murmured. Her smile faded and her hand dropped to her side. "But, Brave Eagle, I wish to be taken to the City of Peace before going to your village. I must see for myself that my sister is alive and well. Please? Will you take me?"

But Brave Eagle was honor-bound not to enter the City of Peace while Running Wolf was assigned his time there. He drew Brietta into his arms. "You will be taken there," he said, running his hand down her back in a caress. "But not by me, my love. We must return to my village. I will assign a warrior to take you there in my place."

"But why can't you take me?" Brietta puzzled, drawing away from him to look up at him.

"I am not allowed to enter the City of Peace at this time of my atonement," Brave Eagle explained. "It is for Running Wolf to be there, not I." He frowned as he looked past Brietta, into the depths of the forest. "Running Wolf does not understand this thing that has been assigned him. Perhaps he never will."

"He is not the only one who doesn't understand," Brietta murmured. "Atonement? Time of atonement? I just can't understand this thing between you and your cousin."

"*O-ge-ye*, it is not something you need to know," Brave Eagle said. "Not until you are taught all ways of the Cherokee, then you will know even that."

"Very well. But Brave Eagle, I am anxious to get to the City of Peace to see about my sister," Brietta said, reaching for her dress. "Can we leave? Now?"

"If she is at the City of Peace, she is safe and there is no cause for you to be so alarmed about your sister any longer," Brave Eagle said, taking her dress from her. "Tonight is ours, my love. We shall sleep in one another's arms beneath the stars. Too soon my duties as son of the chief will be thrust upon me again. Tonight my duty is only to you, my wife."

"As mine is to you," Brietta murmured. "But still I have other concerns." She paused for a moment, then added, "Will you let one of the horses go that you took from Running Wolf's campsite tonight?"

"And why would I do that?" he asked, quirking an eyebrow.

"For Running Wolf to find," Brietta said. "To hasten his return to my sister. I am sure that if he is there with her, she will be much more protected."

"You trust this Cherokee brave so much, who left you to die, and who lied to Brown Cloud about who truly ravaged Brown Cloud's village?" Brave Eagle said scornfully.

"If you trust him so little yourself, Brave Eagle,

269

why didn't you kill him tonight?" Brietta asked guardedly. "He was asleep. Killing him would have been easy."

"It is not for Brave Eagle alone to condemn Running Wolf for his misguided deeds. The council chooses as a whole."

"I hope the council sees the goodness I have seen in the man," Brietta said softly. "He speaks of my sister as though he cares deeply for her."

"In time we shall see," Brave Eagle said.

"Just leave the horse for Running Wolf when we ride onward, Brave Eagle," Brietta pleaded. "It is for my sister's sake that I ask this. It is for my heart's sake—so that it can be at peace while you and I make love again."

"This I shall do, for you," Brave Eagle finally said. "And, *o-ge-ye*, I also promise that soon you will never have cause to beg me for anything again. You will never have need to ask. Everything will be yours."

As he laid her down again on the soft bed of grass, Brietta was persuaded to believe him. He was talented in his persuasions, as always.

"Thank you, darling," she said, twining her arms around his neck as his mouth came to hers in a featherlight kiss, changing then to a kiss of demand, of possession.

She returned the kiss in kind.

The baying of a wolf in the distance, long and drawn-out, disturbed the peaceful silence of the night and awakened Running Wolf with a start. He rubbed his eyes and stretched his arms over his head, yawning, then looked toward the blankets where Brietta had been sleeping. His heart skipped a beat when he discovered that she was no longer there. Bolting to his feet, he snatched up the blankets and stared at the ground where she had lain, so beautiful, so trusting. . . .

"I trust her so much and she flees into the night from me?" Running Wolf shouted, tossing the blankets angrily back to the ground. "This woman who is the world to me thinks so little of me? Is it because I am not as handsome as other warriors, or as gifted with warrior strength? Or is it because I am Cherokee, not white?"

He clenched his hands into tight fists at his sides. "Or was it the white man! Patrick!" he hissed. "Did he backtrack and steal her?"

Seeing slight traces of light along the horizon, proof that daybreak was arriving much too quickly for a brave who was not in his assigned place at the City of Peace, Running Wolf could not go after Patrick. That would take too much time. And he could not let foolish desires for a woman foil his plans to be free of the City of Peace. It was only a matter of weeks before his time of atonement would be past.

"I'll return to the City of Peace now, and when I am set free of the bondages of my people, I will go and find her. I will return her to the land of the Cherokee with me," he whispered to himself as he stamped out the smouldering fire and rolled up his blankets. He rushed to where he had left the horses tethered, paling when he discovered they were gone.

"*U-yo-i!*" he cried. "You even steal my beloved **Appaloosa?**"

271

His head hung, he began walking somberly in the direction of the City of Peace. He had dreamed of Rachel becoming his wife—his Cherokee princess!

Now he doubted that he would ever see her again, much less hold her—and keep her.

CHAPTER NINETEEN

I believe love, pure and true,
Is to the soul a sweet, immortal dew
That gems life's petals in its hour of dusk.

—*Townsend*

Freshly bathed, the stench of the *pe-tsa-ni* washed from his flesh, Brown Cloud walked solemnly toward those who sat in council on rush mats before a fire that was sinking into a pile of smoking coals. His hair was sleeked down with bear grease, and he wore a brief loincloth, as did those young boys who stood back from the old warriors who had been called together by their chief to hold court.

Recalling his own youth, when life was so innocent, Brown Cloud could see himself as one of those eager youths who were standing just close enough to the council to try and enrich their lives, and possibly their futures. As Brown Cloud stepped up to the council, the boys circled around closer, displaying their slender, golden-brown bodies, the bodies of perfect boys. In their eyes he could see eagerness. He couldn't help but wonder if their eagerness stemmed from wanting to see how he was shamed by his chieftain father, or from just being a boy, anxious to become a warrior.

Brown Cloud could not control the hammering of his heart in his eagerness to know how his father was going to accept him back into his life after having behaved so cowardly in a battle that should have brought him back to his father the victor!

But the firewater had been the victor that day. Not Brown Cloud.

Not even Brave Eagle.

And how Brown Cloud was shamed because of the defeat! It would be hard to look into his father's eyes without wanting to flee back into the depths of the forest to hide. Although he had given up the firewater, forever, and the path of his future was no longer encumbered by it, it was the road he had traveled in the past that he could not place behind him all that easily.

Before stepping into the circle of old warriors, his father prominent among them, Brown Cloud looked over his shoulder at the forest and leaned his ear toward it. Since his youth, he had taken omens by listening to the night sounds around him. If he thought he heard a horse or sheep trotting near, that meant success. The cry of an owl, crow, or coyote meant bad luck.

But tonight all omens were elusive to him. All that he could hear was the rustling of the hands of the squaws close by, who were preparing food for those who were in council. He knew very well how the women were experts in making bread called *staninca* with a mixture of persimmon pulp and pounded corn, or *maize*. Brown Cloud hungered for this special food even now, yet wondered if he would be allowed to eat among the old warriors, or be shamed into leaving them.

Brown Cloud's eyes met his father's. He squared his shoulders, trying to appear a warrior whose heart was filled with pride, not shame. His father did not rise as he raised his hand in greeting.

Brown Cloud returned the greeting, so admiring of his father's intelligence and bravery, tempered with the patience that only time could bring.

"Come and sit at my side, my son," Chief Climbing Bear said, touching a mat on the ground at his right side. "Tell me what is in your heart."

Brown Cloud moved to his father's side and sat down. He crossed his legs and folded his arms over his chest, fixing his eyes somewhere above the old warriors whose eyes were on him, in them nothing akin to kindness. But he understood. Word had been brought to the old warriors about his defeat, and why.

The firewater! The firewater!

"I am a warrior who failed," he blurted out, so glad to finally be able to lift the burden of the confession from his heart. He looked quickly at his

275

father. "But Brown Cloud will never fail again. The future is filled with many victories for your son!"

"My son, with every jug of *pe-tsa-ni*, the Osage decrease in number," Chief Climbing Bear said, his leathery face showing no emotion, a look of infinity in his eyes. He had learned long ago not to disgrace himself by shouting at his son. He scolded with a firmness that his son understood well enough. "You know, my son, that drunkenness is considered next to insanity and is a deterrent to building a super race."

"Yes, I understand all of that, father," Brown Cloud said, trying not to let his eyes waver beneath his father's accusing gaze. "Please listen to what I say, father. I vow dedication anew to our people. I will never again drink firewater! I will clear away the cobwebs placed there by the *pe-tsa-ni* and will be a warrior you will be proud to claim as your son. I will make it so, father! I will!"

"And that is how it should be," Chief Climbing Bear said, nodding. "The Osage acquired their sense of destiny and their courage and pride from their forefathers. Always the Osage have been a lordly and dangerous society of fighters and hunters. And so shall you be as lordly—as dangerous to our enemies!"

"Father, your new lodge awaits you in our re-built village," Brown Cloud said, so elated that his father had forgiven him so quickly that he could hardly keep from bolting to his feet and shouting to the heavens of his happiness! "I personally erected your lodge. It is in the exact center of the village facing the Place of the Sunrise. It stands like a blanketed giant chief itself, its scarlet and blue and bright yellow painted symbols awaiting your approval."

He looked at his father's bandaged chest, then back up into his father's eyes. "You are well enough to travel now?"

"Yes, and so we shall, my son, on the dawning of tomorrow," he said. "My son, the winds soon grow cold. Leaves turn many colors. The animals will be waiting for us in winter coats. It is time for fall hunt. Your father is now well enough to ride—to lead his people. Brown Cloud, we will go side by side into the forest soon. It will be time to set carefully tended fires to clear away the underbrush in the chestnut groves to make nuts easier to gather."

"And this we shall do," Brown Cloud said, his heart swelling with pride over being able to sit and talk so freely with his father, knowing that he had once again been forgiven.

But deep down inside himself, he knew that his father's forgiveness was surely at its limit, and that if Brown Cloud did not keep his word this time about the firewater, he would never get another chance with his father again, nor with his people.

Several maidens stepped into the circle of old warriors and placed many bowls of food on the ground before them. The Osage elders began to eat with their fingers from the containers, while a young boy stepped forward holding before him in both hands a long-stemmed calumet pipe festooned with red and white feathers. He handed it to Chief Climbing Bear.

The chief filled the pipe with tobacco and then set it on a sacred bison chip in front of him. He left the pipe there for a moment and shared the food with his comrades and his son.

"It is good that our village is rebuilt," Chief Climbing Bear said, glancing over at Brown Cloud. "There is much teaching to be done, and it can only be done in our dwellings, not in the white man's place of worship." He looked over his shoulder at the steeple rising into the dark heavens from the mission, then his eyes met and held those of Missionary Cutright, who stood just outside the door, witnessing the reunion of father and son.

Chief Climbing Bear nodded, then centered his attention again on his own people. "Our girls must learn the importance of staying at home, converting the fruits of the hunter and fisherman into food and clothing," he said, taking another taste of the *staninca* from his fingertips. He chewed and swallowed, then continued to speak in a monotone. "The boys must be taught to occupy themselves outside the home, to become brave warriors and successful woodsmen by mastering the bow and arrow, war club, spear, traps and snares, and the ways of the forest and its creatures."

He met Brown Cloud's eyes. "Boys acquire both an appetite for praise and the independence to follow lonely winter traplines for weeks at a time. Do you not recall the feast celebrating your first success at killing an animal and catching a fish, my son?"

"Yes, my father," Brown Cloud said, smiling at the thought. "I hear the voice of nature calling me even now, the forest the haunt of the eagle, antelope, and deer."

"We shall celebrate many things this fall, my

son," Chief Climbing Bear said, reaching over to clasp a loving arm around his son's neck. "Father and son. We shall be the leaders, Brown Cloud. Together we shall see that much food is available for our people during the long snows and blowing winds. Our country is rich in nature's food, there for the taking."

Brown Cloud was almost choked up with pride, in that his father would so openly show his affection for a son who had failed him. But he knew that his father did this as a way to prove that he did have faith in him, and he wanted this to extend to all who watched and shared in this special night of camaraderie. Brown Cloud knew now that he never could let his father down again. It would shame not only Brown Cloud, but also the great chief of this band of Osage!

Chief Climbing Bear lifted the pipe from the bison chip and placed the stem between his lips. It was lit from a hot coal brought forward by a young brave.

The chief then raised it out beyond his eyes and offered it to the four quarters, to the Spirit above, and to Mother Earth, then passed it along to Brown Cloud.

Such was the comfort and quiet of the moment that Brown Cloud felt the power and love of the Great Spirit as he took the pipe and puffed on it, drawing the rich, pungent tobacco smoke into his mouth. He then relinquished the pipe back to his father, blowing the smoke into the air.

His father nodded, drew on the pipe himself, and passed it around the row of old warriors who sat in council with them. The tobacco smoke

Cassie Edwards

wafted over their heads into the damp night air.

"My son," Chief Climbing Bear said to Brown Cloud, only loud enough for him to hear. "Always remember that courage is more important than killing. Remember that and never shall you allow yourself to hunger for firewater again, for you know that *pe-tsa-ni* steals away courage."

"I shall remember," Brown Cloud said, nodding in affirmation. "Always I shall remember."

"In all things, my son, you listen with the ears of your heart, and look with the eyes of your soul," Chief Climbing Bear softly instructed. "If you remember these teachings, your life will be blessed."

Again Brown Cloud nodded, then accepted the pipe as it was passed to him again by an Osage elder. He proudly placed it to his lips and sucked the smoke into his mouth, aware that his father had motioned for a young brave to step forth, then sent him away quickly with a message to Missionary Cutright.

When Brown Cloud handed the pipe to his father, he looked warily at the white man whose long black robe swirled around him as he walked toward the conclave of Osage warriors. Within his heart he felt the betrayal that he had felt the day his father had told the man of God that if he brought enough gifts, the enslaved white woman would be his. He had given Brown Cloud no say in the matter, though she was his personal captive!

Then, as now, it made hatred enter Brown Cloud's soul at the sight of the white man. In him, he recalled the white woman all too well and how she had caused so much heartache between himself and his friend, Brave Eagle!

And was it to be now as before? Was the white man going to take away his moment of triumph with his father? The white man sitting in council with the Osage, drawing the attention of the chief away from his son, was another blatant interference!

Missionary Cutright sat down beside Chief Climbing Bear as room was made for him at the chief's left side. "It is kind of you to include me in your time of council," he said, smiling at Chief Climbing Bear.

Feeling eyes on him, Missionary Cutright looked past the chief at Brown Cloud. He smiled kindly at him, even though he could see a keen dislike for himself in the Osage warrior's eyes. "And Brown Cloud, it is kind of you, also, to include me," he said, reaching a hand to Brown Cloud's shoulder, wincing somewhat when he felt the muscles tighten beneath his fingers. "It is good to see you again."

Brown Cloud did not respond in kind, instead brushing the missionary's hand aside.

"And the white woman?" Missionary Cutright dared to say. "Is she in safe hands?"

This sparked Brown Cloud's response. "Do not speak of her to me," Brown Cloud said, glaring at Missionary Cutright. "She has caused nothing but trouble for me and my people!"

Brown Cloud could feel questioning eyes on him and looked slowly at his father, then looked quickly away and stared into the fire as his father and the holy man began talking again, soon forgetting Brown Cloud's presence.

"It is with a humble heart that I thank you for taking my people in during their time of trouble," Chief Climbing Bear said. "One day I wish to repay you."

"Repayment is not necessary," Missionary Cutright said, watching warily as the chief refilled his pipe, fearing that he would be asked to share a smoke with the chief. He taught that the pleasure of tobacco was a sin, yet if he refused to accept the offer to share a smoke with the chief, everything that he had accomplished with the Osage would be in vain.

"You will seal our newfound friendship by smoking from my pipe," Chief Climbing Bear said, holding the pipe as a young brave relit it. He sucked from the stem first, inhaling a great puff of smoke, then exhaled as he offered the pipe to the missionary. "For you. Then hand to my son. His heart will become mellow to you, also, once the smoke is shared."

Hesitating only for a moment, Missionary Cutright took the pipe, gripping the stem tightly between his fingers, then placed it to his lips. Having never smoked anything before, he was not sure if he could tolerate the taste, nor the smoke as it entered his mouth. Timidly, he sucked on the pipe, then was seized by a coughing that he could not hold back as some of the smoke slipped down his windpipe into his lungs.

Still coughing, Missionary Cutright withdrew the pipe from his lips and handed it quickly to Brown Cloud.

Brown Cloud frowned as he looked down at the pipe, then at the embarrassed coughing man of

God. He had no choice but to take a drag from the pipe, for his father was watching him with daring in his fathomless eyes. Was this only the beginning of his father's tests, to see if he was worthy of one day being called chief?

As though a small child again, Brown Cloud relished his father's warm, comforting hand as the chief clutched a hand gently to a shoulder. He had so much to prove, as though he were going to be living his youth over again, for living without the firewater would be like starting his life anew.

CHAPTER
TWENTY

My true love hath my heart, and I have his,
By just exchange one to the other given.

—*Sidney*

Unable to fall asleep, Brietta was acutely aware
that it was the deadly hour of midnight and that
she was surrounded by a dense forest filled with
nocturnal creatures—screech owls, big-horned
owls, bobcats, and timber wolves. She tossed and
turned restlessly in her blankets spread close to
the dying embers of the campfire, aware also that
Brave Eagle was awake beside her, watching her in
her failed efforts to go to sleep.

Smiling sheepishly up at him, she crept into his
arms, snuggling next to him, relishing his close-

ness. Soon she drifted off into a fitful sort of sleep, but the night noises had stirred up too many bad memories, and there was no way to stop the nightmares once they began.

She was back home with Ray and Patrick. Rachel was nowhere to be found. Desperate to find her sister, Brietta was fighting off both her uncle's pawing hands, loathing their touches and the obscene jokes they were teasing her with. Finally getting free, she ran from the cabin into the dark pits of night. Her eyes were wild as she peered into the forest and heard someone sobbing in its dark, haunting depths. Rachel! It had to be Rachel!

She started to run toward the sound, but rough hands suddenly stopped her. She was forced around to look up into the evil eyes of her Uncle Ray, then over at Patrick who held a rope within his filthy hands. As Patrick grew closer to her with the rope, twisting and jerking it as he laughed, she again broke free and began running toward the continuing sounds of sobs.

But again she was stopped, this time tackled by her Uncle Patrick, who pinned her to the ground and leered down at her, revealing his yellow teeth when he laughed. She felt ill at her stomach when Patrick's hand tore the bodice of her dress away and Ray touched her familiarly on her breasts.

Then Rachel was suddenly there with a pitchfork. Brietta watched, screaming as her sister plunged the pitchfork into the backs of their uncles, over and over again.

Brietta awakened, screaming, her brow beaded with perspiration. Brave Eagle swept her more tightly within his powerful arms. "It is all right, *o-ge-ye*," he murmured, gently stroking her hair. "You are safe. You are with your husband. Never shall Brave Eagle allow harm to come to you."

"But what of my sister?" Brietta sobbed, clinging to Brave Eagle. "I just had such a horrible nightmare. My sister was—was forced to do something so out of character. She was forced to kill—"

Brave Eagle leaned over Brietta and placed a finger to her lips, silencing her troubled words. "It was only a dream," he said, looking devotedly down at her.

"But what if Running Wolf doesn't get back to the City of Peace soon enough to look out for her?" Brietta softly cried. "She would be alone again, at the mercy of everyone and anything!"

"Your dreams have filled your heart with so much that you have no control over," Brave Eagle said, turning to face her. "You must learn to place trust in the Great Spirit. He is all things to everyone."

"Sometimes I forget that so much can be resolved through prayer," Brietta murmured, remembering the teachings of her mother as she read aloud from the Bible every night. She looked up at Brave Eagle, somber. "I have learned of late not to trust. How will I ever know that my sister is safe unless I go and see for myself that she is?"

"You shall see soon," Brave Eagle said, drawing her lips close to his. "*O-ge-ye*, perhaps it would be best for you to talk at length about your sister—about your life before we met. That will help purge your soul and heart of hurts and lonelinesses."

"Perhaps so," Brietta said, his arm comfortably around her waist again. She leaned against him, watching the coals of the campfire glowing as though lanterns were lit beneath them. "When we lived in St. Louis, my family was so happy. It was my sister, my father, my mother, and I. We were happy and devoted to one another."

She cleared her throat and wiped a misty tear from her eye. "We lived on a bluff overlooking the Mississippi River," she continued. "Rachel and I would sit for hours on the bluff watching the paddlewheelers plow their way through the muddy waters. Sometimes we saw Indians canoeing to the shores to trade their furs. Always I was most intrigued by the Indians." She smiled shyly over at Brave Eagle. "Like you, my husband, they were always so . . . handsome."

A tinge of jealousy swept through Brave Eagle. He stiffened his shoulders as he frowned down at Brietta. "You find me more handsome than those?" he asked, his voice drawn.

"Oh, yes," Brietta said, turning to give him a big hug. "Always, my darling. Never could anyone be as handsome as you, dark-skinned or white."

Brave Eagle's lips quivered into a smile, then he drew her close to his side again. "*O-ge-ye*, you speak so fondly of this place you call St. Louis," he said. "Why did you ever leave?"

"My father was the adventurous sort," Brietta murmured, her eyes misting again at the thought of her father, once so robust and alive, someone she had put on a pedestal because she admired him so. "When he heard that the steamboats came as far south as Arkansas, and that land was plentiful in the Ozarks, he decided that we would leave

288

civilization as we had always known it and try our luck in the wilderness."

"I have seen these vessels riding the waters," Brave Eagle said. "And you traveled on this strange floating house?"

"No," she said softly. "My father decided against it, after all. He thought it would be better to travel by wagon, saying that it would be more adventurous and he could take more of his possessions than he would have been allowed to carry on the riverboat."

She coughed into the palm of her hand, fighting back a growing lump in her throat at the thought of that day when they loaded their wagons and left for Arkansas. "That the riverboats came to the wilderness was more of a comfort to him than anything," she said. "He knew, deep down, that if he ever wanted to return his family to St. Louis, it could be done quickly by paddlewheeler."

"But he was killed," Brave Eagle said, running his hands down the full length of her arm in an effort to comfort her. "And so was your mother."

"Yes," Brietta said, almost choking in the word. "One morning, when I awakened, I went to their wagon and—and they were dead."

"And you thought it was either the Osage or Cherokee who killed them?"

A sudden hate filled her eyes. "Not truly," she said in a near whisper. "Somehow I always suspected my uncles. But there was no proof."

"Your uncles," Brave Eagle said. "Why were they traveling with you and your family? They were evil men. You are a woman of peace."

"My father felt that we needed the extra men, feeling safer in numbers," Brietta said bitterly. "He said that he preferred paying his own kin than strangers. So my uncles came along, all along plotting against my family."

Brietta sighed and leaned more heavily against Brave Eagle. "The night before I found my parents dead, my sister and I had taken a bath in the river, and after we were dried off and dressed again, we found two baby opossums, orphaned," she said, recalling the thrill of holding the tiny furry animals in the palm of her hand. "I took one. Rachel took the other. We were going to raise them, as pets." She laughed softly. "Rachel took one to bed with her in her bedroll, and I took the other. It was so sweet with the tiny thing snuggling next to me, as though I was its mother. I would have raised it and loved it, had it not been . . ."

She stopped, hate filling her eyes. "I'm sure my uncles are responsible for the death of the opossums," she said venomously. "Rachel and I awakened one day right after our parents' deaths and couldn't find the opossums anywhere. We searched and searched." She swallowed hard. "Then we found them. Their heads had been chopped off."

Brave Eagle felt Brietta's anger, for he never killed an animal, unless it was to use the animal's pelt for warmth, or its flesh for food for his people. "You have been put through much unhappiness," he said. "Brave Eagle is sorry for that."

Wiping tears from her eyes, Brietta looked up at Brave Eagle. "Tell me about yourself," she murmured. She moved around to face him, glad to have a reason to laugh when he lifted her on his lap so that she had to place her legs about his waist. She leaned close to him, twining her arms about his neck. "Tell me, Brave Eagle. I want to know about you. About your people."

With her so close, her trusting eyes gazing into his so lovingly, and her body so vulnerable on his lap, Brave Eagle was finding it hard to concentrate, much less speak. "My people?" he said, pushing a fallen lock back from her brow with a feathering touch of his hand.

"Yes, your people," Brietta said. "You are friends with the white community, yet the Osage are your enemies. Why is that, Brave Eagle? Why can't everyone live in peace and harmony?"

"The Osage believe they are a superior power and continue to fight for that title," Brave Eagle said scornfully. "The Cherokee made peace with the white man so that their Cherokee women and children may not live in fear. We did not want blood spilled on our own land. Many years ago the Cherokee voted at the council for peace."

"And you do not regret that decision?" Brietta asked, seeing a tinge of sadness in the depths of Brave Eagle's eyes as he spoke, his voice solemn.

He turned his gaze to her. He ran his hands gently across her silken cheeks. "How could you ask that?" he said. "Had I not been living in peace with the white community, never would I have been given the peace I have found while holding you in my arms."

"But surely you do feel some anger for having been crowded off so much of your land," Brietta said, melting inside as his hands roved from her face to tenderly cup her breasts through her dress.

"At one time, great herds of buffalo were everywhere," Brave Eagle said, looking across Brietta's shoulder into the dark gloom of night. "Every acre was covered, until in the dim distance they became one black mass extending to the horizon."

His eyebrows knit together into a frown as he once again gazed at Brietta. "The Cherokee shared this land with the settlers, not understanding the white man's concept of ownership, intending only to lend them the use of the land. You see, the land belongs to the tribe as a whole, not to individuals," he said. "As more white men came, they drained the land. Being peaceable and intelligent, we adapted as best we could. To take the warpath with them was but to follow the road to extermination. To save our people from that doom, our warriors were persuaded to put aside their bows and their lances, to make peace with the white man and learn his ways."

"But the Osage didn't," Brietta said. "Yet you have mentioned that you and Brown Cloud were friends. How could that be? You are so different. Brown Cloud even scalped my uncle. You could never do anything as cruel and cold-hearted as that. How could you have ever respected Brown Cloud?"

"Our relationship goes far back into our youth," Brave Eagle said, feeling at peace with Brietta while sharing his past with her. A wife should know all things of her husband. "To our shared boyhood visions."

Brietta scooted closer to him and locked her fingers together behind his neck. "Tell me of your visions, Brave Eagle," she said, her eyes wide with curiosity.

Brave Eagle looked past her again, into the shadowy mists of the forest. "It was not unlike tonight when I left my village and made my way into the forest to seek my vision," he said in a monotone. "For two days and nights I was there. I walked and walked, then sought a place high above the trees on a butte, where I could become one with the heavens. There I began my prayers, asking that a sign be sent to me so that I could know that it was time to leave my boyhood behind me and become a man."

"And it happened?" Brietta said. "You saw a vision?"

"Not only I, but also Brown Cloud," Brave Eagle said, recalling so vividly the moment Brown Cloud had spoken behind him. "We saw the eagle's flight into a mass of dark clouds at the same time. I took the name Brave Eagle because the eagle was brave to fly into the face of such a dark cloud. To interlock our futures forever, Brown Cloud took his name from the cloud. From that moment on, we were destined to be friends, although from separate tribes and cultures."

"That's a beautiful story," Brietta said, sighing.

"A story that has now become ugly," Brave Eagle said, his voice a low hiss. "Because of Brown Cloud's love for *pe-tsa-ni*, everything has changed between us. Had he not unthinkingly told one of his warriors about our special friendship in his drunken state, there would have been no need for Running Wolf to be sent to the City of Peace to atone for my sin of friendship with an Osage warrior. No one would have ever known. Brown Cloud and I spent times together in secret— hunting, swimming, laughing. Now there is no more laughter. Just suspicion, hate, and sadness between friends who are friends no longer."

"Running Wolf was sent to atone for your sin," Brietta puzzled. "Why, Brave Eagle? Why not you?"

"A great warrior is not allowed to atone personally for his crime," Brave Eagle explained. "I am the next-chief-in-line. By family agreement, my blood guilt was shifted to my cousin as scapegoat, and so he has been this past two years hiding from vengeance."

He chuckled to himself. "He is a tricky one, my cousin," he said. "He has eluded many while coming and going from his place of hiding." His smile faded. "Soon he will be returning to our village to be judged again. It would be best if he were forgiven of all wrongdoing. We need all of our warriors to assist in bringing in food for the long season of cold winds and snows."

"Your hunt will begin soon?" Brietta asked, easing from his lap to wriggle up close beside him. She relished the feel of his arm as he wrapped it around her waist.

"When the colors appear in the trees, then the Cherokee warriors will paint their horses yellow and will wear a garb of yellow so that when fringing the edges of the forest we cannot be distinguished from the leaves of the dying year," he said. "The time is soon when I will leave you for the hunt, *o-ge-ye*. But my heart will be lonely until I return to your arms."

"I will be waiting for you with much eagerness in my heart," Brietta said, looking adoringly up at him. "I shall keep your blankets warmed, my love, until your return."

Brave Eagle smiled down at her, ready to kiss her, but discovered that her eyes were fluttering closed. He realized that she was exhausted and needed sleep more than lovemaking. Now that she had promised herself to him, and he believed that she was sincere, they had forever to be lovers.

CHAPTER TWENTY-ONE

I will not let thee go;
I hold thee by too many bonds.

—*Bridges*

Rachel awakened with a start. From her pallet of furs, she peered unblinkingly around her, her body rigid with fright. Then it came to her as, beneath the light of the glowing embers in the firepit, she began recognizing the cavern in which she had been left for safekeeping. A shiver encased her as she rose to a sitting position, wondering just how long she had been asleep. And where was Running Wolf? He had promised that he would return. His promise had seemed genuine. It had given her a measure of peace and hope in this, her time of despair and loneliness.

But the peacefulness within herself had been short-lived. Now awake from a troubled sleep that had been filled with nightmares about her beloved sister, she was beginning to worry that something had happened to the Indian to whom she had given her trust.

What would happen to her then?

Sitting in the cavern, vulnerable to whoever might happen along and detect the smoke from the campfire, she felt like a trapped animal.

"What should I do?" Rachel whispered to herself, running her hands through her tangled dark hair. She looked into the dark depths of the cavern behind her, then looked warily at the entrance, seeing the dark heavens and the shadowed forest beyond.

Where would she be safer, she wondered. Out there among the wild animals, or in here, passively awaiting her fate?

"I can't wait here any longer," she said, choking on a sob of fear. "I must get away. Perhaps I can find Brietta if I wander long enough in the forest." She stifled a sob behind her hand. "Oh, Brietta, where are you? Will I ever see you again?"

She rose shakily to her feet and let her gaze settle on a bundle of Running Wolf's buckskin clothes that were rolled neatly up against the wall of the cave. She tore into the bundle, her heart pounding as she sorted the contents out. She smiled. The Indian was of slight build, which was an advantage to her. She found a fringed shirt and breeches that did not look all that much larger than what she would wear. She slung them across her arms and picked up a pair of moccasins; they also might fit if she stuffed the toes with grass.

"I shall enter the darkness of night dressed like a man," she said aloud, feeling more confident as the moments passed. "Should the moon cast my shadow against the ground, it shall be the appearance of a man should anyone happen along and see me."

Breathlessly, she changed her clothes and slipped her feet into the moccasins. Then, with trembling fingers, she plaited her hair into two tight braids down her back.

When that was done, she stared down at the ashes that outlined the firepit. Remembering the tales of Indians sometimes blackening their faces with ash for various reasons, she knelt before the firepit and sank her hands into the cooled ashes, then spread the soot onto her face. She would blend into the darkness of night, as though an extension of it!

"A weapon," she whispered to herself, wiping the remains of the ash from her hands as she stood up again. Her eyes searched around her, then stopped when she saw something gleaming from beneath a layer of animal pelts.

"A knife!" she said, her pulse racing. She threw the pelts aside and grabbed the knife by the handle. She eyed it warily, not wanting to let it give her a false sense of security. To kill with a knife one must get very close to the enemy. But it was better than no weapon at all!

Taking one last look around the cavern, wondering again about Running Wolf's welfare, a strange sadness swept through her. She would never forget the kindness in his eyes, in his touch, in his voice. If she allowed herself, she could even envision what it might be like to be kissed by him, to be held within his arms, to be told that he loved her. . . .

Shaking off foolish thoughts, knowing that the Indian could never mean anything to her, she fled from the cavern into what seemed the pits of hell, so fiendishly dark and quiet was it as she entered the forest.

The low branches of the trees above her seemed to be twisted, grotesque arms. Eyes shining in the night from the distance sent spirals of fear throughout her. Holding the knife stiffly at her side, Rachel plowed her way on through the thick vegetation, crying out in pain when she became entangled in some blackberry vines, the thorns piercing the buckskin fabric of her breeches. Whenever she tried to dislodge one briar, another would take hold.

And then she heard the neighing of a horse through the foliage, and her heart jumped up into her throat. She stopped her assault on the briars, now afraid to move. She bent an ear in the direction from which she had heard the sound and this time heard nothing. Had she imagined hearing the horse?

Everything was so quiet. So eerily quiet . . .

And then another soft neigh broke through the silence. Panic seized Rachel. Where there was a horse, there was a rider! And out in this forsaken wilderness, all that she could expect was a man!

And she would not let herself believe that it might be Running Wolf. The forest was large. She would not be lucky enough to come across Running Wolf in this vastness!

Rachel took the knife and frantically cut the briars away from her legs, then moved ahead with caution. A smile smoothed out her troubled features when the horse had not met her approach from any direction.

"It must be tethered, not loose and traveling!" she whispered to herself. "Perhaps its owner is asleep! If I can sneak up and steal the horse, my travels will be hastened!"

She had never been as brazen before, having always depended on Brietta for anything akin to being adventurous, and Rachel did not look forward to the chore ahead. She was not at all skilled at riding a horse. If she did even manage to mount the horse, how on earth could she stay atop it? And in which direction would she direct it? In the Ozark wilderness, everything looked the same.

North looked south. West looked east. Even now she didn't know in which direction she was traveling.

Pushing her way through the darkness, her breath caught in her throat when she heard the horse whinnying again, this time surely so close that she could reach a hand out and touch it. She tried to adjust her eyes to the looming darkness, but the moon and its guiding light were hidden from view by the thick foliage overhead.

Suddenly she was taken offguard when she ran bodily into the horse. She stepped quickly away when it bolted from fright and emitted a loud, snappish snort, followed by another whinny.

"There, there," Rachel whispered, after composing herself. She focused her eyes and made out the large figure of the beast. Laying the knife on the ground at her feet, she reached out a trembling hand, palm-side up, testing to see how friendly the horse was by letting its snout nuzzle her hand. She was relieved that it was no longer afraid, but seeming to welcome her company.

Rachel's free hand stroked the horse's mane. "Let's be good friends," she whispered, looking cautiously from side to side, afraid that the horse's owner would soon discover her there. But this was a chance that she had to take. She was determined to make this horse hers! Everything else had been taken from her in life. Surely the Lord would be kind enough to allow her this one mercy!

Finding the horse calm and friendly, and most cooperative to Rachel's plan, she searched for its reins. When she found them dangling loose instead of secured to a tree limb, she was puzzled. Who had been careless enough to leave a horse untethered? Or was it a runaway, also?

She held the reins tightly in one hand, placing her other hand on the pommel of the saddle and a foot in the stirrup, and tried to pull herself up into the saddle.

But each time she almost succeeded, she found that her leg just wasn't long enough to slip over the horse, while the other one remained in the stirrup!

Getting frustrated, afraid that each minute she delayed in her departure meant another minute when the owner of this horse might show up and assault her, possibly shoot her for horse stealing, she forgot the stirrup and tried to pull herself up on her stomach.

But again she failed and found herself standing beside the horse, tears close to falling.

She took a deep breath. She grabbed the reins again. She placed her foot in the stirrup. . . .

A scream froze in her throat when she felt the sharp tip of a knife at the nape of her neck.

She had been discovered!

Running Wolf steadied his hand as he held the knife against the stranger's neck. It seemed that he had found the horse thief, perhaps even the one who had taken the white woman from his campsite! Soundless, like a panther, Running Wolf had moved stealthily through the forest. His eyes accustomed to the dark shadows of night, he had made out the figure of a man whose attempts at mounting his horse had become laughable. Running Wolf had had to hold himself back from catching the thief in the act long enough to stifle soft laughter behind his hands.

But it had become tiring watching the unskilled performance of the man. He had ventured forth, the sound of his footsteps cushioned by the thick padding of damp leaves beneath his moccasined feet, and had stopped the thief before attempting once more to make a fool of himself. Had his father not taught him how to ride from the moment he could walk?

Or had he been too ignorant to learn?

What a fool! To be so ignorant, surely he was of the Osage tribe!

Speaking in the Osage tongue that Running Wolf knew almost as well as his own Cherokee language, Running Wolf told Rachel, in a low growl,

303

to take a slow step back from the horse.

Rachel stiffened inside, unable to understand the language being spoken to her. But was she right to believe it was Running Wolf's voice? This man spoke in a low growl, so that only traces of his speech sounded familiar!

She started to reply, but was stunned to speechlessness when her assailant grabbed her by the wrist and slung her to the ground. Her breath was momentarily knocked from her. She closed her eyes and gasped, then again her breath was stolen when her assailant gave her a slight kick in the ribs.

Doubling over in pain, Rachel winced, then cried out when her normal breathing was restored. "Please!" she begged. "Have mercy! Don't hurt me. You can have your horse! I didn't want it anyhow!"

Recognizing the voice and stunned to find Rachel there—and dressed in man's clothing!—Running Wolf's mouth opened in a shocked gasp. He slipped his knife into its sheath and dropped to his knees beside Rachel. Gently, he lifted her head from the ground, getting close enough to make out her facial features in the dark.

"White woman?" he said, puzzled. First she was with him in camp, then she was here! How could it be? Was she two women, perhaps one spirit, and one real?

"Running Wolf?" Rachel said, rubbing her aching ribs. "Is it really you? For a moment I thought you were an enemy. I thought that I was going to be killed."

Running Wolf's free hand roamed over her,

feeling the breeches and shirt. He recognized them to be his. How had she gotten them?

None of this made any sense.

"You are dressed as a man, and in my clothes?" Running Wolf said, helping her up from the ground to a sitting position. "How can that be? How can you be in more than one place at once? First you are asleep beside a campfire with me in the forest in a dress. Then you are here in man's clothing? I shall never understand, unless you admit to being a spirit who has the power to be in two places at once!"

"What do you mean about me being in more than one place at a time?" Rachel said, feeling much comfort in his arm as he swept it around her waist and held her to him.

"Did I not leave you at the cavern?" Running Wolf asked, peering intensely into her eyes. "Did I not then find you after you fled from the cavern? Did you not agree to return with me again willingly, and did I not then awaken to find you gone yet again?"

"I don't understand all that you are saying," Rachel said softly. "I stayed in the cavern until only a short while ago. I went to sleep and when I awakened and you were not there, I became frightened and decided to leave." She glanced down at her attire, then back up at him. "I chose to move through the forest in men's clothes, thinking that I would be less apt to be harmed should I come across men in my travels. Then I saw the horse. I—I thought it would benefit me to travel on a horse, instead of by foot." She giggled. "But I could not mount it skillfully enough."

"You insist that you only a short while ago left the cavern?" he persisted.

"Yes," Rachel said, puzzled by his attitude.

"It cannot be," Running Wolf said positively.

"Why not?" Rachel asked, becoming frightened.

"Because you were with me."

"That can't be," Rachel argued. "I stayed in the cavern, waiting for you."

Running Wolf scratched his brow, getting more and more confused by the minute. "Did I not promise you that I would return for you?" he scolded.

"Yes, you did."

"And you did not trust me?"

"It was not that I did not trust you."

"Then why did you leave?"

"I told you. I was afraid."

"That is not reason enough. I told you that you were safe in the cave."

"It was because of my sister."

"Your sister?"

"Yes. I needed to go and find her. I miss her so much. She is a part of me—a part of my very soul."

Then Rachel's heart began to pound and her eyes widened. "I am beginning to understand," she said, her voice quavering. "The only answer is that you thought it was me, and in truth it was my sister! Tonight you were with my sister!"

She broke free of Running Wolf and stood over him, so anxious she felt dizzy. "Take me to her!" she cried. "Oh, Running Wolf, take me to her!"

Running Wolf bolted to his feet. "This sister," he

demanded. "She looks so much like you that she seems to be you?"

"She is my twin," Rachel said, a sob lodging in her throat. She explained twins to him, then fell into his arms as he drew her to him. "Our heartbeats were once the same. Even now, everything about my sister is an extension of myself. We must find her, Running Wolf. Please."

"She disappeared from my camp," he said, caressing her back with a gentle hand. "I do not know if she fled by herself, or if she was taken. I did not have time to search for her. I must be back at the City of Peace by daybreak." He held her a fraction away from him and gazed into her eyes. "It was my intent to be there with you, to protect you. Woman with skin the color of winter snows— do you not know that I would die for you?"

Rachel's stomach did a strange sort of flipflop, warming her through and through. She stared up at him, in awe of this man who was still only a stranger to her, yet who confessed such deep feelings for her.

Yet did they not match her own? With Running Wolf, she felt more alive than ever before in her entire life! She felt a gentle peace one moment, then a strange need the next!

Afraid of these feelings, Rachel wrenched herself free and turned her back to Running Wolf. "None of this is right," she murmured, doubling her hands into tight fists at her sides. "My first and foremost thought must be of my sister. Nothing else."

Running Wolf took her by the shoulders and

turned her slowly around to face him. "Beautiful woman, I have no choice but to return you to the City of Peace with me," he said. "Your sister's welfare comes second to me now that I have found you again." He swallowed hard. "Let us return to the City of Peace together. I have risked losing my freedom too often already. Soon I will return to my people a free man and be looked to with much respect for having endured so much for Brave Eagle, the chief's son. I want to return to my village with you at my side."

Rachel questioned him with her eyes, torn with needs. She did not want to make demands of Running Wolf that would jeopardize his future. Yet how could she not go and search for her sister?

A searing pain shot through her ribs suddenly where Running Wolf had kicked while believing she was an enemy—a horse thief. The pain was so severe, she grabbed at her ribs while Running Wolf caught her in his arms.

"You are ill?" he gasped.

"Not ill, injured," she whispered, clutching at her throbbing ribs. "When you kicked me, you . . ."

Running Wolf winced, remembering how hard he had kicked her. He swung her up into his arms and carried her to his Appaloosa. "You should not go around dressed as a man," he scolded. "And there are many dangers in horse stealing! Most would not simply place a knife to the flesh of a horse thief! They would sink it deep into his heart!"

"As badly as I feel, perhaps that would have been best," Rachel said, groaning as he lifted her onto his horse. She leaned against him as he mounted behind her, glad when his strong arm swept around her waist and held her in place against him. She closed her eyes, biting her lower lip to stifle an outcry of pain. She held her ribs as the Appaloosa began to ride away in a slow trot, praying that they would get to the cavern soon. She did not know how long she could bear being jostled about on a horse!

And worst of all dreads was the knowledge that the hunt for her sister was going to be delayed. She had to wonder how long it would take her ribs to heal enough for her to travel again.

CHAPTER TWENTY-TWO

I crave the haven that in your dear heart lies,
After all toil is done.

—Towne

Dawn was breaking along the horizon. René and his slaver friends dismounted in the denseness of the forest, then clasped their firearms tightly and crept onward by foot toward Brown Cloud's village. When they came close enough to see the village through the break in the trees ahead, René became suspicious when he saw no signs of life, nor any smoke spiraling up from the smokeholes in the wigwams.

He turned and looked from man to man. "Damn it," he growled. "Is there one among you who is a traitor? The village seems abandoned! Did one of you warn the Osage? Have they fled from our wrath, or are they hiding even now near us in the forest, ready to pounce on us with hatchets?"

Each man cried out that he was not guilty of such a crime.

Having no recourse but to believe them, René turned and peered back at the village, his heart lurching when he finally saw movement among the wigwams.

And then another. And another.

"Sentries," he whispered hoarsely. "*Oui.* They have left sentries to guard the village." A wicked smile tugged at his lips. "Foolish Indians. No sentries are ever enough to dissuade René and his slavers!"

Raising his rifle in the air, René silently gave the command for his men to follow him. His chest heaving from the exertion, his heavy footsteps crushing the dried leaves of autumn beneath them, René moved from tree to tree, occasionally stopping long enough behind one to get his breath, then resumed his venture toward the village.

Then something strange caught his eye. He faltered in his footsteps as he realized that the chief's lodge was not the same as when he had last visited the village. Though sitting in the same place, in the center of the village, it was now sporting brightly painted symbols in scarlet, blue, and bright yellow colors.

And again, as he had observed about the other dwellings, he noticed that there was no smoke emerging from the smokehole, the lodge fire having been allowed to burn itself out.

René stopped and scratched his brow, wondering about the other changes. The village homes seeming to be newer replicas of the older ones.

"What could it mean?" he whispered to one of his men who stepped to his side. "Where is everyone? Why is everything changed?"

"*Oui*, everything seems changed," his comrade whispered back, his drooping black mustache bobbing as he spoke. "But what does it matter? A new wigwam will burn as quickly as an old one. Let us get on with what we are here for, René, then get the hell out of here."

René smiled. "*Avec plaisir*," he said, nodding.

His men following him, René moved on to the outer edges of the village. They slipped behind the wigwams, and one by one the sentries were knifed in their backs, then kicked aside as torches were lit and set to the roofs of the dwellings.

To be sure that no one was left alive, René checked the sentries again. One by one he kicked them over onto their backs, and when he found one still clinging to life, he removed his knife from its sheath at his waist and plunged it into the Osage's heart, wincing when some of the Indian's blood spurted up onto his face.

Shuddering with distaste, he grabbed a handkerchief from his pocket and desperately wiped his face clean. He shoved the handkerchief back inside his pocket, then rose to his feet and stood back and watched greedily as the flames ate away at the wigwams, the sky filling with the black, rolling smoke.

Afraid of what the smoke might attract, René turned to his men. "*C'est magnifique!*" he shouted.

313

"Now let Brown Cloud and his chieftain father lie to us again! They will know the results!"

He took one last look at the damage that he and his men had done to the Osage village, then spun around and motioned with an upthrust of his rifle in the air for his men to quickly disperse.

When they reached their horses and mounted, René was the first to ride away. He was still puzzling over where the Osage were. He would have delighted in watching the attack on their village! He would even have taken some of the women and children as tokens of his attack!

Anything to show them that he was not a man to be toyed with!

But content enough with his deeds, René rode on into the sweet innocence of the Ozark morning.

Brown Cloud rode tall in the saddle, his father close beside him, his horse moving in a slow canter through the early morning light. On foot, the women and children followed the warriors, some elders being dragged on travoises. It was a day to be proud. It was a day to be thankful for being alive! Father and son had been reunited as though of one heart, one soul.

Brown Cloud felt doubly blessed that his father had forgiven him again, even knowing that this might be the last time that he would be so willing to forgive a son whose weaknesses kept shaming him in the eyes of his people!

But today was different! thought Brown Cloud. He had made it all up to his father by seeing that their village was restored. How his father would praise him when he saw his new lodge, facing the

Place of the Sunrise. Brown Cloud had himself taken great pride in painting the symbols on his father's dwelling.

Ah, yes, wouldn't his father be proud of this lodge that awaited him? It had been built with love and respect by a son who would forever feel humbled in the presence of the great Chief Climbing Bear.

Riding onward into the gray dawning of a new day and a new life for Brown Cloud, he only momentarily glanced up at the building clouds and sharp clicks of lightning that occasionally traversed the sky in luminous white streaks. He would not allow a storm to cast gloom on this day of new beginnings! He would not let himself believe that the lightning was a cause of alarm, perhaps a sign of doom on the horizon of life. He understood that most Osage regarded lightning as the act of a great and powerful spirit who occasionally struck at the earth, splintering and splitting trees, giving the Osage cause never to use the wood from trees that had been struck by lightning, lest it bring them evil or bad luck.

But he would not think of bad omens today! Today was blessed!

No! Today, even if he found a feather at a wrong angle in his path, a sure warning that today was meant for evil, he would not be dissuaded from being happy.

No! Today was a day that he would rejoice in within his heart, a heart that had a corner reserved for Brave Eagle, should they one day be friends again.

Riding onward beside his father, Brown Cloud

315

let himself be caught up in the beauty that surrounded him. For so long, the firewater had blinded him even to this. Along the many rivers were wooded glens and brushy valleys that provided food, water, and cover for the bear, beaver, and other furbearing animals. At favorable locations salt springs emerged to attract the abundant game.

Yes, it was a paradise for the Osage big-game hunter. Buffalo roamed the prairies. In mating season, the vocal outpouring of the mountain lion, bobcat, and tall grey timber wolf echoed back from distant haunts. Great scattered herds of elk grazed the open landscapes. In the spring, pigeons and migratory waterfowl paused on their seasonal treks north or south as the gods of the seasons commanded.

A soft rain began to fall. Brown Cloud withdrew a cloak from inside his buckskin travel bag and slipped it over his shoulders, seeing that his father had done the same. He looked straight ahead again, not flinching when the lightning flashed and the thunder rolled. He did not even care when it began to rain harder. In his mind's eye, he was seeing how happy the women and children would be when they reached their rebuilt village with their fresh, new dwellings!

Yes, he was a part of creating a happy atmosphere for his band of Osage again so that they could walk with the Great Spirit along the peaceful valleys and divides—in the wooded hills, verdant valleys and clear streams. They would solemnly and reverently walk where mother earth of the hills held the sacred bones of their ancestors.

The rain had slacked off. Brown Cloud's pleasant thoughts came to a sudden halt when he saw before him dirty smoke spreading like a stain through the forest, hanging low in the wet air that lingered after the drenching rain.

"Smoke?"

The dreaded word mingled with his father's as he spoke at the same moment, wheeling his horse to a sudden stop beside Brown Cloud's.

"Perhaps it is only fog, caused by the cold rain," Brown Cloud said, hoping this explanation was adequate enough to still the dread revealed in the depths of his father's eyes. As his father knew, and so did Brown Cloud, they were only a short distance away from their village. Soon they would arrive at the break in the trees which should reveal their new village, their sentries proudly guarding it.

"Fog does not carry with it the stench of fire," Chief Climbing Bear said, yet did not falter in his commanding dignity as he peered suspiciously at the billows of smoke rolling toward him.

Dreading what he might find under the pall of smoke, listening for gunfire and watching for some sign to indicate whether he and his father were moving into a trap, Brown Cloud slipped his rifle from its gunboot and cocked it. There were many clicking sounds behind and on all sides of him— guns being prepared for firing, Osage warriors preparing themselves for whatever lay ahead of them.

Chief Climbing Bear turned in his saddle and his gaze wandered from woman to woman, child to child, the air seeming to crackle with a sense of impending danger. "Only the warriors will accompany me and Brown Cloud into the village," he said solemnly. "Women, children and elders, you stay behind until you are sent for."

He saw disappointment laced with fear enter their eyes, yet none defied his order. He nodded, turned to look square ahead, then rode onward. "Let us proceed!" he shouted.

Brown Cloud rode beside his chieftain father, his heart pounding. And when he saw the devastation and death as they moved out into the clearing which revealed the village to them all, he could not help but utter the cry of his soul to the heavens.

And then there was silence as the warriors dismounted and began walking around the ruins of the village. Brown Cloud watched his father dismount, feeling ill to his stomach, knowing who his father was going to blame. And couldn't Brown Cloud, as well?

Brave Eagle! Had Brave Eagle not been satisfied to destroy the village once, but must do it twice?

Chief Climbing Bear went to one dead sentry, and then another, his furrowed face dark with hate, his eyes touched with a deep sadness. Then he walked to the center of the village where his new lodge lay in smouldering ruins.

"It was so beautiful," Brown Cloud said, edging up close to his father. "How could it be gone?" He looked around the village and saw nothing but ashes and ruins. "Only last night it was all so—so new. I could hardly wait for you to see it." He ducked his head and swallowed hard. "You would have been so proud, father."

"Pride seems elusive to the Osage, of late," Chief

Climbing Bear said, his voice wavering. "And there is only one person to blame." His jaw tightened as he turned and gazed at Brown Cloud. "Brave Eagle. He is responsible, Brown Cloud. Within his heart he carries guilt for what he does to the Osage. It is the Osage who will erase that guilt! We shall kill him! He shall never be guilty again about anything!"

"It does not seem a likely thing for him to do," Brown Cloud dared to say. "Surely he does not hate me that much."

"It is not Brave Eagle's hate alone you must consider," Chief Climbing Bear said, clasping his hands onto his son's shoulders. "It is all the Cherokee who hate all the Osage. It will never change, Brown Cloud."

"Brave Eagle was my friend for so long," Brown Cloud said, at least glad that he could voice this aloud now. "How could he become an enemy so quickly? So easily?"

"It is because he was never a true friend," Chief Climbing Bear said. "It was only a boyhood fantasy—one you must forget."

The Osage warriors circled around Chief Climbing Bear and Brown Cloud. Their eyes were filled with rage—with hate! Chief Climbing Bear turned and faced one, and then another. "This time we fight fire with fire!" he shouted, raising a doubled fist in the air. "I will take no more! We will go and destroy Brave Eagle's village! We will take many captives to sell to the slavers! We will spare no one! We will show many scalps on our scalp poles tonight!"

The warriors were separated into two groups.

319

One was sent back to tell the bleak news to those who had remained behind and then to return them to the mission. The other warriors, Chief Climbing Bear and Brown Cloud at their head, would retire to the place of prayer, where a slight butte overlooked their ravaged village. Assembled in solemn conclave to hold communion, they would make their oaths to the Great Spirit, while in the distance a warrior beat his tomtom and others droned song upon song.

Brown Cloud looked to the heavens, trying to will himself to hate Brave Eagle, while deeply within his heart he was recalling that very moment they had met on the day of their vision.

Ah, the majestic flight of the eagle!

The wonders of a sudden camaraderie between two boys of opposite tribes—of born enemies!

No, he could never, never hate Brave Eagle.

"How then can I kill him?" he whispered to himself, tightening inside when he felt the eyes of his father on him.

"You must, my son," Chief Climbing Bear said flatly. "Tell me that it is the same as done, Brown Cloud. Tell me."

Brown Cloud swallowed hard, then uttered, "It is the same as done, father."

Their gazes locked. Brown Cloud could not help the tears that shone clear and sparkling at the corners of his eyes.

CHAPTER
TWENTY-THREE

The happy sweet laughter of love without pain,
Young love, the strong love, burning in the rain.

—*Eastman*

The rain had stopped, yet Brietta still lay snuggled close to Brave Eagle beneath a buckskin covering that he had spread over them just before the storm. The thunder hadn't awakened her. It had been the slight brushing of Brave Eagle's hands and the warmth of his breath on her neck as he had slid beneath the covering to stretch out beside her. When he had turned her so that their eyes met, the delicious memory of her intimate moments with him had swum through her like warmed velvet.

As now, as they peered lovingly into one another's eyes, the storm outside had been weathered. It was the storm within the close confines of the buckskin covering that was about to break now.

"And, *o-ge-ye*, did you sleep well enough?" Brave Eagle asked, smoothing his hands along the slight slope of her cheeks, where color was blossoming to a raging pink.

"Yes," she murmured, overwhelmed with feeling for this man she loved with every fiber of her being. "And you?"

"Brave Eagle did not sleep," was his reply as his hands traveled down, now enveloping her breasts through her buckskin dress, causing her breath to catch in her throat.

"And why didn't you?" Brietta asked, finding it hard to keep her sanity while Brave Eagle was awakening so many wonderful sensations within her. "Was the ground too hard? Was the air too cold?"

"I am used to the hardness of the earth," Brave Eagle said, bending low to brush a kiss across her lips. "I am used to air that blows cold against my face."

"Then . . . why didn't you sleep?" Brietta persisted, breathless as Brave Eagle slipped her dress over her head, his tongue quickly claiming a nipple.

"*O-ge-ye*, it was because of you," Brave Eagle whispered into the cleavage of her breasts.

Her heart pounding, her eyes closed with rapture, Brietta twined her fingers through Brave Eagle's hair. "Because of me?" she said, her voice foreign to her in its huskiness.

Brave Eagle shoved the buckskin cover and her dress aside and rose away from her. Placing his thumbs at the waist of his breechclout, he peered down at her with night-black eyes. "I did not sleep because I watched you through the night," he said, slipping his breechclout off, revealing to Brietta his hard, velvet readiness. "Even in sleep you are beautiful. There is a way you move your lips in your sleep. It is as though you are speaking words of love to me while dreaming."

He knelt over her, the tip of his manhood soon resting against her throbbing mound. "Were you dreaming of me, Brietta?" he asked, cupping her breasts as he slowly pushed his shaft within her as she opened herself to him.

She laced her arms around his neck and drew his lips close, not wanting to tell him the truth of her dreams. Too often they were filled with violence, not with the wonders of Brave Eagle's caresses. She prayed that one day all of her sadnesses could be placed behind her, and that her every thought and deed could be centered on the man she loved!

Like now! How could she feel free enough to be making love with Brave Eagle at the break of dawn when it was time that she should be taking in preparations to move onward, now that her sister was not all that far away.

Her eyes flying open wildly, she shoved against Brave Eagle's chest, trying to wrench herself free of his grip. "Brave Eagle, I mustn't do this," she said, trying not to be dissuaded by the hurt look in his eyes. "My sister! I want to be on my way so that I can see that my sister is safe!"

Brave Eagle looked down at her for a moment longer, then crushed her mouth with a fiery kiss, glad to discover that this was all that was needed to melt her resistance. He held her close, resuming his thrusts within her, his tongue darting between her lips in a love dance, everything within him whirling with pleasure.

His hands moved over her, down her back, across her buttocks, then around to the front of her abdomen, where he placed a hand over her mound of crisp, black hair. He moved his mouth from her lips and bent to suckle one nipple, eliciting a sob of fury from deeply within Brietta.

"Brave Eagle, how can I ever deny you anything?" Brietta whispered brokenly, between her gasps of pleasure. She clung and rocked with him, her whole body quivering as he loved her with his mouth, tongue, and the exquisite agony of his thrusts within her.

He surged into her with even more powerful strokes, his fingers digging into her buttocks, lifting her to meet his thrusts with upward pelvic movements. He fought to go more slowly, his tongue leisurely circling a nipple as its peak grew hard.

But he could not delay the inevitable. He could feel her excitement rising, matching his own. His blood quickened until, unable to hold back any longer, he let the pleasure explode through every cell in his body.

He jerked into her, over and over again, holding her so tightly that she cried out. Then her cries smoothed out into something sweet, something memorable, as she, too, reached that ultimate of feelings between a man and a woman, between a husband and wife. . . .

Still trembling from the ecstasy, Brietta's ragged breathing became slower, then heated up again when Brave Eagle leaned away from her, then over her, and began making his way down her body with his lips, kissing her as though he worshipped her.

And then he moved his mouth back to her lips and kissed her tenderly, holding her close, his fingers twining through her long, lustrous hair.

"My wife," Brave Eagle whispered against her cheek. "You are so much a woman! I am blessed that you are mine. So very blessed."

A surge of ecstasy and well-being welled within Brietta as she clung to Brave Eagle. Surely, nothing on earth compared with this moment of peace and love with him. She was even able to brush another fleeting moment of worry for her sister from her mind in order to relish this time with her husband a while longer. Who knew what the next moment, hour, or day was to bring? She might even lose Brave Eagle, then regret not having allowed herself to be in his arms again!

"I am the one most blessed," she murmured, looking adoringly up at him. "My love, how fortunate I am. At a time in my life when I have been faced with so many sadnesses, you are there, filling my heart with such hope and love. Were it not for you . . ."

Brave Eagle sealed her lips with a kiss, then leaned away from her. "*O-ge-ye*, these moments with you are always so fleeting," he said, regret thick in his voice. "As now, we must move onward. There is much to be done."

Brietta reached for her dress. "Yes, I know," she said, easing the garment over her head. "My sister. If you only knew how anxious I am to see her. She has probably lived through many ordeals since I last saw her." She paused, smiling adoringly up at Brave Eagle. "You see, she did not meet a Brave Eagle in the forest, as I did. Yes, she has become acquainted with Running Wolf. But he is not you, my darling."

"If she had met me first, would she have fought being with me, as you have?" Brave Eagle asked, cupping her chin with his hand.

Brietta lowered her lashes over her eyes. "I was wrong to do that," she murmured. She fluttered her eyes open widely and looked back up at Brave Eagle. "And never shall I again. I trust you, Brave Eagle. Totally."

He smiled. "That is the way it should be between man and wife," he said, then glanced toward the river. "It is time for my morning swim. Then we shall travel onward." He looked back down at her. "You will swim with me?"

Brietta looked at the river, a shiver coursing through her at the thought of immersing herself in water that was surely too cold, now that autumn was nigh, for swimming. "I don't think so," she said, glad to have the buckskin dress back on, feeling warm and snug against her flesh. She looked at Brave Eagle as he walked nude toward the river, oblivious, it seemed, to the cooler temperatures. Soon snows would be swirling from the sky. The rivers would be frozen over.

"You will catch cold if you go into that water," Brietta scolded, rushing after Brave Eagle. She combed her fingers through her hair, trying to remove its tangles.

Her words were unheeded. Brave Eagle walked determinedly onward, the shine of the river near through the break in the trees ahead. Sweeping the hem of her dress up into her arms, Brietta walked across the fallen autumn leaves, crackling in her wake. She could not help but feel passion when she looked at Brave Eagle's lean, copper body, admiring his long, firm legs, his wide shoulders which tapered to narrow hips, and how when he stirred, the muscles moved down the length of him.

And then he was gone from view as he dove headfirst into the river. Brietta ran to the riverbank and waited for him to surface. The trees which lined the river joined to lean low over the water, casting their leafless reflections like mirror images of skeletal remains.

Finally Brave Eagle popped back to the surface and began swimming face down, barely submerged with folded hands on top of his head, which protruded just above the surface of the water. Forever, it seemed, he swam in that position; then suddenly he came to Brietta and smiled up at her.

"Join me," he said, beckoning to her.

"I truly don't want to," Brietta said, shivering as the early morning breeze swept across the lake, leaving a wet coldness in its wake. "Surely I would turn into one large goosebump."

"Do you not see that I am faring well enough in the water?" Brave Eagle taunted, waving both arms in the air above the water line. "Come. Taking an early plunge into icy waters before the morning meal keeps the body clean and toughened so that one can endure the cold and changing weather."

"Perhaps that works for a handsome Cherokee warrior. But surely there are better ways to keep a woman's body clean and toughened," Brietta said, giggling.

"Long Man in the River would welcome you at my side, *o-ge-ye*," Brave Eagle said, not to be dissuaded all that easily.

"Long Man in the River?" Brietta said, quirking an eyebrow. "I have never heard such a term as that."

"Long Man in the River is important. He is a beneficial being whose water in the rite of going to the river cleanses the flesh of sin and sickness," Brave Eagle tried to explain. "The waters of the mountain streams must not be defiled. The rivers are the path to the underworld."

"Oh, I see," Brietta said, hugging herself with her arms to ward off the morning chill. "It is a Cherokee myth."

Brave Eagle left the river and began drying himself off with pine needles he gathered up from the ground. "No, not a myth," he said, now picking up his clothes and dressing. "But for a woman educated in the world of the white man, so many customs and beliefs of the Cherokee must seem no more than myths."

"Oh, Brave Eagle, I'm sorry if I offended you,"

Brietta said, going to touch his cheek gently and flinching at how cold it was.

"You didn't offend," Brave Eagle said, taking her hands. "There is much to teach you. In time, you will know more about our Cherokee culture than about your own."

"I'm sure I will," Brietta said, smiling up at him. "I will be your most apt student, Brave Eagle."

"There are so many things to share with you," he said, his gaze locked with hers. "Did you not hear the thunder this morning?"

"Yes."

"Thunder is incarnate in the Thunder Man and Thunder Boys, who rove the hills, flashing and grumbling, but who never strike a Cherokee."

"How interesting!"

"Stars are also people, with downy, feathery bodies, heads like turtles, and blinking owlish eyes."

"How beautiful!"

"The east is the source of light and life—the west, the domain of death."

There was a strained pause, then Brave Eagle swung away from Brietta. He searched the brush for a long stick, then with his knife carved a sharp point on its tip. Brietta watched him as in what seemed an instant he had a fish flapping on the end of the stick.

"My wife, we have meat for our morning meal, but no fire!" Brave Eagle said, laughing.

Brietta looked around her, seeing that most everything had been wetted down by the early morning rain. Then she shuddered when Brave Eagle thrust the cold, clammy fish into her hands after jerking it from the stick.

"You hold the fish," he said. "I will gather dry wood. Soon we will be eating. Then we will travel on to my village. There a warrior will be chosen to take you to your sister at the City of Peace."

The thought of seeing her sister made her forget the fish. She watched almost dreamily as Brave Eagle gathered together enough wood for a fire, then soon had flames rolling heavenward.

Taking a squat pan from his saddlebag, Brave Eagle placed the fish in it, then set it over the fire. He took Brietta by the elbow and led her down on the ground beside the fire and crept an arm around her waist.

"Soon you will witness the Cherokee Green Corn Dance celebration," he said, gazing with a longing into the fire. "It is a solemn tribal ceremony. Only after this rite in the autumn do the women begin to pound the corn into meal in stumps hollowed out by fire. The meal is used to make cakes cooked in hot ashes."

He glanced over at her, anticipating so much when they could start living the normal life of the Cherokee, once this problem of her sister was solved within her troubled heart. "My wife, there is much about corn that I will teach you," he said. "Some is saved to parch in the ear. Every proper household has earthen jars or reed baskets for the storage of these foods. In our house, food will be plentiful. Even now, my garden overflows with crops waiting to be harvested."

He drew her close. "Upon my return, while you are going to meet with your sister, I will harvest my crops," he said softly. "You will see. My gifts to you, always, will be many."

"And I will be a good wife," Brietta murmured, snuggling closer to him. "You'll be proud of me, Brave Eagle. Always you will be proud of me."

Brave Eagle smiled peacefully, within his mind's eye seeing his father, son, and mother back at the village awaiting his return.

Also Brietta's return, he thought proudly. Because she was now one of them.

CHAPTER TWENTY-FOUR

I love your hair when the strands enmesh
Your kisses against my face.

—*Wilcox*

Shyly, trying to hide her bare breasts beneath her
folded arms, Rachel sat beside a campfire in
Running Wolf's cavern as he knelt behind her,
wrapping her ribs with a tight buckskin fabric.
Glancing over her shoulder at him kindly tending
to her sore ribs, she could not help but be drawn
into deep feelings for him. No other man could be
as kind. No man could be as gentle!

And that he was an Indian was intriguing to her,
his slightness not taking away what she saw as
handsome about him. As his eyes met hers, she

could not deny that the way he was looking at her caused her heart to melt and the pit of her stomach to churn oddly.

"What is it?" she asked, her face flooding with color. She locked her arms more solidly around her breasts. She had felt awkward when he asked her to remove her fringed shirt, yet knew it was necessary for him to be able to bind her injured ribs. "Why are you looking at me in such a way?"

"I found your eyes on me," Running Wolf said, tying the loose ends of the buckskin together. "Why were you looking at Running Wolf?" He reached for her shirt and handed it to her. "I am finished. You can now put your garment on."

Her back still to him, Rachel hurried into the shirt, then turned to face him. "I—I was marveling over how kind you have been to me," she murmured. "How can I ever repay you?"

Running Wolf found it hard not to reach out and draw her into his arms. He had wanted to do so from the first moment he saw her. He stepped around her and knelt down beside the campfire, taking a turtle-hull bowl from the edges of the fire, where cooked meat had been left to warm while he ministered to Rachel's ribs.

"Come," Running Wolf said, ignoring her question.

In truth, he would like her lips against his as payment. But he did not think she was the sort to give of such a gift that easily. He would have to go slowly with her. She was a timid, innocent woman —she deserved to be treated in the same manner. "Let us eat," he urged her. "Soon we must leave again."

Holding her ribs and groaning, Rachel eased down onto a pallet of furs beside the fire. "We must leave again?" she said, hope dwindling that he would help her find Brietta. He had his own life, his own needs. Why should hers be placed before his? In truth, she was nothing to him. "Where must we go?" Hope sprang forth. "You are taking me to search for my sister?"

Placing a serving of meat into a bowl carefully fashioned from a large tree knot, Running Wolf handed it to Rachel, but did not reply. "It is drawing near to the time when I will be able to return to my people, a redeemed man, my two years of punishment for Brave Eagle's careless deed behind me," he said, settling down beside Rachel with his legs crossed, his back straight. He plucked some meat from the turtle-hull bowl and placed it in another wooden bowl and set it at his side. "I must go today to check on several wild horses that I rounded up earlier, to ready them to take as gifts to my people, hoping this will make my return even more accepted."

He turned to face her. "You must go with me," he said. He did not want to take a chance of losing her. He had plans for her—plans that included him! "I no longer feel safe to leave you alone."

"You no longer trust me, you mean," Rachel said, looking quickly away from him. She pinched off a piece of meat and quickly ate it.

"It is not so much that," Running Wolf said, looking into the fire, suddenly awkward with his words. Then he looked at her again, their eyes meeting. "It is because I would not only like to have you at my side while I check on my horses, but also when I return to my people. I would like for you to ride with me in the capacity of—of wife."

Rachel was taken aback by his words. Never in all of her life had she been as surprised as now. "Wife . . . ?" she gasped, paling. "Running Wolf, you barely know me. I—I am white. You are—"

Running Wolf cut her words off by placing a finger to her lips. "You are without a home and family," he said softly. "I offer you both. You will become a part of my Cherokee family."

Still stunned by what he was proposing, Rachel could not find the words that would best fit the moment. She did understand the beating of her heart, though. Never had it thudded so wildly as now. It proved to her that she wanted to be with Running Wolf.

But as his wife?

Until only recently she wouldn't have trusted any man in any capacity.

And now? To become someone's wife?

And not just someone. An Indian's? She had always looked on such unions as forbidden.

Yet when she was with him, anything seemed possible.

"I do have some family left," she finally blurted out. "My sister. And she can't be far from here. Even you have seen her, Running Wolf. I must search and find her. Then my decision can be made as to what the future holds for you—and me."

Running Wolf's insides warmed with hope. Rachel had not flatly refused his offer! In fact, he could tell by the sweetness in her voice that she was truly considering becoming his wife! His life would start anew once he left the City of Peace. He would have atoned for Brave Eagle's sin, and would also have found a woman to love and call his own!

And not just any woman! One whose skin was as white and silken as roses in the spring, and whose heart was innocent and pure!

"Your sister will be found for you," he said, moving to his knees before her. He took her hands, and her fingers trembled in his. "Soon. But today we must check on my horses. They are as important to my future as your sister is to yours. Do you understand?"

"I think so," Rachel said softly, caught up in a gentle passion that she had never thought possible. "Perhaps tomorrow we can search for Brietta? So much can happen in a day. I know. I have experienced many horrors since my parents were slain."

"My woman, if it is at all within my power, I will see that you will experience no more danger," Running Wolf said. "You will become as one with the Cherokee, safe and happy."

"And my sister?"

"She will be welcome in our village, also."

"How can you be sure that your people will welcome us so openly?"

"Many moons ago, the Cherokee and the white people made peace, and since that time we have mingled bloods and vows of marriage," Running Wolf said, smiling. "So you see? It is not an uncommon thing—that a white woman enters our village, as wife."

"If my sister can be with me, then I think it

would be wonderful to go to your village with you," Rachel said, her voice lifting.

"As my wife?" Running Wolf said, his eyes searching her face for answers.

"As your wife," Rachel said, not needing any more time to think about it. In this man, she saw a future of peace, of love, of compassion. How could she ever want for anything else in a man? She even had feelings stirring within her that surely were there because of loving him.

She had made a quick decision, yet she felt that it was a right one!

Running Wolf beamed with happiness. He could not help himself—he drew her within his arms and lowered his trembling mouth to her lips and kissed her, then drew quickly away when she emitted a soft cry of pain.

"My ribs," Rachel said, her face flushed more from the kiss than from the pain. She laughed awkwardly. "They are very sore, Running Wolf."

"Soon they will heal," Running Wolf said, regretting still his actions that had caused her pain.

"How can I ride with you while hurting so?" Rachel said, slightly twisting her body around, testing her soreness.

"You will ride with me," Running Wolf said, leaning away from her to finish eating. "I will hold you in place. When we get to the horses, you will be placed to the ground, where you will then only observe."

"That's a relief," Rachel said, taking up her dish of food.

"One day I will be a rich Cherokee," Running Wolf said. "I will raise and breed an excellent stock of both draft animals and saddle ponies. You and I will own substantial herds of cattle in the pasture, and flocks of poultry in our farmyard." He glanced over at her, his eyes dancing. "We will have many hogs. The Cherokee pork is better than the white man's on account of their chestnut diet."

"It all sounds grand," Rachel said, getting caught up in Running Wolf's dreams. "And I will do everything I can to make life comfortable for you. For you to own so much land, cattle and horses, you will need a wife who will help in many ways."

"The Cherokee do not own land," Running Wolf corrected her. "It is on loan from the Great Spirit."

"Oh, I see," Rachel murmured, realizing that she had much to learn. There would not only be the daily life that would be new to her, but also their religions. She would have to learn how to include Running Wolf's Great Spirit in her time of prayers to her beloved Christian lord.

Running Wolf moved to his knees again before Rachel. He brushed aside her dish of food, then took her hands in his. "It is time for us to leave," he said, looking into her eyes. "But before we go, let me sing a song that I heard my father sing to my mother long ago, before they both were taken from me in the dreaded smallpox epidemic that spread through our camp many moons ago. It is a love song, Rachel. It once was my father's to my mother. Now it is mine to you."

Filled with love and sensual feelings that she could not deny, Rachel listened raptly, her heart seeming to melt into his.

"I see my love at the edge of the prairie," Running Wolf sang in a monotone. "She is more beautiful than scarlet or wampum. I will run after her and she will flee as if afraid. But I see, as she turns her head over her shoulder, and mocks, and laughs, and rails at me, that her fears are nothing but pretense. She is more beautiful than scarlet or wampum. I will run after her until I catch her. She then will be mine."

Rachel drew a ragged breath as his mouth moved toward hers, then touched her lips wonderingly. A sweet current of warmth swept through her as they kissed, realizing now what lay ahead of her when she became his wife—paradise!

Realizing that he was overstepping the boundaries he himself had set with Rachel, wanting to reserve their intimate moments for after they were married, Running Wolf moved away from her. "It is time to go," he said, walking toward the cavern entrance. "Come. Time is wasting."

His abruptness caused Rachel's eyes to waver. She touched her lips, still warm with his kiss. She watched him leave the cavern, then scurried after him, wincing when renewed pain flashed through her ribs.

Following him to his horse, Rachel wondered about his sudden quietness, then saw an awkwardness in his eyes as he turned to her to help her onto the horse. There was a short pause between them, and then they both smiled and sighed, the awkwardness broken between them.

"I will hold you secure in the saddle," Running Wolf said, gently taking Rachel by the waist. He lifted her onto the saddle, then swung himself into it, his arm twining around her slender waist as she became comfortable on the saddle before him.

Soon Rachel forgot her painful ribs—everything but riding with Running Wolf as he led his horse across the vastness of an open stretch of land, toward land shadowed by bluffs. Her hair lifting in the wind, the sun warm on her face, Rachel closed her eyes and enjoyed this special moment with Running Wolf, still thrilling inside from his kiss and his vow to care for her, forever. It was a wonderful feeling, to have someone care that much.

Although her sister had always cared, Rachel now knew that it was not the same as when a man cared.

And then they arrived at a serene, private piece of land fenced off from the rest. Within the fence several horses grazed. Rachel saw another horse, which was set apart from the others, then gasped as she got closer and saw its condition. Its head and body were securely tied to a tree. It looked weak and broken in spirit.

"That horse," Rachel said, pointing to the black mustang as Running Wolf wheeled his horse to a stop. "Why is it—secured in such a way to the tree?"

Running Wolf slipped out of the saddle, then helped Rachel to the ground. He placed an arm around her waist and walked her to the fence, close to the horse in question.

"That horse has been one of my hardest to break," Running Wolf said. "By now, the second week it has been secured to the tree, it should be manageable enough."

Rachel paled. "That seems—so cruel," she said, looking at Running Wolf and wondering if she had been wrong to think he was all that gentle, after all. How could he be so gentle with her one minute, and then so cruel to an animal the next?

Yet, Running Wolf was a man! Had not she seen evil in them all, except her beloved father?

"It is not cruel," Running Wolf said, climbing over the fence. "It is the way of nature."

Rachel scarcely breathed as Running Wolf stepped up to the horse and looked him square in the eye while untying him. She then looked at the horse. It had watched Running Wolf's approach with its ears flattened back. And then, to Rachel's surprise, the horse had whinnied softly and, as its head was freed, began nuzzling Running Wolf's outstretched hand with its whiskered mouth, as though they had been friends for life.

Running Wolf smiled at Rachel, then finished releasing the horse. When it was standing free, gently pawing at the earth with one hoof, its dark eyes peaceful, Running Wolf ran his hands down the mustang's withers, feeling the lean, decisive muscles. He had selected the mustang from all of the others, feeling as if it were his own creation. He passed his hand along the mustang's neck and along its back, feeling the lines of the tough muscles, knowing that this horse would be Running Wolf's gift to Chief Silver Shirt.

At that moment, Running Wolf's future would be assured.

He turned and gazed at Rachel. At that moment even her future would be assured.

CHAPTER
TWENTY-FIVE

Clasp me close in your warm young arms,
While the pale stars shine above,
And we'll live our whole young lives away.

—*Wilcox*

Using the river to silence their approach, the Osage warriors rode toward the outer fringes of the Cherokee village, its semi-circle of dwellings now in sight. His hand clasped hard to a rifle, Brown Cloud rode beside his chieftain father, his heart thumping wildly within his chest. Memories of secret times of laughter and games with Brave Eagle swept through his mind, paining him deep into the core of himself, for he now had no choice but to consider Brave Eagle a staunch enemy. If they came face to face during the battle, this time no life could be spared.

He knew that one of them must die—or perhaps both!

His heart crying silently of the remorse that was overwhelming him, Brown Cloud had to think that perhaps that last choice would be best, if one had the opportunity to make choices. If they died together during combat, neither would be forced to live a life of regret.

Brown Cloud watched as several warriors rode toward the Cherokee horses that were grazing near at hand. They would be a part of the spoils of war, along with the many Cherokee who would be abducted to be later sold as slaves.

And then they would celebrate the greatest prize of all—the many scalps that would soon hang from scalp poles!

It was understood that while an Osage was on the warpath, not only was it important to prove his worth as a warrior by taking scalps, it also enhanced his stature in the eyes of the village maidens.

Scalps were treasured. No matter should that scalp belong to your best friend in the world! Brown Cloud had been commanded to take Brave Eagle's scalp. If he didn't, he would lose face forever in the eyes of his own father. Brown Cloud could never then expect to become chief.

A part of this line of jingling bridles and dark, excited faces, Brown Cloud's stallion was growing closer to the village. His Osage warriors had not yet been detected when he caught sight of many old Cherokee warriors and medicine men sitting in the shade, smoking their long-stemmed, red sandstone pipes. He could see children innocently playing. The aroma of smoke was evidence of meals being cooked in the wigwams by women whose day had just begun.

Still there was no hesitation on Brown Cloud's part to ride alongside his father, who was already aware that the Cherokee village was under minimal guard.

Leaving the river, the Osage slowly, silently, surrounded the village, the sentries' throats now cut by Osage warriors who were moving by foot.

And then the horses stopped. There was only the sound of flintlock rifles being cocked.

Within the Cherokee chief's great lodge, Chief Silver Shirt sat beside the fire in the firepit. He was resting his back comfortably against lattice-work supports made of slender willow rods covered by a long strip of buffalo hide. On Chief Silver Shirt's lap sat his grandson, Rising Fawn, his wife opposite the fire from them, cutting out moccasins from prepared buckskin.

"Your father will be home soon," Chief Silver Shirt said, smoothing his large hand down his grandson's velvety black, shoulder-length hair.

Then, while Rising Fawn sat spellbound on his lap, Chief Silver Shirt resumed making a whistle for him from an eagle's wingbone. "You will then resume life with your father, my grandson," he said, smoothing down the surface of the whistle with a piece of stiff buckskin. "You now have a father and mother, Rising Fawn."

"Soon I learn to shoot crickets with arrows?" Rising Fawn said, his eyes dancing as he looked excitedly up at his grandfather.

"Yes, soon you learn to do many things with your bow and arrow which I have made for you," Chief Silver Shirt said, fastening at the end of the whistle a bit of white down plucked from under the wing of the eagle. He smiled at Rising Fawn. "Like your grandfather and father, you will one day be chief. You must know everything about hunting."

"And warring?" Rising Fawn asked, his eyes innocently wide.

Chief Silver Shirt gave great pause to that question, yet knew that it was a normal thing for a young brave to ask about. Sometimes warring was necessary to survive.

"Yes, you will be taught warring," Chief Silver Shirt said, gently patting Rising Fawn on the back.

A great commotion outside, the thundering of hooves suddenly in the village and great whoops that were so numerous the very air seemed to expand with the din, made Chief Silver Shirt's heart skip a beat.

"What—?" He lifted Rising Fawn from his lap, placing him on the floor beside him. "Who—?"

But Chief Silver Shirt did not have time to rise to his feet, to go to the door, to peer outside. An arrow sliced through the entrance flap of his dwelling, then into his heart. His eyes wild with surprise, he grabbed at the arrow, then slowly crumpled onto his back, the whistle sliding from his lap.

Brave Eagle's mother screamed as she dropped

her sewing. Rising Fawn stood in shock when his grandmother became the victim of a bullet that blasted through the wall of the dwelling and lodged itself in her chest. Terrified, frozen to the spot, Rising Fawn watched as she keeled over, her eyes too soon locked in a death trance.

Instinct soon took over. Rising Fawn stretched himself out flat on his stomach on the floor, hoping that at least he would be spared. He had much to learn! But it seemed that he was learning too soon the horrors of warring!

Sobbing, he hid his eyes beneath his arms, listening to the screaming and gunfire outside the dwelling. "Grandfather . . ." he whispered. "Father, I am afraid!"

Aware of something tickling his nose, Rising Fawn opened his eyes and found the whistle that his grandfather had made for him lying there. Sniffling, holding back another flood of tears, he picked up the whistle and held it tightly, recalling his grandfather's teachings as he had carved the whistle with his powerful hands. The white down feathers from the eagle chosen for the whistle were considered sacred. White stood for consecration—for all things pure.

"I shall remember, grandfather!" he cried. "I shall remember! And I shall keep the whistle with me always!"

Outside the chief's great lodge was a great spinning wheel of mounted warriors and horses tossing heads and dust at tearing gallops. As innocent Cherokees fled, the Osage would head them off until they caught up with them, either rounding them up to take as captives or killing them. The crops in the fields were destroyed as horses trampled them into the ground. The livestock was set free, the Osage warriors hoping that they could come later and round them up, once they had a place to take them to.

Brown Cloud had not yet caught sight of Brave Eagle and wondered where he might be, fearing coming face to face with him again. He clutched his knees to his steed while defending himself, wrestling with the Cherokee warrior who had grabbed him from the ground. Soon he got the best of the man. He raised the butt of his rifle and hit the Cherokee over the head, just as a bullet sank into the man's flesh as an Osage warrior's bullet went astray.

Brown Cloud became sickened when the Cherokee brave fell and writhed for a moment, then grew still in death's grip. Knowing his duty as an Osage warrior, he slipped his rifle into its gunboot at the side of his horse, quickly dismounted, and in an instant had swept his knife from its sheath and claimed the Cherokee brave's scalp as his.

Making a show, he held the scalp into the air as he mounted his stallion again. "E-e-e-!" he shouted, fitting his heels under his steed's muscled belly, lifting his stallion clear off the ground, knowing that his father's eyes were on him—and the scalp!

Hanging the scalp on his saddle, Brown Cloud joined the fight again. Fire arrows and torches were now being set to the village houses, and the wind blowing from the south helped the flames take hold. Smoke billowed high into the sky.

Over and over again, Brown Cloud leveled his slim, heavy weapon, took half a breath, and without further pause, sent a ball cracking to its target, the rifle roaring and recoiling against his shoulder. He closed his ears to the cries and screams of the Cherokee, aware now that Brave Eagle was not in the village, or he would have defended it to the end.

Then Brown Cloud felt a presence at his side. He turned and gazed into the eyes of his father.

"It is time to prove your worth to your people, my son," Chief Climbing Bear said solemnly. He nodded toward Chief Silver Shirt's dwelling that was not yet touched by fire. "It is for you to take the Cherokee chief's scalp. He lies dead. Go. Take it now."

Brown Cloud could not hide his tautness, his every nerve ending crying out against this that was being demanded of him. But he had much to prove to his father to atone for his past weaknesses. If scalping such a powerful Cherokee chief was required, Brown Cloud's best friend's father, then so be it!

"The grandson," Chief Climbing Bear said reservedly. "He is to be a captive. He will be sold into slavery soon."

"Brave Eagle's son?" Brown Cloud said, unable to hide his gasp of horror at knowing the fate of Rising Fawn. "Even he must suffer because of me?"

"It is not because of you," Chief Climbing Bear said, his eyes narrowing. "It is because you are a warrior, proving his worth!"

There was little firing of guns now, and little

349

twanging of bow strings, and not much thrusting of lances. For the most part the fighting was now at quarters too close for this. Combatants pounded at each other's heads with hatchets, war clubs, whip handles, and bows.

And soon the battle was over. The grounds of the Cherokee village were spread with bodies and blood, those women and children and Cherokee warriors who had survived now rounded up, waiting for the march to the mission, where they would be held until the slavers came for them.

Chief Climbing Bear reached a hand to Brown Cloud's shoulder. "Go, my son," he said. "The most coveted spoils of war await you. Take the Cherokee chief's scalp with pride, my son. Wear it on your scalp pole tonight with pride! It is a gift from me to you, for it was my arrow that snuffed the breath from the Cherokee chief."

Knowing that this was a great sacrifice for his father, Brown Cloud squared his shoulders and tried to look grateful. He doubled a fist to his heart, giving his father a final set stare of loyalty, then dismounted and began walking to the chief's lodge.

Out of the corner of his eyes, Brown Cloud felt Rising Fawn's weeping eyes on him and it seemed that a part of his heart was ripping away. He had held this child as though he were his own, one time when Brave Eagle had carried him to their private meeting place for best friends to share in even these sorts of things. While holding Rising Fawn close to his chest, their heartbeats mingling, he had felt the same pride as though he were Rising Fawn's true father.

And now he was betraying one who was like a son! Yet, he must! There was no other way to make things right with his father. Nor with his people.

Inhaling a large, quivering breath, almost choking on the smoke that was swirling and blackening the air from the burning dwellings, Brown Cloud stopped just outside the chief's house.

Then, knowing that everything in the village had become quiet, and that everyone's eyes were focused on him and what he must do, he stepped inside the lodge. His heart lurched when he caught sight of the chief and his devoted wife, both staring at him lifelessly, accusingly.

Turning away from them, trying to compose himself for this chore, Brown Cloud tried to block out all memory of Brave Eagle. This was now. Everything else was in the past, and no longer mattered.

Turning back around, he braced himself for what he must do. He knelt and, in one sweep of his knife, had Chief Silver Shirt's scalp.

In the past, when he had procured scalps during warring, a great pride had seized him. But at this moment he felt no pride, no sense of victory over he who lay dead at his feet. Instead, he trembled inside at the thought of coming face to face with Brave Eagle's wrath upon the discovery of his parents' deaths—and of all those others of his relations and friends in this village of slain Cherokee!

Although Brown Cloud had proven to his father that he was a strong, brave warrior today, inside his heart he was a coward!

Wanting to get everything that was connected

351

with this day behind him, Brown Cloud stepped quickly from the chief's great lodge and forced a triumphant smile as he thrust the scalp over his head so that all could see. He evaded the sorrowful eyes of Rising Fawn, who still stood observing all that Brown Cloud was guilty of. Brown Cloud knew that the child would hate him forever, condemning him for being the creator of the worst day of his life.

Chief Climbing Bear slipped from his saddle and went to Brown Cloud, pride in the dark depths of his eyes. He eyed the scalp, then Brown Cloud. "It is done," he said, clasping a solid hand on Brown Cloud's shoulder. "Now let us return to the mission and make plans to rebuild our village. Never again shall Chief Silver Shirt cause our people grief."

Brown Cloud shuffled his feet nervously. "But what of Brave Eagle?" he said, daring to cast doubts inside his father's heart. "As you have noticed, he was not present today. When he discovers what we have done, he will seek vengeance."

"He is only one man," Chief Climbing Bear said, shrugging. He glanced over his shoulder at the Cherokee captives. "There are none left to fight alongside Brave Eagle. And should he come alone, let him also see the swiftness of our weapons." He walked to his horse and mounted again. "Come, my son. We have wasted enough time talking. It is best that we join our people at the mission, to comfort them. Twice they have lost their homes. We must be sure it does not happen a third time."

Brown Cloud mounted his horse, displaying his

scalps as they swung loosely from his saddle. He did not look Rising Fawn's way as the child walked fearlessly among the other captives toward the mission. Brown Cloud's guilt lay too heavy on his heart already.

And he did not expect to be greeted all that cordially by the holy man at the mission! When he saw the scalps, surely he would refuse entrance to the Osage!

Brown Cloud rode alongside his father, holding his chin high, although his spirits were low. When the mission finally came into view, his insides tightened. When they reached the wide gate that led into the mission grounds, he watched as the Osage women and children began running from the mission to greet them.

And then there was Missionary Cutright, among them.

Brown Cloud and his father stopped their horses just before reaching Missionary Cutright and dismounted. Leading their horses the rest of the way, Brown Cloud momentarily forgot the scalps, so happy was he to see his people so happy, so alive, after having left so many dead Indians behind at the Cherokee camp.

Missionary Cutright stopped and met Brown Cloud and Chief Climbing Bear with wondering eyes. Then he glanced down at the bloody scalps swinging from Brown Cloud's saddle. He paled and looked back up at Brown Cloud, then over at his father, appalled to think they had actually killed, then brought their spoils of war to the house of the Lord!

But he was afraid to turn them away. He reached a trembling hand to the chief. "It is with surprise that I see you and your people again at my mission," he said, his voice drawn. "But of course, you are welcome."

"It was with surprise that I found my village burned again," Chief Climbing Bear said in a low growl, refusing the handshake of welcome. He rubbed his left arm as a slow ache began up and down its full length. He inhaled a shaky breath when a strange sort of pain shot through his chest. While he had been watching the attack on the Cherokee, he had become momentarily dizzied, the same sort of pain he was experiencing now grabbing at his heart more than once.

"It is with surprise that Brave Eagle will now find his village just as burned, just as devastated," Chief Climbing Bear managed in a raspy growl.

"You burned the Cherokee village?" Missionary Cutright said, swallowing hard. He glanced at the scalps again, then back up at the chief. "How many survived the attack?"

Chief Climbing Bear glanced over his shoulder at the captives who were just appearing on the horizon. He turned and smiled knowingly at Missionary Cutright, then moved past him, welcomed by his people with touches and smiles of pride, which made him forget the heaviness that seemed to be pressing in on his heart, and the strange numbness in his left arm. When he served his people well, everything else seemed trivial to him! Even pain.

"May the Lord have mercy," Missionary Cutright

whispered as he watched the downcast Cherokee people moving closer.

Brown Cloud turned and looked at the Cherokee captives, then past them into the dark depths of the forest. He had to wonder how long it would be before Brave Eagle discovered the massacre. Brown Cloud's every heartbeat feared it.

CHAPTER
TWENTY-SIX

With happy tears her bright eyes glisten.

—*Symonds*

The day was bright. Autumn was nigh. The forest leaves were changing to brilliant colors. Brave Eagle riding at her side, Brietta clung to her horse's reins, inhaling the wonderful fragrances of fall and admiring the beautiful leaves. They were like a colorful patchwork quilt overhead.

Brietta looked tranquilly at Brave Eagle. It was now easy to accept him as her husband. Theirs was a special closeness, surely a bond which could never be torn asunder. Her contentment frightened her, and guilt flooded her at the thought that she had yet to actually see that her sister was all right. So much of what she had heard was pure speculation. So much depended on Running Wolf.

Brietta put Running Wolf from her mind, realizing that now so much depended on Brave Eagle and his warriors. They knew where the City of Peace was. Soon, if they realized her concern, they would accompany her there, and she would finally know for sure if her sister was there, and safe and well!

"How much longer before we are at your village?" Brietta asked, disturbing the peaceful silence between her and Brave Eagle.

She tensed when Brave Eagle did not answer her, yet seemed caught up in a sudden worry about something. She could sense this by his furrowed brow, his narrowed eyes, and the set to his jaw as he stared ahead.

"What is it, Brave Eagle?" Brietta asked softly, fear gripping her when he pulled his rifle from its gunboot at the side of his gelding, cocking it.

"Things are not right," Brave Eagle said, sniffing the air. He peered ahead, nudging his horse's flanks with his moccasined heels, riding on ahead of Brietta. Deep within his heart, he hoped that the smoke he was smelling was from fires that his people had set to clear the underbrush in the chestnut groves, to make the nuts easier to gather.

Yet there was so much smoke. And it was not yet late autumn, when the fires were usually set!

Afraid to tarry behind alone, Brietta followed his lead. She snapped her reins and nudged the sides of her steed with her knees, soon catching up with Brave Eagle. "Brave Eagle, you're frightening me," she said, looking at him warily. "Please tell me what is the matter."

Then she looked quickly ahead and gasped when she discovered the heavy pall of smoke hanging low beneath the trees, so thick it looked like an impenetrable screen of grayish black. "My Lord," she gasped, her hands tightening on the reins. "What could have caused such—so much smoke?"

Fear gripping him, the smoke too close to his village not to be cause for alarm, Brave Eagle ignored Brietta and sent his mount into a hard gallop into the smoke. When he broke through to the other side and came to the clearing that led into his village, a sickness spiraled through him when he saw the devastation.

The dead! The burned dwellings! The utter silence!

He looked to the sky, his arms stretched over his head. "*O-yo-i*! Where is the peace?" he cried to the heavens. "Why, *Wah-kon-tah*, why?"

Wildly, he dismounted and began running through the ruins of the village, seeing that the only remaining standing lodge was that of his beloved father. In that lodge had been housed his father, his mother—and his son!

As he drew abreast of the lodge, he stopped and gazed with a pounding heart at the entrance flap, seeing a hole in it the size that would be made by an arrow. But it was the silence that was so overwhelming. He dreaded entering the lodge, fearing what he would find. Should all of his family be dead, could he bear it? Even now he carried within his heart the sadness inflicted when his wife had died. Brietta had helped heal that wound.

But could she heal so many more?

Wouldn't that be asking too much even of her?

Inhaling a nervous breath and clutching his rifle, everything within him rebelling at what he had found on his return home, he finally gained the courage to step into his father's lodge. When he did so, he felt all of his reserves of strength drain out of him and emitted a loud cry of remorse, for at his feet was his father's lifeless body, his scalp removed. Across the firepit was his mother. Even she had not been spared!

"Who did this to you?" Brave Eagle cried, dropping his rifle to the floor. He fell to his knees, cradling his father's head in his lap. "Oh, father, had I been here, it would not have happened! I would have defended you!"

A noise behind him made Brave Eagle turn his head with a jerk. When he saw Brietta step into the lodge, he was seized with a thought that made him die a thousand deaths inside. If he hadn't been with her, spending frivolous moments of the heart with her, he would have been here to protect his father and mother! It was because of her! All of it!

Then he paled, turning his eyes quickly around the lodge interior, searching frantically in its dark depths. "My son," he gasped, his voice breaking. A great sob lodged in his throat. "My son. He is gone!"

Brietta's knees grew weak and she had to fight back seizures of revulsion as she gaped openly at Chief Climbing Bear, scalpless, and the lifeless form of Brave Eagle's mother. She turned her eyes quickly away, covering her mouth with her hand, afraid that she might vomit at any moment.

Then rough hands were on her shoulders, causing her to turn with a start to look up into eyes that
were fiercer than all midnight storms ever experienced. "Brave Eagle, you're hurting me," she
cried, as his fingers dug into her flesh. "Why? What
did I do?"

"You are the cause of all this!" he cried, his voice
filled with venom. "If not for you, there would be
no cause for friends to become enemies." His eyes
wavered as he released his grip, turning to stare at
his father, then his mother, an accusing thought
suddenly coming to him. "Brown Cloud. He and
his people! They came! They murdered!"

Still stunned over what he had said to her,
accusing her of this horrendous crime, Brietta
stood there watching him. Then, knowing that she
must convince him of the full truth, she placed a
gentle hand on his arm. "I am not at fault," she
said, swallowing back a sob. "Oh, Brave Eagle. I
am so sorry for what has happened. How could
you ever think me responsible? From the very
beginning I have been a victim, hardly any different than the loved ones who have been taken from
you. My parents too were murdered! And I did not
mean to cause trouble between you and Brown
Cloud! It just happened!"

Realizing that her words were going beyond his
ears, as though she had not even spoken them,
Brietta dug her fingers into his arm. "Brave Eagle,
hear me out!" she cried. "I love you! Oh, how I love
you!"

Brave Eagle looked down at her for a moment,
then brushed her aside and went outside. As he

began walking through the village, surveying the deaths and the utter devastation, he was torn with what to do. He wanted to hurry away and find his son. He wanted to know how many survivors were now destined for slavery. Yet he felt duty-bound to see to his parents' burial.

Brietta ran outside after Brave Eagle. "Brave Eagle," she cried. "Am I nothing to you?"

She was heartbroken when Brave Eagle did not give her cause to believe that he had heard, or even cared. He continued walking around the village, his head hung as his moccasined feet suddenly came across another lifeless body beneath the thick ashes.

Brietta hurried to Brave Eagle and grabbed his hand. "Brave Eagle," she cried. "You need me now. Let me help you during your time of grief! Let me go with you to find those who are responsible for this—this atrocity!"

Brave Eagle wrenched his hand away, turning to look down at Brietta with what she thought had to be a loathing hate. It stung her as though swarms of bees were attacking her.

Stifling a sob of despair, she backed away from Brave Eagle, then turned and fled to her horse.

Blinded with tears, she mounted the horse, then rode away at a hard gallop, leaving behind her the man she loved—and her heart with him.

Tears misted Brave Eagle's eyes as he watched Brietta ride away. Seeing her long hair blowing in the wind in her flight, and remembering her pleas as though they were arrows piercing his heart, he wanted to go after her and tell her that he was wrong to treat her so unkindly. He loved her. Oh, how he loved her! And deep down inside him, he knew that she was not the cause of this, the most tormented day of his life. It had seemed the easiest thing to do—to blame someone! Anyone! And she had been there, the target of his hate, anger, sadness, despair and total frustrations!

He wanted to go after her, but she was not his main concern now. He had to place his people before the woman of his heart. He was now their chief!

Solemnly, he went back to his father's lodge and knelt between his mother and father, reaching a hand to each of their cold and lifeless bodies. He was duty-bound to see to his parents' burials, but not at this moment. The Cherokee belief was that the souls of the dead were carried on a three-day journey back to the stars from which they came. He could go and search for his son and the Cherokee survivors and still have time to return to bury his parents in the proper way.

"Mother, Father, you are now traveling some-where east," he whispered, bowing his head in reverence as he spoke, tears streaming down his cheeks. He was remembering his teachings as a child, when his mother had told him that it was hauntingly significant to the Cherokee that the East was a land of light and sun—the West the 'darkening land' where lost souls found extinction. "I see you even now, your hands joined, your faces blossoming with peaceful smiles."

Slowly he rose back to his full height. "Forgive me, Father," he said, his voice breaking. "Forgive me for not being here when you needed me. It is with a sorrowful heart that I go now to search for

Rising Fawn. And I will find him."

The click of a gun being cocked behind him, in the doorway of the lodge, made Brave Eagle's heart leap with alarm. He stiffened, not daring to make a move, lest it be his last!

"The smoke lured me to your village," René said, taking a cautious step over Chief Climbing Bear's body, then making a quick turn to face Brave Eagle. "And look what I found. Everyone dead or gone but you. What'd you do, Injun, lay down and play dead during the battle?"

Brave Eagle's eyes narrowed with hate and he doubled his fists at his sides. The Frenchman's words sent renewed spirals of guilt throughout him. Was he doomed to forever regret not having been at his village to help fight off the Osage attack? And Brave Eagle knew that it was the Osage. He could not hold this Frenchman responsible. It was obvious that he had just now happened along. And the white pony soldiers had no cause to lead a senseless attack against the peaceful Cherokee!

René glanced down at the two dead bodies, shuddered and looked quickly back up at Brave Eagle again. "It's a shame, Brave Eagle," he said thickly, truly meaning it. He had lost his own parents long ago at the border of Canada and America. They had been massacred by Indians— the Sioux. "But life does go on."

He motioned with the barrel of his rifle toward the entrance flap. "Get goin', Injun," he ordered flatly. "It seems that the smoke lured me here to catch myself a prize for the slave trade. That prize is you, Brave Eagle. I should get a bundle of money for the likes of you." He forked an eyebrow thoughtfully. "Come to think of it, aren't you now the chief? That should count for something to the lower Mississippi landowners." He rubbed his chin. "Or better yet, perhaps I'll send you to the West Indies for an even greater profit."

Brave Eagle glowered at René, then turned and sauntered to the entrance flap and swung it aside. With his shoulders squared and his chin lifted, he stepped outside and faced several other slavers on horses, gawking at him.

René followed Brave Eagle outside. "One of you get off your horse and bind this Indian's hands," he shouted. "And hurry. We've a ways to go before I'll feel safe. It isn't every day that we have an Injun chief on our hands."

"Chief?" the men said in unison, looking past Brave Eagle at the lodge, then down at him.

"Yes, his father is dead," René said, testing the ropes at Brave Eagle's wrists. When he saw that they were tight enough, he gave Brave Eagle a shove. "You walk ahead of us. And best you don't go too slow. You might get trampled by our horses."

Laughing boisterously, René mounted his horse, then nudged Brave Eagle with the barrel of his rifle, causing Brave Eagle to stumble. He glared up at René, then began his steady gait before the horses, his world having just crumbled around him. In his mind's eye, he was recalling the bliss he had found within his wife's arms, then tortured himself with the picture of the massacre in his village, perhaps being carried out even as he had held and loved his wife.

Nothing could ever be the same again.
Nothing!

Her whole world torn apart by Brave Eagle's
rejection of her, Brietta rode blindly across the
meadow. She felt so empty! So unloved! So totally
alone! Oh, how could Brave Eagle have blamed
her? How could he love her one moment, hate her
the next? It seemed impossible that the man who
had held her with such reverence only this morning could now look at her with a total coldness,
even revulsion!

"It just can't be!" she cried, tightening her reins
and drawing her horse to a shuddering, plunging
halt. "He was behaving irrationally because—
because of having lost his parents." She closed her
eyes as tears threatened to spill from them again.
"And not only his parents, but also his son." She
opened her eyes wildly. "And where were the rest
of his people who were not slain? Will they be sold
into slavery?"

Turning her horse back in the direction whence
she had just traveled, she nudged the sweating
animal with her knees. "Giddyup!" she shouted,
snapping her reins against the animal's sides. She
would return to her beloved. Even if he ordered
her away again, she would not go. He was alone.
He was in total despair. He needed her. And she
would not let him deny himself that need!

Riding into the wind, smelling the smoke again,
she realized that she was nearing the village.
Somehow she would find a way to ease the torment in her husband's heart. She could not let him
suffer in his grief alone. She must find a way to

ease some of his pain. They loved too deeply—too
devotedly. Nothing could break that bond! She
would not allow it to!

A sudden panic seized Brietta. She yanked her
reins and stopped her horse, edging it quickly
behind a tree, stunned to see in the distance ahead
that Brave Eagle had been captured and bound by
a number of white men.

"Oh, Lord, no," she sobbed, covering her mouth
with her hand as she watched the slow procession,
Brave Eagle walked on foot just ahead of the
horsemen. As they grew closer, she recognized
René as the French slaver her uncles had dealt
with.

Scarcely breathing, making sure that she was
hidden well enough behind the tree and tall redbud bushes, Brietta waited for Brave Eagle and the
slavers to pass. When she felt that it was safe
enough, she began following them. She set her jaw
firmly, her eyes filled with a determined fire.
Somehow she would set her loved one free!

Or die trying.

Without him, she was nothing.

Back at the cavern, Running Wolf was restless.
Rachel witnessed this restlessness, unable to quell
it by offering Running Wolf a bowl of her freshly
cooked rabbit stew.

She placed the wooden bowl on the gravel floor,
then went to Running Wolf and followed alongside
him as he began pacing. "What is it?" she asked
softly. "Are you worried about your horses? If so,
why don't you take them to your chief today? Make
him the offering. Surely he will welcome you back

into the village. You said yourself that you had only a short time longer to stay in hiding. What can a few days matter? Surely Chief Silver Shirt will understand your need to be with your people again.''

Running Wolf turned to Rachel. He touched her cheek gently. "I do have needs," he said. "But today it is something more that is troubling me.'' He walked away from her and looked from the cave. "Do you not hear the cry of the eagle sweeping down from the sky? It seems to be beckoning to me! It continues, over and over again. Do you not hear it? Do you not see it?''

Rachel moved to his side and eased her fingers through his, this gesture seeming so natural between them now.

She looked heavenward and caught sight of the eagle as it made another sweep downward, its cries hauntingly piercing.

"Yes, I see and hear the eagle,'' she murmured. She glanced over at Running Wolf. "What do you think it means?''

"It is an omen," Running Wolf said, turning to Rachel. "I must go and see if my people are all right. Ride with me, woman. I do not want to chance leaving you here lest the omen mean bad things for you instead.'' He touched her ribs gently. "You no longer hurt?''

Rachel hid a wince behind closed lips, the pain no less today than yesterday. "The pain is gone,'' she said, forcing a smile. "I will ride with you.''

She frowned. "But I will slow you," she said. "As you know, I am not a skilled rider.''

"As before, you will ride with me, on my steed,''

Running Wolf said, hurrying away from her. He thrust his knife into its sheath and grabbed his rifle. Then he went back to her, his eyes dark with worry as he paused to gaze down at her. But he took her hand and they left the cave together, as the eagle still soared overhead.

CHAPTER TWENTY-SEVEN

I want you when the roses bloom in June-time;
I want you when the violets come again.

—Gillom

The sun was lowering in the sky, casting lengthening shadows along the ground in front of Brietta as she traveled onward, her eyes never leaving the procession of slavers ahead of her. Brave Eagle was still in the lead, on foot. She knew that they soon should be stopping for the night. She would be forced to stop, also, but she would not be able to build a fire for protection or warmth. She couldn't let René and his slavers know that she was there, for she would be forced to join Brave Eagle in his future as a slave.

"What can I do?" she whispered to herself, her skin becoming chilled with the evening breeze wafting across a nearby river, through the pine and spruce trees that towered on both sides of her. "Even though I am following Brave Eagle, I am only one person. How can I set him free without getting caught myself?"

Wearily, her shoulders slumping from tiredness, she urged her horse onward in a canter. She feared the night. If she could only turn back the hands of time to last evening, when she had spent such memorable moments with her beloved. At that time, there had been so much promise for the future—their combined futures!

And now there seemed to be no future at all.

Not unless she found a way to save Brave Eagle, and then his son, and his people. . . .

"I must find a way," Brietta said aloud, determination seizing her. She straightened her back and shook her heavy mane of hair back from her shoulders. "I shall!"

Rachel clung around Running Wolf's waist as she sat in the saddle behind him, her dark hair tumbling in the breeze as he rode in a hard gallop across a straight stretch of meadow. She clung harder to him when he entered the forest again, weaving his Appaloosa around tree after tree for what seemed an eternity.

Then Running Wolf led his horse into the river, following it now instead of riding on land through the thick, darkening forest.

A strong aroma of smoke wafted through the air from somewhere close by, causing Rachel's nose to tickle. She closed her eyes and sneezed several times, then fluttered her lashes open when she felt the Appaloosa come to a sudden halt.

"What's wrong, Running Wolf?" she asked, straining her neck to look around him, seeing nothing but what appeared to be a hanging screen of smoke just ahead. Fear struck her.

"Is it a fire?" she gasped. "Is the forest on fire?"

"I fear not," Running Wolf said, peering at the screen of smoke. "I fear it is something much worse than that."

"What could be worse?" Rachel asked.

"We shall soon see," Running Wolf said, sinking his heels into the flanks of his steed, urging it again through the water.

Rachel clung to Running Wolf for her life when he suddenly turned his Appaloosa to dry land, the horse's hooves slipping in the mud at the river-bank, then finally getting a good grip and bolting on ahead.

"It cannot be!" Running Wolf cried, now able to see the devastation ahead. "It cannot be!"

"What do you see?" Rachel asked, hearing the shock in Running Wolf's voice. She strained her neck around him to see again, this time catching sight of smoking ashes and dead bodies lying among the ash. She felt faint at the sight, relieved when Running Wolf stopped the horse and dismounted, quickly helping her to the ground.

Placing her trembling hands to her cheeks, Rachel surveyed the massacre, then looked at Running Wolf, whose face told the depth of his despair. Tears rolled down his cheeks and his shoulders slumped, as though in defeat. She fought back a sob of regret, then went to Running Wolf and framed his face between her hands, leaning his face against her chest as he wept.

"I am so sorry," Rachel whispered as his sobs of grief tore her apart. "Running Wolf, I am so sorry."

Running Wolf wept for a moment longer, then twined his arms around Rachel's waist and held her close, their cheeks pressed together. "What am I to do?" he said, clinging tightly to Rachel. "Am I the only one left of my band of Cherokee? And what of Brave Eagle? Is he also dead?"

His eyes settled on the one standing lodge. The chief's. He allowed himself a trace of hope as he stared at the lodge.

Breaking away from Rachel, Running Wolf walked toward Chief Silver Shirt's lodge, keeping his eyes straight ahead, for he did not want to see his fallen comrades, some of which were cousins, others good friends.

When he reached the lodge, his hand trembled as he swept the entrance flap aside. With dusk upon the village, there was a gloomy darkness inside the dwelling, the fire in the firepit having burned out, so that Running Wolf could scarcely see.

Moving into the dark void of the lodge, Running Wolf breathed shallowly as he bent to one knee and reached around him. When his hand came in contact with something cold, he wrenched it away, gasping.

Then he felt around again, this time knowing that what he felt was a dead body.

His heart thundering inside him, Running Wolf

reached a stick into the sparks of the dying embers in the firepit and set it afire, then held it over the body, feeling faint when he saw that Chief Silver Shirt had not only been slain, but also scalped. Tears splashing from his eyes anew, Running Wolf leaned the burning stick away from Chief Silver Shirt to see Brave Eagle's mother too lying in a death trance.

"She was also killed?" he said, his voice breaking.

Not able to take any more of the sight, he tossed the stick into the firepit and rushed outside, panting hard. When Rachel stepped up to his side, he looked at her pitifully, then ran behind the lodge and lowered his head, retching.

Not wanting to see the cause of Running Wolf's reaction for herself, Rachel avoided looking at the lodge's entrance flap as she rushed around the dwelling to try and ease Running Wolf's pain with comforting words.

"Life is not easy now," she murmured. "But it will change into something beautiful again one day. I know. I had found nothing but misery until you came my way. Running Wolf, you gave me cause to smile again—and to hope. Please let me give the same to you."

Running Wolf's stomach spasms finally ceased. Breathing hard, he wiped his mouth clean with the back of his hand and looked slowly at Rachel. "You are all that is good on this earth," he said, turning to her. "I will smile again, because there is you."

He walked solemnly away from her and gazed at the devastation that lay around him. "But for now, there is only sadness," he said as she moved beside him. He doubled his hands into tight fists at his sides. "And I must find the ones responsible and make them pay!"

"But you are only one man," Rachel said softly. "You cannot do the impossible!"

A soft neighing from somewhere close by made Running Wolf and Rachel turn with a start. Everything within Running Wolf grew cold when he saw Brave Eagle's gelding move into view, its saddle empty. His heart seemed to drop to his feet. Brave Eagle must have met with foul play also, although he was not among the dead here! That had to mean that Brave Eagle was among the survivors who had been taken from the village. If so, there was yet a chance that Running Wolf might find a way to seek vengeance for his people, and find blessings which would make him a free man sooner than planned. He would search and find Brave Eagle! Forevermore Running Wolf would be looked at with favor by all of the Cherokee nation! He could marry his woman, breed horses, and own many hogs!

Turning to Rachel, he took her hands. "I must go and help my people. I must find Brave Eagle who is now our chief!" he said. He looked at her guardedly. "But this time, I must ride alone."

"No," Rachel said, gasping at the thought of being made to stay behind, not sure if she might be the next victim of those who had so mercilessly killed the Cherokee today. "I'm afraid. I can't stay behind. I can't."

"I did not mean to leave you behind," Running Wolf said, glancing at Brave Eagle's gelding, then back at Rachel. "My woman, you will ride Brave

Eagle's horse. I will ride mine. It is best that we go on separate horses this time. Should something happen to me, you can flee."

"I am so clumsy on a horse," Rachel said, her voice weak. "But I—I will do my best."

"You can do anything you set your heart to," Running Wolf said, touching her cheek gently. He nodded toward Brave Eagle's horse. "Come. I shall place you in the saddle."

Swallowing hard, frightened of the prospect of riding such a large animal for any length of time, Rachel smiled timidly up at Running Wolf as they walked to the horse. When he placed his hands at her waist to lift her onto the saddle, he paused, their eyes meeting in a silent understanding. Holding her close, Running Wolf drew her lips to his mouth and kissed her softly, then set her in the saddle and handed her the reins.

"You will be all right?" he asked, his brow furrowing into a troubled frown.

"For you, I shall," Rachel said, her heart hammering, her lips still moist from his kiss. "I won't let you down, Running Wolf." When he reached a hand to her cheek and touched her again, she leaned into the hand and closed her eyes, everything within her melting with the touch.

"I love you," Running Wolf said, then went to his horse and swung himself into the saddle.

Trembling, fear gripping her when the horse whinnied and pawed at the ground, Rachel willed herself to stay steady in the saddle. With reins in hand, she followed Running Wolf's lead and began riding through the village. She careened back and forth for a moment, but when she got used to the feel of the saddle, she rode up next to Running Wolf, warming clear through when he smiled at her.

"You have made friends with the gelding?" he said. "That is good."

"I told you that I wouldn't let you down," Rachel said, gripping more tightly to the reins when Brave Eagle's horse gave a jerk of his head.

As soon as they were out of the village, Running Wolf stopped his horse, dismounted, and began studying the crushed leaves beneath the trees. Then he swung himself into his saddle again.

"The hoofprints travel in that direction," he said, pointing west. "That is the way we must also travel."

"You truly believe we can catch up with them?" Rachel dared to ask.

"Yes, in time," Running Wolf said, nodding. He urged his Appaloosa into a hard gallop.

Rachel slapped her reins against Brave Eagle's gelding, urging it up beside Running Wolf's. "And when we do, do you truly think we can help?" she asked, eyes wide.

Running Wolf touched the butt of his rifle as it lay in its gunboot, then familiarly touched the knife sheathed at his waist. "Running Wolf will fight until there is no fight left," he vowed. "For my people, I will do this!"

A sudden fearful thought came to Rachel. Through all of the terrifying moments she had shared with Running Wolf, she had somehow placed the concerns of her sister from her mind.

But now, while there was time to pause for thinking and worrying, she could not help but wonder how Brietta might fit into the scheme of things in this land of torment and sadness. With so much warfare and hatred going on, how could Brietta have been spared becoming a part of it?

She shivered at the thought of discovering that her sister was dead, or perhaps sold into slavery.

The moon was just rising on the horizon, and stars flecked the dark sky like twinkling jewels. Chilled through and through from the dampness of the night, Brietta hugged herself as she sat on the ground beneath a tree. She eyed the campfire up ahead, just through the trees. How wonderful it would be to be near that fire! And what delicious aromas were drifting from a rabbit roasting over the flames.

Then guilt swept through her, knowing that neither the comfort of the fire nor the nourishment of the food being cooked was as important as Brave Eagle. Squinting her eyes to peer through the darkness, she could barely make out the outline of Brave Eagle where he stood tied to a tree in the shadows, away from the warmth of the fire himself. Brietta bit her lower lip to keep herself from crying out when she saw one of the slavers lift a whip, the crack of it making contact with Brave Eagle's flesh, sickening her.

"Lord, will this nightmare never end?" Brietta cried to herself. "How much longer until the madmen go to sleep? Only then dare I enter their camp and release Brave Eagle from his bonds." She swallowed hard. "Will he even be strong enough to travel with me? How much torment can he stand before blacking out?"

Someone strumming a guitar made Brietta turn back around and stare at the slavers. They were all now sitting around the fire, eating, joking, and drinking, while the one who had used the whip on Brave Eagle played the guitar. The music was romantic, the sort a gentleman would play for his lady. Brietta could not understand a man who could be cruel one minute, gentle the next.

But that he was leaving Brave Eagle in peace was all that mattered. Time. Brave Eagle needed time to himself, so that he could regain the strength lost with the beating. He needed to be strong enough to flee into the night with his beloved!

A crunching of dry leaves behind Brietta startled her. She jumped to her feet and ran behind a cluster of lilac bushes, watching for the intruders in the night. When the moon revealed who it was, her heart sang with gladness!

CHAPTER
TWENTY-EIGHT

Open thy chamber door,
And my kisses shall teach thy lips
The love that shall fade no more.

—*Taylor*

"Rachel?" Brietta gasped, stunned to see her sister with Running Wolf. Their full concentration had been on the slavers and Brave Eagle until Brietta stepped out into full view, the moonlight spiraling down upon her through the foliage overhead, illuminating her enough so that Rachel could see her.

Rachel faltered in her steps. "Brietta?" she gasped, staring with disbelief at her sister, who stood only a few feet away from her. A sob lodged in her throat as she broke into a mad run, Brietta meeting her halfway. They lunged into one another's arms, hugging and crying, then broke away and looked each other up and down, then laughed softly as they held hands.

"I can't believe it," Brietta whispered, afraid that they had already made too much commotion, afraid of drawing the attention of the slavers. "But, oh, how happy I am that you are here!" She smiled at Running Wolf. "I see that he is dependable after all. He has taken care of you."

"Running Wolf is a wonderful man," Rachel said, blushing, turning to him as he came to her side. "And I trust him implicitly."

Rachel turned back to Brietta. "Why are you here, alone in the forest?" she whispered. She glanced at the campsite where the slavers had now retired to their bedrolls, snores reverberating through the night air attesting to the fact that most were already asleep. She glanced at the Indian tied to the tree, realizing that this must be the Cherokee chief, Brave Eagle.

"Why are you here, with Running Wolf?" Brietta whispered, looking suspiciously at the slight Indian, her trust in him waning again. She couldn't help but wonder if he was here to free Brave Eagle or to see that he was killed so that his vengeance against her beloved would be complete.

"We found the slaughter at the Cherokee village," Rachel whispered, shuddering at the memory. "We followed the tracks which led here. Running Wolf hopes to set Brave Eagle free." She looked adoringly up at Running Wolf. "And then his people."

"That is also why I am here," Brietta said, turning solemnly to look toward Brave Eagle. The moonlight revealed that his eyes were open and alert, which meant that he had not been rendered unconscious by the unmerciful bite of the whip.

But, oh, how he must be suffering!

Anxious to free Brave Eagle, each moment that passed pure torture, Brietta beseached Running Wolf with her eyes. "Thank you for coming," she said, placing a hand on his arm. "Do you think we can get into the camp without being detected?"

"We must," Running Wolf said, having recovered his speech after the shock of seeing these two sisters, who were so much alike in appearance it was as though they had stepped from the same mold! He now understood how he had been mistaken when he had thought one was the other!

"How is it that you are here? A woman alone is powerless!" he added.

"I love Brave Eagle," Brietta said, squaring her shoulders proudly. "I had to do something. I couldn't just—just let him be taken and sold into slavery without first trying to set him free."

"You love Brave Eagle?" Rachel said in a low gasp. "You too have found an Indian to love?"

Brietta stared disbelievingly at Rachel. "You mean that you—you love an Indian also?" she said, glancing at Running Wolf when Rachel looked so devotedly, so adoringly at him. "That man is Running Wolf?"

"Yes—Running Wolf," Rachel admitted, seeing within the shine of his eyes that Running Wolf was proud of her declaration.

But this was not the time to enjoy declarations of

love from the woman of his heart. He had many lives to save. His chief's! His people!

He studied the encampment again, then looked at Brietta with questioning eyes. "There is only Brave Eagle being held captive," he whispered harshly. "Where are the rest of my people?"

"I do not believe the slavers are responsible for the attack on your village," Brietta tried to explain. "I—I believe they only happened along later, and took Brave Eagle captive."

"Then we must set Brave Eagle free and find my people!" Running Wolf growled.

He cocked his rifle, then slipped the knife from its sheath and handed it to Rachel. "You will use the knife if required to," he whispered, imploring her with his dark, fathomless eyes.

The knife felt dangerously heavy in her hand, and Rachel knew she did not have the stomach to thrust it into someone, should she have a need to, so she instantly shoved the knife into Brietta's hand. Brietta had always proven to be the stronger and braver of the two of them. Even now, in the eye of danger, Rachel could not envision herself being brave enough to kill a man, even to save herself.

For a while, away from Brietta, she had thought that she was learning all she needed to know to survive. But now that Brietta was there, ready to take over the role of the stronger sister again, she felt as though she were the same Rachel she had been before the flight from the cabin that fateful night when her world had been turned upside-down.

Brietta questioned Rachel with her eyes as she held the knife, then thrust the weapon back into her sister's hand. "It is up to you, Rachel, to defend yourself with this knife," she whispered. "Nothing is the same between us. Since we've been apart, you have survived well enough without me. So shall you from now on."

Rachel swallowed hard, understanding why Brietta was doing this, yet fearing it. When Running Wolf's arm snaked around her waist, she looked timidly up at him, then met his reassuring smile with one of her own. "I shall defend myself, and also you, my Cherokee hero," she whispered, hugging him hard as he drew her quickly into his embrace.

Brietta was engulfed with wondrous feelings, knowing that her sister had found someone to love, just as she had. And the fact that both men were Cherokee made the discovery even more wonderful. If things ever worked out, they would live in the same village and be able to share the growing-up years of their children.

"We must move onward," Running Wolf said, easing away from Rachel. "Step lightly. The dried leaves of autumn can give us away. One sound and a slaver might be awakened. Our deaths would not come easily, beautiful sisters."

Rachel and Brietta held hands as they moved cautiously behind Running Wolf toward the campsite. The first step they took into the midst of the men awakened René. He jumped to his feet, grabbing for his sheathed knife, his gaze intent on Running Wolf, who was leveling his rifle at him.

Seeing the dangers of exploding gunfire, Rachel ran forth and plunged the knife into René's chest just as the Frenchman pulled his knife from its enclosure. He gasped loudly, dropped his weapon, and grabbed at his chest as he crumpled slowly to the ground.

One of the other slavers was awakened with a start by the commotion. Running Wolf rendered him unconscious with a quick blow on the head from the butt of his rifle, then dispatched another slaver as he also awakened.

As others awakened, rising to back away as Running Wolf held them at bay with his rifle, Running Wolf nodded toward Brave Eagle. "Rachel!" he cried. "Take your knife from the Frenchman's chest. Go and free Brave Eagle!"

Still dazed over having killed a man, Rachel stood frozen on the spot as she stared down at René. Brietta saw the state that her sister was in, and hurried to René. She knelt beside him, placing her hand on the handle of the knife. Gritting her teeth, the sight of the blood seeping from his wound dizzying her, she jerked and jerked on the knife, thankful when it finally came free.

Trembling, she wiped the blood onto the grass, then rose quickly and ran to Brave Eagle. When his eyes locked with hers, and within them she saw so much pain and regret, she could not stop the tears from streaming down her cheeks.

"I'll have you free soon," she murmured, cutting at the rope at his wrists, avoiding looking at the welts across his bare chest, inflicted by that damnable whip. When a burst of gunfire erupted behind her back, she jumped with a start and dropped the knife, turning to see who had been shot. Relief flooded her when she saw her sister and Running Wolf still standing, very much alive.

One of the slavers had attempted to draw a pistol and had been shot by Running Wolf.

"My brave woman," Brave Eagle said, as Brietta picked the knife up and resumed cutting through the ropes. "You have come even after I sent you away while I was consumed and senseless with sadnesses? *O-ge-ye*, you know that I did not mean anything that I said. I do not blame you for anything that has happened. Forgive me?"

"If there is anyone who should be asking forgiveness, it is I," Brietta said, tossing the one rope away and cutting into the one that was tied around Brave Eagle's waist and holding him steadfast to the tree. "I should never have left you alone like that. You were in a state of shock. You needed me and I left you, knowing that you did not mean what you were saying." She swallowed hard and peered up at him. "But your words, your accusations, your coldness, hurt me so, Brave Eagle. I had to leave. Please forgive me?"

"Life is full of regrets and not enough forgiveness," Brave Eagle said, taking a step away from the tree when the rope fell away from him. He clasped his hands to Brietta's shoulders, his chest too painful to draw her into his embrace. "Let us never give each other cause again to have to regret or to forgive?"

"Never," Brietta said, choking back a sob. Her gaze went to the welts on his chest, feeling the pain herself, since everything about him now was an extension of herself. "The slaver hurt you so badly," she said softly. "Soon I shall tend to your wounds and make you better."

"But first, *o-ge-ye*, we must ride to the Osage

village," Brave Eagle said, walking away from her, his steps not as lively, his knees weak from the beatings.

Brietta walked beside him. "The Osage?" she said, stopping when he stopped at Running Wolf's side.

"It is the Osage who are holding our people hostage," Brave Eagle said, his eyes locking with Running Wolf's. "And you, Running Wolf—how is it that you are here instead of at the City of Peace? You take liberties others don't. First you are here, and then you are there! Why is that, Running Wolf? Do you feel more privileged than the others who are serving time at the City of Peace?"

Running Wolf stared into Brave Eagle's eyes a moment longer, then very wisely surveyed the slavers again, finding one reaching for his sheathed knife. "Brietta, Rachel," he ordered. "One by one, remove the slavers' weapons. Bring them to Brave Eagle. Then go and unhitch their horses. Set them free. We want to be sure we do not have the slavers on our trail when we leave their campsite."

"You'd best kill us, Injun," one of the slavers growled. "I'll look for you 'til I die."

Surprising Brietta and Rachel, Running Wolf did not hesitate to pull the trigger. The man's eyes widened in disbelief as the bullet entered his abdomen; then he fell to the ground beside René.

"If any other among you wants to test my courage, step forward," Running Wolf growled, feeling Brave Eagle's eyes on him, appraising him.

No one moved, except for Brietta and Rachel. They scampered from man to man and got their weapons, bringing them back to stack them on the ground at Brave Eagle's feet.

Then they took care of the horses, leaving one for Rachel to ride, and bringing Brave Eagle's gelding to him.

"Running Wolf, it seems you have things under control," Brave Eagle said, unfastening the saddle bag and slipping the weapons inside it. "You have learned much courage and strength while living at the City of Peace."

"Yet you still condemn me for escaping from time to time?" Running Wolf said, frowning. His eyes lowered. "But of course you have cause to be angry—even to hate me. You must now know the lie I told Brown Cloud." He raised his eyes quickly, filled with apology. "But today makes up for all yesterdays, does it not, Brave Eagle?"

"None of what you have done was why you were sent to the City of Peace," Brave Eagle said solemnly. "That was not in the plan. But plans sometimes have to be altered. Like tonight. Thank you, cousin. Now let us ride together and save our people!"

"Side by side?" Running Wolf said, his voice breaking. "You will welcome me at your side?"

"As though we were brothers," Brave Eagle said, nodding.

"Once our people are found and saved, you will then force me back to the City of Peace?" Running Wolf dared to ask, glancing at Rachel, who was awaiting Brave Eagle's reply as anxiously as he.

"No," Brave Eagle said. "You will not be forced to return to the City of Peace. Even without the council's blessing, I will say to you myself, as your

389

chief, that your time has well been served. Now let us look into the future for a time of friendship between us, my cousin."

"You forget so easily that I—I lied to Brown Cloud, causing much trouble between you?" Running Wolf dared to ask, yet needing to be sure the air was cleared about all of his misdeeds.

"There have been many misunderstandings between many people these past several weeks," Brave Eagle said, frowning down at Running Wolf. "You are only a small portion of this misunderstanding, cousin. Let us put it all behind us. Let us go and set our people free and look to all our tomorrows, not back at the ugly past!"

Running Wolf looked humbly up at Brave Eagle, then turned to Rachel. "Our future will be bright," he reassured her, placing a gentle hand to her cheek. "You will see. Chief Brave Eagle will make it so."

Hearing Brave Eagle called 'chief' made pride swell within Brietta's heart. Oh, how badly she wanted to lunge into his arms and hold him to her, repeating over and over again to him just how much she loved him—would always love him!

Yet for many reasons this would have to come later. But she did take the time and liberty to go up to him and give him a sweet kiss on the cheek. "Our life will be wonderful, Brave Eagle," she whispered against his flesh. "Oh, how I adore you."

His hand running down the column of her back in silent understanding was all that it took to make Brietta feel at peace with herself and with the world. She proudly stood back as Brave Eagle and

Running Wolf began securing the surviving slavers' wrists and legs.

It wasn't long before she was riding beside Brave Eagle, while Rachel was riding beside Running Wolf, their destination the Osage village—where Brave Eagle's power as chief would soon be sorely tested!

CHAPTER TWENTY-NINE

> I love you
> For the part of me
> That you bring out.
>
> —*Croft*

Dawn was just breaking along the horizon when they reached the Osage village. Running Wolf was astonished to see the devastation, having received word that the village had been rebuilt. Brave Eagle sidled his horse next to Running Wolf's, silently assessing the situation—seeing the gray mass of ashes where dwellings once stood proud and erect.

"The Osage usually rebuild with a stubborn vigor," Brave Eagle said, having never known the Osage to be lazy, nor to give up so easily. He looked sternly at Running Wolf. "If they are not here, they must still reside in the holy man's religious house! We must go there!"

The sound of an approaching horse made Brave Eagle turn quickly in the saddle, looking past a quiet, patient Brietta and tightening inside when he recognized the one who was approaching. His hand went automatically to his rifle, slipping it quickly from its gunboot and cocking it.

Then he spun his horse around and began galloping hard toward Brown Cloud, his eyes narrowing as he came closer to his old friend, he who wore the same design of tattoo as Brave Eagle on his inner leg.

Why had it come to this? That hate should be so intense between them—that vengeance was sought over and over again between them!

When he came within only a few feet of where Brown Cloud had reined in his horse, Running Wolf now at Brave Eagle's side on his panting steed, Brave Eagle drew rein and stopped to glare into the wavering eyes of his long-time friend, now turned enemy. He held the gun aimed at Brown Cloud's heart, surprised that he had not drawn his weapon to defend himself. He had had plenty of time to do so while Brave Eagle was approaching him.

Brown Cloud sat stiffly erect in his saddle, his face solemn, his reins hanging loosely between his fingers.

"And so we meet again," Brave Eagle said, in his mind's eye recalling the massacre left behind at his village. "Tell me, Brown Cloud, how much Cherokee blood do you have on your hands? How much courage did it take to kill some of my people, and take others as captives? Did it not touch your heart with any remorse at all when my parents died? Did you not know the pain I would feel when I came face to face with my parents' deaths? Friends are supposed to share, but not in this way!"

Brown Cloud squirmed uneasily in his saddle. "It is no different for the Osage than for the Cherokee when wrong has been done them," he said, his voice strained. "The Cherokee moral code is blood law; an eye for an eye. It is the same with the Osage. You came twice and destroyed the Osage village! My father could not stand by and allow it. He ordered the attack on your people! I, being his son, was honor-bound to ride at his side, or forever be shamed in the eyes of not only my father, but my people as well. You are now chief. One day it is also my same destiny! I must deserve the title!"

"It was not in my design to be chief of my people so soon," Brave Eagle said, his voice almost a cry of remorse. "But I am! I am! Because of your father's hunger for Cherokee blood, I am!"

"Had we burned your village twice, your father would have not stood for it, any more than mine," Brown Cloud said, his voice a quiet pleading. "Tell me that what I say is true, Brave Eagle! Tell me!"

"I do not know what you are saying. You talk of my people burning your village twice," Brave Eagle said, "but there was no reason to. My people burned it only once!"

"Then who—?" Brown Cloud said, leaning closer to Brave Eagle. Then he straightened his back again, flexing his broad shoulder muscles. "You are telling an untruth. Your people did it! Your people had to pay, or the Osage would have looked weak!"

Brave Eagle leaned closer to Brown Cloud. "You burned and killed at my village for naught!" he said from between clenched teeth. "Hear me loud and clear, one whose ears seem deaf today. My people are innocent of this crime for which they have paid!"

Slowly Brave Eagle turned his eyes to Running Wolf, a coldness seizing him when another thought entered his consciousness. "You?" he hissed. "You did this, to throw blame my way?"

Running Wolf paled, as did Brietta and Rachel. "Brave Eagle, you cannot believe that I would do this," he said, swallowing hard. "I have never hated you that much. Such an act must have been done by someone else who benefits otherwise from it. Perhaps René, the French slaver?"

Brave Eagle turned his eyes quickly back to Brown Cloud. "Were many of your people taken for slaves?" he asked guardedly.

"No, none," Brown Cloud said, just as guardedly. "We had not yet made our move from the mission. When our village was attacked, no Osage were there to witness the devastation."

"But mine were present," Brave Eagle said in a low snarl, "when you and your warring father arrived and attacked. My son! My people! Where are they, Brown Cloud?"

"They are safe at the mission," Brown Cloud said, lowering his eyes. "I will take you there. I will explain to my father the mistake that has been made. You will be able to be reunited with your people—and with your son.''

"But not my mother and father!" Brave Eagle said, his voice rising in pitch. "They are gone from me forever!"

A sudden gust of wind, which seemed to come from out of nowhere, caused the scalps which had hung hidden in the folds of a blanket rolled up and tied at Brown Cloud's side to flutter free, drawing Brave Eagle's quick, astute attention. His heart became one mass of pain when he recognized the distinctive feathers adorning one of the three scalps. Rage engulfed him.

So quickly, as though he was a flash of lightning sweeping down from the heavens, Brave Eagle thrust his rifle into its gunboot and dismounted, pulling Brown Cloud from his horse. He wrestled Brown Cloud to the ground, knelt over him, pinning him to the ground beneath him, then began pounding his face with his fists. The fight seemed not to be in Brown Cloud. He lay there, accepting the rage his old friend was taking out on him, tasting blood as it rolled from his nostrils into his mouth.

Stunned, Brietta watched Brave Eagle pounding at Brown Cloud. Then, unable to take any more and knowing she could not allow Brave Eagle to kill his old friend with his bare fists, she dismounted and ran to Brave Eagle.

"Brave Eagle," she cried, yanking at his arm. "Stop! You don't want to do this! You will regret it later!"

Panting, his chest heaving, Brave Eagle heard Brietta from what seemed the end of a long, deep tunnel, then suddenly realization of what he was doing came to him with a start. He stopped hitting Brown Cloud as suddenly as he had started and stared down at the blood covering his face.

Brown Cloud looked back at him, non-flinching, the pain on his face nothing to compare with that inside his heart. "The scalp," he finally said, licking blood from his torn lips. "It was taken only because my father ordered me to."

"You killed my parents because you had to follow the command of your father?" Brave Eagle said in a low hiss. "Even though you knew that I loved them so much?"

"It was not I who killed them, Brave Eagle," Brown Cloud said, his voice breaking with emotion. "It was my father." He coughed on blood curling down his throat. "Though I took your father's scalp, never could I have killed your parents. I would have let myself be banished from my Osage family first."

"You say that now, but who is to know how it would have truly been had you been ordered to do the dastardly deed!" Brave Eagle cried, slapping Brown Cloud across the face again. "Do you so easily forget visions of childhood? Do you so easily forget what we have shared through the years?"

"Do you also?" Brown Cloud managed to say, wiping fresh spurts of blood from his nose. "It was you who made that first attack against my people. Was it meant for me to stand by and let you do as you please, while I turn the other cheek in the name of friendship? You know that I could not do that thing, Brave Eagle. Sober or drunk, I could not do that."

"Ah, yes, and there is your problem with *pe-tsa-ni*," Brave Eagle said, pushing himself up away from Brown Cloud. "How much of your actions and cowardices are you going to blame on the firewater?" He spat on the ground close to where Brown Cloud still lay, exhausted from the beating. "I pity you. And because of that, alone, Brown Cloud, I will not kill you."

He gave Brietta a downcast look, then took her by the elbow and led her to her horse. Without even speaking to her, he lifted her back on her saddle, then mounted his steed as he glared down at Brown Cloud. "Get up and accompany us to the mission," he said, his voice lacking emotion. "It will be up to you to ride ahead and tell your father what has transpired between us—that everything that has happened between our bands of Osage and Cherokee has been a foolish mistake."

He rode his mount closer to Brown Cloud, leaning over to give him a helping hand. "I want my people returned to me," he said, his mood softening. "Then I do not want to look upon your face for many moons to come. You can busy yourself helping to rebuild your village and making things right for your people. I shall oversee the building of my village. One day in the future, perhaps we can revisit our youths in our minds, together. But now, all there is between us is pain."

Brown Cloud clasped his hand into Brave Eagle's and moved clumsily to his feet, his face throbbing with pain. "My heart is heavy with regret," he said, his head bent in disgrace. "Some day I shall make it all up to you, Brave Eagle. You shall see."

Brave Eagle wrenched his hand away from Brown Cloud's, then rode up next to Brown Cloud's horse. Taking his knife from its sheath, he reached over and in one swipe he cut the Cherokee scalps from Brown Cloud's saddle. He looked at them for a moment with a deep longing, then tucked them inside his saddle bag.

"Now, Brown Cloud, you do not have the spoils of war forced upon you by your warring father," Brave Eagle said, glaring down at Brown Cloud. "They are now mine!"

He wheeled his gelding around and rode up next to Brietta. Reaching out a hand, he twined his fingers through hers, awaiting Brown Cloud's slow mounting of his horse. "I am sorry that you had to witness this hatred between old friends," he said. "And thank you for stopping me, for had you not, I would have certainly killed him."

"And you would have regretted it," Brietta said softly. "Let us now look to the future. Your son is waiting. I am eager to hear him call me mother."

"His love for you shall soon be as strong as mine," Brave Eagle said, reaching over to kiss her softly on the lips. "And then, *o-ge-ye*, we should plan for more children. Rising Fawn has been without a brother for too long now."

"Or perhaps a sister?" Brietta said, thrilling at the thought of having Brave Eagle's children.

She looked past Brave Eagle, seeing the peace in her sister's eyes as she talked softly with Running Wolf, while everyone waited for Brown Cloud to limp to his horse and mount it. It seemed only a miracle could have sent devoted sisters devoted lovers.

They were truly blessed.

Brown Cloud winced with pain as he pulled himself up into the saddle. His eyes were almost swollen shut. His nostrils were filled with drying blood, and his lips were cut, bruised, and throbbing. Weakly, he lifted the reins and slapped them against his horse. Not looking back, he rode away, feeling as though everything had been taken from him—his best friend, the respect of his father, and surely the hope of ever becoming a proud chief of his people! Never had he desired *pe-tsa-ni* as he did now. He thirsted for the firewater and its ability to make him forget his cares and woes.

Yet he had made promises that he must keep. Especially to himself!

The afternoon sun was hovering on the edge of the land before taking its nightly plunge, splattering the clouds and sky with muted colors as they rode toward the mission. As they rode into the setting sun, the world seemed filled with peace. Yet, Brave Eagle's heart was split in so many ways! A part of it remained back at his village, with his mother and father and the slain Cherokee. A part of his heart was grateful for such a woman as Brietta, and a part of his heart ached to hold his son in his arms again. If anything had happened to Rising Fawn, he would never live down the guilt that would overwhelm him day to day, for those long weeks and months when he had forsaken his son because he feared his presence would make the pain deepen over the loss of his wife!

Never would he separate himself from his son again! Theirs would be a union of father and son as never before since the beginning of time! He was eager to teach Rising Fawn skills with the bow and arrow. He was eager to teach him how to ride!

But, he thought woefully, how he hated to ever have to teach his son warring! If Brave Eagle had the power, warring would be banned forever!

A smile fluttered across Brave Eagle's lips at the thought of what the future held for him and his son. When he felt her eyes on him, he turned and shared that smile and hope with Brietta.

CHAPTER THIRTY

I love your arms when the warm, white flesh
Touches mine in a fond embrace.

—*Wilcox*

The mission stood up like a dark ghost against the
night sky. Although Brietta knew it had been built
as a sanctuary, seeing it tonight along the horizon
filled her with foreboding. Weak and with a heavy
heart, Brave Eagle rode at her side.

What if Chief Climbing Bear chose not to be
understanding? If he refused to listen to Brown
Cloud and would not hand over the Cherokee
captives to Brave Eagle, what then of her beloved?
Of course he would be taken captive also!

The thought sent spirals of dread through Brietta, knowing that Brave Eagle would rather be dead than be a captive of the Osage, to then be sold into slavery.

And what of herself?

She knew that she would not be spared being sold into slavery. Her one hope was the missionary in charge of this mission. Perhaps he could talk sense into the stubborn Osage chief!

Yet it seemed that the missionary was powerless. Hadn't the Osage taken the Cherokee to the mission as captives? No white missionary would condone such an action—therefore, it had to mean that he had been powerless, forced to endure seeing the injustice done.

A terrible thought struck Brietta. Perhaps the missionary was himself a captive now?

As they moved closer to the mission, the air was filled with the sound of mournful wails, the sort that sent chills up and down Brietta's spine. She looked quickly at Brave Eagle, then at Brown Cloud, who rode at Brave Eagle's right side. They were themselves exchanging questioning glances. Then suddenly they broke into a mad gallop together, toward the mission.

Running Wolf and Rachel rode up to Brietta, one on each side of her. "There is meaning in the cries that you are hearing," Running Wolf said solemnly, staring at Brown Cloud and Brave Eagle, who had just reached the gate that led into the mission grounds, and were soon out of sight inside the mission walls.

"What has happened?" Brietta asked. She was amazed at how Brave Eagle and Brown Cloud had ridden away, as though comrades again. Could both have forgotten all the tragedies each had bestowed on the other these past weeks? Both had seemed filled with such hate for each other! Brietta couldn't help but think that their survival depended on both of them offering forgivenesses!

"Someone of great importance among the Indian community has died," Running Wolf said. "Most surely a chief. That has to mean that the dead one is Chief Climbing Bear."

"Brown Cloud's father has died?" Brietta blurted out, interrupting Running Wolf. "It has to be him, for Brave Eagle's father lies dead back at the Cherokee village."

"Yes, it must be Chief Climbing Bear," Running Wolf said, peering through the darkness at the mission. "If so, that means that Brown Cloud is now chief."

Brietta gasped lightly, then inhaled a breath of relief. If Brown Cloud was in charge of all the decisions for his band of Osage now, things would surely be much simpler for Brave Eagle! She was able to truly relax now, for the first time in many hours.

Brave Eagle dismounted quickly beside Brown Cloud, then hurried with him to the mourners. The Osage people parted and let Brown Cloud and Brave Eagle go on to where Chief Climbing Bear was resting in death's sleep on the ground on a pallet of furs. He was clad in a white doeskin shroud, embellished with colorful beads and porcupine quills, his wondrous headdress of feathers on his head.

"Father!" Brown Cloud cried, falling to his knees beside the dead chief. He lowered his eyes to the ground, dizzy with grief.

"He died soon after arriving at the mission," Missionary Cutright said as he stepped up to place a hand on Brown Cloud's shoulder. "He fought one battle too many. His heart failed him, my son. But now he rests in peace."

"You are now chief," Brave Eagle said, kneeling down beside Brown Cloud. "What will your first command be? Let it be to set my people free. Let us be on our way. You have a father to bury. So do I."

"Brown Cloud is not chief!" a great voice boomed out from behind Brown Cloud and Brave Eagle, silencing the mourners and filling the night with a strained silence. "It is I, Blazing Arrow, who challenges Brown Cloud's right to be chief! It is I, Blazing Arrow, who is the next living kin to Brown Cloud, who says that Brown Cloud is not fit to govern his Osage people! It is because of him that so much disgrace has fallen upon them! He is even to blame that his father now wears a death mask!"

Brown Cloud's heart plummeted to his feet and he grew cold inside, not feeling at all fit at this moment to have to defend his right to be chief. His whole body was heavy with grief! He had lost so much, even now his beloved father! Would he now also lose that last possession of value in his world —The title of chief?

Brave Eagle gazed at Brown Cloud, seeing his old friend's torment, and knowing that this was not a good time for him to be challenged by anyone, for anything. Nor was it best for Brave

Eagle and his people! With Brown Cloud as chief, a semblance of peace could be had between their two tribes. With Blazing Arrow as chief, there could be warring as never known before! Blazing Arrow was well known for his fierceness!

Brave Eagle sidled close to Brown Cloud. "You must fight him," Brave Eagle whispered to him. "It is your people's only salvation. And—it is what your father would expect of you!"

Brown Cloud did not respond, only stared at his father, tears streaming down his face.

"You must fight him, Brown Cloud," Brave Eagle said in a sharp whisper. "And you must win! Once and for all, you would prove to your people your worth! Your strengths, not your weaknesses, must rule you now, my friend."

The word "friend" seemed to strike a chord inside Brown Cloud's heart. His eyes widened and his heart began to pound with fervor. His friend was no longer his enemy! He must fight, not only for the sake of his people, but also for the sake of that friendship that he had thought lost forever!

He turned to Brave Eagle and placed a hand on his shoulder. "I will fight," he whispered, smiling. "And I will win!"

Brave Eagle smiled back. He watched Brown Cloud remove his knife from its sheath, then bolt to his feet and face Blazing Arrow, brandishing the knife in the air. The people stepped back, giving space for the two fighters. Brietta hurried to Brave Eagle and stood at his side, her pulse racing as she watched Brown Cloud fight for his life. Running Wolf and Rachel moved quietly to stand beside Brietta and Brave Eagle, their hands joined.

The dueling bodies moved in jerks around each other, thrusting the knives in the air, trying to make contact. Soon wounds were evident on both men, yet they continued to fight, blood blending with sweat as it rolled down their sleek bodies.

Then suddenly Brown Cloud managed to kick Blazing Arrow's knife out of his hand. He moved stealthily around Blazing Arrow, smiling confidently, then tossed his knife away and pounced on him, wrestling him to the ground.

Pinioning Blazing Arrow there, Brown Cloud glared down at him. "Am I foolish for sparing your life?" he hissed. "You will leave, never to show your face among our people again?"

"Kill me!" Blazing Arrow begged, disgraced. "Banishment is not what I seek! Kill me!"

Brown Cloud laughed, reveling in this moment of power while his people looked on, seeing a side of him that made them proud. "Banishment it is," he said, rising away from Blazing Arrow. He kicked dirt on Blazing Arrow, then spit into the dirt. "Leave this place tonight without a horse, and weaponless."

Blazing Arrow rose slowly to his feet, his eyes wary as he glared at Brown Cloud. Then he looked slowly around at his people, seeing shame for him in their eyes. Hanging his head, he turned and walked listlessly away. When he got to the forest he sought the river and walked into it until there was no bottom for his feet to walk on.

Yet he continued onward, making no effort to swim. A black void soon welcomed him as he sank into unconsciousness.

* * *

Brave Eagle knelt to one knee and picked up Brown Cloud's knife from the ground, then went to him. "You fought with the courage of a great chief," he said, offering Brown Cloud his knife. "In the eyes of your people, you have won the title of Chief Brown Cloud."

Brown Cloud stood with squared shoulders and lifted chin as he looked intensely at Brave Eagle. "As chief, I relinquish your people back to your care," he said, accepting his knife. "Go, Brave Eagle. Take your people home. Bury your father. I shall bury mine."

Brave Eagle nodded, then turned to walk away, but was stopped when a hand rested on his shoulder from behind. He turned to Brown Cloud again. "There is more to say?" he asked.

"Our friendship," Brown Cloud said thickly. "It is renewed?"

Brave Eagle stiffened inside, unable to forget the atrocities at his village, and the scalps that Brown Cloud had claimed as his. "We can share a peaceful world, your people and mine, under our leadership," he said, his voice void of emotion. "But never can it be the same between you and me, Brown Cloud. Friends, perhaps. But never comrades in thoughts and deeds again. The instant you placed your knife at my father's scalp, my brotherly love for you was no more. Nor shall it ever be again."

Seeing the hurt and regret in Brown Cloud's eyes was almost more than Brave Eagle could bear, for deep inside his heart his love for Brown Cloud could never totally be banished. They had shared visions, had they not?

Yet that was not enough to sustain Brave Eagle now, fresh from the sight of his slain parents!

Warm fingers twining through his catapulted Brave Eagle back to a world which included Brietta. While Brown Cloud looked on, charged with disappointment, Brave Eagle slipped away from Brown Cloud's grip and gazed down at Brietta as she stepped to his side.

"Let's go and get Rising Fawn," Brietta murmured. "How wonderful it will be to reunite father and son." She smiled sweetly up at him. "And, Chief Brave Eagle, your people await you. How blessed they are to have a man like you for their chief."

Missionary Cutright stepped up to them. "Chief Brave Eagle, I will take you to your people," he said, his long black robe fluttering around his ankles as the breeze freshened into strong gusts of wind. "It is with much regret that I was forced to watch them placed behind my mission and guarded by Osage warriors like—as if they were animals, instead of humans."

"That they had not been herded off to be sold into slavery is a blessing from *Wah-kon-tah*," Brave Eagle said, sweeping an arm around Brietta's waist as he followed the missionary around the large grouping of Osage people who were beginning to wail again, mourning the death of their fallen chief.

Rachel clung to Running Wolf's hand as they also followed Missionary Cutright. Running Wolf kept glancing at Brave Eagle, hoping that Brave Eagle would remember that he had given him a reprieve from his time for atonement at the *City of*

Peace. When Brave Eagle turned his way and smiled, his heart leapt with joy, for in that smile he found compassion, enough to prove that Running Wolf was no longer a condemned man. He was free—free to do with his life as he pleased!

Then he was engulfed with a sudden sadness, remembering what lay ahead of him, Brave Eagle, and their people. The burial of a proud chief. The rebuilding of their village!

But working together, as one force, with one heart, all of this would be done quickly, and with love.

He glanced down at Rachel. And soon there would be a marriage!

A child's voice suddenly exploded from someplace just ahead. Brave Eagle's heart soared when he saw his son running toward him, his arms outstretched. Tears sprang from Brietta's eyes when Rising Fawn came to his father and leaped into his waiting arms, then clung to him, sobbing.

"You came," Rising Fawn sobbed. "Father, you came."

"You thought I would not?" Brave Eagle said, stroking his son's dark, shoulder-length hair.

"I was afraid!" Rising Fawn cried.

Brave Eagle hugged his son for a moment longer, then held him away from him so that their eyes could meet. "There is no need to be afraid any longer," he said softly. "I am here." He looked over his shoulder at Brietta, then back down at his son as she stepped up to his side. "Also Brietta is here. She will make life sweet for you again."

Brietta was touched deeply, her heart melting when Brave Eagle handed his son over to her.

Rising Fawn did not hesitate to go to her. She held him within her arms, looking down into dark eyes which were the mirror image of his father's.

"Everything is going to be all right," she murmured. She could not believe it when he melted trustingly into her arms, hugging her tightly. "Rising Fawn, Brave Eagle and I will never let any more sadness touch your heart. Your life will be filled with love."

To see his wife and son become as one inside their hearts made Brave Eagle's chest swell with pride. He relished this time a moment longer, then turned and looked at his people, whose eyes were imploring him, wanting his leadership, his guidance.

Brave Eagle stepped away from Brietta and Rising Fawn and faced his people directly. He raised a hand in the air and turned his eyes to heaven, silently praying for *Wah-kon-tah's* favor. Then again he looked at his people, and at the trust in their eyes.

"My people, we have burials to tend to and a village to rebuild!" he shouted. "It will be a time of trial and hardships, but a time of oneness between us! We are survivors! Let us go and begin our new lives, even tonight!"

The Cherokee people's reply was an outburst of comaradarie as they flocked around Brave Eagle to touch and hug him. Proudly, Brietta watched the joy among the Cherokee, Brave Eagle's son now standing beside her, clutching trustingly to her hand. Suddenly he had become her son, making her heart soar with a wondrous gladness.

* * *

Brown Cloud stood before his people, his father at his feet. "My people, we have a burial to see to, and a village to rebuild!" he shouted, raising a doubled fist in the air. "Let us return to our village. We shall have burial rites for our fallen chief, and then we will rebuild our lodges! It is a time for oneness between us! Let it be so!"

He could not help but be touched clear to the soul when everyone showed their acceptance of him and came to him with hugs and smiles. Yet it did not seem enough. He had not regained the full measure of friendship with Brave Eagle! Only when he achieved that could his world ever be complete!

He looked past his people as Brave Eagle and his people began a slow procession from the mission grounds. Strange, Brown Cloud thought, how even now, with his people's adoration, there could be such an empty feeling deeply inside him. He could not help a sudden gnawing ache which in the past he could depend on *pe-tsa-ni* to quell.

He licked his lips and ran a hand across his face, emitting a soft groan that only he was aware of, and understood.

CHAPTER THIRTY-ONE

I arise from dreams of thee
In the first sweet sleep of night.

—*Shelley*

ONE YEAR LATER

It was another autumn. The colors of the trees of the forest were a blend of oranges, reds, yellows, and deep coppers. In a clearing, smoke spiraled lazily from the smokeholes of a cluster of wigwams, the Cherokee village having been rebuilt, the people prospering.

Among the wigwams stood two log cabins, side by side, Chief Brave Eagle's great *Lodge of Mystery* only footsteps away from the largest of the two cabins.

Rachel stood beside the bed looking down at Brietta, concerned over her inability to regain her strength after giving birth to a son three months earlier. Rachel and Running Wolf's own three-month-old child, a daughter, Cassandra, lay in a crib close by, contentedly asleep after having just been nursed.

"Don't you feel at all stronger this morning?" Rachel asked, bending to smooth a lock of hair back from Brietta's pale brow. "If you could just get up for a while. Only by doing so will you get your strength back." She glanced at the child at Brietta's side. "It saddens me so, Brietta, when I place Billy's lips to my breast instead of yours."

"That Billy is receiving nourishment at all is what is important," Brietta said, yet deeply sad inside that she was not capable of being a mother in every respect. She had not had enough milk for her child. It not only made her feel lacking as a mother, but less a woman in her husband's eyes!

"You will be able to nurse your next child," Rachel tried to reassure her. "You'll see." Strange, she thought, how fate struck sometimes—strange that it would be Brietta who could not nurse a child, when all through their youth Rachel had been the weaker of the twins.

"If there is even to be a next child," Brave Eagle said, stepping suddenly up to the bed.

When he bent down to kiss Brietta, she could smell the aroma of the fresh out-of-doors, for Brave Eagle had just been outside preparing his gelding for a trek into the forest for pelts. She relished the touch of his lips, and how lean and handsome he was, dressed in his hunting clothes —his fringed breeches and his buckskin hunting jacket decorated with tiny bone buttons and beads and gay-colored porcupine quills.

Then she turned her eyes away as he continued looking at her, so wonderfully handsome, yet so untouchable in her weakened condition!

And that he felt she was unable to bear him another child so tore at her heart! Surely she was nothing but a disappointment to him! She only hoped that he understood her need to name their son with an English, instead of an Indian name. He had agreed, yet only after getting her to agree to their son's name being changed to Cherokee after he sought and found his vision. That seemed only right to her. He was the next chief-in-line, and he was a mirror image of his father, Indian in every feature.

"*O-ge-ye,*" Brave Eagle said, framing her face between his hands. He turned her face so that she was forced to look at him. "We now have two children—two sons. That is enough to make a happy home. But two sons need a mother. You must fight harder, Brietta, to gain your strength back. For me. For our sons, Brietta, you must do this. I see a bright future ahead. You must be a part of that future!"

"Oh, but I shall be," Brietta said, taking one of his hands and kissing its palm. "Just give me time. Each day I feel somewhat stronger."

"You must promise that while I am hunting you will rise from this damnable bed and exercise your weakened legs," Brave Eagle said, frowning down at her. "Rachel is here to help you, Brietta. Let her."

"Rachel should be in her own cabin doing her own wifely chores for her husband," Brietta softly argued, giving her sister a scolding glance. "Running Wolf surely feels neglected!"

Running Wolf walked into the cabin. He had gained several pounds and was no longer the slight Indian that he had been before marrying Rachel. He went to his wife and slung an arm around her waist, their lips meeting in a tender kiss.

Then he smiled from Brave Eagle to Brietta. "Did I hear someone say something about me being neglected by a wife?" he asked, chuckling low. He swelled out his chest. "Now do I look neglected?" His smile faded. "Brietta, do not worry about anyone now but yourself. Your health is of prime importance between close friends and family."

Rachel looked around at each of them, feeling she had never been so loved. She smiled, wiping tears from her eyes. "Now how could I not get well with so many wishing it on me," she said, laughing softly. Then she looked up at Brave Eagle again, gently touching his cheek. "You and Running Wolf go and enjoy yourselves hunting. While you are gone, I shall get out of bed and exercise my legs." She giggled. "Perhaps, I shall even bake you all a persimmon pie."

Brave Eagle's eyes filled with concern. "Do not do too much in one day," he scolded. He looked away from her and down at their infant son, and then at Rising Fawn as he rushed into the cabin, his cheeks rosy from the crisp morning air. He went to his mother's bedside and kissed her with his crisp, cold lips.

"And to make sure that you won't, and to lessen your burden," Brave Eagle said. "I will take both our sons with me on the hunt."

Brietta was only momentarily concerned with this plan, her infant so small and vulnerable. Then she sighed with resignation, understanding and not discouraging Brave Eagle as he fitted a sling onto his back. She did not even discourage him when he swept Billy up from the bed, wrapped him snugly in blankets, and placed him in the sling. She had been in awe of Brave Eagle since long before their child's birth. She had learned that the Cherokee were passionately devoted to their children. The Cherokee, no matter their age or dignity, liked to cuddle the warm bodies of their babies—just as Brave Eagle thought it no shame to sling his infant son on his back in a woman's carrying cloth to take him in the forest to hunt or set traps.

She now realized how it must have hurt him the many months that he had separated himself from Rising Fawn after the death of his wife. Never would she give him cause to separate himself from Billy! She would not die, leaving so much sadness behind!

Brietta smiled a good-bye to Rising Fawn when Brave Eagle took his hand and walked him toward the door.

"Coming, Running Wolf?" Brave Eagle said from across his shoulder. "You will bring your daughter, also?"

Running Wolf chuckled. "It is not required," he said, falling into step beside Brave Eagle as they left the cabin. "It is not important that daughters learn the ways of the hunt. It is best that Cassandra stay with the women and learn womanly chores."

Rachel leaned over Brietta. "Well?" she said, peeling back the blankets. "Wouldn't you say that now is as good a time as any to get started?"

Brietta's heart pounded wildly as she felt the weight of the blankets being taken from her, leaving her free to leave the bed. Her knees weak and trembling, she moved her legs to the edge of the bed, then took a deep breath, her pulse racing, and eased her legs over the sides. Her feet soon touched the bare, cold floor.

Rachel scampered to the other side of the bed and rescued Brietta's house slippers, then took them quickly to her and slipped them on her feet. She grabbed Brietta's soft robe and helped her into it.

And then she stood back, holding her breath, as Brietta pushed herself up from the bed, feeling it important that Brietta do this unassisted.

Sweat pearling her brow, Brietta swayed dangerously as she put her full weight on her feet, then steadied herself. She smiled triumphantly at her sister. Then, from this vantage point where she could see so much of this cabin that her husband had built for her, so that her life as a Cherokee could be much easier, she looked around, so very, very proud, and grateful that her husband, as well as Rachel's, had cared enough to make their wives comfortable. They had built them houses of logs, daubed with mud and weeds, set low on a foundation of bigger logs.

Brietta smiled as she continued looking around at her home. Though it consisted only of two rooms, the furniture sparse—an iron bed, several straight-backed chairs, a table, and a massive fireplace—it was shared with the man she loved.

No, it was not a fancy house, but it was home. And once she was well she could dress it up with lacy curtains, pictures, and bric-a-brac.

Again focusing her thoughts on getting well so that she could enjoy her home and family, she tested her strength by taking a step, smiling again as she found that it was not as hard as it had been yesterday. She was much stronger than she had thought! Her beloved husband was not going to suffer again over another wife's death! At last, she was on the road to recovery!

"That's enough for now," Rachel said, quickly taking Brietta by the arm. "Just stand there a moment and get your breath, then take another step. We must take this thing slowly. We don't want you to have a relapse, do we?"

"What we need is for me to stay out of that dreaded bed forever!" Brietta said, breathing hard as she leaned against her sister.

"Forever?" Rachel teased, her eyes dancing.

"Well, no, I truly don't think so," Brietta said, catching Rachel's meaning. "I don't think my husband would appreciate that." She sighed with a longing long denied. "I do miss being in Brave Eagle's arms, making love." She blushed as she glanced over at Rachel. "Do you mind my talking so openly with you about such a thing, Rachel? It was never a part of our conversation before, as sisters."

Rachel laughed softly, her face coloring with a blush. "No, it wasn't," she murmured. "But never before did we have husbands!"

"You're happy with Running Wolf, aren't you?"

"Wonderfully."

Brietta leaned into her sister's embrace. "Rachel, we are so very lucky," she murmured. "It could have been so different, you know."

"Yes, we could have been forced to live with— with the likes of Uncle Patrick," Rachel said, shuddering at the thought.

Brietta eased out of Rachel's arms, the name Patrick sending a warning through her, wondering where he was, and what evil he was up to. "I must exercise my legs," she said determinedly, forcing herself to walk back and forth before her sister's watchful eyes. "I must regain my strength."

The sun was at the midpoint in the sky. A lone horseman rode a magnificent strawberry roan across a meadow dotted with wild autumn flowers, a hat pulled low over his brow. Pistols hung heavy at his hips and a rifle was thrust into a gunboot at the side of his horse.

Patrick smiled smugly as he glanced down at his fancy attire—at his velvet waistcoat and breeches, the shine from the diamond stickpin in his ascot flashing momentarily in his eyes, adding to their gleam.

Wouldn't his nieces be surprised to discover

that, with a stroke of good luck while gambling on a riverboat, he was now a wealthy Mississippi Valley slaver! And that he now owned vast lands filled with cotton!

His face twisted into an ugly grimace when he thought of Rachel being married to an Indian— the scrawny Running Wolf, no less! Patrick had wanted Rachel to himself for as long as he could remember. Now she had been soiled!

"But I want her anyhow," he whispered harshly to himself. "And Brietta! I fed and clothed them nieces after their parents' deaths! They owe me!"

A raging hunger lit his eyes. He wanted Rachel so badly his groin ached. No number of slaves he had bedded had been enough to erase her from his mind. Always while taking a woman, he had imagined it was Rachel in his arms.

Rachel. His Rachel!

"She will be mine!" he shouted to the wind. "She will be mine!"

Chief Brown Cloud rode far enough back from Patrick not to be noticed, having stalked Patrick since Brown Cloud recognized him and saw the direction in which Patrick was traveling. There was no doubt in Brown Cloud's mind that the evil white man was riding toward Chief Brave Eagle's village—and why.

"He has come after his blood kin," Brown Cloud whispered to himself. "One of whom is Brave Eagle's wife."

Continuing to follow Patrick, Brown Cloud was, in his mind's eye, recalling how he had watched

Brave Eagle's cabin from afar earlier in the day. He had gone there, pining to be as one with his old friend again, yet not having the courage to approach Brave Eagle to see if this was possible. While watching, he had seen Brave Eagle leave with his two sons and Running Wolf, heading out into the forest for a day of hunting and trapping. This had left both wives defenseless, yet Brown Cloud had not thought anything further about this until he had happened to see Patrick riding across the meadow as though he belonged there, a part of the scenery.

He had no doubt as to what the white man had in mind. Brown Cloud reined in his stallion and cast a glance over his shoulder in the direction of the forest. Brave Eagle should still be there, the sun still warm overhead, the day only half gone.

"Yes, I must go and warn my old friend!" he said aloud. He yanked on his reins, and began riding in a hard gallop toward the thick foliage. His heart hammered wildly within his chest, seeing many advantages to telling Brave Eagle about Patrick. It would not only perhaps save his wife from harm, but also it could get him back in better graces with Brave Eagle!

"We can renew vows of friendship!" he said, smiling from ear to ear. "There will be a celebration of celebrations! We will bring our people together, as one! There will be much rejoicing across the land as Osage and Cherokee smoke many peace pipes and share their bountiful crops!"

The thought made him almost giddy with delight. He sank his knees more deeply into the sides of his horse. His future had never looked so full of hope, so full of camaraderie with his old friend! They would hunt together! They would laugh!

Never would they share tears and sorrows again!

CHAPTER THIRTY-TWO

As darkly seen against the crimson sky,
Thy figure floats along. . . .

—*Bryant*

Being out of bed and able to walk freely without assistance was like a reprieve for Brietta. She had begun to believe that she would never live a normal life again. Her recovery had been so slow, she had not even been aware of it.

Not until now. Each step that she took as she slowly paced before the fireplace in her cabin, the warmth of the fire penetrating her flesh, warming her through and through, made her legs feel stronger, more vital!

She felt as though she was being reborn!

"I want to get dressed," she said suddenly, smiling at Rachel, who seemed to be watching her every move as though it would be her last.

When Rachel responded only with a troubled frown, Brietta brushed past her and went to her chest at the foot of her bed, lifted the lid, sorted through the clothes, and pulled free a cotton dress with tiny yellow iris designs embroidered against a white background.

Rachel scurried to her and took the dress, laying it over one arm while she started to help Brietta remove her gown.

"No," Brietta said stubbornly, motioning Rachel away from her. "Just let me be. I'm doing fine."

She was aware that her knees were beginning to tremble and that her breath was coming with more difficulty, yet she would not let anything stand in the way of her newly found freedom from the dreaded bed.

Silently willing her legs to hold her up, she slipped the gown over her head and lay it across the back of a chair. Smiling a thank-you to Rachel as she handed her the dress, she took it and eased it over her head.

"I would welcome your buttoning it," Brietta said, laughing softly. She turned her back to Rachel as her sister's fingers quickly buttoned the dress.

"And now that that is done, I must brush my hair," Brietta murmured, accepting the hairbrush after Rachel got it from the nightstand beside the bed. She began taking long, careful strokes, proud of her achievements this morning. As she continued brushing her hair, her thoughts went to Brave Eagle and their sons. Although she knew that Brave Eagle was capable of caring for their sons, even on a hunting expedition, she could not help but be wary.

She knew that anything could happen in the wilds of the forest.

Anything!

Nervous perspiration pearling his brow, Brown Cloud rode cautiously through the forest, knowing that it was dangerous to be there while his old friend was hunting. His movements could be taken for a deer.

He nudged his horse with his knees and rode more earnestly forward, seeing Brave Eagle up just ahead, kneeling to teach Rising Fawn how to shoot his miniature bow and arrow. Recalling his own teachings as a child, Brown Cloud knew that Rising Fawn's target could be nothing more than a cricket, the usual target for a child just learning the ways of the hunt!

He was catapulted back to the many times that he had met Brave Eagle far away from both their villages, when together they had hunted for much larger game. So often had they spied the same animal at the same moment, both their arrows piercing the flesh simultaneously.

They had laughed and joked about how even while on the hunt, their hearts and minds were joined!

They then had shared their prize, their fathers always puzzling over where the rest of the animal was when they returned to their respective villages with only portions of their day's trophy.

"That was so long ago," Brown Cloud whispered to himself, regret paining his very soul. "But after today, perhaps things will be as they were. Once I give Brave Eagle the warning about the evil white man, surely everything will change and be as it was. Friends forever, all disappointments left behind us!"

Knowing that time was of the essence if his warning was going to be worth anything, for Patrick was too close to the Cherokee village for comfort, Brown Cloud was now close enough to Brave Eagle to shout at him. "Brave Eagle!" he said, his voice alarming and silencing the birds in the trees overhead. "My friend! I have come with a warning!"

Brave Eagle bolted to his feet. Placing his hands to Rising Fawn's shoulders, he pushed his son behind him for protection. With narrowed eyes, his heart pounded with a suspicion he did not want to feel as Brown Cloud reined his horse in close by, quickly dismounting.

"What is this you say about a warning?" Brave Eagle said, squaring his shoulders as Brown Cloud stopped only an arm's length away from him. Although he did not want to feel anything at all for Brown Cloud, fond remembrances of a long time past swept through him. Theirs had been such a special friendship—such a tight bond. How had it gone awry?

"While riding close to your village I saw a man," Brown Cloud said, his pulse racing. "It was not just any man, Brave Eagle. It was the man who once kept me supplied with *pe-tsa-ni*. This man, Brave

Eagle, is kin to your wife. His name is Patrick. Surely he is not traveling toward your village with good intentions."

The news struck Brave Eagle with great alarm. His heart began thudding inside his chest, envisioning Brietta at home, hardly able to get out of bed, much less defend herself!

And Rachel? She would probably swoon from fright the moment she saw her uncle. Never could anyone have left such an impression on two young women as that evil man had!

"I had hoped that he was dead," Brave Eagle said, turning to sweep Rising Fawn up into his arms. "Or had at least forgotten that his nieces were alive."

"What will you do?" Brown Cloud said, looking from Rising Fawn to the infant sleeping soundly in the sling on Brave Eagle's horse. He then looked at Brave Eagle. "I will look after your sons while you go and defend your wife against the man whose heart is black."

Brave Eagle's eyes wavered as he looked down at Rising Fawn, whose face was screwed up strangely as he looked at Brown Cloud, as though he mistrusted and hated the man, though he had surely never come face to face with him before!

Unless he had seen Brown Cloud on the day of the Cherokee massacre, the day that Rising Fawn's grandparents had been murdered, his grandfather scalped.

"No. It is for me to see to their safety," Brave Eagle said, clinging to Rising Fawn, but hating it that he did not have the courage to trust his old friend. He had lost all faith in Brown Cloud. The firewater had been the cause then, but now—?

He gazed more intensely at Brown Cloud, suddenly aware that his eyes were clear and his breath was clean. He had finally given up the firewater! Was he truly a reformed man? If so, the Great Spirit had answered Brave Eagle's many silent prayers for his old friend!

"You cannot return home carrying both sons while the white man is near," Brown Cloud said, taking it upon himself to reach for Rising Fawn. "He would not hesitate to kill them." He flinched when the small child recoiled, wondering why. Then, in his mind's eye, he recalled the day that he had seen Brown Cloud's part in the massacre and fully understood why the child would hate him, perhaps forever.

"You are right, but Running Wolf—"

"I do not see Running Wolf here with you."

Brave Eagle sighed deeply. Running Wolf and he had gone their separate ways, with Brave Eagle having decided not to do any serious hunting today after all, while his children were with him. He had made this a day of pleasure, instead, enjoying the miracle of sons.

"Yes, Running Wolf is not with me," Brave Eagle admitted.

"And time is wasting, Brave Eagle," Brown Cloud said, once more reaching for Rising Fawn. "Give me your trust. I will not let you down."

Brave Eagle watched as Rising Fawn hesitated for a moment longer, then reached his arms out to Brown Cloud as though in his little innocent heart he had forgiven the Osage chief for his past deeds. So then, should Brave Eagle trust his blood brother, who seemed so eager to please—surely as a way to repent his past sins.

"I am displaying the ultimate trust in a friend, Brown Cloud," Brave Eagle said, relinquishing his son to the Osage chief. "I hand over to you the care of my sons, who are life itself to me."

"Brown Cloud is humbly touched by such a trust. I vow to you, Brave Eagle, that no harm will come to your sons while in my care," he said, as Brave Eagle trustingly took the sling in which his son still slept from his own horse and attached it to Brown Cloud's. He paused for a moment of what seemed a silent prayer, kissed Billy on the brow, then went to Rising Fawn, hugging him tightly and kissing his soft cheek.

He then gave Brown Cloud a set stare and clasped his hand to his shoulder. "Thank you, friend," he said, his voice breaking.

Brown Cloud nodded, feeling euphoric as he felt the severed bond between himself and Brave Eagle being repaired. He clung to Rising Fawn as Brave Eagle swung himself into his saddle and was soon riding away in a brisk clip. He unashamedly cried with the joy of the moment, then lifted his eyes to the heavens, giving thanks—and also praying to *Wah-kon-tah* for Brave Eagle's and his wife's safety.

"I feel so much better about myself," Brietta said, laying the hairbrush aside. She hugged Rachel. "I truly believe I'm going to be well."

The door of the cabin opened suddenly with a loud cracking sound as it slammed back against the wall. Brietta and Rachel were wrenched apart by the sound, turning around with a start. They grabbed for one another again when they saw Patrick blocking the door, leering, a rifle aimed at them.

"Now ain't this cozy?" Patrick said, chuckling low. "I see you two finally got back together, huh?"

"Uncle Patrick, what—what are you doing here?" Brietta asked, fear gripping her.

"You need ask?" he said, stepping further into the cabin. While he kept his rifle aimed at the twins, he glanced down into the crib. "And whose little one is this?"

"Mine," Rachel said weakly, nausea sweeping through her at the sight of Patrick looking down at her daughter. "And you leave her be, do you hear?"

Patrick shrugged and stepped away from the crib. "I ain't here for her," he said, his eyes on Rachel, then Brietta. "It's my nieces I've come to lay claim on." He gestured toward the door with a nod of the head. "You two grab yourself a wrap, then go on outside. We've a ways to go to get to my plantation."

Brietta's eyes widened as she clutched harder to Rachel. "You can't do this," she cried. "Leave us be, Uncle Patrick. We've never done you any harm. Let us live our lives in peace."

"Married to Injuns, livin' in an Injun village like heathens?" Patrick said, his jaw tightening. "Now that ain't what your mama and papa had in mind when they come to this Ozark country."

"Nor did they have you in mind for us," Rachel said, seizing of a moment of courage.

"But that's the way it is," Patrick said, yanking two shawls from a peg on the wall and tossing them to Brietta and Rachel. "You're my kin. I'm goin' to see that you have a better life than this."

"I'm not going," Brietta said, stubbornly tossing the shawl to the floor. "You'll have to kill me first."

"And that I'll do," Patrick snarled. "It ain't you so much that I want anyways. I've had my eyes set on Rachel for quite a spell. She'll do me just fine." He cocked his rifle. "Now you understand, Brietta, that if you don't move on outside, I'll shoot you? Just step on outside with me easy-like and get on the horse I have already saddled for you and ride away with me, like it was your idea to do so."

"Brietta, I truly believe he will kill you if you don't do as he says," Rachel whispered. "Let's go. Surely Running Wolf and Brave Eagle can't be that far away. They've been gone an awful long time. They'll be on our trail in no time and save us from this—this animal."

"Rachel, I'm not sure if I have the strength to ride," Brietta whispered back.

"You must try, Brietta, or I'm sure he won't hesitate to shoot you."

Rachel grabbed the shawl from the floor and eased it around Brietta's shoulders, then placed her own around hers. She looked pensively at her child, a sob lodging in her throat, then walked slowly from the cabin with Brietta at her side, Patrick now behind them, leveling his rifle at their backs.

Brave Eagle wheeled his horse to a stop just as he came in view of what was happening in front of his cabin, the other Cherokee people of the village too intent on their daily chores to notice.

Brave Eagle grabbed his rifle from the gunboot at the side of his horse and steadied his aim as he watched with bitter hatred his wife and her sister being forced at gunpoint to mount horses. Without further thought, he pulled the trigger, the explosion of the gunfire deafening.

He became quickly aware of a second blast of gunfire, then saw Running Wolf positioned at the outer fringes of the forest, only a few yards from him.

His attention was drawn again to Patrick, who grabbed for his chest as two bullets pierced his flesh just above his heart. As Patrick dropped to the ground, his rifle fell clumsily beside him, the jolt to the firearm causing it to discharge.

Brave Eagle's attention was drawn quickly elsewhere. Suddenly, everything within him cried out with despair when he saw the rider approaching only a short distance away—riding directly into the line of the stray bullet from Patrick's rifle.

"Brown Cloud!" he cried. "Oh, no! Brown Cloud!" Mortified, he watched Brown Cloud fall from his horse, instantly dead from a gunshot to his head.

And then another thought came to him. His heart throbbed wildly, wondering where his children were! He had left them in Brown Cloud's care! They were not with him!

Tossing his rifle aside, Brave Eagle ran to Brown Cloud. He fell to his knees and cradled Brown Cloud's head in his hands. "Where are my children?" he cried. "Brown Cloud, you promised! You promised!"

But Brown Cloud could not speak, ever again.

He stared lifelessly ahead, all regrets, all sadnesses finally quietened for him.

Brietta had heard what Brave Eagle had shouted. Her insides grew cold as panic seized her. Her children! Oh, Lord, wasn't this tragedy enough today, without also losing her beloved children?

She found the strength to run to Brave Eagle. She grabbed his shoulders, trying to shake him. "Where are our sons?" she cried. "Brave Eagle, where are our sons?"

By now many Cherokee were circling around the arena of death, but it was the appearance of an Osage warrior on horseback, and what he brought to Brietta and Brave Eagle, that drew everyone's keen attention. Brave Eagle laid his old friend's head back on the ground and rose to his full height, standing in awe beside Brietta as the Osage warrior handed Rising Fawn down to Brave Eagle, and then loosened the sling from the side of his horse, handing the infant to Brietta.

The Osage warrior dismounted and went to Brown Cloud and knelt beside him, then rose to his full height again to face Brave Eagle. "The cause of his death?" he said, his dark brows meeting in a frown.

"A stray bullet," Brave Eagle said, remorse thick in his words.

"Then there is no cause to break the peace," the Osage warrior said, folding his arms across his chest.

"How is it that you had our children?" Brietta asked softly.

"I came in search of Brown Cloud to spread the news to our chief that a son was born to him

prematurely while he was away in search of renewed friendship with Chief Brave Eagle," the
Osage warrior said solemnly. "When I found him,
he had your children in his care. He was worried
about your welfare. He asked that I watch the
children while he came to see to your well-being."

"A child?" Brave Eagle said, his voice strained.
"A son? I did not even know that Brown Cloud was
married."

"You have not bothered to know anything about
your old friend for some time," the Osage said, his
voice condemning. He looked back down at
Brown Cloud. "Now it is too late." He went to
Brown Cloud and lifted him into his arms, then
gently laid him across his horse, securing his body
with a rope. Without any further words, he
mounted his steed and rode away.

Filled with regret that he had not allowed a
friendship which had at one time supposedly been
ever-lasting, Brave Eagle cried out to the heavens
with remorse!

Then he began to walk slowly back to his cabin
with Brietta and his sons. When they got to Patrick
and started to step around him, they were stopped
when they heard him laughing a strange sort of
gurgling laugh. Rachel moved to Brietta's side as
they stood over their uncle, whose evil eyes were
looking up at them, daring them, even so close to
death.

"Seems I wasted my time killin' your parents,"
he said, coughing between words. "I didn't get you
all for myself after all, did I, Rachel? Seems the
murder was all for nothing."

Brietta and Rachel were stunned speechless,

even though they had always suspected Patrick and Ray of killing their parents. They stared down at Patrick as he twitched, taking his last breath, then lay quiet, his eyes fixed in death.

"He was such a fiend," Brietta said, sobbing.

"How could he have ever been of any blood kin to us?" Rachel said, sobbing.

"He is not for you ever to think about again," Brave Eagle said, whisking Brietta away from Patrick. He held Rising Fawn in a tight hug. "Let us rejoice for what we have—our sons, Brietta." He glanced over his shoulder at Brown Cloud as he was being taken slowly through the Cherokee village. "Let us think no more of our losses." He was battling deep feelings, those that were tearing his heart into shreds, for at this moment he knew that he could never forget Brown Cloud and what he had once meant to him.

Running Wolf swept Rachel up into his arms and carried her toward the cabin. "My woman, you are now safe with your husband," he said, brushing a kiss across her lips. "Let us get our child and return to our cabin. I've much to say to you."

Rachel closed her eyes and snuggled close to Running Wolf, her beloved hero.

CHAPTER
THIRTY-THREE

There is a destiny that makes us brothers;
None goes his way alone. . . .

—*Markham*

THIRTEEN YEARS LATER,
ANOTHER TIME FOR SHARED VISIONS

Determined to stay another night, awaiting the moment when he would be shown the vision which would make him a man, Rising Fawn smoothed out his bed of dried pine needles on a high bluff and stretched out, marveling anew at the crimson sky as the sun eased toward the horizon.

Placing his hands beneath his head and resting

against them, Rising Fawn sighed. Though dressed only in a breechclout, the whistle his grandfather had made him, with the white down of an eagle at the end, hanging around his neck on a leather string, he did not notice the cooler temperatures. He was too lost in peaceful wonder to feel such an unimportant thing as coldness on his bare chest and legs.

He looked around, content. Ah, but was this not a magical place to be? A magical time? Where one's secrets could be spoken aloud to the Great Spirit? He had searched for hours to find this isolated spot high above the forest that his father had told him about, where he could see across the treetops, as though one with the universe.

If he had wings, he thought, ah, but wouldn't he soar and soar, the wind a soft caress against his copper face? He would join the eagles, the song-birds, the owls. It would be such a time of joy, of total peace . . .

A rustling of leaves behind him made Rising Fawn bolt to his feet and peer down the steep slope that he had climbed to be alone. He had not brought a weapon along, knowing that to prove himself worthy of a sacred vision, he had to spend the long hours in the forest without a defense of any kind.

The crushing of leaves grew louder as someone drew closer, hidden by the thick cluster of pine trees clinging to the side of the bluff. His heart began to pound.

"Who interferes in this, the time of my vision?" he finally dared to say, his eyes widening with surprise when Gray Buck came into view. They

had met many times before when the Cherokee
and the Osage met in council. Rising Fawn had sat
at his father's right side, while Gray Buck had sat at
the side of his distant uncle, the man who now
ruled as chief of the Osage, since Gray Buck had
been too small to accept the duties upon the death
of his father, Brown Cloud.

But that was as far as Rising Fawn and Gray
Buck's friendship had gone, although those moments had proven to be filled with fun and laughter. Rising Fawn had wanted more, yet even the
mention of it had always brought a haunting
sadness to his father's eyes. Loving his father so
much, he did not see that a mere friendship with a
young Osage brave was worth the hurt it might
inflict on him.

Five years younger than Rising Fawn, yet just as
hefty, Gray Buck moved to Rising Fawn and
reached a hand to his shoulder. "It is also my time
of vision," he said, smiling.

"But you are not yet thirteen winters of age,"
Rising Fawn marveled, his eyes widening.

"I must prepare myself early with a vision, for
my uncle is not well, and soon I might be chief of
my people," Gray Buck said, his smile waning.
"Many responsibilities await me, as do they you,
should your father die."

"My father will never die!" Rising Fawn de-
clared, growing cold inside at the thought that one
day he must.

"Never say never," Gray Buck said, sounding too
old for his age. He had been deeply affected by
those who surrounded him, who were filled with
wisdom and advice.

443

A great trembling of the ground and a great gust of wind drew both boys' thoughts away from fathers. They grabbed for one another and clung together as a great burst of light seemed to race across the sky.

Then a large, roaring star fell. It came from the east and shot out sparks of fire along its course. And then it was gone.

"Never have I see anything like it!" Rising Fawn gasped. "It surely was a meteor!"

"No, my friend," Gray Buck said. "Surely that was our vision! Our shared vision!"

Rising Fawn drew away from Gray Buck, recalling his father's tale of another shared vision and the friendship that had begun that night between two boys—one Cherokee, the other Osage.

But that friendship had seemed doomed from the beginning. It had ended in tragedy! Surely the Great Spirit would not let it happen again, in the same way—not since destiny had chosen to make Rising Fawn and Gray Buck *a-na-da-ni-tli,* brothers, in this *un-a-lily,* place of friends.

"My father wears a tattoo on his inner thigh in the shape of a spider," Rising Fawn said.

"And I have been told that my father wore the same tattoo," Gray Buck said.

"Then let us wear the same tattoo as our fathers," Rising Fawn said, filled with excitement.

"That would be grand," Gray Buck said, nodding anxiously. "And also, let us soon choose our adult names, which we shall carry with us throughout our lives!"

Hand in hand, laughing gaily, they fled down the sides of the bluff, vowing to be friends forever.

"Do you see my whistle that I wear around my neck?" Rising Fawn asked, holding the whistle out so that Gray Buck could see it.

"It is a beautiful whistle," Gray Buck exclaimed, his eyes wide with appreciation.

"My grandfather made it for me," Rising Fawn bragged. "He taught me his skill at carving. I shall also now teach you, if you like."

"I would learn quickly," Gray Buck said, his eyes dancing.

Rising Fawn's chest puffed out with pride, no longer worrying about his father's opinion of Gray Buck, and whether or not he approved of him to be Rising Fawn's friend. If need be, it would be a secret friendship!

He smiled at the thought.

Brave Eagle rocked his newborn daughter in his arms, while Brietta looked on from her bed, slipping her breast back inside her gown after feeding her daughter, Lorraine. Brietta could see that Brave Eagle was worried, and she understood why. Rising Fawn had been gone for two days and nights now, seeking his vision.

And he had entered the forest weaponless.

"He'll be fine," Brietta tried to reassure him, leaning up on one elbow. "He is his father's son."

A great burst of light brightening the cabin in this, the time of dusk, sent Brave Eagle to the window. He smiled as he peered out, seeing where the light had been centered. His bluff—the bluff where he and Brown Cloud had shared their vision, the bluff where his son had gone to seek his own vision. He did not worry about the light having been caused by a great falling star, and that some looked on such happenings as a bad omen, for he knew that the Great Spirit was looking out for his son, guiding him at this time when a vision was sought!

"He will be home soon," he said across his shoulder. *Wah-kon-tah* had been kind enough to let him share his son's vision. "He is now a man, Brietta."

Brietta rose from the bed. She slipped into a robe and went to Brave Eagle's side. "I won't ask you how you know this, darling," she said, leaning her cheek against his muscled arm. "That you do is all I need to know not to worry about our son any longer."

Brave Eagle smiled down at her. "Life is perfect now," he said. "So perfect."

Brietta nodded, filled with wondrous thoughts. It was a time of peace, joy, and harmony for herself, her sister, and their loved ones.

It was a time of sweet, savage persuasion.

Dear Reader:

I hope that you have enjoyed reading *SAVAGE PERSUASION*. My next LEISURE book in the continuing "SAVAGE" series, in which it is my endeavor to write about every major Indian tribe in America, is *SAVAGE PROMISE*. This romance will be about the Tlingit Indians of early Alaska and their struggles with the Americans and the Russians to retain their rights to the "brown gold"—the coveted pelts of that region. *SAVAGE PROMISE* promises to be filled with much adventure and passion!

I would love to hear from you all. Please send a legal-size SASE to:

> CASSIE EDWARDS
> R#3 Box 60
> Mattoon, Il. 61938

Warmly,

Cassie Edwards

Cassie Edwards

"May the warm winds of heaven blow softly On your home, and the Great Spirit bless All who enter there."

—*A Cherokee Indian Blessing*